WIPERS GOLD

———∼———

By

Gary Parkins

Copyright © Gary Parkins 2021
This book is sold subject to the condition that it shall not, by way of trade or otherwise, be lent, resold, hired out, or otherwise circulated without the publisher's prior consent in any form of binding or cover other than that in which it is published and without a similar condition including this condition being imposed on the subsequent publisher.
The moral right of Gary Parkins has been asserted.
ISBN-13: 9798590935710

This is a work of fiction. Names, characters, businesses, organizations, places, events and incidents either are the product of the author's imagination or are used fictitiously. Any resemblance to actual persons, living or dead, events, or locales is entirely coincidental.

To my wife Janette, for her unstinting support with this book.

CONTENTS

Chapter 1 .... *1*
Chapter 2 .... *11*
Chapter 3 .... *22*
Chapter 4 .... *31*
Chapter 5 .... *45*
Chapter 6 .... *56*
Chapter 7 .... *62*
Chapter 8 .... *71*
Chapter 9 .... *79*
Chapter 10 .... *87*
Chapter 11 .... *93*
Chapter 12 .... *101*
Chapter 13 .... *111*
Chapter 14 .... *117*
Chapter 15 .... *131*
Chapter 16 .... *135*
Chapter 17 .... *142*
Chapter 18 .... *152*
Chapter 19 .... *164*
Chapter 20 .... *178*
Chapter 21 .... *188*
Chapter 22 .... *195*
Chapter 23 .... *201*
Chapter 24 .... *208*
Chapter 25 .... *213*
Chapter 26 .... *223*
Chapter 27 .... *229*
Chapter 28 .... *234*
Chapter 29 .... *239*
Chapter 30 .... *245*
Chapter 31 .... *254*
Chapter 32 .... *264*
Chapter 33 .... *269*
Chapter 34 .... *279*
Chapter 35 .... *289*

Chapter 36 .... *295*
Chapter 37 .... *298*
Chapter 38 .... *304*
Chapter 39 .... *314*
Chapter 40 .... *322*
Chapter 41 .... *325*
Chapter 42 .... *335*
HISTORICAL NOTE 338
ABOUT THE AUTHOR 345

ACKNOWLEDGMENTS

To Geoff Spencer, John Allen,
and Frank Young for believing in me.

CHAPTER 1

Still they hadn't come.

From his kneeling position in a shallow ditch, beside a rutted narrow country lane, Lieutenant Harry Packard of the First Battalion, The Richmond Regiment, peered across the meadow that spread out before him. It looked peaceful and sedate.

Despite the presence of a peasant village along the lane to his right, beyond the bend and the hedges, it was dead quiet. He closed his eyes and took a deep, sweet-scented breath.

'Bloody Fritzes. Where the hell are they?'

So much for peace and quiet. Sergeant Campbell, by his side, was a thickset, dark-haired slab of no bloody nonsense.

'The buggers are out there somewhere, Sergeant,' said Packard. 'Probably just waiting for their artillery to catch up and give support before they attack. Like as not, there's nothing else we can do for the moment except rest, is there?'

Campbell shrugged his shoulders, yawned, and settled down to rest a few feet away. Tired from the long night march to get here, thought Packard. He stifled a yawn of his own. Like everybody else, he was tired and on edge: now he was here he was itching to get to grips with the enemy.

Packard recalled the exhausting night march of some twenty-odd miles with their packs heavily laden with ammunition. Just before dawn, he had led his company through the village and up onto a slight rise to the north. He'd barely been able to make out the difference between the dark outlines of the hovel-like stone cottages and the pungent smell of cow dung polluting the air from the rickety wooden barns. Nothing seemed to stir in the village, except a frightened dog, which barked, sensing their movement. The village seemed deserted, and probably was, except for a few old people who had stayed behind when the soldiers had come yesterday evening and the noise of battle grew closer.

Packard looked up and down the lane and behind him, shielding his eyes from the sun's glare with a hand. That profound silence, he thought, made it feel as though he were the only person around. Odd, when he could see there were about four hundred other soldiers scattered about in similar defensive positions around the village. The only sound he heard was that of butterflies and other insects buzzing and fluttering around, going about their daily business of looking for food in the warmth of the mid-morning sun.

Packard was grateful that the sun was behind him and not blinding his eyes. He could feel its soothing warmth burning through his tunic and onto his back, giving him some comfort while he waited in this ditch – and giving him a dry ditch to wait in. He realised he was thirsty, so he drank from his water bottle. He replaced the cork, pushed up the peak of his cap, scratched his forehead, and wondered when the Germans would come.

Harry Packard was twenty-five, but looked older, and was not like any other officer in his regiment, or any other officer in the army for that matter. He did not conform to any military standard. His tunic was torn and stained from battle, he wore other ranks' three-inch webbed belt with ammunition pouches and bayonet frog, and he carried a rifle. Around his neck hung a pair of Zeiss binoculars that he'd taken from a dead German officer at Mons. Packard had quickly realised how useless a sword and revolver were in a modern battle compared to a rifle. He kept his Webley revolver but had discarded his Sam-Browne and sword in favour of the Enfield rifle and bayonet, with its long, accurate range and quick-firing bolt action. He'd taken *that* from one of his own dead.

Soldiering came naturally to Packard; he was the best rifle shot in the battalion and had won the rifle shoot competition at Bisley two years in a row. In training, he schooled his platoon on good rifle skills, quick firing, and accuracy. Train hard, fight easy, he kept telling them. In the last few weeks, that training had paid off.

Like Sergeant Campbell, he was a veteran of three major battles now – Mons, Le Cateau, and the Marne – which had left all the officers in his company dead or wounded. As the only officer left, he found himself in command of the company.

Packard placed the water bottle to one side and levelled the binoculars to his eyes, focussed front. About five hundred yards away, he saw in the circle of lenses that the ground dipped then rose again to a ragged line of trees standing sentinel over a winding hedgerow that marked the meadow boundary. Somewhere beyond that hedgerow, there lurked the might of the German army, or so they had been told.

Packard rested the binoculars, then replaced his water bottle and lay down, resting on one elbow next to his sergeant, his rifle close by his side. He began chewing on some hard-tack biscuits taken from his pocket, then decided to take his own advice and rest a while.

All along the ditch on either side of him his men were resting or dozing untidily in the warm sunshine. Some were curled foetus-like and fast asleep, some were cross-legged with their hands behind their heads, caps pulled down over their eyes, while others were resting their heads on their small-packs, nonchalantly chewing on blades of grass. They were regular soldiers; a mixture of old sweats from the

Boer war, a few reservists, some soldiers who had served overseas, and some new recruits.

From the direction of the village, Packard heard the sound of a jingling harness and the heavy fall of hooves. He sat up and twisted round to look as a rider galloped up the narrow lane towards him. He recognised the rider as Captain Denton from Brigade HQ.

'Lieutenant Packard!' the rider was calling out. 'Lieutenant Packard!'

Packard got to his feet, rifle in hand. Campbell stood next to him as the horse came to a sudden halt in front of them. A dust cloud drifted over.

Denton pointed across the meadow. 'Fritz is forming up beyond that hedgerow with artillery support. Prepare your men for action. This position must be held to protect the brigade flank. You understand that, Lieutenant?'

'Understood, sir.'

'Good man, and remember, you're now the OC of this company and it's down to you. It'll be your show. Good luck, Lieutenant.'

Denton tugged at the reins, turned the horse around and galloped back the way he had come.

'Sergeant Campbell.'

'Sir!'

'Tell the men to lay flat in the ditch. When the shelling starts, hands over ears, mouths open. Tell the sentries to keep low and a sharp lookout.'

'Sir.' Campbell went up and down the ditch, giving orders to the men. Suddenly there seemed to be a flurry of activity beside the lane as each man buckled on his webbing and tried to press his body as flat to the bottom of the ditch as they possibly could.

Packard too buckled on his webbing and knelt on the lip of the ditch, binoculars to his eyes, scanning the far side of the meadow for any sign of movement. He noticed a thin dust cloud rising up behind the hedgerow and knew at once that the Germans were positioning their infantry for the assault. He knew this position was going to suffer the concentrated attention of enemy shelling before any assault began. His pulse was racing, and his mouth went suddenly dry, as beads of sweat began to breakout on his brow.

Campbell returned and dropped to one knee beside him. Nervousness was making him pant a little. 'The men have taken cover, sir. The sentries are low but on lookout.'

'Very good, Sergeant. We'd best take cover ourselves. I've a feeling it's going to be pretty lively here at any moment.'

Campbell didn't hesitate; he slid to the bottom of the ditch and wriggled into a flat position, face down, hands covering his ears.

Boom, boom. Boom, boom, sounded the German guns in the distance. 'Heads down everyone!' shouted Packard as he flung himself flat beside his sergeant at the bottom of the ditch; hands over his ears, mouth open to absorb the concussion from blast waves.

A shell whistled in and exploded with a flash in the meadow next to the village. Tons of earth shot into the air. Three more shells pitched in and straddled the village cottages and outbuildings. The ground shook and heaved as shell after shell exploded in and around the village. Flames and smoke rose mushroom-like from the wooden outbuildings with a mad, engulfing roar. Timbers and debris from the barns shot up, twisting and tumbling high into the air. More shells crashed in and began to creep along the lane towards Packard's position, sending a shower of stones and earth lumps scurrying over. Dirty, choking, acrid black smoke drifted and swirled along the lane. For ten long, agonising minutes, salvo after salvo pounded the village and the surrounding area relentlessly. Then, as suddenly as it had started, the shelling stopped.

Packard raised his head, smoke still swirling about him. A trickle of blood was running from his nose, caused by the concussion of the blasts. He wiped it away with the back of his hand. Most of his men would have suffered the same. From somewhere down the line, a voice shouted out. 'Stand to the Richmonds! Stand to!' He recognised it as one of the sentries.

The air was still thick with dust and breathing was difficult. Coughing fits could be heard up and down the lane, mingled with the threats of junior NCOs to ready the men for action.

Packard crawled up to the lip of the ditch, trying to peek across the meadow but it was difficult to see. The acrid smoke was still stinging his eyes and burning his throat, taking away any chance to shout out orders should he need to do so. He felt very hot and dry and his pulse was beating in his neck like a hammer. He wiped his eyes with the palm of his hand and blinked repeatedly against the stinging, dense smoke.

'Here they come!' someone shouted out, and as if by a magic signal, a light breeze got up and the swirling smoke began to clear.

Campbell was beside him now, coughing and spitting, having run up and down the lane to assess casualties. He had a smudge of blood along the top of his lip. Packard smiled at the Scotsman. They had been through hell together since the retreat from Mons and trusted one another implicitly.

'Any casualties?' Packard asked.

Campbell wheezed a bit when he replied. 'No sir. Just a bit dazed from the blasts, that's all. Either Fritz is a poor shot or it was just a fluke they missed us all.'

Packard knew it was a fluke and nodded. Any day the flukes were on your side was a good day. He scanned the meadow with his binoculars and saw a huge mass of German infantry in extended lines heading towards them. More were emerging through the hedgerow – the first assault-wave. By God, he thought, there must be a battalion at least heading towards us. He'd have to cut their numbers down quickly if the company were going to have even half a chance. If too many got close enough, it could be curtains.

'This is it, everybody! Make every round count and cut the blighters down!' he shouted out hoarsely. 'Range three hundred!'

Packard looked about sharply to make sure everyone was ready. Silence descended along the ditch. Then someone down the line started nervously singing, slow and quiet.

'Clarkson!'

'Yes, Corporal?'

'You're not waiting for the pub to open so shut it, and concentrate!'

'Yes, Corporal.'

Nervous laughter rippled out from some of the men.

Packard said nothing. He was glad the NCOs were getting a grip. Fear, he knew, made even the strongest of men dread the start of a battle if they thought they were going to die. The waiting, the stillness, the quiet. Everyone, he knew, was quietly suffocating their fears in their own way – some better than others.

The grey masses came closer and closer. He had to time this right.

Packard shouted out. 'This is it, men. Take aim. Rapid fire!'

An explosion of rifles fired off, then again, and again. Right arms jerked rifle bolts backwards and forwards to load each round into the chamber. The field-grey mass was hammered by the bullets. Individual Germans jerked, spun and pitched down, yet more kept coming, steadily marching over the bodies of their comrades in a mindless courage. Rifle fire crackled all along the ditch as gaps appeared in the ranks of the German assault-wave. The early fear had disappeared, and it was every man now wreaking havoc among the German troops in front of them, with their dead and dying heaped and barely a hundred yards away – and still they came on, one foot after the other like marching on parade. They looked unstoppable and were getting close – too close, Packard thought. If they got to the ditch, the company's resolve would suddenly break and their position would be overrun. He had to take the initiative and take the fight to them. Make the German resolve break first. He shouted, 'Fix bayonets, men!' and looked left and right as the men fumbled for their bayonets. Some were clumsy with fear as NCOs began yelling encouragement at them to steel their resolve for the dreaded close-quarter battle they would have to fight if they had any chance to win the day.

Packard gave the word and another fusillade crackled into the German ranks, then another. This time they could hear the Germans' screams when the bullets hit, and the sickening moans of their dying. The assault-wave suddenly lost its momentum, having lost half its number at least, and the Germans came to a halt, kneeling or standing, and firing back barely thirty yards away, but failing to press the attack forward against the storm of bullets. Was this a sign that most of their leaders were dead and their resolve was cracking? Rapid fire from the ditch cut the Germans down. Some clutched their chest and fell forward. Others twisted their face skywards before falling. But still the Germans stood their ground, face-to-face, bullet-for-bullet, and the air was deadly; it quivered and snapped about them. They just stood there and breasted the bullets that tore through their ranks. It was mindless courage, pure and simple.

But someone will have to give.

A scream came from along the ditch, then another. The company was taking casualties. At what point would courage break and fear take over? Was now the critical time to take the fight to the Germans? Packard decided to take the initiative.

'Prepare to charge!' he roared. The order repeated down the line. 'Here we go then!' he cried out. 'Give them hell. Chaaarge!'

The cry went up along the ditch like a roar. The company scrambled up. Some missed their footing as they climbed out, stumbling, finding their feet again and running wildly, like hunting dogs closing on their quarry. Heads low, eyes narrowed and determined, bayonets thrust forward. The scream of reckless and bitter men was terrifying. There was nothing to do but keep running blindly at the enemy in front of him.

Suddenly they were upon them. A melee of shouts and curses went up like a huge crowd at a football match. Brutal hand-to-hand fighting, arms swinging in a frenzy of clubbing and stabbing in that bitter struggle for life while bayonets thrust and tore into bodies; men going down in screams of agony. Bayonets flashed and glistened with blood as the chilling thud of boots smashed into the faces of the fallen. Bareheaded men with wounds so horrific as to be numbing, but still they fought like demented devils. Crumpled bodies of field-grey and khaki, like bloodied bundles, littered the ground as men fought with sheer madness all around them.

Packard was in the thick of it, thrusting his bayonet into the side of a young German who looked barely old enough to shave. He stabbed another whose face twisted in agony as he fell. He took a swipe with his rifle butt at the face of a kneeling German NCO who was about to knife a fallen Richmond. He missed, then tried to jab his bayonet, but the German ducked out of the way only for the tip of Harry's bayonet to catch his face and open up his cheek in a curtain of blood. He got up and ran off, screaming. Packard's eyes darted about him. Men all around were locked in a private fight of their own.

There was a shout. 'Look out, sir!'

Behind him, a German screamed *'Kamerade, kamerade, nein, nein!'* and before he could wheel round the German collided into the back of him, sending Packard sprawling to the floor. Campbell stood over him, thrust his bayonet into the German's belly up to the hilt. The blood gushed as he twisted the bayonet to withdraw it.

At first Campbell thought his officer was hurt. 'Mr Packard, sir,' he growled, reaching out to help him to his feet.

'I'm all right,' he said, and drew some clean air into his lungs.

Suddenly the German line broke and they began to run. It was every man for himself, leaving heaps of their dead and wounded behind.

'Stand fast the Richmonds!' Packard shouted, and the NCOs repeated it. The men began to cheer. The odd rifle shot cracked in protest. The survivors returned triumphant to their ditch, carrying or dragging their wounded comrades with them.

CHAPTER 2

Packard jumped back into the ditch, white-faced, eyes reddened and wheezing like an old man trying to catch his breath. His head throbbed as he wiped the sweat and German blood from his face with his cuff and tried to steady his breathing, but his heart was still thumping like a jack-hammer. He knew he wasn't wounded but his whole body felt bruised.

Campbell dropped at his side, panting. His dirty face speckled in blood and sweat. 'You ok, sir?' he asked.

His sergeant's concern touched him. 'Yes, I'm all right,' he replied wearily. 'I suppose we should be enjoying the fruits of victory with a tot of rum. If we had any rum, that is.'

'Rum, sir! Right now, I could drink a brewery dry.'

Packard smiled. 'Of course. What was I thinking?'

He peered over the lip of the ditch, looking out in silence for a while. This meadow of rich green grass that just a short time ago was bathed in sunshine was now a hellish human abattoir. Among the litter of German spiked helmets, British caps, discarded rifles and equipment, the dead lay untidy, bleeding out where they fell, the German wounded writhing on the grass, moaning, some shouting out fragile calls for help. His stomach sickened. 'Poor bastards,' he muttered, and slumped back against the side of the ditch.

'Oh, I nearly forgot. We have a prisoner, sir,' said Campbell, beaming. 'Thompson thumped him and dragged him back.'

'A prisoner!' Packard's face lit up. 'Is he fit enough to be questioned?'

'He is, sir. I've sent him back to battalion headquarters in the village under escort with the walking wounded.'

'Well, well, well. A prisoner,' Packard said, delightedly. 'That'll please them back at HQ. I'll see Thompson later and congratulate him.'

'You should be congratulating yourself, sir. You made the Germans pay dear. That bayonet charge was bang on the money. Fritz was too bloody confident at first and then lost it at the end. Our boys did well, though.'

Packard nodded. 'I couldn't have asked for more. How is the company fixed?'

'We got off lightly, considering. We've a number of walking wounded and at least a dozen stretcher cases plus a few dead we need to get away. Corporal Collins has a nasty gash on his arm that's open to the bone,' he said, then added, 'We're short of ammo too.'

'Do you know how many are left, Sergeant?'

Campbell rubbed his chin with his hand and looked left and right along the ditch. 'About eighty, all told. We lost at least a quarter of our number,' he said, 'but we've enough to hold if they attack again, I reckon. I've posted sentries and got the NCOs to do a roll call so I should have a true figure shortly.'

'Very well, Sergeant. Get the stretcher bearers in and send someone to get more ammo. Tell them to look lively. The Germans will shell us again shortly, if I'm not mistaken. Make sure the men rest and have a sip of water, but not too much mind. We've no idea when we'll get our next supply. Make sure they clean their rifles but not all at the same time, and they can have a smoke too. I'll move amongst the men shortly and tell them they did very well. I'm proud of them all.'

'Very good, sir,' Campbell said. 'The lads will appreciate that.' He got up and scurried off in the direction from which he'd come.

The NCOs moved among the men, counting off their names. The walking wounded were bandaged and sent off to the Aid Post just behind the village. Stretcher bearers began to arrive and took the more seriously injured away but there just weren't enough of them and it was taking ages.

Clarkson lifted his canteen to his mouth and was just about to take a big gulp of water.

'Just a sip, the lieutenant said.'

'I know, Corporal, but my throat's as dry as a vulture's crutch.'

'Keep that to yourself, Clarkson, or they'll all want one.'

Subdued laughter bubbled along the ditch.

Thompson, a big brute of a man with a head like a boulder, lit a fag, put a German spiked helmet on his head and started cleaning his rifle.

'Did he give you that?' asked Clarkson.

'Nah, it was the Kaiser, who d'you think.'

'Did you wallop 'im hard then?'

'Who, the Kaiser?'

'No, the prisoner.'

'Nah, he already had a big bump on his head when I found 'im.'

'What caused that?'

'I dunno, but something did.'

'A rifle butt?'

'More like the butt from an elephant gun,' replied Thompson.

Clarkson frowned at him. 'Who's got one of those?'

Thompson shook his head. 'You're priceless, Clarkson, you know that? Just priceless.'

'Officer coming,' someone said, and the men sat up.

Packard knew how important it was to be seen by the men. He

stepped over their legs as they rested. Some were asleep already, faces to the sky at the bottom of the ditch; some were smoking, and some cleaning their rifles. He stopped here and there to give words of encouragement and praise. He noticed faces haggard from the strain and lack of sleep. But the men did pretty well, considering how outnumbered they were.

Wonder what my own face looks like, Packard thought.

He too was suffering from fatigue; fatigue and thirst did funny things to your face and could play havoc with your mind. Along the ditch, he spotted the spiked helmet on Thompson's head. Thompson, like Sergeant Campbell, was a regular soldier. Together they had first seen service in the Boer War, then India, and then Afghanistan. He would make a good NCO, he thought, but Thompson wasn't interested and enjoyed being 'one of the lads' and the banter that went with it, whereas Campbell climbed the promotion ladder. He liked him but was cautious and always said that he was "too cheeky for his own good." Still, Packard was pleased to have him in the company. He was good for moral when the younger ones were feeling a bit jumpy. He stood before him. Thompson looked up. 'Joining the other side, Thompson?' he joked.

'They say the pay is better, sir. Besides, I hear the weather is sunny in Berlin at the moment.'

'I might join you then. First drink on you.'

'That'll be a first, to get a drink out of Thompson,' someone said quietly.

'I heard that,' Thompson snapped back.

Laughter.

'You bagged a prisoner, Thompson. Well done. I've just received a note from battalion. They're cock-a-hoop about it. I see you bagged his helmet.'

'And this,' he said, grinning, holding up a long, dark sausage.

Packard smiled. 'Spoils of war. You're a resourceful fellow; I'll say that for you.'

'You speak German, don't you sir?' Clarkson asked.

'And French.'

'What made the Germans stop like that, sir? They outnumbered us.'

Thompson replied quickly. 'They're a bunch of dimwits, just like you, Clarkson, that's why.'

Everyone chuckled.

'I think it was a lack of leadership, Clarkson,' said Packard. 'We must have killed off most of their leaders during their attack. But what we lacked in numbers we made up for in courage, and I would like to tell you how proud I was of what you all did out there today. You all gave a good account of yourselves.' Packard was pleased to be among the men, cheered that the men were joking. It was a good sign. He nodded. 'Carry on,' he said and trudged his way back along the ditch.

''E's a good sort that one,' said Clarkson. 'I'd follow him to hell.'

'We already have,' quipped Thompson. He shoved the spiked helmet on Clarkson's head and took a big bite from the sausage.

*

For the next two hours the company was rested, resupplied with some food and water, and ammunition was distributed. Most of the company was now asleep apart from the sentries. Packard climbed to the lip of the ditch and took a cautious look across the meadow. The field-grey bundles of German wounded seemed quieter; dying of blood loss from their wounds and thirst, no doubt.

He swallowed hard and his stomach twisted into a tight knot at the thought that it could have been his men out there suffering. The watery evening sun was getting lower in the sky. There seemed to be a lull, and it gave no idea of the German intentions, as if the battle earlier had made them stop and think. Perhaps they were planning a night attack. But he dismissed that thought. No German bombardment as expected. Strange, that. What was Fritz up to? It seemed quiet, suspiciously quiet. He decided to visit the sentries and make sure they were alert. He began to buckle on his webbing. Campbell was snoring next to him. A runner from battalion HQ appeared; crouched low with his rifle at the trail.

'Lieutenant Packard!'

'Yes. Over here!'

The runner went to him, panting, with sweat running down his nose. He caught his breath and said, 'Colonel Drake wants to see you, straight away.'

'Very well.' The runner trotted off in the direction he'd come. Campbell opened his eyes, yawned, and stood up behind him. Packard turned to him and said, 'New orders I suspect, Sergeant.'

Campbell nodded. 'I knew a couple of hours' rest was too good to be true.'

*

It wasn't much of a café, but then it wasn't much of a village. Rubble was strewn about along with timber and broken furniture. Small flames were still licking round some of the piles of rubble. The whole area stank of smoke and cordite. The west side of the village had more damage from the shelling.

A guard stood outside the café and stiffened up as Packard approached. Packard just nodded and entered and was directed by an orderly down a steep flight of steps to the cellar. Paraffin lamps hung on the walls or sat on makeshift tables along with some candles. Cobwebs hung loose in the corners that were heavy with dust. The cellar was crowded and dank and smelt of dirt and sweat and tobacco smoke. Colonel Drake stood over a table with a map spread out, sucking on his empty pipe. He looked up as Packard entered and greeted him. 'Good to see you, Lieutenant. How are you?'

Packard liked Colonel Drake. There was no bullshit with him. He was a commanding officer you could look up to. But Packard was struck by just how old and exhausted Drake now looked. The weight of responsibility to his men and the regiment in this godforsaken war in the last few days had aged him. He was a casualty of war, just like everyone else. 'I'm fine sir,' Packard replied. 'Are you?'

Drake dismissed the question with a wave of his hand. 'I've more things to worry about, Lieutenant,' he said, then added, 'Did you and your men manage to get some rest?'

'A couple of hours, sir, thank you.'

'Good, good. Your company did very well during that attack and stopped the Germans cold. It took the pressure off C Company. Tight spot they were in too, I don't mind saying.'

'What exactly happened to C Company?'

Drake took a breath and spoke quietly, as if to explain the unacceptable. 'C Company's position got overrun during the attack,' he said. 'B Company was in reserve. I had to move them forward quickly to retake the position. In the fighting that followed, the casualties for both companies were simply shocking. Fifty-two men killed, nearly a hundred wounded. C Company lost all their officers: Captain Holder was killed, along with Lieutenants Kay and Blackman.'

Packard slowly shook his head. Holder was an excellent company commander, married with two children. Kay and Blackman had only joined the battalion two weeks ago as replacements for other officer casualties and both had been eager to acquit themselves in the eyes of the men. Now they were dead. What a waste.

Drake continued. 'Lieutenants Scott and North are badly

wounded. CSM Bailey is acting OC. B Company lost Captain Kelsey and Lieutenant Wright. Lieutenants Moore and Crane are also badly wounded and I'm told that Crane is not expected to live.' Packard glanced down for a moment and wiped his face with his hand.

'My God,' he murmured.

'I've sent my adjutant, Lieutenant Deighton, to run B Company. My chief clerk is now acting as my adjutant, but what else can we do except patch up and carry on until replacements arrive. It was a near run thing, I can tell you. Fritz threw everything into the attack and almost succeeded. But, in doing so, he got badly mauled. That's why it's been so quiet these last few hours. Fritz is licking his wounds, but he won't give up yet.'

He coughed. 'Anyway, I've got a job for you,' he said, hastily moving on. 'Look at the map.'

Packard stepped forward and leaned over. Drake was pointing at the map with the stem of his pipe. 'We're here,' Drake said, 'holding this line. Our cavalry scouts are to the north, keeping an eye on our flank just here.' He circled an area of the map with his pipe stem. 'German scouting parties have been seen moving north, trying to find a way to outflank us. About ten miles to our north is a small bridge over a river. Division want it denied to Fritz and held at all cost. That's where you come in.'

An orderly disturbed them with two mugs of hot steaming tea. Packard took it gratefully and cupped it with both hands, immediately taking a couple of gulps.

'I want your company to seize that bridge tonight and hold it until divisional engineers get there to blow it.'

'When will that be?' Packard asked between gulps.

'Tomorrow morning, first thing, but don't count on it. Expect them to be delayed for a few hours at least. A guide will take you there.'

'Once the bridge is blown, what do I do then?'

'Wait until the battalion arrives,' replied Drake. 'Like Fritz, we're all heading north.'

'What about our position here?'

'A company of Fusiliers fresh from England are moving up to replace you,' Drake said. 'They should be arriving any time now. Don't delay, Lieutenant. Get your men ready and make sure they have plenty of ammunition with them. Carry what you can. And here, take this.' He handed Packard a flare pistol with two cartridges. 'Fire a white flare if you're in trouble and need support. Cavalry units nearby will come to your aid. Fire the red one if you lose the bridge. The battalion will join you as soon as we can. About midday, I hope. Good luck, Lieutenant.'

'Thank you, sir.' Packard drained the last of his too-hot tea, saluted, left the cellar, and went back to the ditch.

*

Packard briefed Campbell and the junior NCOs. He didn't mention B and C Companies' losses. They had enough on their plate to worry about. They all scurried off to get extra ammunition and rations. The guide arrived, an orderly from battalion HQ, and Packard told him to report to Sergeant Campbell. Just then a smart but gawky-looking fresh-faced one-pipper with ginger hair and freckles jumped into the ditch beside him. He had the look of having come straight from Sandhurst, with his sword and revolver hanging from his polished Sam Browne. He had cannon-fodder written all over him. Packard wondered what this fresh-faced one-pipper must be thinking about his own appearance. He was unshaven with a dirty, blood-stained tunic with the odd button missing, looking bedraggled and tired wearing an 'other ranks webbing' and holding a rifle.

'Lieutenant Packard?' he asked, with a big toothy smile. 'I'm

Second Lieutenant Walton, Royal Fusiliers. We've come to take over your position.'

Packard looked toward the village and saw a column of men heading his way. He looked at his watch. Four hours to sunset. 'Right, oh,' Packard said, and quickly gave Walton a situation report. Campbell arrived and stood just behind him. 'Ah, Sergeant, tell the men to prepare to move as quick as they can. We're pulling out. I want to get to that bridge before nightfall.'

'Leave it to me, sir.' He turned and started trudging down the ditch shouting for the NCOs.

Walton looked out across the meadow at the German dead. 'We heard it was hand-to-hand fighting. Is that true?'

'It was.'

He swallowed hard. 'My God,' he said, 'I hope that never happens to us.'

'It will. You can count on that.'

'My God,' he repeated. 'Do you think I should arrange a burial party?' he asked.

'No, leave them. That's a German problem, not yours.' Packard heard the coldness in his own voice and inwardly he shuddered at what this war had made him – heartless. 'But they were brave men,' he added. 'Every one of them.'

The company was roused. 'Ah for Christ's sake, no peace for the wicked.'

'Speak for you'self.'

'Come on and look lively there, on your feet!'

The company trudged onto the road and fell into column.

'Where are we going?'

'Paris for the weekend, where'd you think?'

'My prayers have been answered then.'

'All right, keep it down. Fall in there, smarten up.'

Campbell turned to Packard. 'Company ready, sir.'

'All right, Sergeant. Follow the guide. Let's get going and keep a sharp pace.'

'Sir.' He turned and faced the column. 'Company, by the left, quick march!'

CHAPTER 3

'Churchill, Winston Churchill, is he here?'

The Belgian naval officer, in his immaculate navy-blue uniform with a single row of medals across his chest, along with a cabinet private secretary, had been hunting for his man first at his office in the Admiralty, then at Downing Street, before being directed to try at the East India Club in St. James's Square.

Simpson, the head porter sitting behind the reception desk, raised his dark eyebrows towards his short grey hair as he met the officer's eye. Simpson, who had acquired unassailable dignity over 30 years at the club, slowly rose to his six feet two inches. Courtesy edged with forcefulness was his deepest instinct in all confrontations and politely replied, 'Mr Churchill is having lunch with a guest, sir, and left explicit instructions not to be disturbed.'

'He will see me. Disturb him at once!'

Simpson raised his eyebrows even further at this outburst. His experience at dealing with government officials at the club was legendary, but their demeanour told him this was different, and he judged that it could be important – very important. They looked in no mood to be fobbed off by a club porter – even by someone like Simpson. He felt a little uneasy. 'Very well, sir. Whom shall I say is calling?'

'Tell him Captain Andre Dubois, Belgian naval attaché,' said the officer, and handed him his card, as did the government official, Sir Peter Chatsworth, whose card stated he worked for the Secretary of

State for War. 'It is vital that we speak to him.'

When Simpson read both cards, he placed them on a small silver tray. 'Of course, gentlemen. Now if you would care to take a seat, I will inform Mr Churchill that you are here and that you wish to see him.'

Normally, Simpson would have turned them away without batting an eyelid but things were different now. There was a war on, and Churchill was First Lord of the Admiralty in the Liberal government, with responsibility for the entire British navy.

Simpson entered the dining room. Churchill and his guest, Vice Admiral Prince Louis of Battenberg, were sitting in the far corner, away from other diners, next to a window. They had finished their meal and were drinking a vintage port. Simpson was fully aware that Churchill hated being disturbed at lunch, so he approached the table with some apprehension. He stood beside Churchill, who was fully engaged in conversation and had not noticed him. He coughed. Churchill stopped talking and looked up at Simpson as though he were showing disrespect.

'I beg your pardon, sir, but you have two visitors waiting in reception. They are most insistent on seeing you.'

'Who the devil are they?'

'A government official and a Belgian naval officer, sir,' replied Simpson. Churchill saw their two cards on the small silver tray that Simpson had lowered to him. He snatched them up and read them, then showed them to Prince Louis. 'Hmm,' he said. 'How odd.'

Prince Louis nodded in agreement and said, 'Captain Dubois returned to Antwerp last week to organise the gold shipment. It must be urgent if he had to return back to London so soon.'

Churchill flicked the cards with his index finger for a few seconds then said, 'Simpson, is the reading room free?

'It is, sir.'

'Then I'll join them there shortly. See to it that we are not disturbed.'

'Very good, sir.'

'And Simpson …'

'Sir?'

'Four whiskeys in the reading room.'

'As you please, sir.'

*

Churchill and Prince Louis came into the room. It was a bright room with four long floor-to-ceiling windows which opened out to a narrow balcony that looked across St. James's Square. The chairs were comfortable, with red-buttoned leather, and large portraits hung on the walls. A few highly polished tables were scattered around with chairs. Captain Dubois stood up, as did Sir Peter. He had met Captain Dubois before, several times in fact, and had once accompanied Churchill on a tour of the Belgian fleet.

Churchill was thirty-nine years old, slim, with receding hair, and eight years older than Captain Dubois, who looked somewhat out of place dressed in naval uniform in the reading room of a gentleman's club in the centre of London. The three other men were dressed in dark suits.

Churchill cheerfully shook hands with Captain Dubois. 'Good afternoon, Captain,' he said, then turned to Chatsworth and shook his hand. 'Sir Peter.'

'Good afternoon, Minister,' replied Sir Peter. 'Thank you for seeing us.'

Churchill returned to Captain Dubois. 'You know Prince Louis, of course.'

'Indeed, sir. How do you do, Admiral?' They shook hands warmly.

'Please, sit down,' Churchill said. The four men took their places around one of the tables, where a tray and four whiskeys sat in the middle. With a twinkle in his eye Churchill got straight to the point. 'I can see that this is not a social visit, so you had better tell me what you want.'

Captain Dubois began. 'My apologies for imposing on you like this but I have come straight from Belgium; Antwerp to be exact.'

Churchill nodded. 'It sounds intriguing, Captain, but do go on.'

Captain Dubois looked grave. 'We are a small country with limited resources, so our defence against any aggressor would be built around our fortress towns and cities. As you know, King Albert and the Belgian government have located in Antwerp. Our perimeter defence at Antwerp relies solely on the 48 inner and outer fortresses that ring the city. So far, these have held. We have a garrison of 80,000 troops and, as agreed with your government, King Albert has ordered a number of counterattacks from the fortresses against the German flank in an attempt to pull more German troops away from their advance into north-west France. The Germans need all the troops they can muster if their rapid advance into France through Belgium is to succeed.'

'We are relying on Antwerp holding,' said Churchill. 'It is a formidable drain on German resources. The presence of so many Belgian troops on the German flank in that city presents it with a constant threat. Our intelligence tells us that the German High Command has already detached four divisions from their advance into France solely to face attacks from Antwerp. It's slowing down the German advance and it is vital to hold on to Antwerp at all costs.'

Captain Dubois nodded. 'I agree, sir. But for how long. At Liege and at Namur, the Germans used big powerful guns to destroy the defensive fortresses around those cities. In a matter of a few days, the cities were captured. Those big guns are now on their way to Antwerp. Aware of this, King Albert, along with his administration, is preparing to abandon Antwerp to save his army and escape west along the coastal route to Ostend leaving the port to the Germans.'

A chill ran down Churchill's spine. He remembered reading an intelligence report a year ago that the Krupp factory had developed two road-mobile 16.5 inch siege howitzers weighing over 42 tons each, capable of firing a 2,100lb shell over 16,000 yards within 30 minutes once on site with the express purpose of defeating the strongest concrete, stone, steel, or earthwork fortifications liable to be encountered around strategic cities. British military analysis of the report at the time, he remembered, concluded that such a weapon could not be "road-mobile" and would weigh in excess of 100 tons. The logistics of moving the whole weapon around the battlefield would be a nightmare and made no sense. They concluded that, at best, it was purely a weapon designed for coastal defence. How wrong could they be? But survivors' reports from Liege and Namur mentioned big German guns firing shell after shell that smashed into the outer-line of fortresses one by one, ripping armour plate away like wet paper and reducing concrete to dust, leaving behind layers of rubble and twisted steel girders. All within a matter of a few days. It seemed King Albert, doubtless fearful of the consequences should Antwerp be under siege from the two big German guns, had already planned his escape with his government.

'When do you expect the big guns to be at Antwerp?' Churchill asked.

'By the first of October at the latest,' replied Captain Dubois.

Churchill gasped. 'Four days' time,' he said. 'Not long to form a plan.'

'A plan?' asked Prince Louis.

'If King Albert cannot hold Antwerp alone then we must help him. We must buy time. When Antwerp falls, and it will, the Germans can sweep along the coast, cutting our army off from the Channel ports. The war will be lost. Each day Antwerp holds buys us time to plug the gap and secure our supply line.' Churchill looked directly at Sir Peter. 'Is Kitchener aware of this situation?'

'He is,' replied Sir Peter, 'but he can only supply one division. Our losses in France have been significant. All reinforcements are destined for the BEF. This has been endorsed by the Prime Minister.'

'If we lose the Channel ports there'll be no reinforcements and no BEF! Surely he can supply three divisions at least.'

Sir Peter shook his head. 'One division, that's all.'

'We cannot possibly stand aside and watch Antwerp fall, and then watch our own inevitable defeat as the Germans rush into France along the coast and cut off our supply lines. It's madness!'

Prince Louis interrupted. 'Perhaps we can help.'

Churchill looked at Prince Louis with narrowed eyes for a moment then said, 'Us? How can we help?'

'We have two newly-formed naval brigades in England and a Royal Marine brigade that is already in France guarding the Port of Dunkirk,' Prince Louis explained. 'Together with the army division, we could reinforce Antwerp and buy time to plug the gap.'

'But the two naval brigades have just been formed,' he said, 'with virtually no equipment or any experience for such an important task. They've hardly had time to train for war.'

'Cometh the hour, cometh the man,' said Sir Peter.

Churchill looked at their stony faces for a moment. There was no choice. 'Very well, gentlemen,' he said, 'I shall inform the PM that we will mobilise the two naval brigades and the Royal Marine brigade to Antwerp.'

'Thank you,' replied Captain Dubois.

'Should I inform Lord Kitchener or will you do that, Sir Peter?'

'Leave that to me,' replied the civil servant. 'Lord Kitchener will be very relieved.'

'Good. And now,' Churchill said as he reached for a tumbler of whisky, 'let us pray that they arrive in time.'

They all took a tumbler and a sip.

Then turning to Captain Dubois, Churchill said, 'You got the gold away as planned?' Belgian government gold had been moved from banks in Brussels and stored in various banks in Western Belgium, close to the French border to prevent it falling into German hands. But with the rapid advance by the Germans into Belgium, there was a scramble to collect it all and take it to Antwerp to be shipped to England to stop the Germans using the gold to help fund their military machine for war.

'I arrived in Dover with it this morning,' said Dubois. 'But King Albert's personal gold is still in a bank vault in a sleepy market town called Ypres. We have been unable to arrange transport for it. We are still trying but I'm afraid it will be lost. In the next few days the Germans will occupy the town.'

Churchill's eyes narrowed. 'The King's personal gold, to be lost to Germany?'

Captain Dubois nodded slowly. 'I'm afraid so.'

'How much gold?' Prince Louis asked.

Captain Dubois shrugged. 'I'm told it's about three hundred bars along with eight barrels of coins. Two and a half, to three tonnes I should think. Each bar is worth about five hundred and fifty pounds. With the coins it's worth nearly three million pounds.'

'In terms of that weight and transport that would be, what, two lorries' worth?'

'At least,' replied Captain Dubois. 'But we don't have the means to arrange that or the lorries to move it. As I said, the Germans will be there soon so the gold is probably lost. King Albert is fully aware of the situation.'

'Then we must try to get it back,' argued Churchill. 'Why can't we send some troops to get it?'

'We don't have anyone spare, Minister,' replied Sir Peter. 'Besides, we are desperately short of lorries ourselves. We have just commandeered fifty London buses to help transport our troops in France. Now you want two lorries and a squad of men to chase after some gold that is probably going to fall into German hands anyway!'

Churchill looked at Sir Peter with narrowed eyes, he leaned forward and began banging the flat of his hand on the table, saying, 'How many guns can you have made for three million pounds? How many men can you equip? If we leave that gold to the Germans, it will come back to kill us as bullets and shells. We have got to try at least,' he said. 'There must be a small group of soldiers we could pull from the line with two lorries and just go to Ypres and collect the gold. What a triumph that would be! Don't you agree, Sir Peter?'

'Of course, but do we have the time and the resources to do this?'

'If King Albert's gold falls into German hands,' said Churchill, 'the Kaiser will use it as propaganda. Imagine this; the King's personal gold being used to pay for German guns to defeat the Belgian army. It could demoralise the Belgian troops in Antwerp, and if Antwerp falls too soon, then our own army will be outflanked and cut off from the Channel coast and from its vital supply lines.'

'And we all know what that means,' said Prince Louis. 'We would lose the war in a matter of days and the Kaiser takes Europe.'

'If I go to the PM with this,' said Churchill, 'will you all support me?'

They all looked at one another and nodded.

'Very well, gentleman, I shall go immediately to Downing Street, but this has to be kept secret from your staff if there is going to be any chance of success. Agreed?'

Three voices spoke as one.

'Agreed.'

CHAPTER 4

The company had been marching for three hours along narrow country roads. Some were tree-lined, where the shade afforded some respite from the heat of the evening sun. Other roads ran along open fields where the sun burned on their backs. Each man carrying a nine-pound rifle and laden with over seventy pounds of webbing and equipment strapped to his back. They took it in turns to carry the heavy wooden ammunition boxes by rope handles that were swinging to and fro between them. Packard knew the pace was tough; it had to be if they were to make the bridge by nightfall. He put NCOs at their sides like sheepdogs, giving encouragement, and helping to carry the rifles of men who were flagging even though they had two short five-minute breaks during the march.

Packard knew the men were tired, but they had kept up a cracking pace. So far, no man had fallen out. Before leaving to re-join the battalion back at the village, the guide calculated they were about half a mile from the bridge. Packard thanked him and noticed dark clouds starting to roll in ahead of them. They were ahead of time, so he decided to give them a quick break before they reached the bridge.

'Sergeant Campbell, we'll take another five-minute smoke break.'

'Very good, sir.' He turned to the column strung out behind him. 'Company ... companeeee halt!' They all came to an untidy stop. There was a scurry of activity whilst the NCOs stood before Campbell. 'Right, usual routine, sit them down on the grass verge for a fag. Post sentries, and put a couple in the tree line behind us. We've got five minutes. Off you go.' The NCOs fell out and started barking out orders.

Some men lay down exhausted, facing the sky breathing deeply, whilst others just sat there silently with sweat running down their vacant faces. Cigarettes were being lit up, coughing broke out along the line.

'Bloody 'ard going, this is. We'll be in Berlin by nightfall if we aren't careful.'

'I'd rather be in bed snuggled up to a warm, soft, plump woman.'

'Hear that, Ted, he's talking about your missus again.'

'I've nothing to worry about. Once she sees the size of his dick she'll die laughing.' Laughter broke out amongst the men. 'Anyway, he's welcome to her. I'd rather have a cold beer.'

'Me too. I could drink a bloody brewery dry, so I could.'

'Or die trying.'

'All right, keep it down you noisy bastards,' said one NCO. 'Save your breath for marching.'

Campbell lit a cigarette and sat down next to Packard. Sweat was trickling down his face. Packard didn't smoke. His heart still thumped from the hard march as he wiped away the stinging sweat from his eyes. He took off his cap to fan his face. 'The men have done well,' he said. 'We're almost there. I was tempted to push on but we've made good time. We all deserve a rest I think.'

Campbell didn't answer; he just nodded. He cupped the cigarette in his hands, took a drag, and blew a thin stream of smoke in the air. He was still alert and listening for strange sounds about him. Packard looked at him and just assumed he was tired like everyone else and sat in silence except for the soft sound of the wind. The sun was sinking slowly on the horizon and the shadows were growing longer. A cloud of midges gathered in a spill of warm sunshine amongst the trees. A gust got up, leaves and twigs blew about. Suddenly, Campbell stood up, twisting his head in all directions.

Packard looked up. 'Something wrong?'

Campbell stayed rock still and stared up the road. 'I don't know,' he said. 'I thought I heard a horse.' Packard stood up and replaced his cap snug on his head and listened with him for a moment. Nothing; not a thing, except the wind and the rustling leaves. He looked towards the tree line behind them. Nothing but bushes, grass, twisting tree trunks, and shadows. 'Have we got a sentry in there?'

'Yes, of course, sir,' Campbell replied softly, and began to fiddle with his rifle.

Packard knew that wind playing through rustling trees and bushes can play tricks on the tired minds of soldiers. Nonetheless, Campbell's face looked genuinely worried. He was an experienced soldier who cut his teeth in South Africa during the Boer War, then India, and the North West Frontier with Afghanistan, and if he was spooked it was worth being cautious. It made sense for German cavalry to have a scouting patrol out here to watch this road. That thought sent a prickle of fear up and down his spine.

'I don't like it, sir. I feel as if we're being watched.'

Packard knew his Sergeant well enough not to ignore his concern. It wasn't the first time in this war his instinct proved correct, but he could see nothing, nor hear anything except the wind – that and the quiet.

Corporal Hedges got up and sheepishly stood at their side. He was the oldest and most experienced NCO in the company. Like Campbell he was a Boer War veteran. 'What's happening, Sarge?'

Campbell shook his head. 'I don't know, Corporal. Thought I heard a horse, that's all.'

Hedges un-slung his rifle and lifted it into the alert position. 'Shall

I stand the men to?' They remained silent for a while; all movement stopped. Packard turned and looked down the line of men sitting on the grass verge, to his surprise they were all staring back at him. No one moved.

Hedges leaned closer to Campbell, lowering his voice he said, 'Just like South Africa, isn't it? Bloody terrifying.'

'What is?'

'The silence,' he said. Campbell didn't reply but understood well enough. They all felt it.

There was a noise. Two pigeons suddenly burst from a tree above. The men froze. The snap, snap, snap of the birds' wings trailed away as they flew off across a field. 'Fuckin 'ell,' someone murmured. 'Shush,' came a stern reply from Hedges who glared back.

A distant crackling sound made their stomachs turn into a tight knot. Suddenly, a sentry came rushing out of the tree line. 'Sir, sir, two horsemen!' He turned and pointed. Barely a hundred yards away through the gloomy bushes and twisting trunks of the wood, two horsemen were visible. Packard, Campbell, and Hedges gripped their rifles as the two horsemen broke into a trot and headed towards them. Campbell proved right after all.

There was a fractional hesitation of what to do before Packard recognised one rider on the chestnut horse. 'It's all right,' he said reassuringly, 'it's Captain Denton from Brigade HQ.' The other rider was on a bigger mount that was black with a docked tail and he had the rank of major with red tabs on his tunic collar. He looked tall and thin with a big Adams apple and he had a thin pencil moustache along his top lip. His tunic was smart and clean with black shiny boots. His belt carried binoculars, a map case, and a revolver. The saddle and harness were immaculate, but the horse's legs were splashed with mud. Packard suspected he was a staff officer looking over the ground with

Denton before the bulk of the army arrived tomorrow.

They reined in as Denton curbed his snorting horse that was excessively nodding its head. He leaned forward from his saddle and patted the neck, murmuring an endearment to calm it. Unlike the Major, Denton looked more at home in the field; a rifle hung from his saddle, a leather ammunition bandolier slung across his chest, there wasn't a scrape of evidence of spit and polish about him, just a fighting soldier; efficient and sensible. 'Lieutenant Packard,' he said. 'We've been waiting for you.'

'I wasn't expecting to see you here, sir.'

Denton gestured to his left and introduced the rider next to him. 'This is Major Scott-Bardwell,' he said, 'divisional intelligence.' The Major looked down his long thin nose with disapproval at Packard's grubby state and gave a slight nod. He seemed too stuck-up to offer more. Packard was pleased that he had guessed right and just nodded back. He sensed this officer had taken an instant dislike to him. 'Sir,' he said as a means of acknowledgement.

Denton continued, 'We've been on a fact-finding field trip. The news isn't good.' His voice was gloomy. 'It's just our luck that Fritz has got to the bridge before you with a squad of about twenty men. They have a machine gun to cover this road. We waited here to make sure you didn't blunder into it. That machine gun would have cut you down to pieces.'

Packard digested the news. Damn it, he thought. He was hoping to be in a defensive position around the bridge before the Germans got there. Worse still, now it looked like he would have to fight for it. 'I'm grateful for that, sir. It would have been a disaster for us had we done so.' Then Packard lifted his cap and scratched his forehead. 'About twenty men you say, with a machine gun. Must be the vanguard?'

'They'll be waiting for reinforcements to follow them up,' the Major said.

'If that's the case,' replied Packard, 'we don't have a second to lose if we're to take that bridge back.'

'Think you can handle it, Lieutenant?' asked Denton with a rueful smile.

'Of course. I have eighty men. That should be enough, but I'll need to recce the bridge area first.'

The Major frowned and turned to Denton. 'I think this job is too important to be left to a mere half-strength Company led by a lieutenant. Granted that the odds are in his favour, but he'll be going up against a machine gun. It would make sense to wait until the battalion arrives in strength in the morning. We'd stand a much better chance of success.'

'Nonsense,' replied Denton. 'We have to do something now. I know this officer and his men. Lieutenant Packard is perfectly capable of getting that bridge back. I trust him. Besides, we don't have the luxury of time if Fritz is waiting for reinforcements. They could arrive any moment. That bridge is vital to them if they want to turn our flank.'

The Major wrinkled his nose. 'Very well, Captain, if you insist. I think you are both bloody fools. But I want it noted that I objected to this idea.' He then fumbled inside his breast tunic pocket, pulling out a watch and sprang the lid. 'About one hour of daylight left.' He looked up at the dark clouds rolling in. 'Looks like rain.'

'Good,' said Packard. 'I'll recce the bridge in daylight and attack it at night.' He saw the look on the Major's face and suspected that he did not approve. But the Major remained silent. Then, turning to Denton, Packard said, 'If I could hitch a lift on the back of your horse it would save time.'

'Of course,' replied Denton. 'But you'll need to drop off your equipment.'

Packard unbuckled his webbing, dropping it to the floor. 'Sergeant Campbell, take care of this, and move the men into the tree line where they can't be seen from the road, at least a quarter of a mile closer to the bridge. Wait for me there. Keep them out of sight and silent.'

'Very good, sir. Leave it to me.'

'It'll be dark when I get back so we better have a password. The challenge is "Richmond"; the reply is "Bridge". Got that?'

'Got it, sir. Good luck.'

Packard took off his cap and wiped his brow. He flexed his fingers and reached up to get a grip on the back of the saddle. Denton grabbed him and helped haul him up behind him. The horse felt the weight and staggered a bit. He wheeled the horse round and, with the Major, trotted back into the wood the way they came.

Campbell slung his officer's webbing over one shoulder and gave his rifle to Hedges. 'Fall the men in, Corporal. I want a strict silent routine. No noise, got it? Let's get started.'

*

It took ten minutes to get there by horse and another ten minutes to find a suitable position. The major looked after the two horses whilst Denton and Packard rubbed dirt on their faces before going forward to reconnoitre. Packard suddenly realised that he had no weapon. He handed his rifle and his webbing, with pistol holster attached, to Sergeant Campbell before he left. Now, being so close to the enemy, he felt quite naked and vulnerable.

They approached the bridge from a hillside opposite, carefully scanning the ground looking for a shaded spot amongst some bushes with plenty of cover that gave clear views down the slope to the bridge.

The approach was slow going. The evening light was fading fast. The hillside was thick with bushes, long grass, and trees overlooking the river. Packard with Denton crawled the last few yards, occasionally stopping to peer anxiously at the bridge below about two hundred yards away. They found a spot with good foliage cover that was ideal and crawled into it. Denton searched his tunic pocket for his watch, took it out, and flipped the lid. 'About fifteen minutes of daylight left if we're lucky,' he said softly.

Packard nodded and gave himself a moment to control his breathing, not from any real exertion getting to this spot, but from the adrenalin pumping round his body. He eased himself up a little on his elbows, looking around him. He pushed his cap up and lifted the Zeiss binoculars to his eyes. Through the circle of lenses, he focused on the bridge. It was a plain stone bridge with a single arch that spanned a fast-flowing river approximately sixty feet across. It was a hundred years old or more and too well built just to support the fragile local economy. It was probably built to transport Napoleon's army across this natural barrier when the French were the scourge of Europe. Today, it just allowed ease of access across the river for the local village peasants and farmers attending the markets in the nearby towns. Now that the armies were back again, the bridge resumed its true purpose and importance.

The entrance to the bridge had two guards slowly pacing up and down to relieve their boredom. Their rifles slung loosely over their shoulder and tipped with a bayonet. On the left side of the entrance were three stone cottages that were low and squat and had all the hallmarks of poverty. To the right, the three stone cottages were bigger with two floors, the windows lit by lanterns or candles. The pool of pale light spilling onto the road. Smoke rose from the chimneys. There was no sign of the inhabitants. This wasn't unusual.

The Germans would normally kick out any inhabitants they found and send them away to use their homes for a billet.

Along from these cottages were a few rickety outbuildings and two wooden barns that had seen better days. Here, dug-in beside the last barn, was the machine gun pointing south down the road with a good arc of fire. It was cleverly sited and almost impossible to be seen from the road until you got on top of it. By that time, it would have been too late. Again, two guards stood by with their rifles tipped with bayonets and slung over their shoulders. They were wearing the soft peak-less field cap known as the *Feldmutze* that was round and resembled a porkpie. The standard field torch hung from the second button of their tunic. Sitting beside the machine gun, busying with belts of ammunition, was another soldier smoking a cigarette with open tunic and wearing a soft field cap with a short leather peak. He was talking to the two guards. Obviously, the NCO in charge of the machine gun crew, Packard thought.

The cottages to the left of the bridge looked gloomy and deserted with broken roof tiles where grass now grew. He heard the sound of a door slamming shut and swung the binos back to his right. There, two Germans emerged from a cottage and slowly headed to the bridge entrance. One was tall and elegant. He was an officer wearing brown leather gloves and his boots were high and shiny black. He was wearing a pickelhaube spike helmet with a grey cloth cover. On his brown leather belt was attached a large pistol holder and he carried a sword. The other German was short and stocky with a dark bushy moustache, he wore a field cap with a leather peak. His tunic collar and epaulettes were edged in a distinctive white lace. He carried a rifle, and a long bayonet hung from his belt with an NCOs' knot. He was a senior NCO.

They stopped and spoke to the men guarding the bridge entrance and then crossed the bridge to speak to two more on the other side. They returned and slowly walked along the deserted cottages until they reached the end one. There two guards suddenly emerged from a ditch beside the road. After a few moments they returned back to the cottage.

Denton said in a low voice, 'They look quite relaxed.'

'They may be relaxed, sir, but I think we can assume they are not fools. They look disciplined.'

'True,' replied Denton. 'The road south is covered with that machine gun and their billet is right behind it. The road south is where they are expecting trouble. I take it you're not thinking of attacking from that direction?'

'We wouldn't stand a chance. There's no way of approaching from the road without being seen or heard. But I have a much better idea.'

Denton turned to him. 'What's that?'

'Speed and surprise.'

*

Major Scott-Bardwell waited patiently with the two horses. Packard and Denton slowly worked their way back further up the slope. They could still see the road and bridge below between the bushes and the trees. It was almost dark when they breasted the last ridge and reached the major, panting a little.

'Well?' said the major impatiently.

Packard caught his breath and replied. 'The road in is out of the question, that's for sure.'

'Then what's the point?'

'It's a tough nut to crack, sir, but I have a plan.'

'What plan?' he demanded.

'There's no time to discuss it here,' said Denton. 'Let's get going.'

Silently they climbed on the two horses and quietly moved away with only the wind blowing through the tress to stir the leaves and bushes that muffled the hooves of the horses as they tramped along. Packard felt a fleck of rain on his face and lifted his head to confirm it. A moment later he felt stronger rain drops. It was drizzle at first, but it was starting to rain. The stillness of the wood worried him, but rain could hide a thousand noises. A few minutes later they got the challenge.

'Richmond?' The voice was invisible in the darkness.

The hooves stopped. They froze. 'Bridge,' replied Packard.

The shadows of Campbell and a sentry stepped forward.

Packard wasted no time climbing down from the horse, rubbing his backside. If he never rode another horse again, he wouldn't be sorry. 'Got my gear, Sergeant?' He handed it to him. He buckled on his webbing and slung the rifle over his shoulder. His eyes watching dark grey shapes of the men as they moved around him. In a low voice he said, 'Get the men ready, Sergeant, we're moving out. I want total silence. Make sure they all understand that.'

There was a squeak of leather as one of the riders got out of his saddle. A tall figure came out of the shadow and stood next to him. It was the Major.

'Now look here, Lieutenant,' his voice was full of distain, 'where the hell are you going now?'

'Back to where we just came from. I'll brief the men once we get there.'

'For God's sake, man, this creeping around all over the bloody countryside in the dead of night like lost sheep. Do you have any idea what you're doing?'

Packard bluntly replied, 'I do, sir, and we should be thanking God that it's raining.'

*

It took nearly an hour to get the company into the right position. Quietly they counted themselves off in the darkness. All were present. Packard called for the NCOs and invited the Major and Denton to join him. Denton listened intently and felt buoyed up as Packard put his instructions across in a clear, business-like way. He explained the terrain, the cottages, the position of the machine gun and that of the German sentries around the bridge, and that he intended to use stealth to get in close and then use speed and surprise to subdue them.

'It's like this,' he said. 'I don't want anyone to fire a shot unless it's absolutely necessary. The rain will be to our advantage. It'll make the sentries less alert and hide any soft noise from our approach. We go in silently and gently, and just use the bayonet or rifle butt.' He then selected two NCOs. 'Pick three men each; reliable men,' he added. 'There will be four groups of four men. I'll lead one group in to take the two sentries near the machine gun. Thompson's had training on a machine gun so I'll take him with me. Corporal Barlow will take the two sentries at the end of the derelict cottages. Once that's complete, Corporal Johnson will bring in his group to cover me at the machine gun for support. Sergeant Campbell will bring in the fourth group to take the two sentries on our side of the bridge. It will be light assault order so dump most of your webbing; just carry ammo pouches. I don't want anything carried that rattles, bumps, or makes a noise on the approach. You all know what to do, now choose your men and report back here in five minutes.' He turned to Corporal Hedges. 'I want you and Corporal Partridge to follow up with the rest of the men to the start point. Select ten men to follow us to the halfway point so they can cover us should we run into trouble and have to fall back. Got that?'

'Yes, sir.'

'Good man. Major Scott-Bardwell and Captain Denton will remain here with the two horses. I don't want any noise from them that could give us away. Best leave two men behind with them just in case.'

'Very good, sir.'

Once the four groups assembled in front of Packard, he got them to jump up and down and quickly discarded any item making unnecessary noise. Satisfied, he ordered all the men to put a round up the spout of their rifles and lock the safety catches. He and Sergeant Campbell checked every rifle. 'And God help any man I see playing with the safety catch,' Campbell said as he walked the line.

'We'll all go to the start point together,' said Packard. 'And remember, not a bloody sound.'

Denton interrupted, 'I'd like to tag along. Can I come with you?'

'Of course, sir, but the same applies to you. Discard everything you have that could make a noise and just bring your revolver.'

Denton quickly threw off his Sam Brown, binos, and map case and, with his revolver drawn, he jumped up and down.

'Ok,' said Packard, 'let's go. Follow me.' He walked off.

The Major grabbed Denton's arm. 'Wait a minute. You're not seriously thinking of taking part in this foolery, are you?'

'Why not, the plan is sound.'

'Sound, be damned. All this creeping about in the woods in the dead of night will get you all killed, for heaven's sake. This is madness. I say we wait until the battalion arrives in the morning.'

'And if the Germans arrive in strength before – then what?'

Packard returned. 'What's the holdup here?'

'Nothing,' replied Denton. 'All's fine.'

'Well, let's go then.' Packard turned and retraced his steps and led the line of men into the unending blackness in the rain. He could hear their shuffling feet in the long grass, hoping that when the time came for the approach, the German sentries would be too occupied trying to keep out of the rain to notice any soft noise of their footfall coming from the wood. He stared ahead at the dark shadowy trees and bushes and held his rifle at the ready, as did all the men. After ten minutes, Packard raised his arm and they stopped and crouched down. He sniffed the damp air and looked about him. There, through the bushes, about a hundred and fifty yards' away, he could make out a pool of light from one of the cottages the Germans were using as a billet. He turned to Campbell behind him. 'This is it,' he said softly. 'Pass the groups through me and put them into position along here.'

Campbell quietly called the line of men forward and, with an NCO in front, they slowly filed past. Campbell went along the line of men, making sure they were sufficiently spaced apart and in their correct grouping. The two NCOs were called to the middle either side of Campbell for better control.

Packard bit his lip and just listened to the night and the rain for a moment and then, in a whisper, 'OK, let's get on with it.' They all stood up, rifles held at the ready, bayonets fixed, they started their descent down the slope towards the bridge.

CHAPTER 5

Packard looked along the wavering line of shadowy figures, and at Denton beside him, revolver held high across his chest. Stealthily they went forward down the slope with only the sound of their footfall through the long grass, with Packard keeping the pace slow and deliberate. He could hear the occasional stumble and a groan but nothing to worry about. The rain pattering down, along with the breeze rustling the leaves of trees and bushes, would suffocate any such noise.

He heard the men gasping for breath, though not through exertion, but from the fear, and the quiet shuffling of their slow footfall, one careful step after another. Small dark objects scurried away from them. Rabbits, lots of them. Packard heard some of his men take a sharp intake of breath from nerves at the suddenness of this movement before them.

When they were about halfway, he brought them to a halt and cradled his rifle across his arm. Packard stood stock still and felt the trickle of rain running down his neck. They all waited while he listened. Nothing. Only the sound of the men breathing and the patter of rainfall, and no noise coming from the bridge. So far, so good.

Packard's main concern was they hit the sentries with speed and surprise. Without it, they would be doomed, and he prayed that his men would live to see the dawn of a new day. He turned to Denton and leaned toward him and in a whisper, he said, 'Pass it on, we're going in now.'

Packard waited a moment for the message to be passed down the line then he turned to his group and softly said, 'Thompson, stick with me. We'll take the two sentries by the gun. The rest of you follow me.'

They started off with a quick walking pace and as they got nearer the pace quickened until it was almost a trot, their footfall becoming noisier but still masked by the rain. They all looked anxiously at their front, to the dark shape of the cottages with the pale orange light glowing from the windows. They didn't seem to be getting nearer until the shadowy outline of the cottages, outbuildings, and barns loomed up and they crossed the road at a rush. Packard, with Thompson, passed the machine gun and found the two German sentries sheltering from the rain under a rickety awning eating sausage and bread. By the time they knew that Packard and Thompson were there they had quickly clubbed them out cold.

'Good work,' whispered Denton

'Thanks, but we've got to move fast.' He turned to Thompson. 'Get on that gun and get it ready if we need support.'

'Yessir.'

'Jones, gag them,' he whispered, 'tie them up and stand guard over them.'

Thompson swung the machine gun around. They sweated and wheezed, their hearts still hammering in their chests. They were glad the first part was over. The machine gun was now in their hands. Corporal Johnson arrived with his group all panting heavily and reported to Packard.

'Stay here,' he told him, 'and secure this end with Thompson and Jones. Form a defensive position around that machine gun. Under no circumstances can Fritz get his hands on it, understand?'

'Leave it to me, sir.'

'Good man.' Then he turned to Denton. 'Come with me, and careful now, no noise.' Slowly they crept along the side of the barn in the darkness toward the cottages. Suddenly a soldier's silhouette appeared in front of him, seemingly from nowhere. Packard took a sharp intake of breath and quickly raised his rifle butt to lash out as he heard the metallic *click* from Denton's revolver as he pulled back the hammer. 'That you, sir?' a voice said, and they both instantly recognised it as Sergeant Campbell.

'Christ! You gave me quite a fright, Sergeant. I was about to clobber you.'

Campbell said, 'Sorry, sir. Just reporting, we've taken the sentries on the bridge.'

'Good work, Sergeant. Where's Corporal Barlow?'

'I think he's over there, to our left, near the entrance to the bridge.'

'Where's your group?'

'Covering the doorway in case Fritz decides to leave.'

'Good man. Let's take a look.'

Light from the cottage windows spilled across the dirt road and reflected on the faces of the crouching men either side, all staring at him and gripping their rifles tightly. Packard put a finger to his lips and then leaned to the window to look in.

It was difficult to see inside through the heavy lace curtains although he could see figures of men sitting down and relaxing. Few Germans were wearing their tunics. It was all very relaxed but unusually so. The décor was purple with heavy drape curtains at the windows. A girl walked in with long brown hair and went over to a table with three Germans and sat next to one, immediately putting her hand on his thigh. She whispered something in his ear and then nuzzled his neck. He laughed out loud and then kissed her hard on the lips and they both got up, the girl taking him by the hand and leading him out of the room. Then another girl walked in who was a bit plump with large breasts and she too walked over to the table, whispering into the ear of one of the Germans. He nodded encouragingly and he too got up and was led away by the girl. Packard rubbed his chin.

'Well?' whispered Denton. 'What is it?'

'If I'm not mistaken, this is a brothel.'

'A brothel?' Denton leaned forward to get a better look. 'You don't say,' he murmured.

'This changes things,' whispered Packard. 'They'll be easier to take because of their relaxed state. Their minds on other things. They won't be expecting us to come crashing through the door. So, this is the plan. Sergeant Campbell, put a section of men around the back to secure it, then report back here. Quiet now.'

'Yessir.'

'Corporal Johnson?'

'Sir.'

'Captain Denton and I will enter the cottage first. Your section will follow us through. Check every room including those upstairs and bring all the Fritzes into the main front room. Speed and surprise are the key to success, got that?'

'Yes sir, but what about the girls?'

Packard forgot about the girls then made an instant decision. 'Them too. Just put them in the back parlour for now. I'll deal with them once we've all the Germans subdued and under control.' Corporal Johnson grinned and nodded. 'Try not to shoot anyone unless you really have to. Just be assertive with them, lots of authority. Got that?'

'Yes sir,' he replied softly.

Campbell appeared. 'All secure at the back, sir,' he whispered.

'Okay,' then turning to Denton he said softly, 'Ready?'

'Oh, after you, old boy.'

'Very well, here goes.' Packard went for the round brass door handle and gripped it, and slowly twisted it. The door opened slightly, his pulse started to hammer in his neck, he took a couple of deep breaths then rushed in, shouting, 'Hande hoche! Hande hoche!'

Denton was right behind him shouting 'hands up' in German, waving his revolver into the face of every German he saw. Corporal Johnson's men came pushing behind with weapons at the ready. Their boots hammering on bare boards as they rushed inside and spread out into the other rooms with two darting up the narrow stairs. Half-dressed German soldiers in the main room suddenly stood up. Some of the tables turned over along with chairs with tunics over the back of them; wine glasses and bottles smashing on the floor in a cascade of tinkling pieces of glass. For a few seconds, the room was in utter chaos. Girls could be heard screaming around the cottage amid the shouts of English voices putting the frighteners on the German soldiers as they were pushed into the main room naked or dragging on their long-johns or trousers. Suddenly it all went very quiet, partly in amazement, and everyone was brought to their senses. Some of the Germans were standing in the middle of the room covering their genitals with their hands, looking shocked and frightened, while some half-dressed were standing with their hands up along the walls. The room looked a little smashed up and over-crowded and claustrophobic. It smelt of sweat, cheap perfume, and tobacco. A quick headcount by Packard put the German number at eighteen, not including those eight sentries they had captured outside, making a total of twenty-six. Had they got them all, he couldn't be sure at the moment, but one thing was certain – the officer was missing.

There was a thud upstairs and some scrabbling noises. English voices screaming obscenities. Everyone glanced upwards.

'What the hell's going on up there?' asked Denton to no one in particular. And, as if reading Packard's thoughts, he went forward to the stairs and then sped up two at a time. A few moments later a German officer slowly came down the stairs with Denton's revolver in his back. The German had his breeches on with high polished boots, and he wore braces over his unbuttoned shirt. He had blonde hair and looked young and arrogant with a long narrow face.

Denton, smirking, said, 'Trying to hide in a large wardrobe. Had to drag him out. I let him get dressed.'

The German officer stood before Packard and stretched out his hand. 'I congratulate you, Lieutenant,' he said with a thick German accent. 'You took us by complete surprise.'

Packard stared at the outstretched hand for a moment. Denton nodded behind the German and said, 'He asked if I were in charge of the raid. I told him it was you.' The German smiled at Packard and stiffened as a mark of respect. Then Packard offered his own. They shook hands firmly and silently.

Corporal Johnson was gathering the girls into a back room. A tall, striking brunette, about mid-thirties, turned to him and said in English, 'What are you doing, what will happen to us?'

Johnson looked surprised and took a deep breath, 'Blimey, you speak English.'

'I'm half English,' she replied uneasily. 'I'm the accountant here. What is going to happen to us? Can I speak to an officer?'

Johnson broke a smile, 'Now don't you worry your pretty little 'ead Miss, we mean no 'arm. 'Ere, tell the girls to sit down and I'll get an officer to speak to you all.' His words were anything but soothing.

Johnson left one of his men outside the room to guard the girls while he went to the main room. Campbell, with three other men, were searching all the Germans. Packard and Denton stood by.

'Sir, sir!' Johnson said.

Packard looked round. 'What is it, corporal?'

'One of the girls, sir.'

'What about her?'

'She speaks English, sir. Wants to speak to an officer.'

'Speaks English?'

'Yes sir, a lovely brunette and she's a looker.'

Denton was smoking nervously and looked across to Packard, blowing a cloud of smoke before stubbing out the cigarette. 'What do you think?'

Packard shrugged, 'I'll speak to her, see what she has to say.'

'Careful now, Lieutenant. Remember you're an officer and a gentleman. Keep your hat on and take the weight on your elbows,' Denton teased and blew him a kiss.

Packard smiled and followed Johnson to the back parlour. Johnson opened the door and Packard stepped in; Johnson closed the door behind him. The brunette had her back to him and was muttering quietly to the girls. She turned around to face him. They stood close together. Johnson was right about her being a "looker", Packard thought, and was surprised just how natural her beauty was and that her physical presence in the room was enough to make any man's heart melt instantly. He was staring at her without meaning to. 'I'm … Lieutenant Harry Packard, and, your name is?'

'Vanessa,' she replied gently.

Packard smiled warmly. 'Vanessa? Well, Vanessa. I understand you speak English, so, what can I do for you?'

She took a deep breath. 'What is to become of us?'

Packard suddenly felt a bit clumsy and stupid, he realised he was in awe of her. She had big brown eyes and dark curly hair that fell gracefully about her shoulders. She looked a bit older than the other girls, probably about early to mid-thirties, slim, and better dressed. He liked what he saw and he felt a twist in his heart but she looked scared. He glanced around the room, all the girls were scared too; most were hugging each other and sniffling and just wrapped in dressing gowns. 'Well you can't stay here,' he said. 'You're going to have to go I'm afraid. There's going to be a battle here – for the bridge,' he added. His eyes kept scanning the room as he talked. One girl sat on her own in the corner and was quietly sobbing in her hands. 'It will be too dangerous to stay.'

Vanessa looked at Packard with a slight frown on her face. She shrugged. 'But we have nowhere to go. This is our home.'

From the front room came some raised voices. A bottle crashed to the floor. Then more raised voices from Sergeant Campbell and Captain Denton. Then it went quiet again. Vanessa stiffened and glanced behind him and clasped a trembling hand to her throat. 'It's okay,' he said reassuringly. 'We have everything under control. Fritz is being searched at the moment. There's bound to be a bit argy-bargee now they're over the shock of capture.'

'The Germans are pigs,' she said. Her delicate fingers picked at the top of her dress. He saw tears form in her eyes. 'When they arrived, they threatened to shoot us all if we did not co-operate.' She sniffed. 'At first they demanded drink and then some food. Then they wanted the girls. They refused to pay the full price and began shouting that we were "the victors' spoils". Things got a little ugly at first and we felt so helpless about it, but it calmed when the girls agreed to charge them a reduced rate. Over the course of the evening the Germans became more civil from the wine and being serviced one by one.' She wiped her eyes.

'Did any German force himself upon the girls or you in

particular?' Packard asked her in all sincerity – then felt a little embarrassed as it occurred to him that the undertone of his question meant that he only cared for her.

She turned her head for a moment then looked back at him again, her brown eyes looking into his as she flicked a curl from her face seductively, then she shook her head. 'The officer tried to make advances towards me,' she told him, her voice was quiet, calm, 'but I told him that I run the books here, that's all.'

Packard felt the relief unknot itself in the pit of his stomach, then he asked, 'How did you get involved in this place?'

She sniffed. 'I'm a trained accountant, and the accounts were in a mess and this was causing problems amongst the girls so, they asked me to help. I began keeping the books for them – nothing more. I've been here twelve years now and since the Madame had drunk herself to death six years ago, I now run the place.'

'I'm sorry,' Packard said.

She looked up at him, her cheeks wet. 'What do you mean?'

He cleared his throat. 'Well, you are settled now, and this war has come here to you,' he replied awkwardly.

'Yes, the war,' she said. 'But this is our home. We are all happy here. A lot of these girls come from broken homes and have nowhere else to go. They are like family to me. We look after one another. We have a good location with plenty of good regular customers.'

Packard looked around at some of the plush furnishings. 'I'm aware of that,' he replied. 'But tomorrow morning there will be a big battle here and it will be too dangerous for you to stay.'

Vanessa nodded. 'I know. The German officer told us reinforcements for the bridge would be coming soon.'

'He told you that? Did he say when?'

Vanessa nodded. 'About three he said.'

'In the morning?'

'Yes, in the morning – a battle-group I think he said. Before the English arrive, he kept boasting.'

Packard knew what that meant, the Germans were probably sending a battalion battle-group just like they were in the morning. But it looked as if the Germans would beat them to it. It would be up to him to make the next move and buy the time, but could he trust what she was telling him?

The door suddenly opened and in stepped Denton. He grabbed Packard's elbow and ushered him outside the doorway. 'Before you think of bagging that brunette, Lieutenant, there's something you should know,' he said in a hushed whisper. 'One of the prisoners has just told Sergeant Campbell that a battalion battle-group is set to arrive here at three.'

'I know,' replied Packard. 'That girl has just told me.' Inwardly, Packard was pleased Vanessa was honest and telling the truth.

'How did she know?'

'That German officer was bragging to her about it.'

'I see. Even so, a battalion battle-group; we can't take that on, surely. It's bound to have artillery!'

'Two field guns at least, and two machine guns, minimum,' Packard replied, unfazed.

'What are you going to do?' asked Denton.

'Stay and fight of course,' replied Packard. 'Why?'

'I'm not interfering, I just want to know what we're getting into, that's all.'

'If Fritz wants the bridge that bad, he'll have to fight for it. I'll not give it up now. Besides, old Fritz has no idea of our strength and we'll be quite a surprise when he arrives. The darkness will be our friend and buy us time.'

Denton reached into his pocket and brought out a packet of cigarettes and lit one and offered one to Packard who shook his head. 'Well, I hope you're right,' said Denton. 'The engineers may not get here till late morning to blow the bridge and by that time it could be too late.'

Packard frowned and after a short pause replied, 'Then we've got to keep Fritz busy, and far enough away so when the engineers do arrive, they can prepare it for blowing without too much interference.' He looked Denton straight in the eye. 'Right?' Denton looked over his shoulder as Vanessa appeared from behind him. He turned to face her.

'Lieutenant,' she said. 'I know you feel responsible for us, but we don't want to go. No matter what the danger.'

'Vanessa.' Something in his voice as he said her name made her tense. He met her eyes steadily and could feel again that twist in his heart that made him melt instantly. With a calm voice he said, 'This place is going to be a war zone. A battle is going to take place here and you have no idea how deadly and cruel a battle can be. I have enough problems here without worrying about you.'

As she tried to interrupt, he placed his hand on her arm as though pleading with her. His voice was low and gentle. 'You must go, Vanessa. Please go, I beg of you.'

He sensed she was about to protest, but she changed her mind. He withdrew his hand from her arm and as he slowly turned away and went outside with Captain Denton, he felt an affectionate regret that once Vanessa left this place, he would never see her again.

CHAPTER 6

There was a knock on the cabinet room door, and the Prime Minister called out 'enter.' It opened and Kitchener stopped in the doorway while he was announced by the servant, looking every inch the former fighting general.

'Lord Kitchener.'

Suitably announced, the Secretary of State for War gave a slight bow. He looked out of place in uniform, his chest full of medal ribbons, looking like a peacock in the room normally reserved for dowdy old deal-makers in dark coats and trousers.

Kitchener had a face lined by years of service abroad, with a bristling military walrus-style moustache. He stood there, upright, in immaculate field boots, a highly polished Sam Browne and his cap neatly tucked under his arm. A light walking cane hung from his arm as he drew off tight brown leather gloves and tossed them in the cap, placing both cap and cane on the table. He had no intention of sitting down.

Kitchener saw Prime Minister Asquith seated at his usual place at the cabinet table with the Chancellor Lloyd George, Churchill, and Prince Louis sitting opposite; all smoking a cigar. They had a glass of what looked like brandy in front of them. Lloyd George stroked his grey moustached as he entered.

Kitchener had little experience of the cabinet and felt uncomfortable: on his first meeting in this room at the outbreak of hostilities, he'd declared that the war would last for three years, not three months as was the feeling of the political players. He did not enjoy any popularity with the cabinet anymore, though he did usually get on with the Prime Minister and Churchill.

'Ah, Lord K. Just in time,' said the Prime Minister. 'We've been discussing Antwerp and King Albert's gold. Winston wants to reinforce Antwerp with his naval brigades to save your army in France.'

Kitchener was unmoved and spoke with every confidence. 'They'd be more useful helping to plug the gap between the Channel coast and our advance north towards it,' he said, and to emphasize the point he quickly jerked the end of his bristling moustache with a knuckle.

'A good point,' said Lloyd George, who then slumped back in his chair, one thumb in his waistcoat, puffing on his cigar. Then turning to Churchill, he said, 'That would make more sense, don't you think?'

Churchill waved a hand in dismissal. 'I have considered that very point with Prince Louis,' he replied, 'our two naval brigades have just been formed and are not exactly hardened veterans. They do not have enough experience for such a task. However, in a defensive capacity, they would be easier to command and control, and backed up by the experienced marine brigade, they could prove very useful in a fortified defence.'

The Prime Minister inclined his head to Kitchener. 'What do you think, Lord K?'

Kitchener stood solid. This time he wiped his moustache with the back of his hand and stared directly at Churchill. Churchill was right about the two naval brigades' lack of any type of experience or training. They were without artillery, field ambulance, or engineers. They had not been issued with field equipment or khaki uniforms and still had the older charge-loading Lee Enfield rifle instead of the modern short-magazine type, so they would be better used in a fortified defence, rather than soldiering in the field against a determined German army. They offered no other advantage. He knew Antwerp would fall; it was just a case of when. 'How long do you think your naval brigades and the Belgian garrison could hold Antwerp?' he asked.

'How long do you need?'

Kitchener puffed out his cheeks. 'At least seven days. By that time I will have sufficient forces to plug that gap along the Channel coast.'

Churchill glanced at Prince Louis, who nodded. 'Very well,' Churchill replied. 'Seven days it is. Now I would like to ask a favour from you. I want an experienced officer who speaks fluent French with a small squad of men and two lorries to rescue King Albert's gold.'

Kitchener rocked on his heels. He hadn't seen that one coming. 'You want an experienced officer fluent in French *and* two lorries?' he repeated.

'Precisely that,' Churchill said. 'I want that gold rescued before it's too late.'

'You know we have a shortage of army lorries and they are in great demand at the front,' Kitchener said. 'The experienced French-speaking officer I can accommodate you with, I'm sure – but the lorries!' He shook his head. 'Out of the question.'

'Surely two army lorries can be spared for a few days?' asked the Prime Minister.

Kitchener shook his head. 'Out of the question, Prime Minister. The army only had eighty lorries and we took them all to France. We've managed to subsidise those with a few hundred commercial vehicles that are owned by others, with a promise of more to come. I've already requisitioned fifty London buses for troop transports and sent them off to France, and even that is not nearly enough.'

Churchill said, 'It would be highly embarrassing for the Belgian King and his government if King Albert's gold falls into the hands of the Germans. I want to make sure that we are not in a position to lose the war because of it.' He paused. 'It's unthinkable. The stakes here are high; win this, we win the war. Lose this, we lose the war.'

Lloyd George rolled his eyes.

Churchill continued, 'What if I personally went to Antwerp with my two naval brigades, to guarantee you the seven days?' he said. 'Would I get my two lorries then?'

The Prime Minister pursed his lips. 'I'm not sure about that one, Winston. I can't have a cabinet minister in Antwerp when it's about to fall to the enemy.'

Lloyd George removed the cigar from his mouth, puffed the smoke high into the air and grinned. 'Winston being captured again, imagine that,' he said, referring to the time Churchill was captured in South Africa by the Boers in 1899 until he escaped a few weeks later. 'Why, the very nation might fall.'

Churchill ignored the comment and sat facing Kitchener. 'Well?'

The room fell silent as Kitchener slowly walked to one of the windows and looked out over the walled garden and Horse Guards Parade beyond, placing his hands behind his back. He sniffed, and sniffed again. Churchill was right about Antwerp and the need to buy time. His presence there could be vital and help put some starch into the Belgian garrison. Churchill did speak French, although his accent was poor and at times laughable. He could give away the two lorries for the gold but that was not the point. Churchill, he knew, was the only man in the Cabinet to have experienced war. He already held a commission in the Oxfordshire Hussars, a territorial regiment. He was a powerful influence and someone he needed to keep onside, but he was so irritating at times – that and his slight lisping when he spoke.

This war will not be won by meddling upstart politicians poking their noses into military affairs.

He suddenly felt alone among hosts of hostile strangers. King Albert's gold was just a distraction, but it was a political one. Could he really allow the gold to fall into the hands of the Germans without making some effort to rescue it? What would King George think if that happened? And if Antwerp then fell quickly due to a collapse in Belgian morale and the BEF were forced to pull back to the Channel coast … France would be on its own at the mercy of the German army, all for two lorryloads of gold. It didn't bear thinking about. Either way, he had no choice and he knew it. If the gold fell into German hands, he would get the blame, Churchill would see to that. And besides, what were two lorries in the big scheme of things anyway?

A servant came into the cabinet room silently, carrying a tray with fresh glasses and a full decanter of brandy. He put the tray down on the table next to the Prime Minister, poured a shot into each glass, and left.

Once he had gone, Kitchener turned to face them with his back to the window. His eyes moved across their set faces and rested on Churchill's in particular. The Prime Minister broke the silence. 'Gentlemen, I advise caution here.'

Kitchener did not know what he meant by that comment, but it made his eye twitch. 'You'll actually go to Antwerp and help organise its defence with your naval brigades?'

'Of course,' replied Churchill with a half-smile on his face. He could smell victory.

'You think you could hold for at least seven days?'

'Or we'll die trying,' Churchill replied.

'Trying is not good enough. I *need* seven days.'

'You'll get seven days,' said Prince Louis firmly. 'Do we get the lorries?'

Kitchener paused and looked around him at their faces, motionless but for their eyes, which darted between him and Prince Louis. Yet another phase of this war was unfolding, seemingly beyond his control. He cleared his throat. 'For the sake of our army, you get the two lorries. I'll draft a letter immediately saying that the chosen officer is acting on my authority to requisition two lorries, fuel, and any other equipment that he may need from any quartermaster in France to complete this mission. I'll send a copy to Field-Marshall French's Headquarters in France. May I also suggest that he has a similar letter from King George to act on his authority, to get the gold shipped to England as a priority over any other cargo?'

'I'll arrange that letter with the king,' said the Prime Minister. 'However,' he said, wagging his finger, 'I'm not sure about Winston going to Antwerp. There could be enormous consequences if he got killed or captured.'

'It's quite a responsibility, Winston,' said a smirking Lloyd George, still puffing on his cigar. 'Let's hope you are up to it. After all, it's a week's guarantee or we could lose this war. Your words, I believe.'

Churchill glanced around the room from face to earnest face. 'You'll get your seven days,' he said defiantly and added, 'Let's hope we get the gold as well.' He picked up his brandy glass and drained it.

CHAPTER 7

Private Thompson lifted the heavy MG 08 water-cooled sixty-pound machine gun from the sledge mount, placing it gently on the floor. He was preparing to move it, and all the other equipment, including the ammunition, across the bridge. Altogether, the whole contraption, including the sledge mount, the machine gun, the two extra barrels, and the hose attached to the water jacket via a canister, weighed in at 140 lbs. Four men stood by to help carry it once it was dismantled. Even dismantled though, it was heavy.

Captain Denton stood outside the barn, hands on hips, watching as they took it apart. Although the sledge mount was heavy and unwieldy, it could be folded down like a stretcher and carried on the back of a man. Denton knew it could be adjusted for firing prone or kneeling, and was equipped with pads for the elbows, and had its own toolbox. The ammunition was in 250-round canvas belts, stored in a small pile of metal boxes behind the gun, and there were several belts on hand beside the gun for immediate action. Thompson had told him that in rapid fire mode, the gun could easily eat up two belts a minute. 'Good,' he'd said, eyeing the bridge warily. 'We'll need the extra firepower when the German battlegroup arrives.'

He watched the men's faces in the dim light of a hurricane lamp. When they'd captured the bridge, morale had been high, but learning there was an enemy battlegroup on its way had quickly dampened their mood. The thought of the enemy somewhere beyond the darkness heading towards them hung over them like a cloud, and, like everyone else, in his heart, he didn't think they stood a chance.

Packard appeared out of the darkness into the pool of light and stood beside him. 'All ready to move, Thompson?'

'Just about, sir.' Thompson flexed his fingers and gave a grunt as he grabbed the heavy machine gun barrel and heaved it onto his shoulder, adjusted it for comfort, and set off for the bridge with the other four in tow carrying the sledge mount and ammunition boxes, their silhouettes disappearing into darkness.

'Sergeant Campbell suggested that we put the prisoners in this barn under guard,' said Packard. 'He's organising it now.'

'What else can we do with them?' asked Denton.

'Not a lot,' said Packard, 'but if things get too hot around here, they may well be in the line of fire, and I have a duty to keep the prisoners safe.'

The door of the cottage opened, and under guard of Campbell and a few soldiers, the prisoners started to file out, and were led shuffling into the barn. Denton and Packard stared at the swaying figures as they went in one by one.

'What about the officer?' asked Denton.

'I'm keeping him locked in a room on the upper floor under guard.'

With the last one in, Campbell slid a rusty metal bolt across the door. 'That's it, all nice and tucked up for the night.'

Then the girls started to leave the cottage, carrying bags and suitcases. Vanessa was the last to leave. She saw Packard in the light from the hurricane lamp and came over to him. 'We're about to leave,' she said. She took his hand and held it firmly. He made to pull away but she persisted. She leaned forward and kissed his cheek. 'Thank you, Lieutenant, and be safe,' she said softly.

'What the devil's going on here!' bellowed Major Scott-Bardwell, stepping out of the darkness into the pool of light. His dark eyes were hard and angry.

Vanessa quickly released Packard's hand as they both stood perfectly still.

'Well?' he demanded, his eyes quickly flicking from one to the other.

'It's not what it looks like. Nothing is going on here, Major,' Denton explained. 'The girl is about to leave and was just thanking Lieutenant Packard for saving them from the Germans, that's all.'

'That's not how I see it, Captain. One of the lieutenant's men came running up the hill to fetch me and in what can be best described as a highly excitable manner, proclaimed that we had captured a brothel full of girls and we had "better hurry up"!'

'For God's sake, Major, the lieutenant has just captured a vital bridge with nearly thirty enemy soldiers in the bag, and not a single shot fired. I'd call that pretty damn good in any circumstances and the lieutenant should be congratulated.'

'I'll admit the lieutenant has been lucky so far to get us here, but his behaviour with this girl … this *whore*, in front of the men is despicable!'

Denton saw Packard swallow his rage as he looked at a shocked Vanessa in front of him. In that instant Denton knew she was about to retaliate, which was not a good idea, and he tried to distract her. 'You'd best be off,' he said to her quickly. Vanessa ignored him and he could see that she was not yet ready to leave. She took a deep breath. The strange look she gave the major made him suddenly feel uncomfortable.

'First of all, Major, I am not a whore, and your accusations against the Lieutenant and I are monstrous! I can assure you that nothing improper has happened.' She turned away to face Packard and

Captain Denton. 'I'm supremely grateful for what you have both done,' she said in her best English accent, and then walked away and joined the other girls as they slowly walked down the road heading north.

'Where are you heading?' Packard called out. Denton heard a real concern in the tone of his voice.

She turned. The dim light from the hurricane lamp was reflecting across her face. 'Back to Ypres, in Belgium,' she replied. 'I have my uncle there. He's the local bank manager.' She gave Packard a smile and a wave. They watched as Vanessa and the girls faded into the darkness.

'I've never felt warmer in my life than when in that girl's company,' he murmured to Denton.

After a strained silence that seemed longer than it was, the major said icily, 'Lieutenant Packard–'

'This Lieutenant Packard,' interrupted Denton in sudden irritation, 'has just captured a vital bridge from the enemy and is now preparing to take on a German battlegroup heading this way.'

The major gasped. 'A battlegroup?'

'Yes, Major, a battlegroup, and we can't afford to lose any time,' he said, as he took a watch from his breast pocket and sprung the lid. The time was just after midnight. 'The Lieutenant is preparing the defence of this bridge with his men with that captured machine gun.'

'But … but how do you know this?'

'From the prisoners,' Denton explained. He dared not to mention that it also came from Vanessa.

The major shook his head. 'It's ridiculous! A battlegroup will come with artillery and machine guns and at least a thousand men.' Then turning to Packard, he said, 'You have no more than a half-strength company.'

'Yes,' said Denton before Packard could answer. 'We're all nervous about it and no good worrying about it now. The big bonus is that Fritz doesn't know we're here, and in such small numbers. Darkness and surprise will be our strength. Plus that machine gun. The lieutenant believes he can buy enough time for our engineers to get here in the morning to blow the bridge, so we can't afford to hang about. Isn't that right, Lieutenant?'

'I think so, sir.'

'You think so, Lieutenant!' The major's voice squeaked in protest. 'And we're to be thankful for that, darkness and surprise, and a half-company holding a bridge against a strong battlegroup? Such pretensions, Lieutenant.'

'Even with a half-strength company, Fritz will have to fight for it, sir,' said Packard, biting back his irritation. 'The longer we hold, the more chance our demolition teams have to blow it. This bridge is vital to the enemy if he wants to turn our flank and I won't give it up, sir. Not now!'

Denton knew how proud Packard was of his men. He had trained them, led them into battle, and he trusted them, even against an outnumbering enemy heading this way. In the darkness behind him, the men prepared the bridge defensives against that enemy. He could hear their voices, and that of Sergeant Campbell.

A look of annoyance spread over the major's face as if he was looking for nervousness in this young lieutenant. Instead, he saw confidence and pride. 'Don't play games with me, Lieutenant. I'm fully aware of the strategic importance of this bridge. However, in the circumstances I believe that a tactical withdrawal would be suitably justified until our main forces get here.'

Denton said, 'A withdrawing action without putting up any kind of fight? Out of the question, Major. I believe the lieutenant and his men have a chance.'

The major glared at him. 'A chance!' he bellowed, as he looked at one man and then the other. He saw him noting Packard's unkempt appearance in the pool of light. 'As I see it, you have no chance. You may later wish to thank me for such a suggestion to withdraw; the fact remains that the lieutenant is completely out of his depth and involving other people now, like you and me, in this ridiculous nonsense, and you're encouraging him. You may regret that, Captain.'

'I have every confidence in this officer,' replied Denton honestly. In truth, deep down he had doubts about holding the bridge alone for any length of time – he wasn't blind to numbers, after all – but some men, like Harry Packard, were born leaders, he thought. And this man, the little paper-pusher in front of him, wasn't one of them. He knew the major had spent most of his service around the shirt-tails of senior officers at various headquarters in Egypt, India, and Afghanistan, and spent his time mastering maps and pushing paper around while steadily climbing the ranks and growing detached from real soldering. At the outbreak of war, and with no combat experience whatsoever, his military history had left him unprepared to serve in a front-line regiment and he was duly posted to the division as intelligence officer.

'I shall return to HQ and make my report,' huffed the major.

Out on the roadway, a soldier stood quietly holding his horse's reins. The major climbed into the saddle and snatched hold of the reins. The horse in response began nodding up and down.

Denton stepped forward and looked up at the major. 'You'll tell HQ that we need urgent help?'

'Of course,' he said bitterly, and then added, 'Are you staying?'

A clarity entered Denton's eyes as he nodded.

'Very well, Captain.' He turned the horse and galloped down the road, the thudding of the hooves fading away into the darkness.

'Bastard,' Denton said as he turned to look at Packard. 'What a cold, condemning, self-righteous bastard.'

Packard nodded with a resigned understanding.

They made their way to the bridge, Packard leading the way and Denton following. 'So, what's your plan?' Denton asked.

Packard breathed in slowly. 'To deny Fritz the bridge.' His voice had gone flat and distant.

Denton chuckled, but sensed that the lieutenant was a bit uptight. 'No need to worry then, your mission's all but over.' He chuckled again.

They reached the bridge and started to walk across with a line of Packard's men, who were carrying lengths of timber, broken furniture, and doors pilfered from the derelict cottages for building the defences. The machine gun was at the end of the bridge already set up by Thompson, with a home-made barricade built around it. His crew were laying out the ammunition boxes. The night air was chilly and a man yawned. The men were dead-beat but still working. Denton was impressed; there'd been quite a lot going on. Packard stood and hooked his thumbs in his pockets, studying the barricade around the gun.

Denton said, 'I know you're thinking it could have been better constructed with sandbags – if we had some.'

Packard nodded.

Denton asked again. 'Seriously Lieutenant, how do you intend to hold the bridge? What's the plan?'

Boots clumped on the bridge behind him. They both turned. Campbell came with four men carrying containers. 'Any more for any more?' Thompson and his crew stopped working and produced their mugs. Campbell had organised cocoa from a hoard of cans left behind by the girls. 'Any sugar, Sergeant?' Thompson asked.

'Over 'ere, chum,' replied one of the soldiers with Campbell, and spooned a couple into his mug.

'Ah, lovely,' said Thompson, inhaling the fumes and taking a few sips from his hot drink as a line of men formed up behind him. 'Almost as good as payday,' he said appreciatively.

Packard and Denton stood on the bridge with their cold hands around their warm mugs, taking small sips. Denton noticed that after a few sips of cocoa, the lieutenant didn't seem so uptight, and looked rather relaxed. 'The plan,' Packard said quietly. There was no tension in his voice. 'I intend to keep Fritz far enough away from the bridge as possible, so they can't see enough of what's going on.' Then stroked his chin. 'I'm putting forty men under Sergeant Campbell, with two corporals in the treeline across the road about a hundred yards south of the bridge, to cover the left side of the road with the open field along the Germans' approach. They should be the first to engage Fritz once he arrives. I'm placing another ten men on the bridge with a corporal, to support the gun here and give covering fire on the right side of the road and along the riverbank as they approach. The fire from the gun should force Fritz into the open field or the riverbank so that our riflemen can shoot them down, so I'm putting another ten men in the cottage windows with a corporal, overlooking the riverbank, giving flanking fire when that happens. The rest of the men will be on our side of the river as a reserve and to protect our rear.'

'So,' said Denton, 'the gun will sweep the roadway and keep it clear, forcing Fritz into the flanks to be met with a hail of rifle fire for their trouble?'

'Yes, that's the plan. Hopefully, Fritz will think that we're a much larger force and stay back long enough for our engineers to arrive in the morning and rig the bridge for demolition. We need to buy enough time – hopefully,' he added.

'Hopefully?' repeated Denton with raised eyebrows. 'You think your plan will give you that much time?'

Packard paused for a moment, took another sip of cocoa and wiped his chin with his hand. 'Well, they say that the most valuable commodity on a battlefield is time – something that we don't have a lot of I'm afraid, so my plan had better work and give us that time or we'll all be dead meat.'

Denton looked around him, at the homemade defences, the tired men, the loneliness and desperation of their position. 'Then pray your plan works, Lieutenant,' he said, as a lance of foreboding went through him.

CHAPTER 8

Lieutenant Harry Packard was pleased. For the last few hours the platoon had worked tirelessly, preparing their defences as best they could in the little time they had. Several narrow waist-high slit trenches had been dug on the edge of the wood that covered the open field and roadway that led to the bridge on the German side. The spoil was piled up in front for added protection against small-arms fire, as well as giving some modicum of cover from any shelling. It wasn't enough, Packard knew, but in the time they'd had, the men had done well to dig as deep as they had, and were now hunched up at the bottom of the slit trenches, exhausted and fast asleep. What little rest the men got would help to stimulate their strength when the battle started. He'd made sure that they all had some food with a cup of hot cocoa and were now having a much-needed rest.

'Everything is fine, sir,' Sergeant Campbell had assured him when inspecting their position along the treeline. Campbell's group would face the battlegroup first when it arrived. It was quite mad to take on a battalion battlegroup with just a half-strength company and one machine gun, but what else was he to do? Just run? Unthinkable.

With a barricade of sorts around the machine gun, made of old timber planks from the derelict cottages, various bits of furniture, most of the beds and mattresses from the brothel, and another similar barricade across the road nearby, he gave the order for all men to rest apart from the sentries, who had been issued with covered oil lamps taken from the rooms. Two sentries had been sent a few hundred yards down the road on the German side as an early warning of the battlegroup's approach. All sentries were under strict orders not to uncover the lamps and show light unless it was vital to do so.

Captain Denton had just inspected the sentries near the cottages and approached Packard at the machine gun. It was 3 a.m., and still, there was no sign of the Germans. He sidled up to Packard's shoulder, took out a cigarette, lit it, and began smoking nervously, blowing smoke into the night air.

'I've been thinking,' said Denton. 'What if Fritz approaches another way? What if he crosses the river further down and then approaches along the road that we came up? That's our weakest point. We'd be cut off. We've only a few men in the cottage to cover our backs. Do you think we should …?'

Packard cut him off, waving a hand in dismissal. 'If the river was that easy to cross further down, they wouldn't want this bridge. Besides, why risk sending a platoon to secure it in the first place?'

Denton shrugged his shoulders. 'Just thought I'd mention it. With so few men to defend this place, I'm trying to make sure that we cover all options. But you're right of course.' He puffed quickly on the cigarette.

Packard listened to Denton's change of tone. He knew the captain was tired and he was nervous about the strength of the battlegroup, and now that the 3 a.m. deadline had arrived and nothing had happened, his fears were growing. Everyone who was tired and scared suffered from that, he knew. Some handled it better than others. He yawned and pinched the top of his nose with his thumb and finger, then hunched his shoulders and stared into the darkness and thought about Vanessa, and what she was doing now. He quickly dismissed those thoughts, then straightened his back and gazed up at the dark sky. 'It's the best approach for Fritz,' he said. 'Little chance of being bounced by one of our scouting cavalry groups. Still, with us at the bridge, that should surprise him when he arrives and give him a stopping blow. He won't be expecting it.' He heard one of the gun team shifting his boots on the ground and groan as he lay sleeping. He heard Thompson give a little snore. Packard stretched and yawned and wished that he too could sleep but continued in the same unemotional tone. 'Time to make another check around our positions, I think. Care to join me?'

'Of course.' Denton threw the stub-end to the floor and twisted his boot on it and followed Packard in the gloom as they made their way past the sleeping gun team with the sentry and onto the road heading towards the barricade.

They hadn't gone far when a running figure came thumping over the bridge, panting as he ran, rifle at the trail. 'Sir! Sir!' The unmistakable urgent alarm of the sentry's cry sent a shiver down both their spines. They turned around quickly – and held their breath. Packard recognised the soldier's voice and quickly shrugged aside his fear as the sentry hurried towards him. 'What is it, Clifton?'

'Sir, we can hear wagons and horses heading along the road towards the bridge!' Fearfully, Packard's mind quickly heard Captain Denton's earlier words again – 'crossed the river' and 'come up behind' in particular – and felt his hackles rise, but he regained self-control and dragged his thoughts back to reality. 'Are there lots of them?'

'I'm not sure.'

'Did you see them, Clifton?'

The sentry shook his head. 'No, sir. Just heard them in the distance, that's all. They sounded some way off but getting closer.'

'On our side of the river?'

'Yes sir.'

'You sure?'

'Definitely.'

'Who's in charge there?'

'Corporal Hedges, sir.'

Denton gasped. 'God Almighty. You think Fritz has crossed the river?'

Packard wiped his mouth with the back of his hand. 'I bloody well hope not,' he replied scornfully, and instantly regretted his tone while running nagging doubts through his head. Had he got it wrong? Has Fritz crossed the river? There was only one way to find out. 'Come on,' he said, 'let's take a look. Lead the way, Clifton!' They scurried off with Denton bringing up the rear.

Thompson, now awake from all the noise, was standing up with the gun crew around him. 'What's happening?' he called out as Clifton, Packard, and Denton back-tracked across the bridge, their boots ringing on the hard bridge surface as they passed. Packard shouted a warning as he dashed by, 'Stand the men to, Thompson!' and crossed the bridge, turning left towards the brothel, and thirty yards beyond the end of the barn along the road, where he met Corporal Hedges and the shadows of three other men kneeling across the road as a covering party.

Packard dropped beside him panting, with Denton kneeling on the other side. Hedges looked at one and then the other. 'Wagons and horses, sir,' he whispered to no one in particular. 'Coming this way.'

'I can hear it,' hissed Denton, panting mostly from fear rather than exertion as he nervously lifted his revolver from its holster.

Glued to the spot, they listened – hearts pounding, straining their eyes into the darkness as if in a trance. The motion of the distant wagons and horse hooves seemed slow and unsteady. Packard thought they must feel pretty safe, whoever they were, and bit his lip as he gathered his thoughts. Could they be refugees fleeing the war zone? The frustration of not being able to see, and only hear, and dreading what was coming towards him, was grating on his nerves. He made up his mind, took a sharp intake of breath and said, 'Right, that settles it. Corporal Hedges, where's the sentry's lamp?'

Hedges turned to a soldier near him. 'Smithy, get the lamp for the lieutenant.' The soldier got up and went back along the road a few paces, returning with a covered lamp which he handed to his officer. More men joined them from the bridge and Packard gathered them all together. 'Right, listen,' he said in a whisper. 'When they're almost upon us, I'm going to stand up and uncover this lamp to see who they are. Don't open fire until I give the order – or I get shot,' he said as an afterthought. 'Got it?' They all murmured acknowledgement. 'OK, Corporal Hedges, let's get the men to spread out on either side of the road. Quickly now.'

Packard swallowed hard and stretched out the cramp in his leg, then clenched his hands a few times to get the blood back into them. The noise of wagons, horses, and the jingle of bridles seemed like they were almost on top of him. The noise grew louder, and from out of the darkness the outline shadows of horses and wagons started to appear gloomily in front of him. Not a sound came from the men around him, although he could almost hear his heart beating. He gritted his teeth. It was now or never. He took a deep breath, stood up, whipped off the lamp cover, held it aloft, and then braced himself for a sudden bullet.

'Woeoooo!' There were four wagons in a line. The first wagon came to a halt just a few yards ahead of him. There were two horses, one of them snorting in alarm. In the hard glare of the lamp, Packard could see what appeared to be two sitting khaki figures frozen motionless at the front of the first wagon, one built like a bull, the other next to him quite skinny by comparison. They stared back at him like rabbits caught in headlights. Nervously Packard called out as loud as he could dare. 'Who goes there?'

Seconds passed in an uncomfortable silence. The one built like a bull recognised the tone of an English officer and replied with a gruff Scottish voice, 'Sar'ent McWhirter, Royal Engineers. You must be Lieutenant Packard?'

As the relief and elation hit him, Packard felt his toes tingle, and his breath blew out. 'I am,' he acknowledged, and lowered the lamp a little. 'I hope you've come to blow the bridge?'

'Aye, sir. Hope you don't mind, like. We're a wee bit early. Compliments from Major Scott-Bardwell.'

The tingle of relief in his toes surged up through Packard's body, and he grinned. So, the major had sent help to them after all. 'On the contrary, Sergeant, you've got no idea just how happy we are to see you.'

Denton let out a long breath and pushed his revolver into its holster. He looked around, the faces expressionless in the glare of the lamp. Voice low, he sidled up to Packard and said, 'I hate the thought that we may have to do that again when the battlegroup arrives.' He opened a pocket and took out another cigarette and lit it.

Packard didn't reply. It was a dangerous moment and he knew what Captain Denton meant. The whole operation depended on that bridge being blown, and now the sappers were here early, thanks to Major Scott-Bardwell. Turning to Corporal Hedges he said, 'Tell the men from me that was well done. Get them back to their posts and make sure they stay alert. I'll take the sappers to the bridge.' Packard knew the men were far too hyped up now to feel sleepy, but he said it all the same.

'Very good, sir, and thank you.' Hedges started to bark out orders to the men.

Packard led the four wagons to the approaches of the bridge where they began to unload. He noticed the wagons seemed as if they were crammed with everything, including a small boat.

'What are your orders, Sergeant?'

'To blow yon wee bridge as soon as possible.'

'Good. Sooner the better. We have a German battlegroup heading this way, so, if it's all the same to you, Sergeant, I'll leave you to it. You know what to do. Just let me know before you blow it, so I can get my men across.'

McWhirter pushed up the peak of his cap and scratched his forehead. 'Aye, sir. In about four hours, I reckon.'

'Four hours!' Packard exclaimed. 'Bloody hell, Sergeant, we can't wait four minutes, let alone four hours!'

'D'ye think Fritz'll have a' bash before' we finish then?'

'I would think any moment now. We thought you were him sneaking up behind us.'

McWhirter stood with his hands on his hips and stared up and watched small clouds scud silently across the dark sky, and then looked around him. 'Not too worry, sir. We'll blow it in no time.'

Packard stepped aside as the sappers went about their work unloading the wagon. 'I hope you do. Just don't take all night to do it, Sergeant. My aim is to protect you, but I don't have the men to hold Fritz off for too long. So just hurry up and blow that bridge.' He swung on his heel and left.

McWhirter waited until the footsteps had faded away. He sensed the urgency of a man under pressure in Harry's voice, but the bridge would have to be surveyed first to find the weakest points, then he would have to work out how much explosive would be needed, where it was to be placed, how much wire to be laid, a safe spot to blow it from, and it all took time, precious time, and all in the dark.

He turned toward the wagon while some sappers were just standing around it. 'You going to stand around all night? C'mon, get sweating. We've a bridge to blow.'

Clarkson stood next to Thompson. 'Who's that then, Thomo?'

'Bloody pick and shovel mob.'

'Who?'

'The Engineers, dimwit. Don't you know anything?'

'Come to blow the bridge then?'

'Nah. They'll just stand there and watch Fritz march over it, what do you think?'

'Just asking Thomo, that all.' He scratched his chin. 'Think they'll blow it before Fritz gets here?'

'They better, Clarkson, they better, otherwise we're all in the shit, make no mistake about that.'

CHAPTER 9

Packard leaned over the parapet wall of the bridge, listening to the cold flowing river and watching the shadows of two sappers in a boat below him rigging the wire with an explosive charge to vulnerable parts of the arch.

'That's the first charge in,' he heard a sapper say.

About bloody time, Packard thought. He looked up, turned, leaned his back against the wall, and saw the tops of trees framed against the night sky with low scudding clouds drifting along. He wondered if he would still be alive this time tomorrow.

His ten riflemen on the bridge were either lying, sitting, or crouching down next to him, a groundsheet beneath them, some asleep and snoring. He sighed. Lucky buggers. He too felt tired and yawned. He'd had little sleep in the past two days and now he was about to face another battle – to stop a German battlegroup taking the bridge before he could destroy it. What he would give for a break for a few days – a few hours, even. You could only take so much without sleep, then you started to get careless and that thought worried him. Yes, once battle began, the adrenalin would wash the tiredness away. But the price got higher the more you relied on adrenalin to get you through.

Every man in the last few hours had been working hard to dig trenches, as primitive as they were, or form barricades across the river road on the German side and around the gun team. He knew the importance of allowing his men at least a few hours' sleep tonight so they wouldn't get dispirited or resentful and would be fresh when the battlegroup arrived. The battle for the village yesterday had been short, sharp, hard, and gruelling, like most battles in this bloody war. But he knew once this battle began, his men would be wide awake, somewhat refreshed and ready to give a good account of themselves. Adrenalin, the soldier's friend. For a while, at least.

Denton ambled over from the cottages to join him. He heard McWhirter under the bridge swear at one of his sappers. He leaned over to look. 'Thank God they're here,' he said.

Packard looked round and replied gloomily, 'Our only chance. They've been at it nearly an hour and only got one charge in.'

Denton took out his watch and sprang the lid. Another hour had dragged by. 'What's taking Fritz so long to get here? It's almost four and still bloody quiet.' He sounded edgy.

Packard stared at him, knowing his nervousness. 'Fritz is giving us extra time. Don't knock it.'

Suddenly a sentry came running past the barricade across the road, pass the gun team and up onto the bridge. They both stared at him. They both guessed this was it.

'Sir,' he said, panting, 'message from Sergeant Campbell. Stand the men to, we've got company.' He pointed down the river road into the darkness.

Packard felt his lips tighten. The extra time that Fritz had given him had just run out. His tiredness suddenly melted away, like he'd knew it would. 'Very good. Back to your post and tell Sergeant Campbell we're ready.' Despite his tight nerves, he spoke gently and with confidence.

Packard pulled his cap down snug on his head and shouted, 'Right, stand to everyone and keep a good lookout!' He shouted to the gun team, who became a frenzy of activity, feeding a 250-round belt into the gun.

'Your team ready, Thompson?'

Thompson cocked the gun and wiped his lips with the back of his hand. 'We're good to go, sir.'

'Good man. I'm relying on you to hit Fritz hard when he comes.' He rubbed his chin, felt the sharpness of the bristles and tried to recall when he last shaved. It was a silly thought and he dismissed it. He turned and saw Denton running across the bridge towards the cottages, half-crouching with his revolver in hand, calling out in a lowered voice with an undertone of urgency, 'Stand to, stand to!'

Packard had suggested to the captain that he take command of the defence of the cottages along with the German prisoners, and act as a rear-guard and a reserve, which he'd readily accepted. With Sergeant Campbell, Packard had reconnoitred the Germans' approach to the bridge. They had been together since this war started two months ago with the battles of Mons and Le Cateau. They trusted each other and now they put themselves in the place of the German battlegroup commander and considered what he would do.

The river on the German left flank was too deep and flowed too fast. An unsurmountable obstacle. If they kept to the road, their line of attack would be too narrow and easy prey for Thompson's gun team on the bridge. They only had one choice – to outflank the bridge defences by crossing the open field in front of the wood and using its undergrowth to shield their infantry sufficiently to charge the bridge from the flank.

That was what Packard wanted them to do. He gave Campbell the flare pistol to fire the moment the battlegroup came marching along the road. In the cold glare of light, the front column of the battlegroup would be fired on remorselessly by his riflemen, while Thompson's gun team would chop Fritz to pieces if any attempt was made to push their way forward along the river road. Campbell's team of riflemen would then cut them down if they made any attempt to cross the open field for cover.

British Infantry battalions carried two machine guns and the Germans knew that. With one machine gun firing at them, the German battlegroup commander just might think that half a battalion were holding the bridge. This deception, if it worked, just might give them a little more time to rig the bridge for blowing.

Then there was the reticence factor. German commanders had learned to fear the accuracy and the rapid rate of fire from twenty-five aimed shots per minute that British infantrymen could put down with their bolt-action Lee-Enfield rifles' ten-round magazine. Whereas German conscripts, at best, with their bolt action Mauser rifles' five-round magazine, could reply with just about ten shots per minute from a defensive position. But on their bridge approach, they would not *be* in a defensive position; they would be walking in extended attack lines across an open field, and Packard hoped Campbell's handful of men would cut them down enough to make them think they were facing a much larger force than just forty men. The wood, he knew, besides giving some protection from observation and German artillery fire, would also give some cover when Campbell's men had to fall back to the bridge before it was blown.

That was the plan.

Packard stood at the centre of the bridge, waiting and listening, looking around him in a slow circle to his left, and then to his right. The whole place was silent but he could sense, rather than feel, that something was not right.

Denton strode from the cottages and joined him on the bridge. The captain's footsteps seemed deafening after the silence all around him and Packard cringed at the noise. He was about to speak when a white flare shot into the night sky. It was bright – they froze – everyone looked skyward with one eye closed to help protect their night vision.

Packard turned to the gun team and shouted. 'Right, Thompson, let 'em have it!'

Thompson shouted back, 'But there's nothing there, sir. The road's empty!'

Packard quickly made his way to the gun team and stood behind them. He raised his field glasses and began looking down the empty river road in dismay just as the light from the flare was beginning to fade, the area turning back into darkness. His first thought was that Campbell had fired the flare too soon. 'Bugger!' he cursed.

Denton joined him beside the gun team. 'I don't think that flare was fired by Sergeant Campbell – much too far away,' he said. 'I think it was fired by the battlegroup.'

Stunned by that idea, Packard quickly lowered his glasses to his chest saying, 'By who?'

'The battlegroup,' Denton repeated. 'I think they fired the flare!'

Suddenly another red flare was shot from an upper floor window of one of the cottages. They all stared mesmerised as its blazing glow arched high into the night sky. Denton turned to Packard. 'Oh my God,' he said. 'That's got to be that bloody German officer. He's fired a warning signal!'

Packard swallowed hard. In his heart, he knew the captain was right. He remembered his own orders to fire red flares if they lost the bridge to the enemy. Only this time, Fritz had got in first.

*

Denton wasted no time and sprinted across the bridge. Ahead, he saw the shadow of a soldier enter the cottage and heard the door bang open as the soldier rushed inside. A few seconds later, Denton followed him in, revolver in hand, and went up the stairs two at a time. Another door banged open along the landing above him amid shouts and curses as furniture and china crashed to the floor. He entered the German officer's room, trying to control his breathing, and looked at the scene. There, backed up against the far wall with his hands straight up, was the German officer, looking decidedly fearful and shaking, the point of Corporal Hedges' bayonet firmly pressed under his chin, with another young soldier at the ready standing close by. The window was wide open, as were the two doors of the wardrobe, with scattered girls' clothing on the floor. A small table by the open window was on its side. Among the clothing on the floor was a smashed china water jug and bowl, along with a flare pistol.

'The bastard signalled the battlegroup, sir. I've a good mind to run him through!' Hedges spat out in frustration.

They all stood motionless for a moment and then Denton released a deep sigh. He holstered his revolver, crossed the room, bent down to pick up the flare pistol and examined it in his hand. He shook his head. 'Now I know why he was in the wardrobe when we arrived, he was looking for the flare pistol, to fire it when we burst in. No doubt of that, and we didn't search it.' A burst of anger swept up from his stomach to his throat at the blunder they had made. He felt like killing the German officer on the spot, but then dismissed that thought. He was no assassin. He looked at Hedges. 'Take him to a different room and search him thoroughly. Search the whole bloody room – everything, d'you hear, everything!'

The young soldier backed away from the Captain's anger. 'Yes, sir,' replied Hedges. 'Right, c'mon, Fritz.' He pushed the German officer out of the room.

*

Packard was about to dispatch a runner to Sergeant Campbell when

Denton approached him on the bridge. It was more of an unhurried stroll than a stride. He handed Packard the flare pistol with three unused cartridges then tugged down the front of his tunic before inhaling and said, 'I should've checked and made sure his room had been searched thoroughly. He's made idiots of us.'

Packard nodded, and saw the disappointment in Denton's eyes, but granted him a benevolent smile. 'Well, at least we have more flare cartridges.' He handed them to the runner. 'Give them to Sergeant Campbell. He knows what to do with them.'

'Sir.' The runner turned and trotted off in the direction of the wood.

'Now that Fritz knows we're here, it must change things,' said Denton.

'It changes nothing,' replied Packard with some confidence. 'Sure, Fritz knows we're here now, but don't forget, he doesn't know our strength. We might be outgunned and outmanned, but Fritz doesn't know that – not yet, anyway, and until he does, the plan remains the same.' Even in the darkness, Packard saw Denton's look of surprise. 'We all know what to do, so let's do it.'

It seemed an age before Campbell fired his first flare. Small groups of German soldiers had tried to cross the open field with one group attempting to push their way up the river road. In the cold light of the flares, they were cut to pieces by Campbell's riflemen and Thompson's machine gun. The fight only lasted a few minutes, but the skirmish was swift and brutal. There were at least thirty enemy dead and wounded. 'They're trying to find our positions,' remarked Packard.

'And assess our fire power,' Denton replied gloomily.

'Well, now they know,' Packard said fervently. 'If they want this bridge, they're going to have to fight for it. Which leaves Fritz with little choice.'

'And what do you anticipate he'll do?'

Packard scratched his chin. 'If he has artillery, he'll be ranging his guns on Sergeant Campbell's positions along the treeline to soften it up prior to his next assault, only next time he'll mean to take that position and cut through the wood to the bridge.'

Denton took out his watch and sprang the lid. 'Dawn will be breaking in about twenty minutes.' Suddenly a flare went up from the German side, quickly followed by two flashes in the distant darkness and then two loud booms. Both shots screamed into the canopy of the trees and exploded harmlessly at least fifty yards behind Campbell's position. The flare died out. 'Using the brightness of the flare to observe their fall of shot and make adjustments,' Denton muttered to Packard. Another flare and two more shots, this time exploding in the field just short of the treeline.

'That's it – they've got the range of the treeline,' remarked Packard in a heart-rending tone. 'Now they'll blast it.'

Denton put the watch away and stared helplessly into the darkness. 'I pray to God that Fritz misses,' he said.

Packard replied, 'Let's hope He hears you. I'll thank God if just a quarter of those men survive.'

He felt bad about leaving Sergeant Campbell to face the full force of the German assault and had discussed the danger of it with him. He knew casualties would be high but what else could he do? He had to buy time for the engineers to do their job. His job was on the bridge, directing and controlling its defence – and its destruction when that time came. Now, as he watched the German gunners zero in on his sergeant's position, he felt a sickening ache of hopelessness, responsibility, and guilt in the pit of his stomach as shell after shell rained down.

CHAPTER 10

Sergeant Campbell, along with his 40 riflemen, hunkered down on the floor of the trench as it heaved and shuddered, stinking of cordite and filling with smoke. The men coughed and gasped for breath as blast after blast roared above; the trees were splitting like matchwood, the blasts showering great clods of earth, branches and huge sharp splints of wood over the trench. A man screamed, and then another. They were taking casualties, but nothing could be done. They all pressed their hands hard over their ears, mouths open wide, some shouting and swearing in a feeble attempt to stop the deafening bellow and torment from the blast waves all around them. In an endless pain, the pressure from the blasts hurt their ears like hell, while grit and soil stung their faces. Part of the trench wall collapsed, burying four men alive. A frantic scramble began to quickly dig them out by hand before it was too late. They were coughing, spitting, one spewing up as each man was dragged clear of the clinging earth, but the last one had succumbed and remained lifeless.

A shell hit a tall tree that split in two as if a giant axe had chopped it, and the heavy trunk swung down across the trench in a crash of leaves and splitting wood; its thick branches crushing and burying two men huddled beneath it. The air was foul with cordite, the trench clouded in thick dust and smoke and the men's faces covered in sticky blood that ran from their noses and ears. The minutes crawled by. Was this never going to end? The earth lurched one final time and then, just as suddenly as it had started, it stopped. The roar echoed away across the field, the smoke slowly clearing to show that dawn was breaking.

Campbell wondered how he was still alive. The silence was unnerving. It made him tense. Somehow he had survived that onslaught of shellfire – the worst he had yet experienced. With eardrums ringing, he could taste blood in his mouth and spat it out, instinctively checking that he wasn't injured. Was there anyone else left alive?

Then men could be heard moving about, some moaning, some coughing, spitting, cursing, some too weak to move while others lay dead. The soldier beside him had a head wound and looked dazed and nervous. Campbell placed a comforting hand on his shoulder and the soldier slowly lifted his head. His face looked awful, shocked, but he nodded that he was alright.

Campbell looked around him and could see the damage done to the trench and the places where it had caved in, with half-buried equipment and lifeless bodies sticking out like discarded ragdolls. He knew that the whole operation to blow the bridge depended on making time with his defence at the treeline. Had he enough men left to give the engineers that time?

He felt a nudge and turned to see a corporal with a dirty blood-smeared face standing over him. 'You okay, Sarge?' he asked.

Campbell nodded and reached up and the corporal grabbed his hand and pulled him to his feet. 'Thanks,' he said, and started to brush loose earth, twigs, and leaves from his shoulders and tunic with his hand, his ears still ringing from the sound of the shell blasts.

'Blimey, Sarge, that was a bit lively,' the corporal said.

Another voice chimed in further down the trench. 'Bloody hell, Corp, you can say that again!'

The men sheltering at the bottom of the trench from the blasts were now slowly getting to their feet and helping the half-dozen or so wounded. Now that the enemy artillery had stopped, it was time to worry. An assault by German infantry was imminent. Campbell instructed the corporal to do a quick head count, check their weapons, and report back. He poked his head over the lip of the trench and for the first time he had a chance to study the terrain in the dawn light, but what he saw were dark columns of German infantry forming up across the other side of the field – masses of them. He swallowed hard. This time there would be no messing. They meant business, one attack, straight at the treeline, then on through the wood, and then on to the bridge. And the only thing in their way was his handful of men.

He cupped a hand to his mouth. 'Stand to!' he shouted along the trench. 'Stand to!'

The dark mass of German infantry started moving towards them. The corporal fell in at his side. 'We've twenty-five effective men left. We've six dead, nine wounded, and three of those are very serious and can't be moved. Everyone has got the wind up after that blasting,' he said in short breaths, then jerked a thumb towards the lip of the trench. 'We're not staying here to face that lot, are we Sarge?' he said in exasperation.

'We can't hold them, that's for sure,' Campbell replied, 'but we'll fire a few volleys to cut them down a bit. Once they're close enough, I'll give the order to fall back to the bridge as planned. Timing has got to be right, mind. Two sections of five men each and we'll skirmish in turn to cover our withdrawal like we discussed. I don't want the walking wounded slowing us down when we have to make a run for it, so send them back to the bridge now.'

'Right oh, Sarge.' The corporal dashed off down the trench line, sending the wounded back. Three were limping, a fourth was being carried by two men with head wounds. The three seriously injured men he left at the bottom of the trench. There was nothing he could do for them.

Campbell didn't want to tangle with the overwhelming numbers of German infantry heading towards them. His men wouldn't stand a chance. A crackling sound came from his right flank. Captain Denton's riflemen in the cottages had opened fire. Thompson was firing short bursts into the German infantry's flank but he wouldn't be for long; it would soon be out of sight. The German guns were beginning to fire on the cottages to support their infantry and to suppress any interference from that quarter. He could hear the loud explosions as the HE shells tore into the brickwork. The German Battlegroup Commander was no novice.

Campbell looked left and right. There was no sign of the Germans trying to outflank him and get behind. They were coming straight in. It was time to give the order. He cupped a hand to his mouth and shouted down the trench.

'Get ready!' He looked left and right. 'Load – take aim – fire!' Twenty-five rifles cracked as if they were one, then they fired again, and again, and again into the dark massed ranks advancing towards them. Germans could be seen going down, but it wasn't enough. They fired again, and again, and again, and more Germans went down but there was no flinching. They kept coming like a dark grey tidal wave, getting closer and closer. If there was one thing he had learnt in this war it was that German bravery knew no bounds, they had lots of pluck and just kept coming, and Campbell looked on in awe, picking out individual faces and ranks on their uniforms as the grey tidal wave advanced, getting close to breaking on the treeline.

Then at the crucial moment, he cupped his hand to his mouth again.

'This is it boys, fall back as planned – fall back!'

They didn't need telling twice. Almost as one, they turned around and quickly scrambled out of the trench, darting back into the wood away from the treeline. Within a few seconds, the first of the German infantry began jumping the trench, with many more following behind. Campbell's men ducked and darted through bushes and around trees. Fifty yards later, they entered a small clearing with daylight shining through and quickly gathered together on one knee.

'Right,' said Campbell, panting. 'Section one and section two, form a line on the other side of this clearing and conceal yourselves.' He pointed towards a bush line. It was just ten men. 'When Fritz enters the clearing, give him five rounds rapid and then skedaddle. Got that?'

They all nodded.

'The rest of you, follow me.' They all got up and darted through the bush line, leaving the two sections to take up kneeling positions concealed among the bushes, all squinting through their rifle sights.

The seconds seemed to tick by slowly – and then.

'Here they come!' shouted the corporal. 'Rapid fire!' It was just like a wild pheasant shoot, with gunfire blasting away at the first German soldiers who broke into the clearing, hitting a wall of bullets. Several fell down instantly, while others clutched at arms and legs, but it was enough to stall their advance.

'Back, boys!' the corporal shouted. The two sections got up and beat a hasty retreat into the wood as German rifle fire was returned. Bullets zipped and whizzed past, stripping leaves and twigs from the bushes and trees around them as they ran. At least three men cried out as they were hit and went down. 'Keep going, don't stop for the wounded,' the corporal roared. They met up with Campbell, who already had another two sections forming a new concealed defence line and waiting. He yelled, 'Pass through, pass through!' then watched grimly as they darted between them. He could hear the men calling one another. There had been casualties. Of the ten men, he only counted five. Once they were through, he got up and joined them. But would they make the bridge?

CHAPTER 11

The walking wounded had just made the bridge. They looked grim. Packard rushed to the barricade and yelled, 'This way!' He ordered some men from the bridge defence to help bring them in. He knew it was bad from the sound of gunfire coming from the wood. He was desperate for news of his sergeant.

'What's happening?' he asked anxiously to the first limping soldier to reach him, sweaty and breathless with threads of blood streaking his face and neck. His uniform was fouled with dirt, splattered in blood spots and other horrors. He had a crude bloodstained bandage wrapped around one leg.

'We're under attack by a huge force,' the limping soldier gasped, sucking in air to form the words. He tried controlling his breathing. 'We couldn't hold them, sir. Sergeant Campbell is fighting a delayed withdrawal through the wood. He should be right behind me … and Fritz is right behind him.' He looked back. 'It's developing into a running fight. I hope they make it.'

Packard took off his cap and wiped his forehead with the back of his hand.

'God Almighty,' he whispered, then quickly trotted over to Thompson, who sat crouched behind the gun, waiting with his crew. 'As soon as our men are through, give Fritz hell!'

Thompson nodded, then they all ducked and turned their heads as a screaming shell went in and exploded in a flash on the cottages with an ear-splitting roar. They heard rubble, breaking glass and masonry crashing to the ground. Dirty grey smoke billowed above the now roofless building. The barn was on fire, flames cracking and roaring as they took hold of the wooden frame. He saw Denton running towards it and shouting at two men. A moment later, German prisoners were running away from the burning barn, helping each other, coughing and spitting, some being dragged in almost total collapse. Denton had had the foresight to release them from the barn before they burned to death. The battlegroup's guns kept up their efforts though, raining shells on the cottages and outbuildings. Shells exploded all around, but none too close to the bridge so far.

Packard stared mesmerized at the roaring, blazing barn and cottages, but there was no time to mess about. Stray bullets whizzed over his head. Packard knew that his time for holding off the battlegroup from the bridge was fast running out. Thompson's gun team was key to holding off Fritz until they could blow the bridge. He went to the bridge parapet, leaned over, and, cupping a hand to his mouth, he yelled above the din of battle at two sappers working below.

'How much longer?'

They looked up. One sapper shouted back, 'Almost ready, sir. Five or six minutes!'

Packard was relieved at that news and felt that they just might pull it off in time. He turned sharply as Thompson's machine gun opened fire behind him. Sergeant Campbell, he saw, was now at the barricade, yelling encouragement to those near him, with just a few of his men returning fire at the Germans who were pursuing them. It was an odd feeling, but he felt strangely elated that Campbell had made it. He immediately went to him. 'You made it then!'

Campbell turned to face him and nodded, his eyes wild and red with sweat. He looked pale under the streaks of blood about his sweaty face.

'I almost left it too late, sir.'

Packard thumped him on the shoulder. 'You got back in one piece. That's all that matters. Anyway, we're about to blow the bridge. Hold them off until we're ready. I'll be back!'

The rapid fire from the rifles at the barricade and the bursts of fire from Thompson's machine gun devastated the German soldiers as they broke the treeline, their bodies hammered by bullets as they went down in heaps. Campbell knew from previous battles that a machine gun was particularly lethal against this type of attack at close range and after a few minutes he saw the attack stall, the Germans falling back into the wood. The German dead and wounded spread out before him like a grey carpet of horror and misery. The loss of life was startling and appalling to him, but they were German and not his men out there, which was all that really mattered to him at that moment.

The Germans began firing back from the cover of the wood. The stutter of incoming small-arms fire was either lacerating the ground before them, zipping overhead at lightning speed or slamming into the barricade. Campbell and the men at the barricade were exchanging bullet for bullet. Thompson's machine gun was adding to the catastrophic din.

'Bloody 'ell', one man shouted. 'Those bastards are really up for a fight!' They were his last words. His head jerked back in a red spray of blood and he fell heavily on the ground.

Campbell took a second to look around him. At least half the men manning the barricade had now been hit, including three of Thompson's men who were sprawled on the ground, one face down, the other two flat on their backs. If they didn't get the call to withdraw soon, he thought to himself, it would be too late. Glancing across the bridge, now almost covered by black smoke from the blazing cottages and barn, he saw Lieutenant Packard break through and come running towards him. A series of explosions near the bridge made him throw himself to the ground as earth rained down upon him, but when the shockwave died away, he scrambled up and completed the dash to Campbell's side almost breathless.

'Start pulling the men back, Sergeant,' shouted Packard above the din. 'The sappers are ready to blow the bridge. The smoke should cover your withdrawal!'

'About bloody time,' Campbell yelled back. 'I'll get Thompson with Clarkson to cover our withdrawal!'

'Good idea. I'll tell them. You'll see Captain Denton the other side of the smoke. Form up with him to cover me and the gun team.'

'You staying with Thompson?'

'Of course. He's a good man to have around in a situation like this, now go, Sergeant. I'll be right behind you!'

'Right oh, sir!' Campbell went along the barricade and started sending men back. Packard was now with Thompson and Clarkson at the machine gun. Campbell turned from the barricade. He made sure he was the last, and he started running back over the bridge through the pall of smoke. Some men fell as they ran, hit by bullets that were zipping all over the place. Some were being half-carried or half-dragged by friends. Behind them, Thompson, with Clarkson feeding the belt into the gun, was hammering away at the treeline to cover their withdrawal. Explosions were ripping up the earth on the far side of the bridge and raining soil and clods of earth everywhere. The whole area was covered in a grey and black pall of choking smoke. The smell of cordite was thick in the air. The first men reached Captain Denton, coughing, spitting, and gasping.

'Where's Lieutenant Packard?' he cried to one of them.

'He's behind us sir, with Sergeant Campbell.'

Once Packard saw Sergeant Campbell go, he slapped Clarkson on the shoulder. 'Go man, go.' Clarkson picked up his rifle and ran back. Thompson still kept his finger on the trigger, hammering the treeline. Packard shouted above the din, 'That's it, Thompson, let's go. That's an order!' The machine gun suddenly went silent apart from steam hissing from the connector of the water hose attached to the gun. Thompson quickly picked up two thick gloves, slipped them on and started to disconnect the gun from the water hose, then disconnected the gun from the mount.

'What the hell are you doing?' Packard cried out.

'I'm not leaving the gun to Fritz, sir!' Thompson explained, releasing the gun from the mount. A cloud of steam spurted from the connector as he lifted the gun and carried it to the parapet of the bridge. With all his strength, he heaved the gun above his head and hauled it into the swirling river below.

'Well done, Thompson,' yelled Packard. 'Now run man, run!'

Thompson turned, grinning with satisfaction, and went back to the gun pit to grab his rifle. Breaking into a run, he raced to the other side of the bridge. Packard let him pass by and had a quick glance back at the barricade to make sure no one was left behind apart from the dead. Just as he began running and picking up speed, a small tied bundle of stick grenades was tossed over the barricade into the gun pit by a German sapper. It exploded with an almighty roar. The bridge lurched and the shockwave tossed Packard in the air and dropped him heavily to the ground. The gun parts and wooden bits from the barricade fell about him in a wide arc.

Thompson had passed through the drifting smoke, heading for the other side of the bridge when he heard and felt the explosion behind him. For a split second, he thought the engineers had blown the bridge under him, not realising that his officer was down and hurt. He reached Captain Denton and Sergeant Campbell with Clarkson behind a makeshift pile of logs and boulders and jumped over to join them, his face streaked with dirt and sweat. Shells were still exploding on their side of the bridge.

'Where's Lieutenant Packard?' Denton asked.

Thompson looked towards the bridge and the drifting smoke, hoping that his lieutenant would suddenly break through.

He didn't.

Catching his breath, he said, 'He was right behind me, sir.'

Campbell got to his feet. 'Something's wrong then,' he said. 'He's not bloody there!'

Thompson got up beside him. 'I'll go back,' he said, but Campbell held him back by grabbing his arm and shot a glance at Denton for approval. Just then, the engineer corporal appeared crouching low and went to where Denton was kneeling. 'Sir, sir, we can't delay any further. From the firing point we can see German sappers under the bridge pulling away our explosives and wires. We've got to blow the bridge now!'

All eyes turned to Captain Denton. Would he give the order to blow the bridge or delay and rescue their officer?

'That's why Fritz hasn't followed us over the bridge yet,' said Campbell. 'They're waiting for their sappers to remove as much of the explosive as possible before they cross. They fear we'll blow it when they try. Now's our chance, sir, let me get the lieutenant?'

'The bridge, sir, the bridge,' intervened the engineer corporal. 'We don't have time. We've got to blow it now!'

Denton licked his dry lips, looking anxiously about him from one face to the other, trying to be calmer than he felt. Either way, there was no easy answer. He looked straight at the engineer corporal. 'Okay,' he said nervously, 'I hear you loud and clear, but if that was me out there, Lieutenant Packard would delay and attempt a rescue. I know he would. So,' he said, turning to the sapper corporal, 'wait until I give the order.' Then turning back to Campbell, he added, 'Two minutes, Sergeant, got that? Take Thompson with you and find out what's happened to him. Two minutes, that's all!'

Campbell nodded. 'C'mon,' he said to Thompson, and both men got up and raced back into the gloom of swirling smoke from the burning cottages drifting across the bridge. As they broke through into the clear air, they saw their lieutenant face down with the gun pit wrecked and smoking behind him. They could see no movement. They rushed over to him. Packard was lying in the gun pit's scattered debris. His back was covered in grit, wood pieces, and soil.

'Sir, sir, are you alright?' Campbell asked, and gently gripped his shoulder. He turned him over with the care that he would give a sleeping child and could see that Packard had a gash across the side of his head, with blood streaking down the left side of his face. He was moaning, slipping in and out of consciousness. Campbell whispered gently to his ear, 'It's all right, sir, we've got you.' He bit his lip and gave a quick glance over him, especially his legs, but could see no other signs of injury apart from the gash where a piece of debris had struck him, but it didn't mean that he didn't have any. He knew that to carry a man with an unsupported broken leg was almost certain death for that man. The jagged bone would sever the artery and the casualty would bleed to death long before he got to an aid station. He'd seen that too many times on the battlefield, but there was no time to check further. The seconds were speeding by. He had to get him out of there quickly if they were all to survive. He took a chance.

'Grab him, Thompson,' he said, and they hauled him to his feet. Packard let out an agonising moan as Thompson threw the lieutenant over his shoulder in a fireman's lift and started to carry him back across the bridge. Packard's legs dangled normally to Campbell's delight as he started to follow them.

Men began shouting in German behind them. Campbell took no notice until a bullet zipped past his head, and then another. He turned towards the barricade and saw three German soldiers in their grey-covered spiked helmets climbing over, with another taking pot shots at him. He stopped, dropped to one knee, lifted the rifle firmly into his shoulder, took careful aim and shot the shooter behind the barricade. He knew he only had three bullets left from his ten round magazine so he quickly pulled back the bolt to eject the empty .303 cartridge case and pushed the bolt home to pick up another. Then, one after the other, as they were climbing over, he shot two more in quick succession. He was out of ammo. No time to reload. But something caught his eye. He lifted his chin slightly from the rifle and saw about a dozen Germans starting to climb over. Fritz was going to go for it and storm the barricade. He knew the bridge must be a heartbeat away from being blown. He lowered the rifle, got up, turned and ran like hell, disappearing into the swirling smoke.

CHAPTER 12

Thompson returned to Captain Denton with his lieutenant slung over his shoulder and gently lowered him to the ground beside him. Blood and sweat streaked Packard's face but his bloodshot eyes were open in a staring gaze.

'Is he hurt badly?' asked a concerned Denton.

'A gash on the head and a bit concussed, that's all, sir,' replied Thompson, regaining his breath. Then a grin spread very slowly across his battered face. 'He's tough, that one. He'll be fine after a short rest. You'll see,' he added.

Denton breathed a sigh of relief and hoped no one noticed.

Packard's senses reluctantly returned slowly as he started to become aware of his surroundings. Somebody spoke. He was conscious of voices talking around him that started to come clear and he tried to focus on them, straining his ears – first Thompson, then Captain Denton. He blinked in the smoky sunlight, listening to explosions and ragged gunfire, and tasted the smoke drifting about him. The bitterness of cordite raked his tongue. He began to move and felt a comforting hand from Thompson on his shoulder to steady him as he struggled to sit upright on one elbow. He shifted his glance to all the grim-faced men around him and began flexing his fingers to draw life into them, felt a throb to the side of his head, reached up and touched the gash. He saw blood on his fingers.

'You're going to be all right.' It was Captain Denton's voice, calm, reassuring. 'A minor wound,' he added.

Packard heard someone cry out. He needed to know what was happening and turned his head as a khaki figure rushed towards them from out of the smoke and jumped over the logs and boulders to land next to him.

It was Sergeant Campbell. He was gasping. Grimy sweat was running down his face and nose. 'Fritz is over the barricade,' he reported. 'We've got to blow the bridge, sir. It's now or never!'

They heard the popping of a motorbike engine coming up the road. They watched as a speeding Triumph suddenly appeared through the haze of smoke from the burning cottages to career drunkenly around the shell holes and debris that littered the road.

'Dispatch rider,' said Clarkson, flatly.

'I 'ope it's a message the war's over. We can all go 'ome and get some bloody sleep.' The name of the hopeful soldier wouldn't quite come to Packard in that moment, but he smiled at the thought.

They all watched as the rider skidded to a halt right in front of them, engine popping with legs spread out for balance. He raised his goggles and twisted around in the seat, glanced at their grimy faces and saw an officer with captain's pips on his sleeve. He swung round a canvas bag that was slung over his shoulder, untied the flap, and retrieved a buff-coloured envelope. Then he crouched low over the handlebars as a shell screeched overhead, exploding with an almighty crash by the ruined cottages, near the engineers firing position. He felt the Triumph buck from the blast wave.

'Christ,' he muttered. More shells began pitching in all around the place. He raised his head gingerly with wild brown eyes looking at the huge pall of drifting smoke and dust against the sky, looked down and eyed them gravely. They all looked back, dead-beat.

'Sir?' he said to Denton. 'I'm looking for Lieutenant Packard. I've an urgent message for him.'

'Give it here,' said Denton, reaching out to take it and glancing quickly to Packard. 'Shall I open it?' he asked with hesitation.

Packard agreed with a nod.

Denton tore it open, removed the white flimsy and began to read. He slowly removed his cap and looked solemnly at Packard beside him. 'It's from Divisional HQ.' He swallowed hard and held a grim stare. 'They want the bridge held at all cost.' He heard everyone gasp and freeze. He continued, 'Reinforcements are on their way to support us.' He handed the white flimsy to him.

Packard read it in silence. He bit his lip, then glanced at Denton and slowly shook his head in disbelief. Behind him, he heard some of his men protesting. After what they had been through, they had plenty to moan about. Good friends were lying out there with their heads and bellies open.

'Is there a reply, sir?' asked the dispatch rider. He offered the lieutenant a message pad and the stub of a pencil. He looked eager to get away from this hell hole.

Packard read the flimsy several times. There was no time stated as to when they could expect their reinforcements. It didn't make any sense, they could be minutes or hours away and besides, it was too late, Fritz was already on the bridge and there was nothing he could do about it except blow the damn thing. Most of his company were dead or wounded and the dozen or so left were in no shape to put up much of a fight and the ammunition must be getting low. There was no time for a discussion, it wouldn't help anyway. He nodded.

'Yes, there is,' he said, somewhat subdued, and took the message pad. He could hear the croakiness in his own dry voice. He took a deep breath and exhaled very slowly as to what to write. He looked first at Captain Denton and then Sergeant Campbell for support. Their faces intent and anxious. They all felt it was cruel and unfair.

He wrote, *Heavy fighting.* Stop. *Company reduced to a dozen all ranks.* Stop. *Enemy about to take bridge.* Stop. *Will make a last stand and then deny enemy the prize!* Stop. He read out the message so they could all hear it. Packard saw the surprise on the faces of his men when he passed the message pad back to the dispatch rider. With a dry smile he said, 'Good luck.'

'Thank you, sir, and good luck to you.' The rider revved the engine and set off in a wide circle and a haze of blue smoke, headed back the way he'd come. Everyone watched him. Suddenly a shell pitched in with an almighty roar, and the blast was deafening. The dispatch rider was flung high into the air, disappearing in the flame, dust, and smoke. Seconds later, human remains, bike pieces, and other debris started falling to earth. A large piece of motorbike, with the attached back wheel spinning, landed and bounced toward their position.

'Bullseye,' Thompson muttered coldly.

Packard wiped his forehead with his sleeve, leaving a smeared bloodstain. He felt pity for the dispatch rider but at least it was quick. He swung round to Campbell and looked at him gravely. 'Share out the ammunition, Sergeant. Then we'll get that bridge blown.'

Campbell understood. One last blast at Fritz as he crosses the bridge then blow it. He bared his teeth in a grin and replied, 'Yes sir!'

Denton asked, 'You intend to make a last stand?'

Packard shook his head. 'Once Fritz crosses that bridge, we'll blow it to blazes.' He got up and dashed over to the engineers' firing point.

The engineer corporal was kneeling in front of the plunger-type exploder box with his hands on his hips when the lieutenant knelt beside him. 'Ready, Corporal?'

He turned and smiled. 'Yes, sir.' He yanked up the handle. 'Shall I blow it now, sir?'

'Not yet.' He looked around. 'Where's Sergeant McWhirter?'

Packard saw the grim expression as the sapper corporal jerked his thumb over his shoulder at a body under a groundsheet with a pair of boots sticking out. 'He's dead, sir. Shell blast about ten minutes ago. The others are dead too. It's just me and 'im,' he said, pointing to a lonely sapper nearby who was propping himself on his elbows behind some boxes as the odd shot pinged by.

Packard bit his lip as he glanced at the groundsheet. He'd forgotten just how dangerous the sapper's job was, preparing the bridge for demolition under fire. They rigged the bridge without protest and just got on with it. He felt a pang of guilt – or did he? The sappers were dying doing their job just like his men were dying doing theirs. There was an uncomfortable silence then Packard said, 'Reinforcements are on their way, but I don't think they'll get here on time. I intend to blow the bridge the moment Fritz crosses.'

A few bullets whimpered past. The corporal glared at him. 'We don't have that time, sir. Just give the word. German sappers are already tearing away our charges from under the bridge. If we don't blow it now—'

He didn't finish – a shell exploded nearby, sending a shower of stones, earth, and grit over them. Packard bowed his head and grimaced. 'Dammit,' he cursed, as the shockwave made his head throb, and then he heard a dull thud. A shell splinter pierced the corporal's chest, right through the heart. Packard recognised that sound and lifted his chin just as the body of the corporal went down from the impact, his face turned towards the sky and then toppled forward over the handle of the exploder, pushing it hard into the box.

At first nothing happened, then the ground heaved and a monstrous, majestic roar erupted around the bridge, sending flame, billowing smoke, huge stone pieces, timber, and bodies whirling up into the air. Packard, still kneeling, was watching the spectacle in awe as the debris lifted slowly upwards, high into the air before falling to earth with a crash. The explosion rumbled gently away along the river valley, and then silence fell upon the area. The bridge crossing was still in a thick haze of dust and smoke, its destruction totally obscured.

Packard stayed motionless at the firing point as thousands of gold, yellow, red, and brown autumn leaves from the tall trees around began slowly fluttering down all over the bridge area like paper confetti at a wedding. He looked at the twisted face of the dead sapper slumped over the plunger. He'd died without even a cry, and Packard had seen enough men die like that in this war.

He slowly stood up, not knowing he had moved, and forced a smile. His ears were still numb from the explosion when Denton came over to join him and grasped his arm. In a spirit of jubilation, he pushed up the peak of this cap and said, 'Bloody hell Lieutenant, you've done it! By God you've done it!'

A bugle blared across the river. It was German. A rallying call, perhaps?

When the smoke and dust finally drifted clear, the bridge was badly wrecked but the main span connecting both banks was still standing. It had great jagged holes along it, but with care it was still crossable!

Both men stood like statues looking quizzically at the wrecked and crumbling, featureless stonework of the bridge, trying to work out what had gone wrong. Were they overconfident? Did they allow too much time for the German engineers to remove the explosives and wiring? Whatever the reason, the grim reality was that the bridge was still standing and Fritz was on the other side just waiting to charge cross. Packard only had a dozen or so men left that were able to put up a fight and they were very short of ammunition. He twisted round to the engineer taking cover next to the firing point. 'It didn't go down, dammit!'

The sapper looked up to him. 'It just happens sometimes, sir. Nothing you can explain.'

Packard swung on him angrily, and instantly relented. It wasn't the sapper's fault, but it was incredible that after all that fighting, the loss of life on both sides, and the effort made by the engineers to wire and charge the bridge under fire, the bridge was still standing. He started to walk off towards Campbell in silence, kicking small stones and masonry across the roadway.

'Sir!' called Campbell. 'A Fritz officer is coming over the bridge under a white flag!'

He spun around to look. There, gingerly picking his way over rubble and around gaping holes, was a German officer in a field-grey uniform, silver epaulettes, and a cloth-covered spiked helmet. Following closely behind him was a German sergeant with a dirty white cloth attached to a large stick that he was slowly waving from side to side.

Denton ambled up and stood beside Packard. 'My God. I don't believe it. Fritz is surrendering!'

Packard looked at him dully. 'That may be wishful thinking. More like a truce, I'd say.'

They both stood quite still until the German officer reached their side of the bridge. He stopped and looked around him. The air was heavy with dust and grey smoke from the smouldering charred ruins of the barn and cottages that drifted in the light breeze. Amid the rubble and stones and the lunar landscape of shell holes were the bodies of British soldiers like discarded rag dolls, some sprawled in grotesque shapes. Just as on his side of the bridge, it was carnage.

'Are you ze officer in charge?'

Packard regarded him calmly and replied in German. 'Yes. What do you want?'

The German officer's epaulette showed he was a lieutenant and his tunic was carrying an adjutant's lanyard. Unlike Denton and Packard, his uniform was not corrupted by the filth of battle. He carried no sidearm and gave a slight bow from the waist before speaking again in English. 'You speak German. That is good. My colonel sends his compliments. We are both exhausted and fight very hard, yes?'

Packard nodded heavily. In truth, his men, or what was left of them, were worn out from battle, the forced marching, and the lack of any decent sleep. They had been on the go for days. 'What is it your colonel wants, Lieutenant?'

The German officer gave a small smile. 'A truce to clear our wounded and collect our dead. You agree?'

Packard had guessed right, but it was still so unreal and vaguely absurd. Enemy officers meeting out here in some sort of civil ceremony with pleasantries, where minutes before, they were all blasting one another to hell – literally. Now all Fritz had to do, if he still had the manpower to do so, was cross the bridge or what remained of it, and there would be bugger all Packard could do to stop him. But clearly Fritz was hurt and had no more will to fight. It was over.

Denton muttered, 'Careful what you offer him. It might be a trick.'

'I don't think so,' whispered Packard.

'Maybe, but all the same …'

'How long?' Packard demanded.

'One hour. Maybe two?' said the German.

Denton and Packard whispered to each other, then Denton

replied harshly. 'One hour, that is all.' He had argued with Packard that at any time now reinforcements would be arriving. This type of thing would be scorned by the brasshats. Packard had argued that chivalry in battle still had meaning.

'Very well, one hour,' said the German. 'Our engineers say the bridge is too kaput for any use and my colonel congratulates you on its defence.' He clicked his heels and threw up a smart salute to show respect. Packard and Denton instantly returned the salute.

So, chivalry in battle still had meaning after all.

As the German officer carefully made his way back across the bridge, he left a heavy silence. Then Denton ran a hand over his brow, rubbing sweat and grime and mud across his forehead, and said, 'Well I'll be blowed, Lieutenant, you pulled it off. Took on a German battlegroup and defeated the buggers. I'm going to see you get a gong for this. My God, you deserve it.'

Packard, head bowed replied, 'I lost my company, my precious company, and all those men. No medal is worth that.' Then he strode off towards his men. The place smelt of cordite and death and Packard was keen to get it cleared up. 'Sergeant Campbell!'

'Sir!'

'We've brokered a one hour's truce with Fritz to attend our wounded and gather our dead. See to it.'

'Very good, sir. And what about the prisoners?'

Packard had forgotten about them. The last time he saw them they were escaping from the blazing barn. He was glad Campbell had reminded him. With so few able men left, he made a quick calculation. 'Get the prisoners to help, or what's left of them.'

'Most of 'em are still hiding in the wood behind us,' said Campbell, 'but I'm told the officer has scarpered with a few others.'

'Can't say I blame them,' replied Packard. 'I wouldn't have hung around.' Packard was about to walk away. He stopped. 'And Sergeant …' Something in his tone made Campbell stare at him.

'Sir?'

Packard took a pace towards him. 'On the bridge … when I was down.' He extended his hand. 'Thanks.' They looked into one another's red-rimmed eyes and shook hands firmly.

'You'd have done the same for me,' Campbell said honestly, and Packard nodded slowly with a slight smile.

'Yes, I suppose so.'

They both turned away. There was work to be done.

CHAPTER 13

It was just before midnight when Churchill arrived by car outside Lord Kitchener's home in London. As he climbed out and looked up, he saw the lights burning in all the windows. To Churchill, they burned with gloom. He began searching his thoughts for some reason why he had been urgently called back to the Kitchener's home, and not 10 Downing Street as he would have expected. The Foreign Secretary's car, parked a few feet away with the driver idling his time smoking a cigarette, made him feel even more uneasy, and he sensed that something profound had happened in this war since he'd left London by train just a few hours ago.

He turned and leaned into his driver. 'Thank you, Freddie. Wait for me.' He quickly went up the few steps, two at a time, to the large black door that was opened for him by a house servant.

Earlier that evening, Churchill, along with his Naval Secretary, Rear Admiral Sir Horace Hood, had been on a train bound for Dover for a quick trip to France to visit some of his naval gunnery and air units stationed along the coast. His train had been intercepted at a station in Kent and ordered to return to London.

Churchill was silent as he walked through the familiar door into the bright hallway, allowing the servant to lead him to a large room on the left. The servant gently pushed open the double doors into a spacious room and stepped to one side as they entered. Churchill saw a fire burning invitingly in a grate beneath a large ornate clock on the mantel, and above that, a large portrait of Lord Kitchener with a backdrop of Khartoum in the Sudan.

The conversation in the room suddenly stopped.

Churchill swivelled his eyes, first to the Foreign Secretary, Sir Edward Grey, standing next to the fireplace, dressed in a black suit with a white winged collar and tie, and then to Lord Kitchener, who had his back to Churchill, but turned when he entered. Kitchener looked immaculate in his military uniform. Both men were holding a tumbler of brandy. Churchill could feel the tension in the room, and for some reason, he felt like an intruder.

'Mr Churchill, m'lord,' the servant announced as he entered.

'A glass of brandy for Mr Churchill,' said Lord Kitchener.

The servant nodded and retreated behind the doors.

'I'm sorry to have to call you back like this, Winston,' Lord Kitchener said with sincerity. 'It must have been quite a wrench for you, but something very disturbing has come up.'

Churchill noticed that as Kitchener spoke, he was nudging the corner of his moustache with his knuckle, as he always did when he was irritated.

Churchill shrugged. 'I assumed this was not a social invitation.'

'Quite so,' replied Lord Kitchener, his face impassive as he strode across the room to a corner desk, picking up a telegram and handing it to Churchill. 'Here, read this. I received it today from Colonel Dallas, my War Office representative in Antwerp. He's heard that King Albert and his government intend to evacuate Antwerp on the third of October – that's tomorrow. And if that didn't cause enough consternation, Sir Edward then received a telegram from Sir Francis Villiers, our Ambassador in Belgium, confirming the Belgian government's intentions to evacuate Antwerp, including its field army, approximately 65,000 men. Apparently to Ghent, to protect the coast – their escape route!'

Churchill was shocked as he read the telegram. This was devastating news, and exactly what he was trying to avoid. The capitulation of Antwerp by the Belgians before the promised reinforcements arrived. 'What about the French division promised by Marshall Joffre?' he asked. Marshall Joffre was head of the French army and was heavily engaged holding onto the hard-won ground of the Marne battle, and now, along with the British, he was chasing the Germans in a series of clashes in the "rush to the sea".

'I've already contacted Marshall Joffre,' said Lord Kitchener. 'His army is under severe pressure all along the front and he cannot release a division for at least another seven days.'

'Seven days! That's much too long. By that time, we could lose the war!'

'And what about your Naval Brigades, Winston?' said Sir Edward. 'When are they due to reach Antwerp?'

Churchill felt uneasy. He knew Sir Edward was a devious, capable, intelligent politician, and he respected his views. Was he about to swing some blame his way? Churchill answered carefully. 'In two days' time, on the fourth of October. They're in transit now and I shall join them on their arrival as promised,' he said. 'The Belgians can wait that long, surely?'

Lord Kitchener said, 'If the telegrams are right, and I believe they are, your presence may not be necessary.'

Churchill squeezed his eyes shut for a moment and shook his head in despair. 'Belgium's capitulation of Antwerp at this moment could spell the end for us all,' he stressed. 'We've got to buy time and make them stand firm for a few more days, it's vital.' Then, looking straight at the Foreign Secretary, he asked, 'Has the Prime Minister not contacted King Albert about this?'

'He has,' replied Sir Edward, 'and he's on his way here now to brief us. My fear is it's too late. Tomorrow, the Belgians will capitulate the port of Antwerp to the Germans and if we don't get to the Channel coast first, it too will be up for grabs and could mean our army will be cut off.'

The ornate clock chimed midnight and they all listened intently as each chime sounded with a slow foreboding. Sir Edward and Churchill both took out their pocket watches, sprung the lid, and checked the time.

'Midnight,' said a subdued Churchill. He looked up. 'I fear it's no longer tomorrow … our destiny is today.'

At that moment, the doors swung open. 'The Prime Minister, m'lord,' announced the servant, and Herbert Asquith entered the room, looking decidedly shaky. They all acknowledged the Prime Minister as he stepped in, and he gave a defeated sigh.

'I've been in contact with King Albert and his Prime Minister, Charles de Broqueville. They do intend to leave Antwerp tomorrow,' he said. 'They have not got the promised reinforcements in time.'

'That's today, Prime Minister,' Churchill said glumly.

The Prime Minister looked at Churchill. 'Indeed Winston, and we're all upset about it, I'm sure.' It probably wasn't *meant* as a put down but there was an exhausted waspishness to Asquith's manner.

Lord Kitchener nudged his moustache. 'Do you think this is a bluff to get a last-minute rescue – I mean, to get the promised reinforcements?'

Taking a deep breath, the Prime Minister considered for a moment and replied, 'I think they're serious. King Albert explained that the big German gun is starting to destroy their ring of forts one by one, at least on their outer defensive perimeter, and time for them is fast running out, along with their options … and, if truth be told, so are ours.'

'Then let me go tonight,' said Churchill, determined. 'Telegraph King Albert and tell him I'm on my way with the promised reinforcements.' He looked around to each man for support. They stood there, faces glum. Then turning back to the Prime Minister, he said, 'Delay him somehow, and make him wait for me at least.'

The doors to the room swung open again and the servant entered, holding a silver tray of fresh glasses and placing them on the desk. He poured brandy into each glass, handed them round, and left.

'I'm still troubled by your presence there at such a critical time,' said the Prime Minister. 'What if you're captured?'

'What if we lose the war?' retorted Churchill.

There followed an uneasy silence and then Lord Kitchener said, 'I think Winston should go, Prime Minister. It's a risk worth taking.'

'I agree too, Prime Minister,' said Sir Edward in support. 'As you rightly said, our options are fast running out. We can't afford to lose the war. It's worth a try, don't you think?'

The Prime Minister nodded slowly, then stared silently into his glass, preoccupied as he swirled the brandy around, thinking about his options – or lack of them as the situation in Antwerp continued to deteriorate. 'If Antwerp falls in the next day or two, and the Germans take the Channel coast, it would be catastrophic for the army as well as for France. The war would indeed be lost. Britain and France would be forced to sue for peace and that would never do.' He looked up to face Churchill and sighed. 'I should not allow you to venture on this journey alone.' He held Churchill's gaze, emphasizing his words. 'You can't make too many promises, Winston. Just encourage the king to hold on until your reinforcements arrive and at least resist for a few more days.'

Churchill gave a small smile as a rush of pleasure swept over him. 'I'll beg him if I have to.'

'How soon can you leave?'

'Right now, Prime Minister. I have a car waiting outside and a train waiting for me at Victoria Station. My companion in the train is Admiral Hood, my naval secretary.'

'Ah, excellent,' said Lord Kitchener. 'Isn't he an expert on gunnery in fort defences?'

'He is, and should prove very useful in Antwerp.'

'Then it's settled,' said the Prime Minister, and he raised his glass. 'To Winston. May he succeed and grant us a few more days' reprieve in Antwerp.'

Lord Kitchener and Sir Edward Grey raised their glasses – 'To Winston,' they all said, and downed their brandy in one.

CHAPTER 14

The last two days had been the fastest that Packard could ever remember. He'd spent most of that time asleep – or eating. The Company, or what was left of it, had been billeted in a local village some four miles away where the Divisional Quartermaster had set up a base. Apart from the usual military supplies, there was a place to have a bath, field kitchens to eat in, and stores with a good supply of clean uniforms, and replacements for lost or damaged equipment.

The wounded men at the bridge were collected by a fleet of horse-drawn ambulances and taken to a casualty clearing station that was set up close by the village. The dead were collected for burial by horse carts and transported to the field hospital. Once their names had been recorded, they were buried in a field at the back, in a long trench with each man wrapped in his personal field-grey blanket, then carefully lowered and laid together side by side. Everyone attended the service, including the colonel with his headquarters' team.

They stood solemnly in their battle-soiled uniforms. Packard looked around him at their grey, weathered faces lined with pain and tried to gauge their sadness, their shame, and pity for their dead comrades, while the chaplain took the service, reading out the names, including the thirteen men who were listed as missing.

And Packard felt it too. Right or wrong, their deaths were his responsibility, and his alone, and he tried to gauge his own feelings and doubts about the way he'd conducted the battle. When the service was over and the men started to shuffle away, he stood alone.

The silence covered him like a blanket, except for that scraping sound as the grave was filled in. When they were all out of earshot, Campbell looked at his lieutenant's profile, alone and solemn, and went to his side.

'You OK, sir?'

Packard tugged down the peak of his cap. 'Sure. I'm fine.'

'War sir, it's all blood and guts no matter what you do.'

Packard nodded but was still peering down, quite moved by his sincerity. He knew what he meant. They both stood in silence for a few minutes, deep in their own thoughts until Packard turned to his sergeant.

'C'mon, let's get on with it.' They collected the wooden crosses that had been dropped off by the quartermaster near the grave site. They placed each cross, one by one, along the trench that marked the spot where each man lay. It was the least they could do.

It was two hours after the truce with the Germans before reinforcements began to arrive at the bridge, led by the Richmond Regiment. What they found on their arrival was a scene of utter devastation. The row of cottages used as a brothel, with the large wooden barn at the end that held the German prisoners, was completely consumed by fire and resembled nothing more than a pile of charred and broken bricks with a single blackened brick chimney stack sticking up defiantly, surrounded by a haze of dirty grey whispery smoke. Thank God the girls could not see it now, thought Packard.

The Richmond dead, along with the dead sappers, had been collected and laid out beside the road into a line under groundsheets, with just their boots sticking out. It had been a gruesome task for those seventeen fit and able men left from a half-company of eighty, to gather each dead man, a personal friend, a fellow soldier, one who had shared the same fear, the same horror of battle. The dead had been treated with the utmost respect and Packard, along with Campbell, had the unenviable task of searching each man brought in for their personal effects such as letters, photographs, money, and any other items that could be sent home to their families and loved ones back in England, before they were collected for burial.

The area around the bridge was pock-marked with shell craters and covered with stones, broken roof tiles, great lumps of turf, masonry, planks of wood and bricks, together with all other sorts of debris from the battle, including thousands of spent bullet cases, discarded equipment and caps, a few broken rifles, and bloodied body parts. The whole place reeked of cordite, smoke, and corruption.

Packard was adamant that the truce he'd made with the Germans be respected, even though it had gone over the hour they'd agreed. 'Beyond the bridge,' he had argued, 'Fritz has an awful lot of wounded and dead to clear and should be given the time to do so.' Grudgingly, the colonel had relented.

After the burial, the men were bathed and given clean uniforms. Under Campbell's keen eye, they cleaned their weapons and what was left of their equipment. They were fed a hot meal of stew and bread and then bedded down. Some men fell asleep instantly, exhaustion taking its toll, but some couldn't; just lying there, their closed eyes recalling the battles with a sickening clarity and terror.

Packard had a room to himself in one of the cottages owned by an elderly couple and felt out of place after spending most of his time in the field. He had slept for eighteen hours before he woke up and now it was daylight. He reached out, picking up his pocket watch and springing the lid; the time was just after six. Was it a.m. or p.m.?

His whole body seemed to ache, and he felt shaky. Over and over again he criticised what he had done at the bridge; that nagging doubt that cut into your confidence like a sharp knife, the accusation that any part of your planning might have been at fault for the losses. He sighed and threw his legs over the side of the bed, yawned and stretched, and then stood up and crossed the room to a dresser and had a drink of cool water from a jug. He felt hungry too. He looked at himself in a wall mirror. His hair was unruly and he ruffled it. The lines in his tired face made him look ten years older. He rubbed his jaw with his hand and felt new bristles breaking through. He needed another shave and recalled his hot bath and shave the day before, then a clean shirt and uniform to wear. Such utter bliss, he thought. He had not felt that clean since his arrival in France some six weeks' ago. His "officer's trunk" had been delivered to him yesterday, containing a clean spare uniform, shirts, socks, shoes, and underwear, among other delights like toothpaste and cologne. He would make the most of it and go and have another bath and shave and have breakfast or lunch or dinner, depending on what time it was.

It was 6 p.m.

After dinner, he inspected his men and their personal equipment with Sergeant Campbell. Everyone looked clean and tidy but the strain still showed on their faces. Afterwards, they both went to the field hospital to visit the wounded. Four serious cases had been moved earlier that day to a general hospital for further treatment and possible passage home – if they lived that long. Six of the less seriously wounded were returned to unit for light duties. Packard returned to his billet that evening and until the early hours he wrote letters to the relatives of the dead.

The following morning, Campbell organised a game of football; he led one side, Packard the other. Packard's team lost 3-1. After lunch Packard was organising a cricket match for the afternoon when a dispatch rider handed him a message flimsy. He had orders to report to Major Teller, an intelligence officer at Divisional Headquarters, in an hour. Transport would collect him at his billet.

It was a motorbike with sidecar, and they trundled along the leafy, winding roads for a couple of miles until they reached a large red-brick building behind a whitewashed stone wall just on the edge of a town. It was a hotel – or had been, but now that war had come, it had different guests. They coasted up to the black wrought-iron gate, where a guard was mounted by three members of the Military Police. Two outside and one behind the gate. Both men outside were tall, both had bushy moustaches, to make them look older, Packard thought. One was a full corporal, the older of the two. He snapped off a salute and Packard handed the message flimsy to him. The corporal read it, handed it back, turned to the third guard behind the gate and said, 'Open up,' then stepped back and saluted again.

The gates swung open and the motorbike revved and went in. It was a very short distance to the front door. There were various large pot plants and shrubs either side of the hotel entrance. Lots of uniforms, officers mainly, hanging around outside talking, smoking, or walking in pairs around the small garden. Hardly anyone noticed as Packard climbed out of the sidecar and adjusted his tunic, his best one but with a few creases in it from being in his trunk. His Sam-Brown also lacked that polished finish. He went up the few stone steps of the entrance and through the large wooden glass-panelled door. Inside the foyer, the flagstone floor had a large square patterned carpet in the middle with various leather chairs around a small low table. There were two large decorative urns each side of the sweeping stairs, with tall ferns fanning out. Packard looked around. The foyer was a hive of activity. Officers and senior NCOs were everywhere going about their business in a calm manner. It was hard to believe that a few miles down the road there was a major war taking place.

He reported to an immaculate lieutenant sitting behind a reception desk of dark oak. No foot slogging for endless miles, sleepless nights, shellfire, bullets, or muddy ditches for him, Packard thought. The lieutenant glanced up as Packard handed him the message flimsy.

'Ah yes, we've been expecting you,' the lieutenant said. 'Up the stairs, first floor, first room on the left. Major Teller, Intelligence Section. You can't miss it.'

'Thanks.' Packard made his way up the stairs, turned left in the corridor, saw the door, and knocked on it.

'Enter,' came the muffled reply.

Packard twisted the large ornate brass handle and entered into a bright room with floor to ceiling windows. The room smelled of cigarette smoke mixed with cologne. A large dark wooden desk, with papers and maps spread across it, was in the middle of the room, with a major sitting behind it. The major looked up. He had dark slick hair, a pencil-thin moustache, an eyepatch, and the one good eye was dark and piercing. A row of South African and Indian medal ribbons spread across his chest. One South African ribbon had the distinctive oak leaf that denoted him as being Mentioned in Dispatches (MID). He looked every inch a grizzled veteran. The major's tunic looked immaculate, in comparison to Packard's crumpled uniform.

Packard stood in the doorway. 'Major Teller?'

'Yes, and you are?'

Packard saluted. 'Lieutenant Harry Packard, sir. Reporting as ordered.'

Teller regarded him calmly. 'Marvellous. Come in and take a seat.'

Packard closed the door behind him, crossed the floor, and sat on the chair in front of the desk, removed his cap and placed it on the floor beside him. As he did so, he noticed a full ashtray on the desk.

'I expect you're wondering what this is all about, so I'd better get on with it. You speak French very well, correct?'

'I do, sir, and German,' Packard replied, a little bewildered.

Teller smiled. It was a smile without warmth. 'Ah yes, German too. Good, then we have a job for you. You've been recommended by Captain Denton and your own colonel. They both rate you as first-class. A good job done at the bridge. Most impressive, Lieutenant.'

'Thank you, sir.'

'Fact is, our government think we have a small crisis unfolding just north of here in a Belgian town. We think you are the man to solve it.'

'Me, sir? I know nothing of politics.'

'Just read two reports about your service here in France in the last six weeks,' the major continued. 'One from your adjutant, the other from Captain Denton. By all accounts, good stuff.'

'Thank you, sir.' Packard felt a little flattered. It wasn't every day that you received a pat on the back in this war.

'Let me explain something to you.' Teller picked up a silver cigarette case from the desk, opened it, and offered Packard one.

'I don't smoke, sir.' Inside, Packard winced a bit. He hadn't meant his answer to sound so condescending.

'Umm, very well.' Teller took one, lit it, and blew smoke into the air, then leaned back in his chair and crossed his legs. 'Just before Fritz invaded Belgium, top banking officials prepared to move their country's gold bullion, around hundred tonnes of the stuff, to the west of the country and place it into a bank vault in a large town near the border with France. The idea was it would be close enough to move to a channel port if invasion occurred and shipped on to England should it be necessary to prevent it falling into German hands.' He took another drag on his cigarette and blew the smoke to the ceiling. 'When the invasion came, the gold was hurriedly loaded onto the first available train out of Brussels, an old freight engine that had seen better days. After a few miles, the train broke down in the middle of nowhere. Boiler trouble, by all accounts. They contacted the army, who commandeered every available mode of transport they could lay their hands on but it wasn't nearly enough. It took four days to move the bulk of the gold northwards to the nearest port of Antwerp, which was where the Belgian army was heading, along with its government and its king. But with Fritz approaching fast and about to cut off that route, the bank officials panicked. So, as planned, they moved the last three tonnes of gold to the border town at night in two army lorries. There it remains. Got the picture?'

Packard took a deep breath and guessed that Teller wanted him to recognise why he was telling him this. 'I think so, sir. And … you want me to get it?'

Teller nodded and smiled wolfishly. 'Exactly. It would be tragic if it fell into German hands.'

Packard said, 'I'd have thought the Belgians would have moved it across the border themselves by now. So how come we have to do it?'

'Transport.' Teller took a long drag on the cigarette and blew the smoke high into the air. 'Transport, Antwerp, and secrecy are the key factors here. They don't have the lorries anymore. Once they got to the town and unloaded the gold into the bank's vault, the army left. They only had enough fuel to get back to Antwerp, where the bulk of the Belgian army is fighting a defensive position and saving our bloody necks, and besides, the bank manager doesn't want anyone else to know what he has in the town's bank vaults, especially if Fritz gets to hear about it, and he probably will – sooner rather than later.'

Packard's forehead creased. 'In the great scheme of things, does it really matter if Fritz picks up a couple of tonnes of Belgian gold, sir?'

Teller leaned forward on the desk, his one good eye dark and serious, and lowered his voice slightly and said, 'This gold is different. It belongs to the King of Belgium and must not fall into German hands. Imagine the German propaganda on that one.' He leaned back in the chair and took another long drag. 'To lose three tonnes of Belgian gold to Fritz would not be a disaster, but the king's gold …' He took a deep breath. 'That's a different matter.'

Packard sighed. 'So, it's for political reasons that we recover the gold.'

Teller smiled and nodded his head. 'It's bloody political alright, make no mistake about that.'

Packard thought about it for a moment. It sounded too easy. He said, 'Ok, so I collect the gold. Where do I take it?'

'Across the border into France to the port of Dunkirk. Here, look at this map.' Teller unfolded a map on his table, stood up, and turned it round for Packard to see. He pointed with his finger, and then ran it along. 'We're here,' he said. 'Travel northwards along this route until you reach the town of Ypres.'

'Ypres!' exclaimed Packard.

Teller looked up in surprise. 'You know this town?'

Packard's faced flushed with embarrassment. 'Well, no, not exactly.'

'Well, what then?'

Packard reddened even more and then admitted, 'It's a girl I know … or knew,' he corrected himself. 'I met her at the bridge.'

'A whore?'

Packard felt anger at that remark and wanted to defend her, but he thought better of it and suppressed his feelings. 'No – nothing like that. She just ran the brothel, accounts and things for the girls.'

'And?'

Packard felt awkward. 'Damn,' he spat out. 'When I made the girls leave, I asked her where she was heading.' Packard swallowed hard. 'She told me her uncle was a bank manager in a sleepy market town called Ypres and she was going to join him.'

Teller straightened up and put his hands on his hips. 'My word, Lieutenant, you are full of surprises. What's the girl's name?'

'Vanessa.'

'Vanessa,' repeated Teller in a mocking tone. 'Well, this Vanessa could prove useful I suppose. Can she be trusted?'

'I think so,' replied Packard in all sincerity. 'It was she who told me of the German battlegroup.'

Teller nodded slowly. His eye went back to the map then he glanced up and gave him a hard look. 'This is a serious operation, Lieutenant. One that reaches out to our government and the Belgian royal family. This has been sanctioned from the very top – Downing Street and Buckingham Palace. It cannot be jeopardised by some floozy running the books at some chicken-shit village brothel. You understand that?'

'Of course, sir.' Again, he felt hurt by Teller's remark against Vanessa. He shrugged. 'The girl means nothing to me,' he lied. 'But she was born in England to an English mother and Belgian father and I think she's trustworthy.'

Teller slowly sat down, pushing both hands together in front of his face, two fingers forming a steeple. There followed several long seconds of silence. The cigarette burning close to his fingers. 'Let's hope she is, Lieutenant,' he said finally, then scratched at his moustache and stubbed out the cigarette in the crowded ashtray on the desk. 'Your orders are simple. Take two trucks with two drivers and eight men and drive to Ypres. Make contact with the bank manager, load the gold onto the trucks and drive to Dunkirk. At Dunkirk, load the gold onto a British ship, preferably a British warship, and return the gold to England. From there, load it onto a London-bound train and deposit the gold into the vaults at the Bank of England. Any questions?'

Packard chuckled. 'Just like that?'

Teller, straight-faced, replied, 'As a matter of fact – yes.' Before Packard could protest, Teller held up a hand. 'I was being sarcastic,' he admitted. 'Ok, I have something to give you.' He opened a drawer and took out three white envelopes, laying them on the table. 'Number one.' He picked up the first envelope and handed it to him. 'This letter is from Lord Kitchener, Minister for War. He effectively gives you the power over any rank to requisition anything you want from the army to carry out your mission. Anyone, regardless of rank or position, who does not comply with your request, will have to account to him personally. The letter is also countersigned by Field Marshall Sir John French, our Commander-in-Chief of the BEF in France. Underneath his signature is the telephone number of his headquarters. Identify your mission with this code word "Falcon". Got that?'

Packard nodded. 'Falcon,' he repeated. 'Yes, sir.'

'Good. Now, number two.' He picked up a second envelope and handed it over. 'From The First Lord of the Admiralty, Winston Churchill. He effectively gives you the power over any rank to load the gold onto any British warship that sails to England. Any naval officer, regardless of rank, who does not comply with your request will have to account to him personally. Number three,' he pushed on with a third envelope, 'is from His Majesty, King George, and counter-signed by Prime Minister Herbert Asquith. They effectively give you the power to load the gold onto any British *cargo* ship bound for England, and any train bound to London.'

Packard opened all three envelopes and read them in silence. When he finished, he looked up, open-mouthed and stunned. 'I ... I don't know what to say.'

This was no jolly trip up to Ypres to collect a few dozen bars of gold, he realised. This was a very serious and a potentially dangerous top echelon political operation he was about to get involved in. Possibly war-winning. The three letters confirmed that.

Teller scratched at his moustache. 'Right now, you are the most important British soldier in France, with the most absolute power. Anyone, and I mean anyone, who fails to comply with a request from you will be for the high-jump, regardless of rank – and that includes Field Marshall French.'

Packard swallowed hard.

'Yes,' said Teller, 'even Field Marshall Sir John French. In fact, for the duration of this task and until the gold is safely in London, he has promoted you to acting major with immediate effect.'

'Bloody hell,' Packard said.

'Yes, bloody hell indeed ... Major,' Teller said, emphasising the rank, then continued. 'This gold has priority over any cargo, men, or equipment and it's your duty to make sure that it's transported safely to London. Any obstacles, anyone not wishing to comply with your request ... use these letters like bullets. Got that?'

'Eh ... of course, sir. Umm, just a few things. I take it the gold is in bars?'

'Bars and coins, I believe.'

'Are they in crates or just loose?'

'The bars are in manageable crates and the coins are in small sacks stuffed into kegs. Light enough for a man to carry, and lots of them, so I'm informed.'

'And the trucks, sir, where do I–'

Teller cut him off. 'Motorised transport is rare in this army, as you know, but the Army Corps has about thirty trucks in a motor pool just outside town. Go there, choose two trucks with drivers. You won't be popular, I can tell you. But needs must. And don't be fobbed off. You have the letters, use them! Anything else?'

Packard slowly shook his head. 'I think that's it for the moment.'

'Good. That's settled then. Now a few other points. You can't tell anyone what your mission is.' He tapped the side of his nose with his finger to emphasise the point. 'It's top secret and that includes the men you take with you until you reach the bank. But they don't need to know who the gold belongs to, just that it has to go to London. Clear?'

Packard nodded, but then said, 'Do I get to choose the men?'

'Of course.'

'In that case I would like my sergeant to be my number two.'

'As you wish.'

'Should anything happen to me,' he continued, 'then he could continue with the mission.'

'I see,' said Teller. 'But that would mean briefing him of the facts of this operation – correct?'

Packard nodded. 'Yes, sir.'

Teller paused, sucking his teeth as he worked it through in his mind.

'Alright, I see your point,' he said, 'but you are not to tell him who the gold belongs to unless it's absolutely necessary – clear?'

'Clear, sir, and thank you.'

Teller nodded. 'Before you leave this building, I've arranged for the divisional tailor to sew your new rank on your uniform. In the morning, I'll give you a despatch of the latest intelligence of German movements in that area before you go. Don't leave until you get it. Is that clear?'

Packard nodded. 'Yes, sir.'

'Splendid. A number of officers throughout the army were considered for this job, but in the end, it came down to you.' Teller stood up and reached across the table to shake his hand. 'Good luck, Major.'

Packard stood and they shook hands firmly. 'Thank you, sir.' He picked up his cap from the floor and slowly headed towards the door, thinking of the scale of what he was getting into.

Before he reached the door, Teller called out. 'Oh, and one more thing. In Ypres, apart from the bank manager, be careful with who you trust.' He tapped the side of his nose again. 'Secrecy is key here. Got that?'

'Of course, sir,' Packard replied. Then he opened the door and left.

CHAPTER 15

Teller took another cigarette from the packet on his desk, lit it, walked to the window and looked out. It was a grey day but dry, thank God. At least life for soldiers holding the line would be more comfortable, but it also helped the scouting patrols to keep watch on enemy movements. But in his busy mind he reflected on the events that were due to take place in the town of Ypres. The gold, that precious gold, just sitting in a bank vault, a literal king's ransom, just waiting for someone to collect it. British or Germans? Us or them.

Politics, he thought. The army was fighting for its life against an aggressive enemy, dealing with shortages of men, artillery, shells, and motorised transport and what did the politicians back home do? Send one of their best fighting officers on an errand to collect some foreign royal gold in two desperately needed trucks that were vital to supply the fighting soldier at the sharp end. He shook his head. It just didn't make sense. He took a long drag on the cigarette and blew the smoke high into the air. He turned his back to the window, stubbed out the cigarette in the crowded ashtray, and went to the door. He went out and down the corridor to the operations room. There he found Major Arnold Scott-Bardwell with a small team busily typing up field intelligence reports they had gathered from their scouting patrols. He crossed to his desk as Scott-Bardwell stifled a yawn.

'Fritz keeping you busy, Arnold?'

Scott-Bardwell looked up. 'Field officers are always busy. Unlike some I could mention.' He gave a half-smile. 'What can I do for you?'

Teller didn't flinch at that comment. He knew that Scott-Bardwell harboured a deep resentment of successful soldiers who gained status or glory through combat, particularly close combat, along with any gallantry award pinned on their chest, like his oak leaf attached to the Boer War campaign medal ribbon. It had cost him an eye getting that oak leaf. Scott-Bardwell never sought to get involved in a fight with the enemy, but he was good at collating intelligence and accessing its importance. Everyone knew that.

'Can you get me the latest report on any German cavalry activity near or around the town of Ypres?' Teller said – technically it was a request, but he made it sound more like an order, just to grate on Scott-Bardwell's nerves.

The major eyed him curiously. 'So, you've got someone for that job?'

'Yes, someone you know actually. Harry Packard.'

'Packard!' he groaned. 'The man's a risk-taker. Trying to make a name for himself. An adventurer, a wartime wonder. Nothing short of that.'

Teller had anticipated that reaction. From the moment Scott-Bardwell reported back from the bridge, he'd been slating the plucky, or the lucky, lieutenant. But to give an air of competence and the impression that he grasped the situation, he'd also ordered the engineer team to leave headquarters for the bridge immediately, while recommending no reinforcements.

'Maybe,' said Teller, 'but Corps like him and chose him and you must admit he did an excellent job capturing that bridge and defending it prior to its destruction, despite receiving that odd message to hold the bridge at all costs. Which we still haven't found the source of.' Teller searched Scott-Bardwell's face for a reaction to his implication.

None came.

He continued. 'But division have confirmed having a dispatch rider missing which we presume was the one killed at the bridge. There's talk upstairs with the brass-hats of some form of recognition for Packard. After all, he did severely maul a German battlegroup, capture a bridge from the enemy without firing a single shot, and put a dozen or so prisoners in the bag. Not bad for a wartime wonder, I'd say.'

'Packard was lucky getting that machine gun, that's all,' Scott-Bardwell said grudgingly.

'Sometimes, all you need is a little luck. So, let's hope Major Packard's luck lasts long enough for this operation.'

'I think you mean Lieutenant Packard,' corrected Scott-Bardwell.

Teller shook his head with a slight smirk. 'Not anymore. Oh, sorry, did I not mention it? Sir John promoted him for the duration of this job. Acting rank, of course, but still, you know how these things tend to stick if a chap survives.'

Scott-Bardwell just grunted.

Teller knew that hit him like a sledgehammer. 'If I can have that cavalry report by 7 a.m.?'

Scott-Bardwell just nodded and continued with his report as Teller left the room.

*

Scott-Bardwell banged a clenched fist on the desk and cursed. He was conscious of his subordinates looking at him.

'Got work to do?' he growled.

They suddenly all looked busy. Scott-Bardwell was typing up a report of a large German cavalry brigade seen near the area of Ypres, possibly up to 8,000 men. It was no threat as such, probably just plugging gaps between here and Antwerp with scouting patrols he suspected, just as they were doing. It was the sort of information that Packard would need and perhaps might make him alter his route to swing around the longer way to the west, rather than just going north directly to the town. They would be watching that main road for troop movements. This type of intelligence was his domain. He had the responsibility of gathering it together and assessing it for distribution to other intelligent sections.

But this was one piece of information that, he decided, would be just too late for Harry Packard.

CHAPTER 16

Just over one hour later Packard left the building with three rows of rank distinction lace and an embroidered crown sewn on the cuffs of his tunic, denoting his rank of major. The motorbike with sidecar was waiting for him. He jumped in and headed for the motor pool outside town.

The motor pool was housed on a farm that had a large farmhouse with several barns and sheds in a 'U' shape around the gated yard. Motorised trucks, vans, motorbikes, a few cars, and plenty of bicycles were parked up neatly across the large cobblestone yard. When Packard arrived, he was stopped by a guard at the gate and directed across to the farmhouse to see the transport officer.

Packard walked into the farmhouse. It smelt musty and dank and was lit by candles. A short stocky sergeant with red hair and a ginger moustache behind a desk in the hallway stood up as he entered. 'Sir?'

'Who's in charge here, Sergeant?'

'Captain Brook, sir.'

'I would like to see him.'

'Very good, sir. And your name is?'

'Major Packard, Richmond Regiment.'

'If you would wait a moment, sir.' The sergeant went into a corridor behind him and knocked on a door, then went in. A few moments later, he came out again.

'Captain Brook will see you now, sir.'

Packard went into what turned out to be a small room that was bright and airy from a large window, but much cluttered, with clipboards on the wall and paperwork on the desk, almost obscuring a telephone. The captain stood up as Packard entered, something he wasn't used to from a ranking officer.

'Good afternoon Major Packard, please take a seat.'

Packard stood, creating the dominating effect he wanted to convey to the captain. 'Thank you, Captain, but I'll come straight to the point. I need two lorries for the next few days, plus two drivers. This is my authority.' He handed him the letter from Lord Kitchener. Brook took it and read it, raised his eyebrows, and looked up.

'Is this some kind of joke, Major?'

'No joke, Captain. It's real, I can assure you.'

Brook shook his head a little timidly and his cheeks coloured. Packard could see he was nervous about the letter and the fact that he was being outranked.

'Without a form requesting motorised transport signed by my colonel, I'm afraid I can't help you,' said Brook, handing the letter back.

'Really? And this letter means nothing?' He held the letter up to emphasise the two signatures, and to push home who it was from. 'Lord Kitchener and Sir John French?'

Brook frowned, considering the letter for a few seconds, but then shook his head timidly. 'I don't know where you got that letter from, Major, but it cuts no ice with me.' He licked his lips nervously. 'Motorised transport of any sort is in short supply and in great demand in this army at the moment. Nothing, and I mean nothing moves unless my colonel authorises it. And that goes for your letter.'

Packard noticed Brook looking nervously at him and the letter he was holding. He pointed to the telephone on the captain's desk.

'Captain, telephone your colonel right now, and then hand him to me.'

The captain stared at him suspiciously, then said, 'Now look here…'

Packard held the letter closer to the captain's face and said, more forcefully, 'If you don't, I will, and then there will be consequences for you – that I guarantee,' he emphasised, remembering to use the letters like bullets.

They stood staring at each other in a silent awkwardness for a moment. Then the captain grudgingly relented and said, 'Very well, Major. If you insist.' He picked up the phone arm from the cradle, put it to his ear, and wound the handle at the side of the phone.

'Hello … hello, it's Captain Brook here, put me through to Colonel Bingham, it's urgent.' After a short pause, his tone changed. 'Hello, sir, Captain Brook here. I've got a Major Packard who wishes to speak to you about transport.' Then he handed Packard the phone.

Packard explained who he was and relayed the details of his authorising letter from Field Marshall Sir John French, including the telephone number of his headquarters. The colonel took some persuading but in the end he said that he would check his story with headquarters and ring back.

Packard sat in awkward silence with Captain Brook as the minutes ticked past. He now realised that he could have got things done quickly and efficiently with less confrontation by going to the man at the top, the Quartermaster-General, rather than Colonel Bingham or Captain Brook, who had no choice but to conform to their superior's instructions regardless of what the letter said. Next time he would do things differently.

When the telephone started ringing, Packard had to drag his mind back to reality as Brook quickly picked it up to his ear. Packard could hear the agitated voice of Colonel Bingham on the line. Without realising it, Brook had got to his feet and looked startled and shocked, then his mouth fell open and in an incoherent mutter he began to reply.

'Of ... of course, sir,' he stuttered. 'I ... I fully understand, sir ...'

Packard quickly stood up and snatched the phone from Brook before he'd finished speaking.

'Major Packard here, Colonel. Do I get what I want?' Packard heard the acknowledgement and replaced the phone arm on the cradle. A small smile tugged at the corner of his lips.

'Right, we're in business,' he said.

Brook looked very pale and stunned. 'Bastard,' he murmured. 'The bastard threatened to have me shot.'

Packard chuckled a bit and tried to make light of it. 'Look on the bright side, Captain, Sir John French probably said the same thing to Colonel Bingham, eh?' Then he hurried a shocked Captain Brook out of the office into the cobbled yard of parked vehicles. 'Who are your best drivers?' he asked.

Brook looked around and silently pointed towards two men in shirtsleeves securing the side panel of a lorry.

'You there,' said Packard as he approached with Captain Brook. Both men looked around, startled, and then stood to attention. He saw concern in the men's eyes.

'What's your name?' he asked the tall one on the left.

'Driver Steed, sir.'

Packard turned to the other shorter one. 'And you?'

'Driver Joyce, sir.'

'Good. So, which are the two best lorries here?'

The men looked at one another silently.

'Come on,' he demanded. 'Which are the two best lorries here? I need something that can carry about two, maybe three tonnes?'

'The two Dennis three-tonners are the best lorries we have,' said

Steed. 'This one and the one behind, sir.'

'Ah, yes, the Dennis three-tonner. I've heard of them. Good. Are they reliable and can you fix the engine if it breaks down?'

'Yes, sir,' they said in unison. Joyce added, 'The Dennis lorry is one of the best in its class and very reliable.'

'And we're both mechanics,' added Steed.

He nodded. 'Good. That meets my requirements. Now then, I've got a job for you both.' He told the two drivers to fill the lorries with fuel and carry spare cans in the back, along with any other spare parts they thought the lorries might need in an emergency. They were to report to him in the village square at 6 a.m. the following morning. They could be away for a few days so they were to bring their kit with them. Rations would be supplied.

'Any questions?'

They both looked at Captain Brook for approval. He nodded.

Packard turned to Brook and shook his hand. 'Thank you, Captain.'

He climbed into the waiting sidecar and roared out of the yard into the lane.

Brook looked at both men coldly. 'Report to the sergeant and tell him what's what. And in the morning don't be late, got that?'

They stiffened and saluted. 'No, sir.'

*

The motorbike with sidecar was waiting outside the headquarters of General Sir William Robertson, the Quartermaster-General for the BEF in France, known throughout the army as 'Wully'. Wully had started as a private in a Victorian army and worked his way up to General.

In his office, Wully took the letter from Packard and read it. He was a good-looking man, Packard thought, with dark hair, strong features, and a small dark moustache. He was also an imposing figure and had a no-nonsense air about him. He looked up. 'That damned fool Colonel Bingham called me about this letter earlier,' he said irritably. 'After I phoned Sir John French to confirm it, I rang him back. He criticized the Field Marshall's letter and his decision to give you the two Dennis lorries. How dare he? Let me assure you, Major, that I gave Colonel Bingham both barrels over the phone. If he did not comply, I told him, I'd have him shot!'

Packard smiled a little. So, it was Wully who'd said that, and not Sir John French as he'd first thought. He would have loved to have been a fly on the wall in that room when Colonel Bingham got his blasting.

'I don't know what the hell is going on, Major, but that's a powerful letter you have there. Whatever your task, it must be very important.' He handed the letter back to him and leaned back in his chair. 'Obviously, you haven't just come here for a social visit to show me your letter. So, how can I help? What exactly do you want from me?'

With a little nervous concern, Packard said, 'Well, sir, it would be easier and quicker to acquire the equipment I need if you contacted the appropriate quartermaster first. A word from you would save me a lot of time and anguish.'

'Hmmm ... I see.'

'Otherwise, sir, every quartermaster I visit in the next few hours will continue to bother you to check that this letter is legitimate.'

Wully thought about it for a moment, showing no expression on his face. Then he said, 'Yes, you're right. It makes sense. Do you have a list of requirements with you?'

'I do, sir.' Packard handed him a list. Wully studied it.

'Very well, Major. Consider it done. I'll personally make the contact to give effect and if any quartermaster gives you any trouble whatsoever, contact me immediately, and not the Field Marshall. I will personally deal with them, regardless of the hour.'

Packard was relieved and pleased that Wully approved of his idea. 'I'm grateful, sir. Thank you,' he said, then he saluted and left the office. With the Quartermaster-General's input it would entitle him to ask for whatever he wanted and when he wanted it. They could not refuse him anything – not now.

CHAPTER 17

The Burgomaster of Antwerp greeted Churchill and his Naval Secretary, Rear Admiral Sir Horace Hood, with great enthusiasm when they arrived on a chilly morning. They had left Victoria Station at 2 a.m. on a special train that took them straight to Dover. Without delay, they boarded a waiting naval vessel that sailed overnight to the port of Antwerp. Tired on their arrival, they were buoyed up by the warm and affectionate reception of the burgomaster with local dignitaries and a small crowd.

A line of Belgian Marines stood as a guard of honour along the quayside and tensed as the order to 'Present ... arms!' was given when Churchill and Hood stepped from the gangway, and a uniformed civilian band crashed out their version of *God Save the King* and the Belgian national anthem, *La Brabançonne*. Churchill removed his hat and Hood saluted. As Churchill stood there, he feared he would have to make a speech, and tried desperately to wrestle his weary mind to form some cheerful and rallying words.

Once the band had finished playing, the burgomaster, in a black top hat with a bright sash across his chest, led the small gathering in giving 'three cheers', then stepped forward to greet them both with a big smile, kissing both men on the cheek and shaking their hands vigorously, exclaiming, 'Welcome, gentlemen, welcome to the city of Antwerp'. Then he squeezed between both men to pose with a smile as a photographer with a boxed camera on a tripod stepped from the gathering of dignitaries. The camera flashed and then moved back into the small crowd.

'This is a great honour, Mr Churchill,' said the burgomaster as he led both men through the throng towards a fleet of waiting cars. Churchill acknowledged the crowd with a broad smile and by waving his hat high in the air, relieved that there was no time for speeches.

'Your arrival has boosted the spirits of our people in this great city,' the burgomaster said cheerily. 'Our king and Prime Minister await you.' He ushered them both into the first car that headed into the city, followed by a small convoy of local dignitaries.

The convoy of cars stopped outside Antwerp's huge Festival Hall. The front of the building was an eclectic design, while the interior was neoclassical with a large sumptuous hall, an impressive marble staircase and gilded decorations that had made it a very popular location for high-level parties or balls before the war. Now it was a temporary home for the army, the royal family, the Belgian Government, diplomats, and their families.

Churchill and Hood were taken to an upper floor, where they entered a large ornate room and were presented to King Albert, who was dressed in military uniform. Beside him stood his Prime Minister, Baron Charles de Broqueville, wearing a black suit. He was fifty-three, with dark hair, and a dark bushy moustache that turned up at the ends.

'Your Majesty,' said Churchill, removing his hat as he bowed his head. Admiral Hood stood beside him and saluted.

'Mr Churchill,' King Albert said, by way of greeting. 'You know my Prime Minister.'

'Of course,' said Churchill, and moved forward to shake de Broqueville's hand warmly. de Broqueville, Churchill knew, came from Belgian nobility, and inspired confidence anywhere he went. It was de Broqueville who had overseen Belgium's mobilization just prior to its invasion. He opposed King Albert's suggestion of deploying the Belgian army along the German border. Instead, he placed the tiny Belgian army throughout the country. He did not want neutral Belgium to be seen as being provocative. After the German ultimatum to Belgium on 2nd August, de Broqueville told the Belgian Parliament that they would fight any invasion with all their strength. Two days later, the Kaiser had invaded and with the rapid advance of the German army quickly overrunning Belgium, de Broqueville's government had followed the king and the army to their National Redoubt at Antwerp to continue the fight.

Churchill now turned to the King. 'This is my Naval Secretary, Admiral Hood, an expert on fortress defensives,' he explained.

King Albert acknowledged the admiral with a nod, then Hood warmly shook hands with the Prime Minister.

King Albert said, 'Let's not stand on etiquette, gentlemen. The battle is going on and we are losing. I no longer have any reserves to continue. If we do not get immediate assistance from our Allies, then disaster shall befall this great city and our army within it. I've already made preparations to evacuate my army at the earliest possible moment should that occur.'

Churchill could see that King Albert was anxious. 'Your army has made a magnificent fight of it and inflicted great losses to the Germans. Indeed,' he continued, 'their brilliant counterattacks have become a painful thorn in the side of the Hun, without which, they may very well have reached the Channel coast by now and cut off our supply lines.'

'My business is to save my army,' King Albert said. 'All I've received so far from my Allies has been promises of reinforcements in the hope that our sacrifice will save theirs, while in the meantime the situation here continues to deteriorate.'

'It is with gratitude that I come here today, your Majesty,' Churchill replied. 'My marine brigade should arrive here by train from Dunkirk within the next few hours, followed very shortly by a landing of two further naval brigades. We do not intend to stand aside and leave our friends to their fate.'

He dared not tell the king that the two naval brigades were poorly trained and equipped, with most not even having fired a rifle and not suitable for any type of warfare, let alone front-line combat in one of the most critical points in the war so far.

'Our government,' continued Churchill confidently, 'has also set aside a further infantry division and a cavalry division to arrive here in the next few days.'

He didn't specify that their main role was to occupy and defend a corridor to the west of the city, some fifteen miles towards Ghent, as an escape route for his marines and sailors should they need it.

Admiral Hood glanced around before speaking and looked eagerly at the king, keeping his voice low. 'Your Majesty,' he said, 'we have also mounted several naval guns on a train to give support to your army against the German field guns and their attacking infantry. They should be arriving any time now.'

Churchill nodded approvingly and hoped that news of reinforcements and commitment from Britain could bring a little cheer, if only for a few days. It seemed to work. He noticed that the king and de Broqueville brightened visibly and the king's scepticism about his ally's promises looked to be overcome – for now. Even so, Churchill knew that he had to tread carefully and not promise too much or give too much hope, but just buy enough time for the British army to reach Belgium and put the Germans under extra pressure.

'What about the French?' King Albert asked. 'Are they not going to support us?'

Churchill sensed a nervousness in the king and replied, 'They are sending two divisions in support. I have no idea when they expect to arrive.'

'Nor do I,' said King Albert. 'They've probably got lost on their way here,' he replied carelessly, then slowly walked to one of the large elegant windows and opened it. He gestured to Churchill and Admiral Hood to join him. 'Listen,' he said. 'Can you hear the cannon fire?' The distant booms were very audible. They listened in silence for a few moments and then they heard a large powerful boom in the distance.

'That,' said King Albert, 'is the German big gun slowly destroying our defensive fortresses.'

'That 16-inch gun we all believed would be too heavy and impossible to be transported by road,' said Hood ruefully.

'Exactly,' replied the king, sounding amused. 'That gun. You have no idea how much damage it is doing to my army's morale, let alone the destruction to our defensive fortresses.'

Admiral Hood took this revelation with a slow nod. Some of Britain's main battleships carried this armament. They were very powerful and very destructive. The Antwerp fortresses had not been designed or built to withstand anything larger than an 8-inch gun.

de Broqueville said, 'With your help, Winston, we may be able to hold our city for another three days, but not much more.'

'Then pray that our army in the south reaches Antwerp in time,' replied Churchill.

'And if it doesn't?'

Churchill thought about his answer very carefully. If the Channel Ports fell into German hands in the next day or two it would be a disaster for the Allies. It was in Britain's interest that he had to buy those three days at least. 'Very well, Prime Minister, if you are confident that you could hold out another three days, then hold out for those days. If, by that time, Britain and France cannot offer you the assurance of relief from our armies in the south, then you are under no obligation to stay. Indeed, my forces will help you withdraw, and you will be free to abandon Antwerp.'

de Broqueville slowly nodded his head and turned to look at his king for acceptance. King Albert gave a gentle nod of his head. 'Then we have a deal, Winston,' said de Broqueville, and they shook hands firmly.

'Let us hope that Antwerp holds until she can be relieved,' said Churchill. 'For all our sakes.'

The next two days passed swiftly. Admiral Hood toured the fortresses in a motorcar, in the company of a Belgian colonel of engineers. Churchill too went out most of the time with his marines, who had arrived in fifty brand new London buses, and were followed later by the two naval brigades – a total of 10,000 men, visiting and inspecting their newly-found defensive positions with their commander, General Archibald Paris. Occasionally, this group came under rifle and artillery fire. Churchill never flinched and just puffed on his cigar, waving his hat on his stick. The men loved it and cheered.

They held the defensive positions around the town of Lierre, on the River Nethe, about twelve miles south of Antwerp, a vital spot should the Germans launch an all-out attack. As Churchill glanced at the trenches there, he could not help but notice how shallow they were, with hardly any cover from artillery, and barely any barbed wire in front of them. Churchill was full of excitement when his naval brigades and marines had arrived and rushed into the front line. But seeing for himself the meagre conditions of the defensive trenches was quite an anti-climax.

'It is very precarious,' General Paris told him as they toured the line, and he had to agree. Apart from the marines, his naval brigades, dressed in blue with their flat caps, were not hard-core veterans in any shape or form. Churchill knew that Britain's very existence depended on them holding this line for as long as possible to keep the threat away, but with the resources they had, that did not seem possible.

Churchill returned to his accommodation in Antwerp at the Festival Hall in a sullen mood, only to find Hood waiting for him, looking very serious. Churchill could feel the tension in the room as the door closed behind him. He felt as though the admiral was going to give him a severe dressing-down. Inside, he shivered as a cold chill ran his spin. More bad news? It couldn't get any worse, surely? He gingerly took off his hat, his head shining in the light, and then his coat, and placed them on a chair beside him.

Churchill prepared for the worse and said slowly, 'You have the look of a man who has grave news?'

There was a nervous tightening in his jaw as Hood nodded. 'I'm afraid I have.'

Churchill sighed and turned away to a drink stand on a table and poured a large brandy. He gestured to Hood to join him, but the admiral shook his head and stood in silence while Churchill poured his drink. Churchill took a large swallow then licked his lips and felt the burn linger on his tongue.

'All right, Admiral, make your report.'

Hood kept his face impassive, his dark features set in concentration. 'I've just spoken to Antwerp's military governor, General Deguise, about the so-called fortress redoubt around this city and my inspection of it.'

Churchill sat heavily in a chair, knowing, with that context, the news was going to be dreadful.

'He confessed to me that much of the 1906 Government Plan to update and complete the Antwerp defences exists mainly on paper, and that nothing much has been achieved since then. Shortly after he took office on the outbreak of war, and knowing the state of the fortress redoubt, he ordered immediate entrenchments between the fortresses, but it was not nearly enough. My inspection has revealed that some of the rotating gun turrets have not yet been concreted in. There are gaps in the telephone and electricity supplies to the fortresses. Trenches that should run continuously between the forts have hardly been started. There is only one cannon per mile of front. The fortresses are garrisoned by the oldest of Belgian troops, who are under-trained, poorly armed and supplied. Quite frankly, Winston, the fortresses are obsolete by today's standards and, in my opinion, not able to withstand a 6-inch gun, let alone anything the size of the big guns now possessed by the Germans.'

Churchill swallowed hard and held up his hand for him to stop. 'You paint a gloomy picture rather well,' he said.

'And that's not the half of it, not by a long chalk,' Hood added forcefully.

Churchill slowly stood up and poured himself another drink. He cleared his throat noisily. Grim-faced, he said, 'That's not all, Admiral. I've just been informed that Prime Minister de Broqueville and his government left Antwerp yesterday and are now in Ostend.'

Hood's face flushed angrily. 'You could hardly credit it,' he said. 'The bastard knew the state of these defences when we arrived. He had us greeted at the dockside like royalty, and all the time he knew. That's why they were eager to go a few days ago. Our arrival did not alter their plans.'

'I'll say no more,' said Churchill, diplomatically, 'but King Albert and Queen Elizabeth intend to stay until the last moment.'

'At least that's something, I suppose,' said Hood bitterly.

'The longer we hold,' said Churchill with some concern in his voice, 'the more chance we have of not losing this war.'

Hood huffed. 'Hold on, you say, but with what? Our own naval brigades are not much better equipped or prepared than the Belgian fortress troops I've seen. One strong push by the Germans and this whole rotten fortress redoubt will just crumble, and the Germans will march straight into Antwerp. Mark my words.'

Churchill dropped his eyes with despair and hooked his thumb into his waistcoat pocket. 'I know. I've seen our men in their trench defences. Pathetic scrapes in the ground with little artillery cover. But their morale is high and they're spoiling for a fight.' He shook his head, biting his lower lip. 'They seem eager to get their heads shot off.'

'Huh, trenches! Nasty things,' Hood said. 'It seems an odd way for a sailor to fight a war.'

Churchill looked up and smiled a little. 'Indeed it is, Admiral, indeed it is, but very necessary at the moment.'

Hood nodded, and, as if reading Churchill's thoughts, he asked, 'Does London know of the nightmare situation here?'

'They do,' answered Churchill quickly, 'and that's not all. I sent a telegram earlier offering to resign my post in the Admiralty and take command here.'

'Good God. What did they say?'

'I got an immediate reply. Downing Street has ordered us back to London. They're sending a boat. I tried to resist it, but they are adamant we return. I have informed General Paris that his naval brigades will come under the command of the Belgians. He told me that he would stick it out until the last moment and try to evade capture and get his men away.'

'It makes sense under these circumstances,' Hood agreed.

'But I have some good news,' said Churchill, forcing cheer into his voice. 'I've received a telegram this morning that we have chosen a gallant officer with a small team to rescue King Albert's gold.'

'Good for him,' replied Hood. 'I wish him the best of British.'

'Yes,' said Churchill, 'and so do I. I took the liberty of informing King Albert, believing it would bring him some cheer, but he seemed indifferent and dismissed it as an "unimportant matter".'

'Oh dear,' said Hood. 'Personally and politically, I think he's wrong.'

'I think so too,' Churchill replied. 'To lose his gold now to the Germans would really upset the morale of his men in Antwerp, and could speedily advance their collapse, but I did not emphasis that point with him. All we need is for Antwerp to hold a few more days, that's all.'

'We've been lucky so far,' said the admiral. 'The Germans don't know just how weak the defences are here. Let's hope it continues for the next few days.'

'In my experience,' said Churchill, 'luck rarely lasts,' and he raised his glass. 'Let's hope our officer has more success securing that gold than we're having here.'

He tossed down the last drop of brandy and poured himself another.

CHAPTER 18

'This is a .38 Webley revolver Mark 4 with a lanyard fitted,' Packard said. 'The lanyard goes over the head like so.' He demonstrated the action to the small group in front of him. 'So, if some clumsy so and so drops the revolver, it will dangle and not be lost. Now try it.' Some of the group responded woodenly. One man managed to get the lanyard entangled and ended up dropping the revolver on the ground.

Campbell sighed. 'You dozy individual, Norris. Pick it up!'

Norris cringed as if he expected to be punished.

Harry looked down for a brief moment to hide a smile. When he looked up, he was composed. 'Good. Now place the revolver into the leather holster on your belts and secure the flap like so.' Again, he demonstrated the action. Norris ended up putting the revolver in the holster back to front and couldn't secure the flap. Everyone was waiting for him. He looked up and flashed an apologetic smile as Campbell went straight to his side, twisted the revolver around into the right place and shoved it down. 'There,' he said through gritted teeth, sounding exasperated. Leaning forward, he whispered into Norris's ear, 'If we have to use these pea-shooters in anger, make sure you're in front of me. Got it?'

Packard continued. He undid the flap, retrieved the revolver, and turned it around so that the 4-inch barrel was facing him. He moved closer to the group so they could all see. 'This is the hammer,' he pointed out, 'and on the left side is the stirrup catch. Press the stirrup catch down with your thumb and the revolver will break in two. It's called a "top break action". Now watch.' The revolver broke in half and Packard bent it all the way. 'In a nutshell, this action allows you to do two things quickly,' he explained. 'One: to load. Two: to eject spent cartridges. Now try it for yourselves.'

Campbell and Packard went around the group to make sure that they had the action right. Some needed more help than others. Packard returned to the front. 'Now snap it shut like this,' he said, and everyone followed his instruction. 'Ok, just practise that for a while.'

After a few minutes he said, 'Ok, I have a bag of spent cartridge cases so I want you to practice loading like this.' Taking six spent cases from a small pouch on his belt, he began loading the cylinder, then snapped it shut, pointing the barrel into the air in the safety position. 'Ok, practice that and remember, always keep your finger away from the trigger unless you intend to fire it.'

They practised for the next ten minutes, loading and ejecting the spent cases again and again until it became second nature to them.

Packard continued. 'The .38 is a low-powered cartridge that doesn't have much of a kick when it fires, or a particularly loud bang,' he said. 'There is a fixed blade on the top of the barrel at the front and a notch at the rear for aiming. It should have an effective range of about fifty yards if you're lucky, and with practice, you can fire twenty to thirty rounds a minute. If you have to use this weapon in anger it will probably have to be up close and personal for it to be effective. So, extend your arm fully to steady your aim, looking along the barrel and centralising the blade in the rear notch, then pull the trigger to fire.'

For the next few minutes, they all practiced taking the aim to fire standing up and kneeling, and clasping the gun with both hands, legs apart, to steady their aim.

'Good. Well done everyone.' Then, turning to Campbell, he said, 'Very well, Sergeant, they're as ready as we can make them in the short time we have. Lead them off to that makeshift range at the back of the barn and we'll have a practice shoot at some tin cans.'

A small cheer went up from the group. 'At last,' someone said.

'All right, cut it out,' said Campbell. 'Holster your guns and form up in two ranks, look lively now.'

Then turning to Packard, he said, 'Do we have to take Norris, sir? The man's useless.'

'Like turning a sow's ear into a silk purse?'

'Something like that, sir. He's not cut out for front-line duties, that's for sure.'

Packard had taken Norris on the recommendation of General 'Wully' Robertson. One of his backroom staff spoke fluent French and German and thought Norris might come in useful. Packard hadn't hesitated. Having another French and German speaker on the team could prove very useful if he was incapacitated for some reason. Private Percy Norris, a plump bespectacled redhead, was a loner who came from a good upper middle-class background and had been educated at a good private school. Apart from that he was a naturally clumsy boy who could not grasp any aspect of life other than his love of books. Exasperated by his son's inability to hold onto a job, his father had pushed him into the army. Norris had failed his officer training selection miserably and was about to be kicked out when a friend of the family who was a serving colonel in Corps Headquarters Intelligence took him on, and Norris was fast-tracked through his basic training as a private to end up working for him. Norris, he knew, had a panache with languages, and with the threat of war looming, the colonel had set him working on the German section, interpreting messages until he was handed over to Packard.

'He'll be fine,' Packard said, half-smiling. 'It'll be the making of him.'

Campbell gave the order for the team to march off. Then, scratching the back of his ear, he said gloomily, 'Heaven help us when Norris fires that gun. I'd stand well back if I were you, sir. Well back.'

Packard smiled and could find nothing useful to say. The cruel thing was Campbell was right.

The idea of issuing revolvers to all the men came to Packard when he was riding in the cab of a lorry with his rifle upright between his knees during the battle of Le Cateau in August. The lorry had just set off when it was nearly overrun by German infantry. Packard had pulled his Webley from its holster and shot two German soldiers as they attempted to drag out the driver. They got away – just, but in that situation, the rifle was useless in the confined space.

Getting his small band of eleven men issued with service Webley revolvers caused quite a stir at Corps Headquarters Armoury. Although the armoury got the call from 'Wully' Robertson's office to assist Major Packard with whatever he wanted, the Regimental Quartermaster Sergeant dug his heels in when Packard asked for eleven Webleys with leather holsters and one hundred rounds of ammunition for each gun to be issued to his men.

The RQ was a long-serving African Wars veteran. A somewhat fearful-looking big brute of a man with a barrel chest, sporting a long dark moustache that narrowed to a point at each end. He was almost stunned into silence when Packard asked for eleven revolvers. His nostrils flared wide open with outrage and he'd answered, 'Really!'

He refused to issue a single revolver or bullet unless he received the order in writing, despite Packard's repeated orders and showing of the letter of authority from Field Marshall French.

'Revolvers are for officers and military police, not enlisted ranks,' the RQ kept repeating. The man was remorseless. In the end Packard sighed, shook his head and made a phone call from the armoury to General Robertson's office.

It took a few moments for the return call but when the telephone rang, the RQ immediately answered it. At first, he looked puzzled, then his faced turned purple and he looked as if he was about to have a heart attack. After he returned the phone to its cradle, a short silence followed. Apologetically, he turned to Packard and choking the words out he said, 'How ... exactly ... can I ... help you, sir?'

Despite his resentment, he reluctantly issued the revolvers, the holsters, and ammunition.

But it wasn't always this bad. Packard got the rations and petrol he required with no problem. He asked the cooks to prepare his men a hearty breakfast at dawn prior to their departure. No problem. He asked the cooks for all their empty cans and had them delivered at the back of an old barn in the village. No problem. He got the engineers to set up a twenty-five-yard range at the back of the old barn. No problem. Packard even arranged for every man to have a fresh uniform and to have sufficient hot water for every man to bath before breakfast. No problem. Some officers did complain, but when Packard showed his letter of authority they backed off.

After the firing range, at which Packard got his men to fire off thirty-six rounds each from various firing positions – sitting down, knelling down, standing up, and firing behind cover at tin cans – they were marched back to their billet to clean the revolvers and bed down for the night. Packard and Campbell were very pleased with the results. The men had thoroughly enjoyed the experience with the Webley, and their accuracy and handling of the weapon had vastly improved as the day had gone on – including those of Percy Norris.

At first, Norris didn't hit a thing and kept turning around with the loaded revolver whenever Packard or Campbell gave him an instruction. On the third occasion that he turned around, Norris, frantically nervous, pulled the trigger and accidentally let off a shot that pinged off a stone wall and ricocheted somewhere between them. Packard and Campbell dived for cover. 'What did I tell you?' remarked Campbell. Packard grunted as he got to his feet. That was enough: Campbell was ordered to stand right behind Norris and gave him a one-to-one instruction throughout the range session when it was his turn to fire. It worked. Norris felt the stirrings of confidence and began hitting the targets. Even Packard and Campbell began to realise he could do it.

*

'Once you've bedded down the men, Sergeant, I would like you to join me at my quarters in the village to discuss our mission in more detail.'

'Very good, sir.'

Campbell arrived an hour later. Packard pulled a cork from a whisky bottle and poured a shot each into two glasses on a small table, handing one to Campbell. 'To us, and to absent comrades,' he said, and they both raised the glasses to their lips and emptied them in a swallow.

'That's better,' Packard said as the liquid burned the back of his throat. 'Now, tomorrow morning after breakfast, I'll brief the men.' Packard poured another generous shot into the glasses, then corked the bottle. 'They don't need to know where we're heading until we get there. Just in case.'

'Just in case? Sounds like you're expecting trouble on this trip, sir?'

Packard nodded. 'I am. So, I'm now going to take you more into my confidence. Should anything happen to me, it's vitally important that you take over and complete this mission, regardless. You understand that?'

Campbell nodded slowly, as if a cold feeling was sweeping over him.

'I haven't been honest with you, Sergeant.' Packard's eyes began to twinkle. He lowered his voice, hoping he wasn't going to sound too dramatic. 'That vital equipment we have to recover in Ypres tomorrow – it's gold.'

Campbell swallowed hard. 'Gold?'

'Yes,' replied Packard, grinning as he turned his head quickly to look around the room. 'About three tonnes of the stuff. Bars and coins, worth nearly three million pounds.'

Campbell thought for a few seconds. 'Is it Belgian gold?' The words barely tumbled out.

'Of course, but this gold is different. It belongs to King Albert of the Belgians,' he explained, now buoyed up. 'Royal gold,' he said with a wide grin. 'Got left behind and hidden in Ypres a few days ago. They fear Fritz will get his hands on it and use it for propaganda purposes to reduce the morale of the Belgian Army in siege at Antwerp.'

Campbell whistled softly. 'So, it's bloody political then,' he said. 'That accounts for those letters you have from the likes of Asquith and Churchill. I thought it was a bit strong issuing those to you, and with the instant temporary field promotion to major. It all adds up now.' He chuckled. 'Bloody gold, and royal at that, eh? It'll make a change from fighting this war, that's for certain.'

'Apart from us, no one else must know,' Packard stressed. 'Providing the Intelligence boys are right, it should be an easy job.'

'But you have doubts about that?'

Packard sighed. 'It just sounds too easy, that's all. It could all go terribly wrong.'

Campbell shrugged. 'Like what, for example?'

Packard swirled what was left in his glass and drank it in one. 'For example, what if Fritz gets wind of the gold? What if a criminal gang decide to have a go and steal it?'

'Is that likely?'

'When war comes knocking on your door, there's no bloody law and order in these towns and villages. We know that from experience.'

'That's true enough,' Campbell replied. 'The local criminal element always sees the opportunity to make a few extra shillings.'

'Exactly. That's why I need the men to carry a sidearm at all times – hence the revolvers.'

Campbell looked hard at him. 'Do you *really* expect trouble on this trip?'

Packard smiled awkwardly. 'Let's say I'm being cautious. Major Teller will bring us the latest intelligence in that area in the morning before we leave, but I'll take nothing for granted.' He reached out for the bottle and uncorked it. 'Another before you go?'

Campbell nodded and smiled. 'Why not?'

*

The two Dennis three-tonner lorries arrived in the village prompt at 6 a.m. as ordered, fully fuelled and with spare petrol cans in the back. Both drivers, Steed and Joyce, were issued a revolver with ammunition and taken away by Campbell for instruction in its use and a practice shoot at the makeshift range. Thirty minutes later, they re-joined the group for a hearty breakfast. The cooks did not let them down.

It was a clear, cool, crisp morning and there was excitement in the air. They all felt it. Packard got Campbell to parade the men at the makeshift range for a quick brief before departure. They all looked clean, smart, alert, and eager to go with their Webleys holstered, lanyards around their necks and rifles at their side. Even Norris looked good and soldier-like for once. Campbell brought them to attention when Packard appeared and then stood them at ease.

Packard looked at the assembled group. Corporal Hedges was there, along with Corporal Ratcliffe, both Boer War veterans and in the thick of it since this war started, and Thompson, with Clarkson at the end of the line. A few other battle-experienced and hard-bitten old sweats like Private Gower. From what was left of his platoon made up the number. Hand-picked by him and Campbell. Four men in the back of each truck, with one corporal. Packard would take the lead truck and sit in the cab with Driver Joyce, while Campbell would be in the cab with Driver Steed in the second one. Twelve men in total.

Packard introduced the two drivers to the group and explained their mission to collect vital equipment from a Belgian town near the border with France. He never mentioned the name of the town, only that they had to remain very alert at all times. He deliberately did not offer them the chance to ask him questions. He took a quick glance at his pocket watch. 'Time to load up, Sergeant Campbell,' he said.

'Sir!' Campbell saluted.

Packard returned the salute and walked off.

By the time he reached the two Dennis lorries, a motorbike with sidecar had roared in and pulled up beside him. Packard felt tense as Major Teller climbed out, looking sharp as a pin with his jaw jutting out, a thick white scarf around his neck, tight brown leather gloves on his hands and motorcycle goggles covering his eyes.

'Major Packard,' he said. He lifted the goggles over the peak of his cap. His one good eye was clear and steady as a rock while he adjusted his eyepatch over the other. 'You ready?'

Packard felt a little awkward in front of Major Teller as he stood to attention. He stopped himself saluting him. After all, they were of the same rank, only Teller was a real major. 'I'm ready, sir,' Packard replied. 'We're just about to load the lorries and then we're off.'

'Good show. I hear HQ had a few phone calls yesterday regarding your requests. Got what you wanted?'

'Yes, sir. Everything.'

'Good. Fine.' Teller started to walk slowly, and Packard fell in step beside him. Once they were out of earshot of the motorbike Teller stopped, loosened his scarf and looked at him. 'Things may have changed,' he said cautiously. 'I got word last night from Belgian Intelligence that one of the soldiers who transported the gold to Ypres had been captured making his way to Antwerp. Not good.' Despite the negativity of his news, his face was devoid of expression. 'On top of that, our scouts have reported that a large force of German troops, brigade strength, is heading to your area.' He paused and then said, 'Major Scott-Bardwell, remember him?'

Packard nodded. 'Yes sir, I do.' Packard's mind quickly turned to the night they captured the bridge and Scott-Bardwell's scathing assessment of his decision to do so.

'He said not to worry about it, just routine stuff. He seems to think this large brigade force is just positioning itself to fill the gap between their army and the Channel Coast. But still, worth mentioning.'

Packard regarded the news calmly but inside his nerves began twisting into a tight knot. 'Of course, sir. Thank you.'

Teller paused, and as an afterthought he said sharply, 'But I don't buy it. If I could, I'd send a large force to secure the town and grab the gold, but we can't. We can hardly spare your little group, let alone a brigade.' Teller turned serious. 'Get to Ypres as quick as you can, grab the gold, and get the hell out of there. Got it?'

Packard was stunned at that sudden outburst and felt the apprehension suddenly boil up inside, that left him tongue-tied and unable to answer except with a nod.

Teller looked towards the motorbike and beckoned it with a hand. He glanced around him, making sure they were still alone. 'If I was in command and it was my decision, I'd just call this bloody thing off and take my chances.' He grinned and then said more seriously, 'But I'm not in command, and we don't have an army to send – just you.' His tone was flat and unfeeling. Then dropping his voice a little, he said, 'I want you to understand that in the next day or two your actions could very well decide if we lose this war or still have a stake in it.'

The motorbike pulled up beside him. He peeled off a glove and reached out and shook Packard's hand firmly. 'Well, good luck, Major,' he said, then he plucked at his moustache before dragging the tight leather glove on. He placed the goggles over the peak of his cap to cover his eyes, tightened the thick scarf around his neck and jumped into the sidecar. He looked up at Packard. 'You take care, Major Packard, and God help you if you foul this up!' He tapped the arm of the driver, who revved up the engine and they roared off into the distance.

Packard stood there for a moment. Silent. Staring blankly and seeing disaster ahead of him. That old feeling of tension and fear creeping under his skin before battle. It never left you. Packard always fought it, drawing strength from his sense of duty and the need to get on with it. The silence was broken by the comforting sounds of Campbell's voice barking out orders in the background. He turned and headed towards him.

As Packard approached, Campbell said, 'All loaded and ready to go, sir.' He knew straight away that something was wrong. Harry tried to smile but it would not come.

'Something wrong, sir?' he asked in a quieter voice.

Packard's eyes met his and he took a deep and meaningful breath. 'You may well ask, Sergeant. Remember last night I told you that I thought it was too easy, and it could all go terribly wrong? Well, I've just been told by Major Teller that Fritz is moving a large force, brigade strength, towards the town. We could be heading into trouble, Sergeant. Lots and lots of trouble.'

CHAPTER 19

Monsieur Henri Renard, the bank manager of Ypres, had a great affection for his niece, Vanessa. She visited Ypres during the school holidays with her parents when she was a little girl. Uncle Henri was well known in the town and would take her on visits to his customers and introduce her as his favourite niece, on holiday from England. To be fair, Vanessa was his *only* niece. He had no children of his own, his beloved wife and daughter had died in childbirth. He'd never remarried, never wanted to, and had thrown himself into his work as the town's bank manager, an important and respected position. When he received a telegram that she was on her way to see him, and would be arriving later that day, he was truly delighted.

*

By the time Vanessa reached Ypres, and presented herself at his front door, her hair was a mess, her feet were dirty and sore, her coat was splashed with mud, and she was exhausted.

Her journey to Ypres had been a nightmare. From the brothel at the bridge, she had walked nearly ten miles at night in almost pitch darkness. Her shoe heel had broken and she'd carried a heavy suitcase to the nearest town with a post office, to send a telegram to her uncle in Ypres to expect her. She was tired, thirsty, hungry, and her leg muscles ached. Her feet were sore and her coat was soaked from a heavy rainfall. She managed to wangle a lift on a cart taking milk to another town a short distance away that had a railway station. There, she'd been able to buy a piece of cake and a hot coffee from a small but busy café next to the station before her train arrived. The train was delayed for five hours due to war action further down the line. She tried sleeping in the crowded waiting room, but it was too noisy with children playing with their bored parents. The day was cool and drawing in as the sun started to sink over the rooftops. When the train eventually reached Ypres, it was late and dark.

When she arrived at her uncle's house, his expression was of sheer joy, his arms reached out to embrace her. Now warm and dry she had some hot food and went straight to bed, exhausted.

*

Next morning, she got up and took a long soak in a hot bath and had some breakfast. Uncle Henri was at the bank, but he'd left her a note to join him for lunch. Vanessa got ready, left the house, and walked, still wincing on feet that would take days to forgive her for her trek, into the historic town centre, with its gothic style and medieval buildings.

Vanessa remembered Uncle Henri telling her that during the middle ages, Ypres had been a Flemish town called Ieper, a name derived from the local river. It had been occupied by French forces several times, growing to around 40,000 French-speaking inhabitants, and so had changed its name to the French, Ypres.

Ypres, Uncle Henri had always boasted, had become the gateway to Europe, criss-crossed by roads, rivers, and a canal leading to Holland, France, and the English Channel, just 40 miles to the north. It soon became an important hub for the lace, cloth, and wool trade routes into Europe. The town's wealth was reflected in the erection of a magnificent gothic-style Cloth Hall with a large belfry tower, next to one of the largest market squares in Belgium. The Cloth Hall had spacious ground floor halls where cloth, wool, and lace were bought and sold. It also housed the town's archives, the treasury, an armoury, and a prison. Uncle Henri told her it was probably the finest specimen of Gothic architecture in Europe, but then he would say that – he was furiously proud of the town.

Trade had diminished over the last forty years, and now there were only around 18,000 people living in Ypres. The imposing architecture remained though, surviving the high days of trade and giving Ypres a sense of grandeur that now felt a little incongruous. The grandeur extended to the bank building where Uncle Henri worked, with its large basement vaults that were once filled with the town's wealth of gold, silver, and bullion, and had armed guards to protect it. Today, the bank vaults were mostly empty, save for around 100,000 francs and old bank records that were archived there and historical papers from the abbey. Market traders still used the grand market square to buy and sell goods on their stalls but never in the quantity that the square had originally been designed for.

Beside the imposing bank building ran the road Rue St Jacques, that led to the Rampart Road and the Lille Gate to the south. At the front of the bank, running from the grand market square heading east, was the Menin Road leading to the Menin Gate. Immediately behind the bank building stood the magnificent Royal Benedictine Abbey, with its large gardens and corner cemetery, two barns and outhouses, where lived a community of Irish nuns known as Les Dames Irlandaises – the Irish Dames of Ypres.

As a child, Vanessa had visited the abbey with her uncle and met the Reverend Mother Prioress. Uncle Henri had dealt with the abbey's accounts for nearly twenty years and met with the Reverend Mother once every two weeks to discuss the abbey's monetary affairs, refusing to take any payment for this service.

The Reverend Mother had been very kind to him when his wife and daughter died. He'd never forgotten her kindness and always balanced the abbey books with a little charity and cleverness. He made sure the Irish Dames of Ypres had no debts and he, along with the mayor, were great supporters of their charity work in the town and with some of the poorer farming communities in the villages beyond the ramparts.

She remembered the Reverend Mother as being elegantly tall and slim in a nun's dark habit. She had a kind, smiling face with a soft, gentle voice, and told Vanessa that in Greek, the meaning of her name was "butterfly".

It seemed special, and every time the Reverend Mother saw Vanessa, she called her "my little butterfly".

Vanessa entered the sunlit grand square. She felt relaxed and happy and realised the world could be wonderful. Could it possibly be just a few days ago that war, with all its horrors, had come knocking at her door. And Harry Packard ... she smiled primly, embarrassed at the way her heart beat faster, making her spine tingle when she thought of his name.

She was just approaching the town hall when she heard the throb of an engine above her. Like everyone else in the busy square, she gazed skyward. She stood and watched, unable to take her eyes off the aeroplane as it turned in a tight circle about three hundred feet above the square, like a predator bird waiting to strike its prey. She felt a nervous twang in the pit of her stomach, like a small cry of alarm, that took her mind straight back to the bridge when the Germans appeared. And what of Harry, was he alive or dead? And that of the girls – most having come from broken homes. Where were they now? That thought made her shudder and she clutched at the collar of her blouse.

The bi-plane, with big black crosses under the wings, circled the grand square several times. Most of the town's people were looking upwards, shadowing their eyes with their hands, some pointing. The mayor, Monsieur Colaert, a tall slim man with a neat grey beard, came onto the street with his clerks from his lawyer's office, all staring skywards just a few feet away from Vanessa. The bi-plane made one last circle, levelled out, and headed east, disappearing over the town's rooftops.

As the engine noise faded into the distance, Vanessa saw him. He looked frightened and pale. She heard him say to his clerks, 'That's the second time in two days.' 'They're surveying the town.' All his clerks nodded nervously in agreement.

She called out, 'Monsieur Colaert! Monsieur Colaert!'

At first, he looked startled. Then he spun around to see Vanessa eagerly walking towards him. 'Bless my soul! Vanessa!' He reached out and they embraced. 'How long has it been?'

'Too long,' she replied. 'How is your wife and children?'

'My wife is fine and my children have grown up too quickly. They're with their cousins in France at the moment. So, how about you? When did you arrive? Your uncle never mentioned to expect you?'

'Well it was all last minute and much too long a story to explain here,' she replied, honestly. She gestured towards the sky. 'I sense that aeroplane is trouble?' she said.

Colaert's face flushed and his eyebrows drooped. For a moment he seemed unable to speak. There was the sound of running feet heading towards them, and the voice of Uncle Henri's chief clerk shouting, 'Monsieur Mayor! Monsieur Mayor!'

Colaert let go of Vanessa and swung round.

The chief clerk stopped to catch his breath.

'What is it?' said Colaert.

'The chief of police wants you to meet him in the bank, right away,' gasped the chief clerk, breathlessly.

'Okay, okay. Tell him I'm coming.' Turning to Vanessa, Colaert said, 'I must go. We'll speak later,' and dashed off with the chief clerk.

She was slightly taken aback. Something was wrong at the bank. She had to find out what. 'Wait for me,' she called. 'I'm coming too!'

When they arrived at the bank, three gendarmes with carbine rifles slung over their shoulder were outside, puffing anxiously on cigarettes.

The mayor strode past them into the bank and hurried upstairs, two at a time, and Vanessa trotted after him. As he opened the door, she saw her uncle and Chief of Police Marcel Du Mont sitting at a desk, the room thick with smoke as both men took nervous, rapid drags of their cigarettes.

Colaert was closing the door behind him when Vanessa squeezed in. Her sweeping gaze took in all their nervous faces. 'What's happening?'

Marcel narrowed his eyes. 'What is she doing here?'

Her uncle immediately stood up from behind his desk, holding up his hands as he stepped forward. 'Vanessa, you must leave,' he said. 'We have important matters to discuss.'

'What's happening? What's going on?'

'It's urgent town business, Vanessa,' said her uncle in a calm voice. 'Now please, go home and wait for me there.' There was something in his voice that alarmed her. Vanessa didn't say anything. There was nothing to be gained by trying to stay. Reluctantly she nodded, turned, and left the room, the door closing behind her. She left the building, her face ashen. She suddenly felt angry with herself for her foolishness. What right did she have to burst in on an important meeting?

*

Colaert sat down and was the first to speak. 'That plane,' he said, 'the second one in two days. I think we have trouble.'

Henri looked at Colaert, seeing the strain in the mayor's eyes. 'Undoubtedly,' he said.

Marcel said, 'I was told earlier that German cavalry patrols have been visiting the local villages this morning asking questions. I was on my way to tell you when that plane flew over again.'

Colaert raised his eyebrows in surprise. 'Questions? What kind of questions?'

Marcel scratched the end of his long nose and replied, 'Things like are there any soldiers in town? Is the town being defended? Those type of questions.'

They were all stunned into silence for a few seconds.

'My God,' said Henri. 'They could be here today or early tomorrow.'

Colaert was fiddling with his coat buttons. 'Then what are we to do?' he demanded, wiping small beads of sweat from his brow with a pocket handkerchief, like a conspirator about to be caught.

Marcel turned to Henri. 'When are the English due to collect the gold?'

'Tomorrow,' he said. 'About lunchtime.' He took out a pocket watch. 'Another twenty-four hours at least.' He sounded worried. He sat down behind the desk again and stubbed out his cigarette in the ashtray.

Marcel thought about it for a moment. 'Either we move the gold and hide it, or we delay the Germans somehow until the English get here.'

'If they get here,' Colaert said, running his finger around his collar. 'And anyway, where could we possibly hide about three tonnes of gold and keep that a secret?'

'The Cloth Hall?' Marcel suggested.

Colaert wagged a finger. 'Too obvious, the first place the Germans would look.'

'Then hide it in a whore's knickers for all I care,' Marcel replied, his voice harsh. He stubbed out his cigarette in the ashtray on the desk and sat back. 'The fact is, the English won't be here until tomorrow and we're running out of time.'

'And options,' added Colaert, his face set in a frown.

'Marcel is right,' said Henri. 'We should hide the gold.'

Colaert frowned. 'Hide it? But where?'

'How about the abbey, with the Irish nuns?'

Colaert glanced at Marcel and saw his grim expression. Marcel shook his head and said, 'The Reverend Mother would never allow it. She would not want to get involved.'

Colaert considered it for a moment, then looked meaningfully at Henri. 'You know the Reverend Mother better than most, Henri. What do you think?'

Henri shrugged his shoulders. 'I think it's worth a try. I could speak to her. What have we to lose?'

'The gold, for one thing,' Marcel grunted testily, 'and possibly our lives.'

Henri stood up and said, 'It's time to make decisions. I'll go to the abbey now and talk to her and see what she says.' He went to the door, grabbing his hat from the hat stand.

'Then good luck,' Colaert said. 'Better to get it done now. Time is not on our side.'

*

The room was sparse with whitewashed walls, a table, and two chairs. Light came from a small arched window high on the wall. Under the window hung a small portrait of the first Irish Lady Abbess, dated 1682. Below it hung an ancient wooden crucifix. The door opened and the Reverend Mother Prioress came in, her long dark habit almost touching the floor. A black wooden rosary hung from her waist.

Henri, standing there, holding his hat, gave a slight bow. 'Reverend Mother,' he said.

She smiled and offered her hand. Henri took it and shook it gently. He felt a slight tremble in his hand as he did so.

'Is there something wrong? You wanted to see me urgently.'

Henri smiled at her awkwardly. 'I'm sorry to have disturbed you, Reverend Mother. Sister Margaret informed me that you were praying.' His faced reddened.

'Indeed I was, Monsieur Henri. Praying that this war will soon end.'

'Of course, Reverend Mother. That's what we all want.'

'What can I do for you?'

Henri took a breath. 'I'll come straight to the point. I have a certain something in my bank that I don't wish the Germans to have. The English are due to collect it tomorrow, but I fear they will not get here before the Germans do. I have spoken to Rene Colaert, and Marcel du Mont, the chief of police. They have asked me to approach you for help.'

The Reverend Mother looked at him curiously. 'You want *my* help?'

'Yes, we do.'

'I see.' She began to fiddle with the rosary at her waist. 'What help exactly do you want from me?'

Henri gulped, his eyes darting away from her. He gave a short sigh, then looked up, meeting her eyes. 'What I'm about to tell you is of national importance. I'm holding the king's personal gold in the bank's vault, waiting to be collected. We think the Germans will be here before the English, so we need to hide it.'

There was complete stillness in the room for a moment, then she said, 'And you want to hide it in the abbey?'

He nodded slowly. 'Yes – yes we do.' He was silent for a long moment. 'I know it's a lot to ask, but we have no alternative. It's either that or–'

'Or the Germans get the king's gold.'

'Indeed, Reverend Mother.'

She nodded, taking time to answer. Slowly she crossed the room, approached the portrait of the first Irish Lady Abbess and crossed herself. She said, 'Many times the Irish house at Ypres has been threatened by siege, hostility, and war in the last two hundred and fifty years, and now it has come again. But we have survived. I shiver at the thought of a visit from the dreaded German Uhlans, ransacking the abbey looking for the gold. They would take their revenge on us.'

Henri saw her tense and shiver.

'The Belgian Royal Family have been good to the abbey over the centuries, and publicly supported our Irish community of nuns at the abbey. How could I let them down now? What is important is doing the right thing – no matter the risks.' She turned to face him and met his gaze. 'When?' she said.

Henri let out a sigh of relief. 'Thank you, Reverend Mother. We need to do it straight away.'

'How much gold is there?'

'About three tonnes in small crates and barrels.'

'That's a lot of gold to hide.'

Henri nodded. 'Can you hide that amount?'

She did not answer at once, then shrugged acceptance. 'Very well, bring it to the small gate in the north wall, the one opposite the bank. I'll meet you there. I know a good place to hide it.'

'We are indeed in your debt, Reverend Mother.'

She held out her hand. Henri took it, stiffened, and gave a slight bow. They looked at one another and shared a grim smile.

*

Henri returned to the bank where Marcel and Colaert were waiting.

'Well, what did she say?' said Colaert, as soon as Henri closed the office door behind him. Henri grinned.

Marcel said, 'That's it then. We hide it in the abbey.'

'It must be now,' said Henri. 'I'll close the bank and get my clerks to move it.'

'They'll need help,' said Colaert.

'I'll give you some of my gendarmes to give you a hand,' volunteered Marcel.

Henri shook his head. 'No, just us and my clerks. The less people know, the better. Agreed?'

Colaert and Marcel looked at one another. 'We agree.'

'Good,' said Henri. 'I'll close the bank and we'll get started. It's going to be hard work, gentlemen.'

Marcel organised his gendarmes to block the tiny road behind the bank from any onlookers. Sister Margaret opened the ancient wooden door at the back as the small crates and barrels were carried through by Henri, Colaert, Marcel, and four bank clerks, who stacked them just inside the abbey in the cemetery corner on a pathway by the door. Even going only that far, it took two hours to complete the transfer.

Henri, red-faced, sleeves rolled up, wiped away the beads of sweat on his forehead with his handkerchief. In front of him stood about twenty nuns with the Reverend Mother, all surrounded by headstones, tombs, stone angels, and crosses in a beautiful corner garden of flowers, plants, scrubs, and small trees. Colaert, Marcel, and the four clerks stood behind him, all red-faced and sweating.

'It is done, Reverend Mother,' said Henri, almost breathless.

'Where shall we put it?'

The Reverend Mother moved forward to examine the crates and barrels. 'Leave it to us, Monsieur Henri. We will take it from here.'

Colaert stepped forward and said, 'But Reverend Mother, the crates and barrels are quite heavy, even though they are small.'

'Monsieur Mayor, I thank you for your concern, but my sisters are used to heavy work. Now I ask that you please go, so that we can move the gold to a safer place.'

Before they could protest, they were ushered out.

*

They all returned to the bank. So far, there had been no further news of any German activity outside town. Henri sent the clerks home, while Colaert and Marcel slumped into chairs in the office upstairs. Henri entered the room with a tray of three glasses and a jug of water. He poured water into each glass and handed one to them. The water felt cool and was gulped down.

'I've been thinking,' said Colaert. 'In a few hours it will be early evening, and dark. This town will be lit up like a beacon to the Germans. What if I was to issue a notice to the town that no strong lights should be seen from the outside? Let's say, six in the evening till the following day?'

'Good idea,' said Marcel. 'Make the German bastards try and find us in the dark.'

'I agree, but what about the town's noise?' said Henri.

'Noise? What noise?' asked Marcel, his brow furrowed.

'Church bells, including those at the abbey. You can hear them ringing the hour for miles.'

'Good point,' said Marcel. 'If the town is in darkness it should be quiet too.'

Colaert stood up. 'You're right. I'll get on to it straight away.

Perhaps your gendarmes will help my staff get the message around town?'

Marcel stood up. 'Of course. Let's get on with it.' All three left the office.

Henri first went to the abbey and spoke to the Reverend Mother, who agreed not to ring the bells to summon the nuns to prayers. Colaert went to the caretaker of the Cloth Hall to stop the large bells ringing in the belfry. Marcel went to the churches and all agreed to keep their lights low and not to ring the bells. An uneasy feeling of uncertainty took possession of the town, and rumours had spread like wildfire that German Uhlan Cavalry had been seen outside.

*

A few hours later, Henri returned to his house.

Vanessa had pulled all the curtains, so very little lighting could be seen on the outside. She waited for him in the parlour. He looked tired and worn out.

'I've kept some food warm for you,' she said.

He nodded. 'I could smell lamb cooking when I came in. I'm famished. You're good girl, Vanessa.'

He ate his food in silence and, when he'd finished, Vanessa cleared away the plates and joined him in the parlour. Henri was smoking a cigarette, sitting by the fireside, watching the flames flickering in the grate. She could see by his stiff demeanour in the chair that he was all pent-up from strain, that something very important was troubling him.

She sat on a small stool just behind him. 'Is this town going to be invaded by the Germans?' she asked, softly.

He did not turn but stared intently at the flames. 'Yes, I think it is. You've come at a bad time, Vanessa.'

'Tonight?'

'Maybe tonight, but most probably tomorrow.'

'And you were discussing this with the mayor and the chief of police today?'

He nodded.

She looked at him more closely. 'Is there something else troubling you? Apart from the Germans?'

Henri swallowed. He looked down as she touched his forearm. He seemed to struggle to find his words and then said, 'When the Germans come, I expect to be their centre of attention.'

She tensed, a little startled. 'But why?'

Henri shook his head and said nothing. She sensed the danger but decided not to push it. In a small voice she said, 'If there is anything I can do?'

He half-smiled. 'If only, Vanessa, if only.'

She removed her hand slowly.

Eventually, she went to bed. Her thoughts turned to tomorrow, and her eyes brimmed with tears for what the day might bring for them all.

CHAPTER 20

The two Dennis lorries had been on the main road for about three hours. The final leg of the journey had been slow. For the last half hour, the four men sitting in the back of each lorry had bumped, bounced, swayed, and shaken against the rough jolting of an uneven dirt track that Packard had taken to avoid the main road into Ypres from the south, on the grounds that the main road might be patrolled by German cavalry scouting parties. With about three miles to go, the discomfort of the ride came to an end. Packard decided to stop for a quick brief with his sergeant and the two NCOs just before the dirt track joined the main road through a clump of tall trees and low bushes that gave cover from the main road. He told Joyce to keep the engine ticking over as he stepped down from the cab to look around.

As he did so, he thought he heard a faint engine noise in the sky. He froze on the spot, straining to hear against the throbbing lorry engines. The noise got louder. Before he had a chance to react and hide the lorries under the canopy of a tree, an aeroplane appeared low over the treetops at about 100 feet and flew directly above them.

Campbell got out of the lorry behind him, rifle at the ready, twisting his gaze skyward in all directions, the engine sound disappearing over the treetops into the distance. 'One of ours or theirs?' he asked.

'Theirs,' Packard replied grimly, still looking up, shielding his eyes. 'Ruddy great black crosses on the wings. It flew over so quickly, I just hope they didn't have time to notice us.'

Packard bit his lip. Inwardly, he was cursing himself, thinking of the time during the retreat from Mons six weeks earlier, when the Germans had used spotter planes to follow their progress. Aeroplanes in war were a new phenomenon then, and nobody took much notice at first and didn't consider them to be too much of a threat. But the pilots dropped messages to their forward patrols and it wasn't long before small clashes occurred with the regiments covering their backs. Now, soldiers knew that aeroplanes were a vital source of intelligence, and that, in their role as an airborne spy, they should not be underestimated.

'Right, let's get the lorries tucked under those big trees over there with the wide spreading branches, and post two sentries front and back. Then join me with the two NCOs for a quick brief. It'll give the men a five-minute fag break. Make sure they stay under cover and don't move away.'

'Very good, sir. They'll appreciate it after that last bit of the journey. Quite a bumpy ride.' Campbell banged on the side of the lorries and started barking out orders. 'Ok, five-minute smoke break, an' keep under cover. Hurry up, we ain't got all day! Norris! Clarkson! As you two don't smoke, take sentry duty. Clarkson, take the main road, Norris to the rear, and keep a sharp lookout!'

'About bleeding time,' said Thompson, as he climbed down from over the tailboard onto the road, followed by the others, yawning and stretching, their unwilling limbs stiff and lame from the journey. Some men went behind the bushes for a pee before lighting up a fag.

Ted Gower, a tall lanky lad from Kingston, and one of the returned wounded from Mons, said, 'Bloody lorries and their hard seats. My arse feels like it's had a good pounding.'

'Ask the sergeant if you can walk then,' replied Thompson, and the men chuckled.

Packard went to the main road with Clarkson, where he positioned him by a road sign that said "Ypres 5km". He looked up and down the road. Nothing, just an empty road going north to Ypres and south to Lille.

Packard crossed the road to climb a high wooden fence and lifted his binoculars to scan the open fields that rose and fell with the land's contours. Nothing was stirring, not even a farmer or any labourers working the land that he could see, just birds grazing on the fields or flying overhead. He scanned skyward; no sign of that aeroplane. All quiet and peaceful. He still felt nervous about it. This was ideal cavalry country. The dips in the landscape could hide a whole squadron of cavalry and they could be on to you before you knew it. He turned and faced north. To his left, woodland, tall trees, bushes, and scrub. That at least gave some modicum of cover.

He headed back to the lorries. 'Keep a sharp lookout, Clarkson,' he said, as he passed him, 'especially across those fields. I don't want to be caught out by cavalry.'

'I've got it, sir.'

'Good man.'

He returned to the cab of his lorry, grabbed the map from his seat and told Joyce to take a smoke break before spreading the map over the bonnet.

Sergeant Campbell, Corporal Hedges, and Corporal Ratcliffe came to his side. All three were old campaigners, and without announcing it, Harry began his brief.

'We're here,' he said, pointing at the map. 'Just shy of entering this town from the south, about three miles up this road.' They all leaned forward to see.

'Wipers?' murmured Ratcliffe.

Packard grinned. 'Yes, you could call it that, but the 'Y' is pronounced like an 'E', Ypres.'

'Ahh.' They all nodded.

He continued. 'We're going into Ypres to the main bank in the town square to pick up nearly three tonnes of gold in small crates and barrels and ship it to England by this evening.'

Surprised, the two corporals looked up. 'Gold, sir?' said Hedges. 'And back to England? That including us?'

'Spot on, Corporal.'

'Blimey.'

'Yes, that's one way of putting it. Now, I don't want the men to know about the gold until we get there. Fritz has cavalry patrols in this area, and I suspect they will be particular about the main roads near this town, hence the cross-country trek for the last half-hour. But now we have no choice. We have to take the main road right into the southern part of town, through the Lille Gate. So, from now on, keep your eyes peeled for enemy cavalry until we get there. Clear?'

'Yes sir,' replied both corporals as one.

'Good. I'll be relying on you two to chivvy the lads on to get us loaded as quickly as possible. Once we're loaded, we won't hang around. Any questions?'

They all shook their heads.

Packard folded the map. He wiped his mouth with the back of his hand. 'Right, let's mount up and get cracking.'

There was an alarmed shout from Clackson. 'Riders!' he yelled and sprinted up to his officers. 'Riders, sir! About 'alf dozen of 'em!' He pointed across the open field. 'Over there! Coming straight out of that dead ground!'

They all turned and stood stock still. Their bodies rigid, faces tense, like death.

Packard's fear had come true. *Damn that aeroplane.* They'd been spotted, he was sure of it.

'Get the men in, quickly,' he barked to Campbell and the two NCOs, then dashed across the road, stepping up to the fence in a flash, lifting his glasses up to scan the field.

Through the lenses, he counted eight riders carrying lances with small swallow-tailed squadron pennants fluttering just below the spearhead, about four, maybe five hundred yards away. They wore the characteristic square-topped lancer helmet bosses and Ulanka-style double-breasted grey tunics. German Cavalry. Uhlans. Heading straight for them.

Tipped off by that bloody aeroplane.

Coming over to investigate the lorries' presence. He swallowed hard. Uhlans were a highly trained elite German cavalry regiment with a ruthless reputation.

They were close enough now for him to hear the soft thump of their hooves; he saw them kicking up small clods of earth as they galloped across the field towards him. If they caught his squad out in the open like this, they would use those lances to good effect, and spear his men without mercy. They'd be dead meat in seconds. He had to act fast. Get the lorries moving. They would be a much harder target for riders with lancers, which would give him some advantage. It was their only chance.

He cupped his hands and shouted, 'Sergeant Campbell! Eight Uhlans coming straight in. Get the men in the lorries and be quick about it!' Then, remembering that rifles were too unwieldly in the confines of a lorry, he added, 'Engage close quarters, revolvers only!'

'Sir!' Campbell turned to shout orders to the men – not that they needed telling. Every man scrambled to the lorries and jumped in. He heard Ted Gower say to Clarkson, 'Uhlans. Sod this for fun and games,' as he climbed up over the tailgate.

Engines revving, the lorries set off with a jerk.

Packard jumped into the cab as it hit the main road. Looking to his right, he saw the riders galloping across the field were almost upon them. 'Foot down, Joyce, give it all you've got, and stop for nothing!'

Packard knew they had some protection from the wooden fence, which was too high for horses to jump. But how long would that luck last? One mile, maybe two? The Uhlans were level now. Harry could see the first of them driving their spurs hard into their horses' flanks, urging them on at full pelt to keep level, great earth clods kicking up from the field as they galloped along. They turned a bend in the road. A farmer was driving four cows into the field; the gate was wide open. The cows scattered in panic as the Uhlans galloped through without hesitation and onto the road like steeplechasers in hot pursuit. The two lorries were surrounded by thundering horses, jangling harnesses, fluttering pennants and hooves clattering on the metalled road. The Uhlans looked bloodthirsty and in a determined mood, like horsemen from hell.

Packard heard a sudden bang! Then another, then several more. The boys in the back were engaging the riders, and cheers went up as one by one the Uhlans went crashing down. The training with the revolvers was paying off. One Uhlan slumped in his saddle, grasping his neck as thick red arterial blood pumped from a gaping wound. He slowly leaned sideways and fell out of his saddle. Their leader, a sergeant, with the distinctive white lace edging his collar and epaulette, drew level to the cab of Harry's lorry.

In those few short seconds Packard unholstered his revolver. The Uhlan sergeant leaned down, gritting his teeth before he could dip his lance to spear Joyce. He jabbed the sharp four-edged spear-like lance-head into the open cab, just missing the driver, but clumsily striking the top of the steering wheel. Joyce, terrified, swung the steering wheel to one side and began frantically zig-zagging along the road to get away from the glittering, lethal lance-head. The men yelled in alarm as they were thrown about in the back of the lorry, lurching from one side of the road to the other.

'Damn it, man, drive straight!' Harry cursed, desperately clinging on himself in the open cab. 'Let him get close enough so I can shoot the bastard!'

Joyce looked at his officer, his eyes wide and questioning.

'Drive straight, damn you!' Packard yelled again, this time grabbing the steering wheel to keep it straight. 'Do it!'

Joyce stared straight ahead, too frightened to look as a horse's head inched its way forward beside him with flared nostrils, wild eyes and ears pointing back. The Uhlan sergeant was back, spurring his horse forward, his face a mask of anger as he readied his lance to jab it into the cab again, only this time he was determined not to miss. Joyce sat there, foot hard on the throttle, cringing, and waiting for the fatal blow from the sharp German lance.

Packard read the signs, and with revolver in hand, he swung his gun-arm straight across Joyce's chest, fired off two quick shots before the Uhlan sergeant could react. The shots in the cab were deafening.

The first bullet struck the sergeant in the upper arm. He gave a yelp and lost his grip on the lance, which clattered to the ground. The second bullet hit the horse in the neck behind the ear with a loud smack. The horse screamed as its front legs crumpled. It fell thrashing to the road in a gut-churning shriek of agony. The Uhlan sergeant was catapulted headfirst for several yards, arms and legs flailing, and hit the road with a heavy, bone-breaking crash.

Then another Uhlan suddenly appeared at Harry's left side,

inching its way forward, trying to spear him with his lance. Harry seized the lance-head with his left hand as it poked in and tugged it hard. The Uhlan desperately pulled it back. Harry swung his gun arm round, aimed along the lance at the rider's head, pulled the trigger, and fired at almost point-blank range. The .38 bullet smacked into the Uhlan's face with a bone-crunching thud. The back of his skull exploded into a red spray of blood, and he instantly toppled over in his saddle, falling hard to the ground and somersaulting into the bushes.

The horn was tooting from Sergeant Campbell's lorry behind. Hedges poked his head through a slide-hatch at the back of the cab.

'Sergeant Campbell wants us to stop, sir!'

Packard twisted around, looking from one side to the other, making absolutely certain there were no more Uhlans around his lorry before he told Joyce to pull over and stop.

Joyce slumped forward on the steering wheel, breathing heavily, resting his head on his forearm.

'You all right, Joyce?'

Joyce slowly looked up, breathing deeply, his face pale. 'Never been that close to the enemy, sir. Never been that frightened.'

Packard slapped him on the shoulder. 'You did well, Joyce. You held your nerve. That took guts to do.'

Joyce did not seem cheered by his officer's opinion. He closed his eyes and just nodded.

Packard jumped out of the cab, revolver in hand, and went to the back of his lorry as Sergeant Campbell pulled in behind.

'What's up?' he asked. 'Casualties?'

Campbell climbed out of the cab and shoved his revolver back into its holster. 'No, sir. The boys are fine. They did a bloody good job with those revolvers. The Uhlans didn't know what hit them.

Rifles would have been bloody useless firing from the back of a moving lorry.'

'Well, what is it then?'

'We got them all,' Campbell explained. 'All eight, but some are just wounded.'

'So what? You don't expect me to go back and help them, surely?' Harry heard the callousness in his own voice.

Campbell shook his head. 'No, sir. But when their friends find them, they'll know that two lorries of British soldiers are heading for Ypres. We're the only British in this area. They'll come after us if only to find out what we are doing so far north of our army.'

Packard raised his eyebrows. 'You mean go back and despatch the wounded? Make sure they don't talk?'

Campbell nodded. 'Harsh, I know. It's a thought, sir. Just might give us a bit more time. That's all.'

The men in the back of the lorries were jubilant, cheering, laughing, and swapping stories of who had killed who, and how the Uhlans had fallen from their horses. The noise irritated Campbell, who banged his fist on the side of his lorry. 'Hey! Keep it down in there! Anyone would think you lot had just won the bloody war!'

Packard pushed up his cap and scratched his head, trying to think it out. He could go back and give the Uhlan wounded the coup de gras, but what for? It was only another twenty minutes' drive to Ypres, if that. They would be wasting time searching for the wounded and dispensing with them, and leaving themselves wide open again to get spotted and attacked, only this time it could be by a much larger force. If he thought for one moment it would be the right thing to do, and that the wounded Uhlans posed a real threat to their mission, he'd do it without hesitation. In war, things go wrong, but there was nothing to suggest that things had – at least not yet. As far as he could read it, the completion of this mission was his first priority and getting the gold was vitally important. Killing the enemy in battle was one thing; killing the wounded in cold blood without a good enough reason … He shook his head and replaced his cap.

'I see your point, given the circumstances we find ourselves in,' he said, 'but, I don't think it necessary. We'll crack on to Ypres. We're almost there. Let's get on and get this mission over with.'

Campbell shrugged. 'Just thought I'd mention it, that's all, sir.'

Harry nodded, then looked back down the road. In the distance he could see three of the horses standing forlorn, with one horse lying on its side, thrashing its legs in agony, and scattered crumbled grey bundles, the Uhlan dead and wounded. At least two of them were moving. Too late anyway, he thought. It was time to move.

Packard turned and faced Campbell. 'Let's get on!'

They mounted their lorries and set off for Ypres.

CHAPTER 21

After ten more minutes, they could see the town of Ypres before them, the moat with its stone ramparts, old rooftops, and church spires beyond. They turned onto the moat bridge that led to the arched Lille Gate dating from 1385. Two gendarmes smoking cigarettes, carbines slung on their shoulders, with two bicycles leaning against the rampart wall, waved them to a halt. Quietly, Packard breathed a sigh of relief. They had made it this far at least.

The gendarmes looked at Packard curiously, then recognised the uniform. 'Ah, English soldiers,' said the elder of the two. 'We were told to look out for Germans, not the English. The mayor seems to think the town is going to be occupied by the Germans.'

Packard frowned. 'Today?'

The guard shrugged. 'Maybe. Maybe tomorrow. We've been waiting since yesterday, all night and all morning, and seen nothing except their aeroplanes flying over. That's all I know.'

It occurred to Packard that since they had been on the main road, they'd seen no civilians, apart from that farmer with the cattle. Obviously, people were too frightened to be outside their homes with German aeroplanes flying above and Uhlans patrolling around. And looking through the Lille Gate, he noticed that it wasn't much better in town either.

'Are we free to pass?' he asked.

'Of course, monsieur. You know where you are going?'

Packard nodded. 'I've got a good idea. We're going to the town square.'

'Ah, yes, the square. Straight ahead, and don't leave it too long, monsieur. The Germans.' He spat on the floor. 'I'd hate them to find you here,' he warned as he waved them through.

They drove down the old narrow cobbled street. There were a few people about, looking frightened and hurrying along. A few moments later, they got to the square and stopped. The town square was huge. The Cloth Hall was to their left, dominating the centre of town with its large gothic architecture and belfry tower. Here too, there were very few people about. Most scurried away when they saw them, unsure who they were.

'Turn right here,' he told Joyce, and Joyce turned the lorry eastward towards the Menin Gate.

Packard saw the "Bank" sign in bold lettering outside a big impressive gothic building on the corner of the square, and told Joyce to park outside, but keep the engine running. He stepped out of the cab and looked about him gloomily. The town square was almost deserted and still, apart from the throbbing pulse of the two lorry engines. There was fear in the town. He could almost touch it.

Campbell was now at his side. 'Eerie, isn't it?'

Packard nodded. 'They're expecting Fritz today,' he said, 'so we'd best get on. The sooner we get out of here the better. Tell Corporal Ratcliffe to stand guard here with the two drivers, with rifles and bayonets. The rest in the bank with me.'

Campbell turned, barked out some orders, and the men leapt from the tailgates and onto the pavement outside the bank.

Packard went towards two huge brown wooden doors, opened one and stepped in. There were two glass inner doors and, beyond them, a large room with a long dark oak counter on the opposite side, with glass panels that had slits cut into them. Sitting behind the glass panels were three bank clerks. Packard pushed open the glass doors and they all trooped inside and filled up the room. He went up to the nearest clerk, who looked terribly nervous, his eyes wide and staring like dark buttons.

'I'm looking for the bank manager,' he said. 'Monsieur Henri Renard?'

The bank clerk suddenly brightened. 'You are English?'

'Yes, we are,' Packard replied.

The clerk smiled, clasped his hands together, then stood up and went to a side door, unlocked it with a key and came into the main room, securing the door behind him. 'Ah, welcome, sir,' he said with a big toothy smile. 'We have been expecting you. Come this way,' he enthused, leading them to the stairs.

Packard turned to Campbell. 'Wait here. I'll find out what's happening.'

He followed the clerk up the stairs. The clerk knocked on a door marked "Manager", and went in, then turned back to Packard, smiling, and beckoned him into the office. Once he was in the room, the clerk nipped back past him, quickly shut the door, and scurried away.

It was a pleasant office with a large desk in the corner and three chairs spread out along the front. Sitting behind the desk was the bank manager, dressed in a black suit, who stared at him, face pale and drawn.

'Monsieur Henri Renard?' He saw the bank manager hesitate at first, and then he rose silently behind the desk. He looked at Packard, his uniform and demeanour.

In almost a croak he said, 'You are Major Harry Packard, English army?'

Packard nodded. 'Yes, that's me. I've come to collect the gold.'

Henri brightened visibly. A big smile broke his drawn face and he quickly went around his desk and shook Packard's hand vigorously. 'Thank God you have arrived. I can't tell you how happy I am to see you.'

Despite the vigorous handshake, behind the gleeful expression, in the bank manager's eyes, Packard could see he was nervous. He didn't want to waste time and got straight to the point. 'I understand you are expecting visitors, so can you take me to the gold? I want to load up as quickly as possible before they get here.'

'Visitors, Major?'

'I mean the Germans.'

'Ah, yes, the Germans. English sense of humour, no?'

'English sense of humour, yes,' Packard replied with a half-smile.

'The gold, but of course. You have lorries outside, no?'

'I have two lorries outside, yes,' replied Packard, now a little irritated by this game of yes and no.

'Good,' said Henri. 'We expect the Germans here any moment. We have hidden the gold somewhere in town. We must hurry.'

Packard frowned. 'You mean the gold isn't here at the bank?'

Henri shook his head. 'No, Major Packard. We were fearful the Germans would come here and take it, so we moved it yesterday to the abbey. A convent of Irish nuns is looking after it.'

Packard digested the news for a few moments. 'Irish nuns? Here in Ypres?'

'Of course,' replied Henri. 'They've been in the abbey for two hundred and fifty years. Now come, we must move quickly. Follow me.'

As they left the office, Henri grabbed his hat and trotted down the stairs, quickly followed by Packard. As he passed Campbell he said, 'Back on the lorries, Sergeant, the gold isn't here.'

'What?'

'Haven't got time now. It's somewhere else. You'll see when we get there!'

With everyone back on the lorries, Henri squeezed into the cab on the bench seat with Packard, the lorries turned about and headed down the Rue St Jacques. There was a long red-bricked wall about ten feet high, with a gated entrance of two large black wooden doors, edged in studs and iron brackets. They pulled up in front of it.

Henri got out and went to a hanging chain with a handle and began pulling on it, ringing a distant bell. A few moments later, a small slit in the door was pulled aside. Two inquisitive eyes peered out.

Henri looked closer. 'Sister Margaret, is that you? It's me, Monsieur Henri Renard, the bank manager. Open up. The English soldiers have arrived.'

They waited while heavy bolts were slid back, which seemed to take ages. After one minute the left side yawned open first, followed by the right. Henri jumped into the cab, they drove in and onto the gravel entranceway.

Ahead of them was a picturesque abbey surrounded by beautiful gardens, sheds, and two barns tucked away at the side by the outer wall. Packard was surprised just how spacious it was, considering the abbey was in a walled garden inside a walled town. They stopped outside the abbey building, and a tall elegant nun came out of the entrance. Her stiff coif framed her smiling face and gave it an egg shape, and the black veil dropped down her back. The brilliant white wimple gave coverage under her chin and down her chest. A woven belt with an old wooden rosary attached hung limp from her waist.

Henri went forward. The abbess proffered her hand. He removed his hat and gave a slight bow, shaking her hand gently. 'Reverend

Mother,' he said gleefully, 'the English are here.' He turned. 'This is Major Harry Packard.'

Packard stepped forward, finding this all surreal. Twenty minutes ago, he had been fighting for his life, killing Germans, and now ... He'd never been introduced to a nun before and certainly not a prioress. He took his lead from Henri as to what to call her.

Packard managed to force a half-smile and shook her hand. She seemed almost saintly. 'I'm pleased to meet you, Reverend Mother,' he said.

'Thank you,' she replied with a warm smile. 'I'm glad you have arrived. Perhaps your soldiers would like some refreshments after their journey?'

'That's very kind of you, Reverend Mother,' replied Packard. 'But we would like to get loaded and be on our way as soon as possible. Some other time, perhaps.'

She nodded. 'In better circumstances,' she said.

'Of course,' replied Packard. 'It would be a pleasure, I'm sure.'

There was a shout from the half-closed gate, and a bicycle bell rang wildly. It was the older gendarme from the Lille Gate, red-faced and peddling like mad. He rushed through and skidded to a halt beside them, sending a scurry of stones everywhere. 'Monsieur! Monsieur!' he yelled to Henri. 'The Germans, they are here! They are marching into town. They'll be passing the abbey any moment!'

At first Henri thought he had misheard. 'Germans? Here already? Are you sure?'

Packard's stomach suddenly twisted into a tight knot as he spun around on the spot, looking towards the half-closed gate. They could hear the sound of marching feet, wheels of carts and horses' hooves on cobbled stones slowly approaching. For a second, no one moved, not believing their ears.

'The gate!' Packard shouted, and in that instant, he drew his revolver. With Sergeant Campbell and Henri, he ran to help close the other half, as Sister Margaret struggled alone to secure the bolts of the half-closed gate.

They closed it and secured the bolts in time. A dog was heard barking somewhere and a German voice shouting out. This was followed by some distant laughter.

Packard pushed the slide open about an inch to peer outside. He was panting slightly as they came into view, a long column of infantry on one side of the road, and on their flank, supply wagons, cavalry, and some field artillery, all heading for the town square.

Must be brigade strength at least. Thank God they were in the abbey. Another minute or so … it didn't bear thinking about. He bit his lip and glanced down angrily, closing the slide with some bitterness. He looked back into the fearful faces of Sergeant Campbell, Sister Margaret, and Henri who stood there next to him, stock still, staring at his grim face.

He said nothing, just breathing deeply, still trying to come to terms with what this meant. Time had run out. They were trapped.

The German army had arrived in Ypres.

CHAPTER 22

It was nearly 1 p.m. when Vanessa peered out of the parlour window, and the weather looked fine. No rain. She went to the table where she'd prepared a packed lunch of bread, cheese, some sliced meat, and pickle for Uncle Henri, placing it all in a basket under a napkin.

Her thoughts went back to the breakfast table that morning. Uncle Henri just picking at his food. When he finished, he just sat there, quietly brooding, drinking coffee, his demeanour that of a man who had the whole world's problems resting on his shoulders; his red-rimmed eyes, the paleness of his cheeks. Obviously, he'd not slept well. She was worried about him.

She'd suggested taking him for lunch. 'I can meet you at the bank and we can enjoy lunch together,' she said cheerily. 'There's that lovely little bistro in the square, next to the bakery. We'll go there. My treat.'

He didn't look up, just dismissively shook his head.

'I will not take no for an answer,' she countered.

Picking up his cup, he drank the remains of his coffee, placing it back on the table. 'I'll be too busy for lunch today,' he replied.

She noticed he began fiddling with his watch chain, something he always did when he had something pressing on his mind. 'I should not pry,' she said softly, 'but there must be a reason why you are like this?'

He pushed his plate and cup away and looked up at her. 'There is,' he responded.

He sounded fearful. Something was weighing heavily on his mind.

'What would you say,' she said, 'if I was to make a nice packed lunch for you and drop it off at the bank?'

He took a deep breath, pushing his fingers together in front of his nose like a church with a spire, thought about it for several seconds and replied, 'You're a good girl, Vanessa.' And with a slight smile he said, 'Very well, if you insist.'

Vanessa smiled back at him. 'Good, that's settled then.'

With that he got up, left the table, went to the door, grabbed his hat and coat and left for the bank.

*

When Vanessa left the house and made her way to the square, the town was still quiet. The streets were almost deserted. And the square was no different, just a few people scurrying around the food shops. The fear of German occupation had kept most people in their homes. It was actually Wednesday lunchtime, but it felt more like an early Sunday morning before church.

She entered the bank, and that too was empty except for the three clerks who sat stony faced behind the glass screen staring at her. 'Good afternoon,' she said, smiling. 'I've come to deliver lunch for my uncle,' she explained, placing the basket on the counter in front of them.

'He's gone to see the prioress at the abbey,' said the chief clerk. 'Should be back soon if you'd like to wait?'

Vanessa was just about to answer when she heard a bicycle bell ringing like mad in the street outside. Five seconds later, she heard boots clattering in the entrance and a gendarme came rushing through the door, bicycle clips on his trousers, red-faced and panting.

'Where is Monsieur Henri?' he gasped.

'What is it? What's wrong?' the chief clerk fretted.

'The Germans,' said the gendarme, still breathing heavily. 'They're here. Heading straight into town. Hundreds of them ... no, *thousands* of them. I've been sent to warn him!'

Vanessa raised her hand to her mouth and gasped. 'My God!'

'He's at the abbey!' the chief clerk yelled back. 'Go, and hurry up!'

The gendarme turned and ran out.

The three bank clerks spun into action, grabbing money by the handful from the tills, then quickly making their way from behind the glass screen, locking the door behind them.

'What are you doing?' Vanessa said with a scowl. 'That's the bank's money!'

The chief clerk's face looked grim. 'I know, I know,' he said, 'but it's instructions from your uncle.'

He ushered her outside, then began looking up and down the street. There was no sign of the Germans, so he locked the main door. He shoved a bunch of keys into her hand. 'Give these to your uncle. Tell him we've gone,' he said, and all three scurried off in different directions.

Vanessa watched them go and suddenly found herself alone. The square was deathly quiet, empty, not even a bird in the sky. For one terrible moment she didn't know what to do, and she felt a tremble in her hands. There seemed little choice; she would have to go to the abbey and find her uncle.

Then she remembered that she had left the basket of food inside the bank.

She was just about to unlock the door and go back inside to retrieve it when she heard the faint sound of horses' hooves and hobnailed boots ringing on the cobbled street from the direction of the Menin Gate. She craned her head to look, and there in the distance was a grey column of marching men, with riders on one side holding lances, their pennants waving lazily in the small breeze. Her mind raced as she recalled the night the Germans stormed the brothel. She stood there transfixed, a choking sensation clawing at her throat, her anxious fingers clutching at the collar of her coat. She felt sick with fright.

She had to get away, so she headed for the side street that led to the abbey. As she did so, she saw another grey column of marching Germans, with horse-drawn wagons, all heading for the square.

She stood frozen on the corner for several long seconds. Then she looked towards the Menin Gate and then the abbey. A feeling of dread twisted in the pit of her stomach, her heart thumping against her ribs.

The Germans were at the square now, forming up into columns as though they were on a parade ground. Orders were shouted in German. The two columns merged at the corner where she stood. It seemed endless. The gendarme was right, there were thousands of them. It was as if the whole German army had come to Ypres. The ground trembled under her feet as the mass of marching men, horses, and heavy supply wagons went rolling by.

'Bonjour fraulein! Bonjour fraulein!' some of the soldiers cheerfully shouted out to her as they marched by, some whistling and most smiling. They all marched into the square and were then detailed off into smaller groups and sent to different parts of the town.

Vanessa watched the spectacle unfold before her. She took deep breaths, calming herself, turning her fear to action. Slowly, she walked off in the direction of the abbey, and as she got closer, her pace quickened until she reached the abbey gate and her calm broke. She rang the bell desperately, repeatedly.

It took an agonising three minutes before the viewing slide moved across, and two eyes peered out like dark buttons. 'Who is it?' hissed a female voice.

'My name is Vanessa. My uncle is the bank manager, Henri Renard. The bank told me I'd find him here. I must see him.'

The two peering eyes blinked several times, and the slide closed.

Nothing happened for two further minutes. Vanessa rang the bell again.

The slide opened again. This time Vanessa recognised the eyes. 'Uncle Henri, Uncle Henri, it's me, Vanessa. Let me in, I need to see you!'

'Wait,' he said. 'Can you see any Germans nearby?'

She looked about, craning her head left and right. 'No,' she replied.

She could hear the sound of heavy bolts being shifted. Then the left door partly opened, enough for Vanessa to squeeze in, then it was pushed closed quickly behind her by Sister Mary.

She reached out and embraced her uncle. Vanessa squeezed her eyes shut for a moment, her heart beating like that of a small terrified child. 'Are you all right?' he asked.

She opened her eyes and looked up to him, wiping a tear from her eye with her hand. 'The Germans are here, thousands of them,' she said with a tremble in her voice. 'I've been so worried for you.'

Someone moved behind Henri and when she looked, she gave a gasp! She stepped away from her uncle, eyes wide, with both hands covering her open mouth. She was stunned. Harry Packard was standing there with the prioress.

She saw him swallow hard when he saw her face, and he broke into a half-smile. She felt his eyes on her. 'Hello, Vanessa,' he said softly. 'We meet again.'

Vanessa was almost too afraid to breathe when she heard Harry's voice. All that pent-up fear she had, suddenly draining away. 'But… but…'

Her uncle cut in. 'You know this officer?'

Vanessa smiled girlishly and nodded, not knowing what to say. An awkward silence fell between them.

They all turned as the abbey clock in the tower began striking the hour – it was 2 p.m.

'It doesn't matter now,' Henri said. 'I'd better get back to the bank. May I suggest, Major, that you get your men hidden in the abbey until we know exactly what to do.' Then, turning to the prioress, he said, 'Reverend Mother, I can't apologise enough for what has happened. It was very foolish and unforgivable of me to involve you. It seems I have placed you and the sisters in grave danger.'

The prioress replied, 'I am no fool, Monsieur Henri,' she said. 'When you came to me yesterday, I knew exactly what I was doing. As long as we keep our heads, and I pray to God that we do, I'm sure this will be resolved. In the meantime, I will offer the Major and his men our protection.'

'Are you sure this is what you want to do?' Harry asked.

'Of course. Now, let's hide your lorries in our two barns, and find a safe place in the abbey for you to stay.' She turned to Sister Mary. 'Let's prepare some hot food for our soldier guests.'

'I'll see you both later,' said Henri. 'Come,' he said to Vanessa, and they were let out of the gate.

CHAPTER 23

They walked on in silence, passing small groups of patrolling German soldiers with rifles slung over their shoulders, tipped with bayonets. The square was still crowded with soldiers, wagons, and cavalry. When they got to the bank, she gave him the bunch of keys, Henri unlocked the main door and they went in. Vanessa went to the counter and picked up the basket of food. 'A strange thing happened,' she said. 'When the Germans arrived, your clerks emptied the tills and shoved the money into their pockets. They told me you had told them to do that. Is that true?'

Henri nodded.

Vanessa frowned. 'But why?'

He took a deep breath. 'You're asking too many questions, Vanessa. It could be dangerous for you.'

She was peeved by his remark and wasn't going to let go. 'Last night you told me that you might be the focus of the Germans' attention. What's going on, Uncle? Why are English soldiers hiding in the abbey?'

'You must never repeat to anyone what you saw,' he replied quietly. 'Never.'

They heard vehicles stopping outside the bank, with orders shouted out in German. Hobnailed boots jumping onto the pavement.

Vanessa was about to speak again when Henri pushed a finger to his lips. 'Shush! Listen,' he said.

The main door opened and in stepped a tall slim man in a long black leather coat wearing a black fedora. Behind him came a bull of a sergeant with a waxed moustache. He and six other German field police in their spiked helmets, wearing distinctive dark green tunics with a hanging silver gorget around their necks, formed a ragged semi-circle behind him. They held their rifles at the ready in case of trouble.

Vanessa stared nervously at the man in the black coat. She judged him to be in his early thirties, and under the brim of his hat, his dark beady eyes shifted from her to her uncle.

'Are you Monsieur Henri Renard, the bank manager?' he growled.

Henri had a sudden feeling of panic. His throat went dry, he swallowed hard and his pulse began to thump. He'd been expecting something like this. 'I-I am,' he replied.

'Good. Let me introduce myself. I'm Captain Max Hoffmann, German Intelligence.' He looked at Vanessa, and in a dismissive tone he said, 'You may leave, fraulein, my business here does not concern you.'

At first, Vanessa didn't move. Then Henri started to usher her towards the door, 'It's better you go,' he said.

As Vanessa went forward, Hoffmann grabbed her arm. 'Wait!' he snapped, and yanking the basket from her, lifted the small napkin that covered the top and looked inside. Vanessa stood there glaring at him.

Henri stepped forward. 'She's my niece,' he said. 'She was just dropping off some lunch for me.'

Hoffmann studied the contents carefully. Satisfied it was all food, he handed it back to her and shrugged. 'One can't be too careful, fraulein.' His lips curled with contempt. 'And as you're related to the bank manager, perhaps it's best you stay.' Hoffmann turned to the big barrel-chested sergeant standing behind him, whose waxed moustache turned up in a comical fashion. 'Fetch the prisoner.'

'Jawohl, Herr Captain,' the sergeant said stiffly, and left, returning thirty seconds later with a Belgian soldier who was frogmarched into the room by two burly field policemen. His head hung low to one side.

Vanessa's heart sank when she saw the state the soldier was in. Clearly he had been roughed up. She could see that his left eye was swollen almost closed; his bottom lip was split, and his short goatee beard was caked in dried blood. His dark hair was also matted in dried blood with some straw sticking to it. The uniform was dirty and speckled with dried mud and blood, and most of his tunic buttons were missing. Obviously, he had been given a hard time during questioning.

Hoffmann took a small red velvet pouch from his pocket and displayed it on the palm of his hand. 'This was found on the prisoner when he was captured,' he said. 'As you can see, it has the Belgian royal coat of arms. Inside are five gold coins. This information was handed to my department. After I questioned this soldier, he admitted he stole it from a huge consignment of royal gold he had escorted to this town.'

Hoffmann placed the red pouch in his pocket, turned to the prisoner and said, 'Is this the bank where you dropped off the gold shipment?'

The Belgian soldier stood there weakly and made no response.

Hoffmann grabbed the soldier's hair and yanked his head up to face them. 'Answer, you dolt!'

Vanessa gasped. Henri bit his lip and laid a hand on her arm, to stop her protesting.

'Well!'

The soldier's bloodshot eyes fearfully looked around the room briefly and he stammered, 'Y-y-yes.'

Hoffmann pointed directly at Henri, saying, 'And was the gold shipment handed to this man, the bank manager?'

The soldier weakly murmured, 'Yes.'

'Louder!' insisted Hoffmann as he tightened his grip.

The soldier's face twisted in pain. 'Ahhhh! Yes! Yes!'

A crooked smile of satisfaction broke over Hoffmann's face. He let go of the soldier's hair, jerked a thumb over his shoulder, and the Belgian soldier was marched back out by the same two burly field policemen.

Hoffmann gave Henri a cold, hard stare. 'So, monsieur, you received the gold shipment. Now you know why I'm here.'

Henri suddenly went cold, but he could feel small beads of sweat breaking out on his brow. With a tremble in his voice, he said, 'But we don't have the gold anymore. It was collected by the English a few hours ago, before you occupied the town.'

They stood in silence for about ten seconds, Hoffmann's steely eyes still watching him. 'Is that so?' Hoffmann said angrily. 'Then what if I told you that for the past two days, I've had cavalry patrols keeping watch on all roads leading into this town – and *nothing*, I repeat *nothing*, has been reported to me of any English vehicle entering or leaving! I will not tolerate my time being wasted with these lies!' He pulled a Luger pistol from his coat pocket, stepped forward and pressed the short barrel into Henri's forehead.

Vanessa dropped the basket to the floor with a crash and went to her uncle's side. 'No! Please, no!' she screamed.

The sergeant rushed forward, grabbed Vanessa by the arms and pulled her away screaming.

Hoffmann changed tack, and turned to Vanessa instead, pushing the Luger's barrel hard into her right cheek. She saw the coldness in his eyes as he looked at her, then turning to Henri, he sneered, 'Your choice.'

'It's– it's the truth,' he said, 'I swear it. I'll show you the bank's vaults. You'll see for yourself they're empty.'

Hoffmann eyed each one in turn and nodded. 'Very well, monsieur. I'll see the vaults. But any tricks by you and I shoot the girl.'

Henri took a deep breath. 'I understand. This way,' he said. They all followed him.

Henri turned up the gas light above the set of stairs that led down to the vaults. Despite the gas lighting, it still looked creepy and shadowy. At the bottom, they came to a wide steel door with a large brass handle in the middle. There were three locks on the left side, one above the other.

Hoffmann had his Luger in Vanessa's back. He sniffed the musty air while reading the black painted gothic lettering above the door, 'Strong Rooms,' he murmured.

Henri unlocked the doors, then swung the brass handle to the side with a loud metallic *clunk*. The wide door weighed over three tonnes, and Henri leaned backwards to get momentum to open it. There was a grille-gate inside that he unlocked, pushing it inwards so they could all go through. He turned up the gas lighting on the inside. There were two large chambers, each about 20 feet square.

Henri turned to Hoffmann and said, 'The room on the left contains archive filing, paperwork, and all the old leather-bound ledgers from the abbey. The room on the right stores safe deposit boxes and our cash. It was here that the gold was stored, but as you can see, it has now gone.'

Hoffmann frowned. 'So I see.' He glared around at the room's emptiness and spotted a large green steel locker in a shadowy corner. 'What's in there?'

'Our cash,' replied Henri. 'We keep it locked until we need to replenish our tills at the front counter.'

Hoffmann went over to the cabinet, pushing Vanessa ahead of him. 'How much cash does it hold?'

Henri replied, 'It can hold half a million Francs. At the moment, there's about 75,000 in there.'

He turned to Henri. 'Open it.'

Henri walked across the room and unlocked the cabinet, swinging open the two doors. Piled on two shelves was the cash in neat bundles.

There was no hidden gold, and Hoffman's frown deepened. Then he turned and gave a quick glance to the sergeant. 'Send someone to the trucks and get some sacks, we'll take the money.'

'You can't take the money; it belongs to the bank!' Henri protested.

'Silence!' Hoffmann pushed Henri to one side.

The two field policemen returned, one with a handful of sacks, and they began emptying the cabinet and bagging the cash.

Once they'd finished, Hoffmann ordered the two policemen back to the trucks. Then he snatched the bank keys from Henri. 'You will be detained until further notice,' he said, then turning to his sergeant he ordered, 'Take him away.'

Vanessa and Henri exchanged worried glances, and she watched in horror as he was led out of the strong room.

'And you, fraulein,' said Hoffmann, his voice suddenly light and convivial, 'you may go about your business.'

'What will happen to him?' she asked.

Hoffmann grinned. 'Your uncle will assist with my investigation as to the whereabouts of the gold.'

'You will beat him, you mean?'

Surprised by her defiant tone, he replied, 'That depends how uncooperative he is. In the meantime, I will have this town searched, end to end if necessary.' He nodded to a field policeman standing by the entrance. 'Escort her out.'

When Vanessa stepped out of the bank, she could see her uncle being marched to the Cloth Hall. She heaved a long, trembling sigh, and tears streamed down her cheeks. She took a handkerchief from her coat pocket to dab at her eyes. Now she had some understanding of why Harry and his men were hiding in the abbey. They'd come to collect the gold. Vanessa composed herself and headed to the abbey. Where else was there to go?

CHAPTER 24

The first thing Packard noticed as he stepped inside the abbey was the smell of the beautifully arranged fresh flowers everywhere – that and beeswax polish. It reminded him of his local church in Mortlake. A large marble crucifix was hanging on the opposite wall in the entrance, and underneath was a dark wooden table where two large church candles were burning, one at each end. Between the candles rested a portrait of the Virgin Mary.

He removed his cap and his men followed suit, walking in a single file behind him. Sister Mary opened a small arched door by the entrance with a large ancient key and led them down a narrow flight of candlelit stone steps into the crypt. At the bottom, a long narrow shadowy passageway, like a mine tunnel, ran the length of the abbey building, with small dark wooden doors on either side. Single candles burning along the wall gave off the faintest of lights, the flames fluttering as they walked past. The place looked and smelt old, and so it was; nothing had changed much since the abbey was first built, over five hundred years ago.

Sister Mary stopped at a door, opened it, and went inside. Packard stopped in the doorway while Sister Mary lit the church candles in the large room that brightened the room and seemed to make it come alive. He sniffed; the room smelt musty and unused and felt devoid of warmth. Stacked against the back wall were dozens of base bedsprings with two piles of iron bed ends, and a stack of thin mattresses. Two tall, ancient-looking wardrobes stood next to them.

Sister Mary turned to Packard and said, 'These are our spare hospital beds. There's plenty for your men. Pillows and bed linen are in the wardrobes. We have a room next door for you and your sergeant.'

'That's very kind of you, Sister Mary,' he replied. 'We are very grateful.'

'In twenty minutes, I will collect you all for a meal,' she said. 'Hot broth and bread.'

Packard nodded, 'Once again, we are in your debt. Thank you.'

Sister Mary smiled and left as the men began to file in.

Campbell got the two NCOs to organise the men with erecting and making the beds.

'Home sweet home,' said Thompson as he reached for a bed end.

'How'd you know? Thought you lived in a cave,' responded Ted Gower.

'You'll be sleeping in a coffin tonight, if you're not careful,' Thompson replied.

Laughter broke out among the men.

'All right, keep it down,' said Corporal Hedges. 'Let's get the beds made and have a hot meal afterwards.'

'What's the meal then, Corp?' asked Clarkson.

Hedges replied, 'I dunno really, but Sergeant Campbell said it's hot, brown, and there's plenty of it.'

'Horse meat and axle grease then,' replied Clarkson.

A voice in the background said, 'Sounds like the stuff my missus cooks up.' More laughter.

Packard made sure that all the men carried their revolvers when they went upstairs to eat. Campbell warned them that he'd wring the neck of any man who used bad language in front of the nuns. They went into a hall with a high ceiling, and sat at a long, highly polished wooden table. The nuns sat at another long table on the other side of the room and were curious about their presence, turning around to look at them whenever they thought they could get away with it. One man stood guard at the entrance while the others ate, just in case they had a visit from the Germans.

After they'd eaten, the Reverend Mother invited Packard to her office to discuss the situation with him and to formulate boundaries and routines. They had just started assessing the situation when there was a knock on the door.

'Come in,' answered the Reverend Mother.

Sister Mary paused in the doorway. 'Vanessa is here, Reverend Mother, and would like to see you.'

'Of course. Come in Vanessa, and sit down,' said the prioress with a warm smile.

Packard stood up as she came in, grabbed a chair from the corner of the room and placed it beside the desk near him. He could see she had been crying.

Vanessa took a deep breath and said, 'They've taken Uncle Henri. They searched the bank and found no gold and arrested him.' She began sobbing. Packard leaned over to comfort her, and she tilted her head towards his shoulder.

The prioress was dismayed. 'So, the Germans have taken him.'

Vanessa raised her head, her cheeks wet with tears. 'Yes. A man called Hoffmann, Captain Hoffman of the German Intelligence Service.' She told them about Hoffmann and what happened. Both listened intently, without comment.

When she finished, Packard turned to the prioress and said, 'This changes things, now that they know about the gold. How can I get a message to my headquarters in France?'

'We have a post office in town, next to the railway station,' the prioress said. 'They have a telegraph. But it would be too dangerous for you to go dressed like that, and at this moment, I cannot risk one of my sisters.'

'Then I will go,' said Vanessa. 'The post office is near to our house.'

'Jacques is in charge of the post office,' said the prioress, 'but would he contact British Headquarters in France on a request by you? And besides that, this town is now occupied by Germans. It would be a big risk for him.'

Packard looked straight at Vanessa. 'Then I must go with you and convince him to do it.'

The prioress considered the matter then said, 'Very well, but you will have to change clothes. We have plenty of old clothes in storage that have been donated to us from the town's better-off families to help the poor. Perhaps, Major, you may find something suitable to wear.'

Packard nodded slowly. 'It sounds like a plan. Where are they?'

'Come,' said the prioress, 'I'll show you where we keep them.'

Twenty minutes later, he was back in the office in a dark blue suit, wearing a white shirt with a high-winged collar. 'How's this look?' he asked.

'Splendid,' replied the prioress. 'It will certainly do.'

Vanessa moved to him and plucked at some fluff on his shoulder. 'You must look your best if you are to be seen in town with me,' she remarked with a smile.

He stood there smiling, looking down at her hand.

'You must have a cover story if you are stopped by the Germans,' said the prioress.

Harry and Vanessa looked at each other, then he suggested, 'I could be your fiancé?'

Vanessa smiled. 'Yes,' she said, 'you'll do fine.'

The prioress nodded. 'And where do you work, if asked?'

Vanessa quickly said, 'I know, he's a lawyer from Poperinghe, the next town down the road. That way it will be difficult for them to check.'

The prioress nodded. 'Good idea, that's settled then,' she said.

There was silence as Harry and Vanessa looked at each other, then the prioress said, 'I will pray for you, and wish you God speed.'

'Thank you,' they both replied.

CHAPTER 25

Vanessa waited for Packard at the abbey entrance while he went off to brief Sergeant Campbell of his intention to contact headquarters in France using the post office in town.

'Make sure the men don't wander around,' he stressed to Campbell, 'and keep a sentry posted just in case.'

'I've already issued a rota for sentry duty, while the others are cleaning and making our rooms tidy. Keeping them busy with a routine down here is key, otherwise they'll end up getting on each other's nerves. Then bad feelings set in and fights start to break out.'

'And that'll never do,' said Packard. 'Keep them busy where possible.'

'Oh, and one more thing before you go, sir, Norris is Catholic and would like to attend Mass with the nuns?'

Packard rubbed his chin. 'Speak to the Reverend Mother and ask if she can accommodate him. But I don't want our presence here compromised because of it, make that clear to them both.'

'Of course, sir.'

Packard picked up his revolver from his bed and put it into his pocket. They shook hands and Campbell wished him good luck.

*

The post office in Ypres had been run by Jacques as long as anyone in town could remember. He had snow-white hair, snow-white bushy eyebrows, and a snow-white bushy moustache, although the edge was stained by nicotine, and he always wore a waistcoat and shirtsleeves when working. When Packard and Vanessa entered, Jacques was sitting behind the counter counting recent payment slips. There was no one else in the post office. He looked up. 'Madame, monsieur, how can I help you?'

Vanessa spoke first. 'My friend here needs to send an urgent message of great importance.'

Jacques raised his eyebrows questioningly. 'Of great importance, you say, Madame. To whom is this urgent message to be sent?'

'British Headquarters in France,' she replied without hesitation.

His white eyebrows rose even higher to meet his white hair. 'British Headquarters!'

Vanessa nodded. 'Yes, that's right, British Headquarters in France. Can you help us?'

Jacques looked at Vanessa and then to Packard. He leaned forward and said softly, 'Are you mad? The town is full of Germans.'

'It's vital that we send this message,' said Packard. 'Will you help us, yes or no?' He winced, hearing how abrupt he sounded.

Jacques leaned back in his chair and scratched his moustache, giving Packard a hard stare. 'And who are you, monsieur?'

'He's my fiancé,' Vanessa replied, 'but never mind that, would it help if I told you my uncle is the bank manager, Henri Renard, and he has been arrested by the Germans.'

Jacques swallowed hard. 'Henri Renard arrested? For what?'

'Do we have to discuss this here?' hissed Vanessa. 'Is there somewhere private to go?'

Jacques looked at them both, scrutinising their faces with a mixture of curiosity and uncertainty. He grunted, stood up, pointed to a door marked "Private". 'In there, both of you.' They went behind the counter and into the room used as an office, feeling the warmth from a fire burning in the grate. It was a cluttered room of chairs and desktops piled with paperwork, ledgers, and files. In the far corner on a desk was a telegraph, and next to it was a large upright safe.

Stern-faced, Jacques asked, 'Now, what's this all about?'

Packard realised his tone had not helped and he didn't want to unsettle Jacques any further. 'We were told that you would help us.'

'By whom?' Jacques retorted.

'By the prioress at the abbey,' said Vanessa quickly.

Jacques raised his eyebrows. 'The prioress?' Vanessa's answer had startled him.

Packard made his tone gentler. 'I can't tell you any details but sending this message would be doing this town and your country a great service.' He handed Jacques a piece of paper with the message written on.

Jacques read the message and looked up, seeming unsure. 'What does all this mean?'

'For your own safety I cannot tell you what it means,' Packard said, 'but it's vital that you send it.'

Jacques scratched the back of his white head. 'It's vital, you say?'

'Very,' Packard replied. 'It has to be sent word for word. Will you do it?'

Jacques scratched the end of his nose for a long moment. Then he looked up to Packard and reluctantly nodded. 'Very well,' he said, and crossed the room, sat down at the telegraph and began tapping.

When he'd finished, Packard asked, 'How long for a reply?'

Jacques shrugged his shoulders. 'The message will have to be relayed from one telegraph station to another. One, maybe two hours, who knows?'

'Would you bring the reply to us as soon as you get it?' Vanessa asked, a note of sweetness in her voice.

He nodded. 'Of course. Where are you staying?'

'At Uncle Henri's house, just around the corner from here. Do you know it?'

'Yes, I know it. Leave it to me, I won't let you down.'

'Thank you,' Packard said. 'Just bear in mind that no one must know of this, otherwise you could be putting people's lives at risk, including your own and those of your family.'

Jacques nodded his head gently. 'I understand, monsieur.'

Packard extended his hand and Jacques shook it firmly. Then he and Vanessa left the post office.

When they approached the house, a large group of German soldiers were in the street knocking on doors. Three were knocking on Henri's door.

'What do you want?' called Vanessa and she approached them.

'You live here?' a German Corporal asked.

'I do, along with my uncle,' she replied.

'Good. We are billeting our soldiers in people's home for the night. You'll be paid for it. You have these two,' he said.

'I think not, Corporal,' she replied. 'There are only two bedrooms here. One for me and the other for my uncle. He's the town's bank manager, and at this moment he's in the company of your commanding officer,' she lied.

The corporal stiffened. 'Those are my orders, madame.'

A young lieutenant approached. 'What is going on here?' He nodded acknowledgment to Vanessa and Packard.

'I was just explaining to this corporal that we only have two bedrooms in the house, for me and my uncle, who is the town's bank manager, presently being entertained by your commanding officer,' Vanessa repeated.

'I see,' said the lieutenant. Then turning to Packard he said, 'And you are?'

'He's my fiancé, Monsieur Antoine Verlinden,' Vanessa cut in. 'A lawyer from Poperinghe.'

The lieutenant nodded his head to Packard. 'Monsieur Verlinden, very nice to meet you.' He turned to face the corporal. 'May I suggest that you find another billet for your men.'

The corporal clicked his heels and led the two soldiers away.

'Thank you, Lieutenant,' Vanessa said with a smile.

The lieutenant clicked his own heels and bowed slightly. 'Madame, monsieur, have a pleasant afternoon,' he said, and strode away.

Vanessa unlocked and opened the door and they both went inside.

'Phew! That was close,' Packard said. 'You think fast on your feet, I grant you that. Careless mistake on my part, I'd not thought of a name for myself. Excellent choice by you, though. You really are quite a girl, I say that for you.'

Vanessa took off her coat and hung it on the back of the door. 'I'll make some coffee,' she said, and went to the kitchen. 'Would you like some cold meat with bread and pickle?' she called out to him.

'That would be lovely,' he replied.

Ten minutes later she came into the parlour, placing a tray on the table of coffee with two plates of food: cold ham, slices of salami, two different cheeses, pickle, bread, and butter. They sat down and started to eat.

'So, you came here to collect the gold?' she asked in a gentle voice.

Packard nodded while buttering his bread. 'Yes, that's right, but so far it's all gone terribly wrong. We're trapped in the abbey surrounded by Fritz, and there doesn't seem to be a way out. Coupled with the arrest of your uncle, it's all a mess.' He put down his knife and took a sip of coffee, then said, 'Add to that, I still haven't seen the gold.' He bit into the cheese and pickle and began chewing.

Vanessa's brow rose in surprise. 'You don't have the gold?'

Packard was chewing on some ham and shook his head. Once he finished chewing, he said, 'Not had a whiff of it so far.'

The answer was so unexpected it left her open-mouthed for a few seconds. Astonished, she said, 'But Uncle Henri told Hoffmann that you collected it before they arrived.'

Packard half-smiled, while still chewing. When he swallowed, he said, 'Not quite right. Your uncle moved the gold to the abbey for safe keeping until we got here. By the time we went to the abbey, Fritz was arriving. So, we haven't seen the gold yet.'

Vanessa's astonishment changed to utter disbelief. 'You mean the prioress is in on this and hiding the gold?'

'Apparently. That's why we were there in the first place, to collect it from the abbey.'

He turned his head away to chew something then looked back at her again. Then he asked, 'How did you get involved in that brothel?'

She sniffed. 'My father is from Belgium and comes from this town. His brother is Uncle Henri. My mother is English from Hove in Sussex. Do you know it?'

'Yes, I do.'

'My father was a businessman. We lived in England until I was fourteen then we moved to Brussels where I studied accounting. My father died suddenly, and my mother was in poor health with her breathing. It was her heart. We had some money, but father had some debts which almost left us penny-less. Our doctor recommended that my mother move to the countryside for the better air quality. Shortly after we stayed a few days at the small village near the bridge. She had a heart attack and died. I was on my own with no real means to support myself. I was desperate and about to return here to my uncle in Ypres for help when I met one of the girls in the village. She took pity on me and introduced me to the Madame running the brothel. She was old and an alcoholic. The accounts were in a mess and this was causing problems amongst the girls, so, to earn my keep I began keeping the books for them – nothing more. It was only supposed to be a short time until I had earned enough money to support myself. I was there nearly twelve years and, since the Madame had drunk herself to death about six years ago, I started to run the place.'

Packard cleared his throat. 'I'm sorry,' he said.

'What do you mean?' she asked.

'About prying into your background at the brothel. I didn't mean to–'

He didn't finish. 'Forget it,' she said, interrupting him. She met his eyes. 'I was going to ask about you and your family and what did you do before the war?'

He nodded with a smile. 'I see, well not much to tell really. My family own a large piece of land and a house alongside the River Thames in Mortlake village. They're market gardeners, one of the biggest producers in the area. I didn't get on with my father who wanted me to study business practice. Instead, I wanted to read languages at university with the intention to travel and work my way around the world. It caused a blazing row with him as you can imagine, so I joined my local regiment to spite him and here I am.'

There was an urgent knocking on the door. Packard and Vanessa froze. More urgent knocking.

Vanessa stood up. Packard put down his knife and fork, feeling the weight of the revolver in his pocket.

'I'd better answer it,' she said. 'It could be Jacques.'

She went to the door and carefully opened it. Jacques pushed in and went straight to the table where Packard was sitting. Vanessa closed the door as Packard rose to his feet.

Jacques shook his head grimly. 'The Germans are pigs,' he said. 'They came bursting into my post office, shoved a gun into my ribs, and demanded the safe. When I opened it, the pig said, "Where's the gold?"'

'Who said that?' asked Vanessa.

'This pig of a German in a black leather coat. "Where's the gold," he kept demanding. "Who's hiding it?" "I know nothing of any gold," I said. He took all the cash from the safe, about 200 francs, they smashed the telegraph, cut some wires, and left.'

Vanessa looked at Packard. 'Sounds like Hoffmann,' she said. 'Was this German on his own?'

'No, he had field police with him. You know, they have a silver gorget around their necks. If ever I get hold of them, I'd like to put a rope around their necks, the filthy German pigs!'

'That's torn it,' judged Packard. 'Now the telegraph's busted, we won't get a reply.'

'Ah, yes, a reply,' said Jacques. 'I nearly forgot. I was just about to close the shop to come here.' He fumbled in his waistcoat pocket and pulled out a slip of paper. He tapped the side of his nose with his finger. 'They don't know about this,' he said, grinning. 'I received this just before the pigs came.' He handed it to Packard.

Packard unfolded the slip of paper and read the message. *'Find a way out at all cost. FSL."*

He showed it to Vanessa and whispered, 'From Churchill. First Sea Lord.'

'The pigs have arrested the mayor and the chief of police. They're holding them in the Cloth Hall.'

'Did the Germans tell you that?' Vanessa asked.

Jacques shook his head. 'No, one of my old customers came in and told me shortly after you left. She saw them being led away.'

Vanessa sighed. 'They've now got all three.'

Packard frowned, not understanding.

'I'll explain later,' she said.

Jacques continued. 'That's not all, the pigs have ordered 6,000 loaves of bread from the baker and taken all the food from the shops. They've paid the shopkeepers in German tokens, to exchange for money when their paymaster arrives tomorrow. Huh! They'll pay them with the cash they stole from my safe, the filthy robbing pigs.'

Jacques took a watch from his pocket and studied the time. 'I must go before it's too late,' he said. 'The pigs have put a curfew on the town tonight, starting in two minutes.'

Packard gasped. 'A curfew! In two minutes!'

Jacques nodded. 'They're starting to clear the streets now, warning everyone to stay inside until 6 a.m. or be shot. I'd best be going.'

Packard held out his hand and Jacques grasped it, giving a firm handshake. 'I'm very grateful to you, Jacques,' Packard said sincerely.

'Well, good luck to you, monsieur, whatever you are doing.'

Vanessa gave Jacques a brotherly hug and thanked him before he left.

She stood facing the door for a few seconds before turning around. Packard was looking at her, almost pleading to be let out.

'You can't risk the curfew,' she said. 'The abbey is too far away, and I couldn't bear to see you shot, not now, not ever.' She lifted her hands to cover her eyes and cried.

She felt the tears running down her cheeks. She looked up and saw him picking up a napkin from the table and he went to her, dabbing her cheeks dry, but she could still feel the wetness in the corner of her eyes. He looked at her and touched the tousled black curls that lay gracefully on her shoulders and curled round her face.

She looked directly into his face as if it were the first time and touched his lips with her fingers, as if to catch the kiss she knew was coming. There was a pause, then she lifted her face to him. She saw the deep blue-grey of his eyes. She felt that mix of fragile innocence and honest desire. She swallowed the lump that came to her throat. She could feel her eyelids flutter and then close. She found his lips and gave a gentle kiss. It wasn't enough.

She murmured, 'Kiss me again,' and crushed against him, pressing her mouth to his.

She felt his hands going to her waist, then to her breasts, and he began to work the buttons on her blouse. His fingers touched her bare skin and she began to tremble. He was now working her breast, his tongue travelling the curves, and it felt like a thunderstorm of pleasure tingling, flashing, building through her body.

She took a deep breath of pleasure as he raised his head onto her smooth shoulder and found the elegant curve of her neck, her pulse throbbing hard.

'I want you,' she whispered. 'Take me, Harry, please take me.' He lifted her up and cradled her in his arms, her dark hair cascading down as he carried her to the stairs, and took her to her room.

CHAPTER 26

Captain Hoffmann was summoned to the hotel overlooking the square, where Generalmajor Wolff Vogel, commanding the German troops in and around the town, had set up his headquarters on the first floor.

Hoffmann clenched his teeth at the thought of meeting him. Vogel has a no-nonsense reputation when dealing with subordinates, especially those from the Home Services, like Intelligence. His brigade had been pulled out of the line to rest after hard and bitter fighting with the British, when they were recalled for this mission to occupy Ypres while the gold shipment was seized, and to safely transport it back to Germany under their escort. Hoffmann would have to report that he still had no idea of the whereabouts of the gold shipment, despite rigorous questioning of the town's leaders.

He approached the hotel from the Cloth Hall, saw the generalmajor's car parked outside, and a guard at the hotel door who checked everyone before they were allowed inside. From the hotel lobby, the generalmajor's adjutant, Leutnant Otto Haas guided him up the stairs to the generalmajor's suite where one room was converted into a makeshift office. Haas knocked on the door.

'Enter!'

Haas opened the door and stepped inside. The generalmajor looked up.

'Herr Generalmajor, I present Captain Hoffmann, as requested.'

Hoffmann stepped in, removed his fedora, stiffened and clicked his heels.

'Herr Generalmajor,' he said sharply. It was the first time he'd met the general, who sat behind a table looking serious, with various paperwork piled on top of an open map. The generalmajor's face was roundish, with a thin duelling scar running down the side of his right cheek, he was probably in his mid-to-late forties. He had a close crop of iron-grey hair that was cut flat across the top. Typical Prussian old school, Hoffmann thought. He noticed that the generalmajor's collar patches, a gold embroidery tassel on a red background, stood out from his plain field-grey tunic, and apart from a line of medal ribbons across his chest, he wore a 2nd class Iron Cross ribbon of black and white stripes through a button hole of his tunic.

The generalmajor sat back in the chair and ran his eyes over him, and he could feel the man's scrutiny, just as he could sense his dislike of his authority over the gold shipment.

'Hoffmann,' Vogel said, his face impassive. 'We meet at last.'

'We do, Herr Generalmajor, and it is a pleasure to meet you.' Hoffmann tried to hide his unease.

Vogel stared, his eyes locked on him, his dark pupils like cold glass. 'So, no gold found at the bank? Now what?'

'I'm questioning the bank manager, the mayor, and the chief of police,' he said, his voice leaping half an octave round the tightness in his throat. 'If anyone knows where the gold is hidden, it will be them.'

'And what have you gleaned so far?'

Hoffmann cleared his throat and replied, 'I've searched the bank, the Cloth Hall, the post office, and I've raided the large jewellery shop in town. Anywhere that holds a large safe. I've even searched the mayor's office, the civic building, and the police barracks, but found nothing. The mayor and the chief of police admit that the gold shipment from Brussels was stored in the bank's vaults but insist they don't know of its whereabouts now. Interestingly, the bank manager claims that English soldiers arrived this morning in two lorries, taking the gold with them just before we entered the town.'

Vogel raised his eyebrows. 'Is that so? Do you believe him?'

'Of course not,' Hoffmann snapped. 'Had the English been here this morning I would have known about it. As you are aware, Herr Generalmajor, I've had every road into this town covered by cavalry patrols, with aeroplanes flying above. Nothing could have entered or left this town without my knowledge.'

'Suppose the bank manager was telling the truth?' said Vogel, his voice flat and toneless.

Hoffmann knew better than to argue with him, and remained silent.

'I say this, Hoffmann, because …' Vogel paused as he glanced down at the papers on his table and picked up a folded sheet of paper. 'Twenty minutes ago, I received this report.' He looked up at Hoffmann. 'About midday, one of your aeroplanes spotted two lorries hiding under trees on the Lille Road heading for this town. It dropped a message to a nearby cavalry patrol to investigate. As the patrol approached the two lorries, they drove off. The patrol gave chase. English soldiers in the back opened fire on them. Eight men in all. Five dead and three wounded.' Vogel offered the report to Hoffmann, who craned forward and took it. Vogel added with a cold grin, 'The reason why I summoned you here.'

Hoffmann unfolded the paper, read it in silence, and felt his heart stop. Tight-lipped and grim-faced, he read the report several times.

Vogel sat back with his arms folded, staring at Hoffmann's grave features and said, 'You look troubled? It seems the bank manager was telling the truth after all. The English beat you to it, eh?'

Hoffmann shook his head slowly and looked up. 'Timings,' he

said. 'The timings are wrong.'

Vogel's eyes narrowed. 'What do you mean, the timings are wrong?'

Hoffmann coughed to clear his throat. 'While I now accept that the English did arrive here first, there is no way they could have loaded the gold and left town before we arrived. Not according to these timings. There just wasn't the time to do all that.' He folded the report and handed it back. 'If I'm right, and I believe I am, the gold is still here, and I intend to find it.'

Vogel sighed. 'I thought you'd searched all the places in town where you expected the gold to be hidden?'

'Exactly, Herr Generalmajor, where I *expected* the gold to be hidden. I was not looking for two lorries. The next search will be different, that I can assure you.'

Vogel unfolded his arms, took a cigarette from a silver box on the table, and lit it. He didn't offer Hoffmann one. 'How different?' Vogel asked.

'I'll consult a map of this town and pick out areas of interest and conduct a search of large storage areas like warehouses, large sheds, stables, schools, barns, that kind of thing. Anywhere that could hide two lorries.'

'And English soldiers,' said Vogel.

'Of course, Herr Generalmajor, and English soldiers.'

Vogel glanced at the paperwork on his desk, shuffled a few papers around and unfolded the report that Hoffmann had given back to him, considering it for a moment. He took a long drag on the cigarette, looked up, blowing smoke into the air. 'We were given twenty-four hours to occupy this town, find the gold and leave.' He sniffed up, then leaned back into the chair. 'The longer my brigade stays in this area, the more vulnerable it will become to the English army who are just a few miles down the road. A breakthrough by them, just two days, and they could quite easily cut us off. We came here with very few rations and had to confiscate all food in the town just to feed my soldiers. There is not enough for two days' rations in this town or for the two-day march back to our lines. Therefore, I took the liberty to contact Berlin by the town's telegraph that you so conveniently captured, giving an update of the situation. Berlin confirmed we're to leave tomorrow lunchtime, with *or without* the gold.'

Hoffmann was surprised and angry and puffed out his chest. 'I'm sure I do not need to remind the Herr Generalmajor that my orders come directly from the Kaiser himself. The capture of this gold is a personal instruction from him, and it could be a huge propaganda weapon to demoralise the Belgian army holding out in Antwerp, and—'

Vogel held up a hand. 'Stop there, Captain. I know all this. That's why I contacted Berlin. They confirmed the Kaiser has been notified and that nothing has changed. My troops leave tomorrow as planned. However, I've been instructed to tell you that *your* mission remains the same. Find the gold or find out what happened to it. That's from the Kaiser himself.'

Hoffmann beamed. 'That's good news, Herr Generalmajor. I have most of tomorrow at least to find the gold.'

'If it's still here,' Vogel sneered, cocking an eyebrow.

For a few seconds Hoffmann said nothing. 'Herr Generalmajor, if that cavalry report is correct, the gold is still here, and I shall find it.'

Vogel nodded slowly. 'Then good luck, Hoffmann,' he said. 'Until tomorrow.'

He returned his attention to the paperwork on his desk.

Hoffmann stiffened, clicked his heels, turned, and made for the door. Just as he opened it, Vogel said, 'Oh, one more thing, Hoffmann?'

Hoffmann turned to face him. 'Herr Generalmajor?'

'Ask Haas to come in.'

'Of course, Herr Generalmajor.'

Haas was in the next room, the door wide open. Hoffmann peered in. Haas was sitting at a table and looked up when he entered.

'He wants to see you,' he said.

Haas acknowledged the instruction with a nod, and Hoffmann left.

*

When Haas entered the room, the generalmajor was standing at the window, hands behind his back, looking down at the square.

'You sent for me, Herr Generalmajor?'

Vogel didn't look round. 'There is a Benedictine abbey behind the bank in the Rue St Jacques, run by Irish nuns. Ask the Reverend Mother if I can take Mass there this evening. Make the arrangements and be sure to tell her I'm Catholic.'

'Of course, Herr Generalmajor. I shall see to it at once.'

CHAPTER 27

The bell was ringing. Sister Margaret went to the gate, pushed the slide across and peered out. A black car was at the gate with a tall young German officer standing beside it.

'Can I help you?' she asked.

The German officer craned his head towards her. 'I'm Leutnant Haas,' he said, 'adjutant to Generalmajor Vogel, commanding the troops in town. I would like to see the prioress.'

'Wait, please,' said Sister Margaret, who turned to face the abbey and made the prearranged signal of a flat hand towards the entrance.

Clarkson, on guard duty at the entrance, saw it, signalled back with his flat hand, and quickly disappeared down the stairs to the crypt, making sure the door was closed behind him.

'Sarge! Sarge!' he called out in a hushed whisper as he ran down the shadowy corridor, his hobnailed boots ringing on the flagstones.

Campbell came out of his room with the Webley in his hand. 'What is it, lad?'

'We've got Fritz at the gate! Sister Margaret is talking to them.'

'Any idea how many and what they want?'

Clarkson shook his head.

By this time everyone was spilling into the corridor and crowding around the doorway.

'Right, stay in your rooms everybody, and stand to!' He looked around. 'Corporal Ratcliffe, where are you?'

'Here, Sarge!'

'Good. Stay here and get the men ready, pistols only. Got that?'

'Leave it to me, Sarge.'

Campbell was spinning his head in all directions again. 'Corporal Hedges?'

'Here, Sarge!'

'Good man. Get your belt kit on and come with me.'

Carrying their pistols at the ready, they went to the bottom of the crypt stairs and climbed them slowly, careful not to make any noise. Campbell felt his heart thumping with every careful step he took until they got to the top. Hedges was right behind him. Campbell's mouth felt dry; he licked his lips, leaned an ear against the door, and listened. Hedges did the same. They heard Sister Margaret talking to the prioress in the abbey's entrance. It was too muffled to clearly understand all what was being said, but they heard footsteps fading away and crunching onto the gravel drive outside the entrance. Then silence. About ten seconds later, they heard footsteps approaching the door again. The handle moved and both Campbell and Hedges stepped back, lifted their pistols, ready to shoot. The door yawned open, flooding daylight into the stairwell, blinding them for a few seconds, and Sister Mary gasped with fright as Campbell and Hedges, both blinking madly, pointed their guns straight at her.

She took a deep breath to counter her shock. 'My goodness,' she crossed herself. 'You gave me such a fright!'

'What's happening?' Campbell said in a whisper. Sister Mary waved her hand, shooing the guns away. Campbell and Hedges withdrew them and he asked again, 'What's happening?'

She dropped her voice. 'There's a German officer at the gate who wants to speak to the prioress,' she said. 'Stay in your rooms and don't come out until we tell you.' With that, she closed the door and plunged them back into darkness.

'Living in this crypt is like being buried alive,' Hedges whispered.

'We will be if we get caught,' Campbell replied. 'Come on, let's wait at the bottom of the steps.'

*

The gate was opened and the black car drove in, stopping at the entrance to the abbey. The prioress was waiting. Haas got out from the back of the car and approached the prioress while peeling off his grey gloves. He looked immaculate in his black spiked helmet with the spread of a silver eagle's wings covering the front, and the lanyard curled around his right shoulder of his tunic, denoting him as an adjutant. He clicked the heels of his black shiny boots, saluted, and gave a slight bow. 'Reverend Mother, I'm Leutnant Otto Haas. Thank you for seeing me.'

The prioress nodded and extended her hand. Haas shook it firmly.

'How can I help you, Leutnant?'

Ten minutes later, Sister Mary opened the crypt door and went down the steps. Campbell and Hedges were still waiting at the bottom. 'It's alright,' she said, 'the German has gone.'

'What did he want?' Campbell asked.

'Their general wants to take Mass here this evening, in about thirty minutes' time. The Reverend Mother has asked that you all stay down here and keep very quiet until the general goes.'

Campbell nodded. 'Very well. Any news of Major Packard?'

Sister Mary shook her head. 'We suspect your major is hiding in town with Vanessa, possibly at the house of Monsieur Renard, until the curfew ends in the morning.'

Campbell nodded. It sounded plausible. He waited until she had gone and then left Hedges there on guard while he went back along the corridor to their rooms.

*

Generalmajor Vogel arrived on time, his staff car crunching on the gravel drive as it swept in from the gate. The driver opened the door and Vogel got out from the back with Haas, who introduced him to the prioress. They shook hands warmly, and she led him and Haas into the abbey for the service. Haas handed their spiked helmets to the driver to look after, then stood guard just inside the entrance.

*

Campbell and his men remained hidden in the crypt below, lying on their beds, talking in whispers.

'I don't think much of all this religious lark,' Thompson hissed 'Here we are, hiding from Fritz, and all this time Fritz is up there praying to God, wanting to kill us all and win the war, the same as our bloody generals, I suppose.'

'There's got to be something in it,' reasoned Gower. 'Under fire I pray all the time that I get through. It's like a comfort, something to hold on to when I'm scared.'

'Well, Norris is a believer, ask him,' Clarkson volunteered.

Thompson looked around the shadowy room. 'Norris? Where are you? Norris?'

Campbell was in the next room with Ratcliffe and Hedges when Thompson appeared at the door.

'Hey, Sarge, any idea where Norris is?'

'He's with you, isn't he?'

'No, Sarge.'

Campbell froze, took a deep breath, slapping his hand to his forehead, 'Christ! I forgot, I sent Norris up to help the sisters with this evening's meal.' He glanced first at Ratcliffe, and then Hedges. 'He's up there now, in the kitchen! I'm tempted to go up there and get him.'

'No,' said Ratcliffe. 'It could make matters a lot worse. Let's hope the nuns warn him, so that Norris can hide somewhere safe until

Fritz goes.'

'Different if Norris gets caught,' said Hedges, 'there'd be no choice, we'd have to shoot our way out.'

Campbell sighed deeply. 'You're both right, of course. I suppose we'll just have to sit it out and wait. But just in case, make sure the men are ready.'

CHAPTER 28

Forty minutes later, the service finished and the prioress and Sister Margaret escorted Vogel to his car. The driver stiffened at the entrance as the generalmajor slowly walked by, pulling on his grey gloves. He handed the generalmajor's helmet to Haas, then quickly went to the car, opened the back door, and stood at attention. Vogel turned to the Reverend Mother.

'A delightful service. It gave me a spiritual uplift from my present duties. I'm grateful for your time. Please pass on my sincere thanks to all your staff. They are wonderful.'

'It's been our pleasure to have you join us,' replied the prioress. 'I trust we will see you again soon.'

Haas handed him his spiked helmet, and Vogel carefully placed it on his head, looking every inch an old Prussian officer.

'I'm afraid not,' he replied. 'My orders are to leave by tomorrow lunchtime.' He saluted. 'Goodbye, Reverend Mother, until we meet again.'

A truck swung quickly into the open gate with some speed, skidding to a halt behind the generalmajor's car, sending a shower of stones everywhere. Hoffmann jumped from the cab onto the gravel drive, pistol in hand, and immediately froze when he recognised the car and saw the generalmajor standing behind it with the prioress. The field police jumped down from the back of the truck, along with the sergeant with the waxed moustache, and stood behind him, their rifles at the ready.

Vogel narrowed his eyes at Hoffmann, who now stood, grim-faced.

'What is the meaning of this interruption?' Vogel barked out. 'What do you think you are doing? Explain yourself, Hoffmann!'

Hoffmann, red-faced, stiffened, and at first seemed to have some difficulty getting his words out. 'H-Herr Generalmajor, I-I'm merely carrying out a search of all premises in this town that have a large enough space to store two lorries.'

Vogel's eyes narrowed even more. 'How dare you suggest that this sacred convent is being used for subversion. Have you no shame, Hoffmann?'

'Herr Generalmajor, please let me explain,' Hoffmann replied, like a man about to face execution and pleading for his life. 'I apologise for my sudden entrance, but everything about this place is ideally suited to hide two lorries full of gold. It has the space, the secrecy, barns, large sheds, a building that could hide a small army, it's next to the bank and all this run by Irish nuns. Just think about it for a moment? It is the last place in town anyone would suspect.'

Vogel stood quietly for a few seconds, his arms rigid at his sides, fists clenched into tight balls. At first he didn't know how to react in front of the nuns to what Hoffmann was accusing them of, and he began looking around; firstly at the prioress and Sister Margaret, who were both standing serenely behind him, then at the abbey building, the two barns and large sheds dotted around, the beautifully kept garden with its large space to grow vegetables, a quiet cemetery in the far corner, the back of the bank building on the other side of the perimeter wall, and of course, the sisters themselves. All Irish. To Vogel, it all appeared peaceful and idyllic, and not corrupted by man, politics, or war. The whole place was spiritual and given to God's good work. It was absurd, what Hoffman was suggesting. It was unthinkable.

He turned to face Hoffman, his voice dangerously calm. 'May I suggest, Herr Hoffmann, that you take your men to look elsewhere. This abbey is not to be desecrated by your foolery.'

Hoffmann swallowed hard as Vogel's eyes narrowed and bore into him. The silence stretched, and Vogel read the man like a book. Tomorrow, the generalmajor would be leaving with his troops. Hoffman would do as he pleased then, tear the sacred place apart if he had to, grubbing for gold.

But not today. Not while he stood here, freshly blessed by God and standing between Hoffman and the fulfilment of his heathen intent. *Not today*, Vogel said with his eyes. *You will not do this thing while I am here.*

Hoffmann broke the awkward silence, he clicked his heels and gave a slight bow to the generalmajor. He turned to his sergeant behind him. 'Get the men back on the truck, quickly!'

The sergeant barked out orders and the field police turned around and scrambled back onto the truck. Hoffmann replaced the pistol in his pocket, climbed into the open cab and sat stony-faced as the engine revved up, and the truck turned on the gravel drive and headed out through the gate.

Recovering control of his anger, Vogel turned to the prioress.

'Forgive their nonsense, Reverend Mother, that type put a dark stain on the reputation of the German army.'

The prioress stared at him for a few seconds, then managed a little forced smile. 'I'm grateful for your support, Generalmajor,' she said, 'and pleased that you were here. I hope we have the pleasure to welcome you to our abbey for prayers again.'

Vogel smiled back warmly and gave a slight bow. 'It would be my honour, Reverend Mother. And rest assured, you will not be bothered with the likes of him again, certainly not while I am in command here.'

He threw up a salute, turned, and got into the back of his car. The driver closed the door, got in behind the wheel, started up the engine, turned a circle in the drive and left through the gate.

The prioress and Sister Margaret went forward and closed the gate together. Sister Margaret let out a sigh of relief and crossed herself. 'A close call, I think. I was trembling inside so bad I almost passed out when Hoffmann accused us of hiding the gold, along with the English soldiers. His eyes looked so cruel.'

The prioress nodded as she crossed herself, and lifted the crucifix hanging from her waist to her lips, kissing it. 'And we can all thank God for sending Generalmajor Vogel for evening prayers. But still, we can't take any chances. Hoffmann will return, only next time we won't have Generalmajor Vogel to protect us.'

Sister Margaret clasped a trembling hand to her neck. 'But what can we do, Reverend Mother? Every minute the English soldiers stay in the abbey puts us more in danger. We must do something.'

Someone coughed behind them, and they turned to see Sister Mary, the youngest of the nuns.

'Can I let Sergeant Campbell know the Germans have gone?' she asked.

The prioress smiled. 'Of course, my child, and bring the sergeant to my office. I need to speak to him.'

Sister Mary bowed respectfully and shuffled away.

*

Norris was standing in front of Campbell when Sister Mary came for him. He was explaining that he'd been hidden in the toilet of the large hall by Sister Teresa when they were told about the Germans' visit. Campbell just grunted and accepted that it was the right thing to do. But he was still worried about it, and it made him think that he must have a better plan of action for when it happened again.

Sister Mary led Campbell to the prioress's office. He was not surprised when she told him what had happened, and about Hoffmann in particular. He sat and listened, his face passive, and accepted that the game was up. Hoffmann, whoever he was, was on to them, so they would have to leave tomorrow.

'It's a risk, I know, but we'll have to be loaded and ready for the moment the Germans leave town,' Campbell said. 'We can't afford to waste time knowing that Hoffman could be back at any time after that.'

'I agree,' the prioress said. 'First thing in the morning, we'll transfer the gold onto the lorries and wait ready until we're certain the Germans have left town.'

'I just hope that Major Packard has returned by then,' added Campbell.

The prioress nodded. 'Of course. But if Major Packard doesn't return for some reason, what will you do?'

Campbell glanced at the crucifix on the wall. 'If he's hiding while the curfew is on, he'll be back sometime after it ends, I should think. If he doesn't show for some reason, I'll have no choice but to go ahead without him.' He said that to give comfort to the prioress that they would leaving tomorrow either way. But deep down, he knew he would not leave the town until he found out what had happened to his officer.

CHAPTER 29

Hoffmann loosened his collar and smiled grimly.

Henri Renard was tied by rope to a chair, and now on his side, face down on the cold damp flagstone floor, his matted grey hair caked in blood, his face swollen.

Hoffman got down on his knees, his head almost level with Henri's. 'Why put yourself through this?' he whispered softly in his ear. 'Do you think I enjoy doing this to you? Just answer my questions and all this unpleasantness will stop.'

Henri groaned.

Hoffmann stood up and gestured to the sergeant with the waxed moustache. The sergeant grabbed the chair from behind, and, with another field policeman, they lifted the bank manager back up to the sitting position. They stood each side, both big men, their faces blank. The sergeant held a small rubber cosh in his hand.

Hoffmann stood in front of him. Even compared to his experiences of having people tortured back in Germany, Henri was a pitiful sight. His bloodied bare feet showed dozens of small round burn marks and his toes had been slowly crushed by the twisting heel of a hobnailed boot. His face was very white, with day-old stubble covering his chin, and rivulets of blood were streaking down from his head wounds. His right eye was swollen shut; his left was half-closed and bloodshot like a red marble. His nose, or what was left of it, was smashed flat like that of a bare-knuckle boxer, and caked in congealed blood; both lips were split and bleeding, and he'd lost most of his front teeth.

Henri's head hung low, with strings of phlegm mixed with blood dangling from what was left of his nose and mouth, and the only sound in the room was his ragged breathing. The flagstone floor beneath him was splattered with droplets of blood, phlegm, froth, and bits of teeth.

The small room had once been part of the medieval prison complex in the basement of the Cloth Hall and was now being used by Hoffmann to torture the bank manager to make him confess the whereabouts of the gold shipment. The cell was lit by candles, throwing shadowy light across the dark brick walls covered in damp and mildew. It stank of neglect, like old rubbish left in the rain of an alleyway; dead, forgotten, and rotting.

Henri had been suffering for the six hours since Hoffmann had returned from his confrontation with Generalmajor Vogel at the abbey. He was convinced the abbey was hiding the gold, and it was more than just a mere hunch. There were too many coincidences for him to be wrong. At first, Henri Renard had admitted to working on the abbey's accounts, and Hoffmann knew now that he had lied to him about the timing of the arrival of the English to collect the gold. So, it was likely the gold was still in town. From local enquiries, he'd discovered that the nuns enjoyed the support from the Belgian royals, through their charity work in the local area. Hoffmann had searched every other space in town big enough to hide the English with their lorries, and the bank backed onto the abbey's perimeter wall, where a small door gave access into its garden. That garden and that building had space enough to hide two lorries and a group of English soldiers – and he could not ignore the fact that the nuns were Irish. But he needed the confession of the bank manager if he were to raid the abbey while the general was still in town. Once the army left, there would be too little time so it was vital that he get the confession now.

Hoffmann craned down close to Henri's ear. 'Is the gold in the abbey?'

Henri said nothing.

'Are the English hiding in the abbey with the gold?'

Henri still said nothing.

Hoffmann bit his lip in frustration, then grabbed Henri's hair and yanked his head back. 'Answer me, you swine!'

Henri's blood-streaked face twisted in pain, but he said nothing.

Hoffmann let go, stepped back and looked to the sergeant, giving him a nod.

The sergeant lifted his right arm high above him and swung it down to deliver a stinging blow to the right side of Henri's face. It hit with a sickening *smack*.

Henri screamed and rolled over, but the field policeman behind him grabbed the back of the chair, stopping it crashing to the floor.

Hoffmann nodded again and the sergeant delivered another sickening blow to the left side of Henri's swollen face, and he let out another agonised scream.

'Answer me, you dolt!' Hoffmann yelled in frustration. He began pacing up and down in front of him. 'Where is the gold?'

Henri grunted something unintelligent and began coughing, trying to clear his throat of the blood and mucus that was forming there, and then gave out a slow, pitiful groan.

Hoffmann stopped pacing to glare at him, huffing and puffing bitterly. He would try the soft approach again. He bent down to Henri's face, close now, staring at him, hearing his rasping breath. Blood and phlegm were constantly dripping on the floor. 'Is the gold in the abbey?' whispered Hoffmann again, waiting for him to answer the question. 'Tell me what I want to know, and all this pain will stop.'

Henri said nothing, not even a groan.

Hoffmann stood up and grimaced. He gave a nod, and the sergeant delivered another blow to the left side of Henri's face that sent him crashing sideways. His head hit the flagstone floor with a resounding *crack!*

They all heard it – and for five seconds, they stood stock still.

A pool of blood, like a small crimson lake about the size of a Victorian dinner plate, was slowly spreading out from under Henri's head.

Hoffmann took a sharp breath and craned forward for a closer look. He could see that Henri's mouth was partly open in a mocking half-grin, and he didn't appear to be breathing or making any noise. He wasn't sure if the bank manager was alive or dead. He kicked him in the stomach and got no reaction. He stood there, examining him, tilting his head to one side, hoping to see some sign of life, a twitch, a blink of an eye, a groan – but there was nothing, no sound, no movement.

The sergeant looked at Hoffmann. 'Is he still alive, Herr Captain?'

There was a long silence, about ten seconds before Hoffmann shook his head. 'I don't know,' he answered. 'Lift him up and let's see.'

They grabbed the back of the chair and raised it to the sitting position. The body was lifeless and hanging forward in the chair. Blood poured down the face from the gaping cut on the head, as well as from the nose and ear. Hoffmann took a closer look one more time and grimaced. It was obvious that the skull had badly cracked in the fall. There were no more questions to ask. Henri Renard was dead.

Hoffmann sighed in exasperation and threw his arms up angrily. 'Wonderful!' he said. 'Now the swine is dead.'

The sergeant looked worried, as if he might be blamed. 'Herr Captain?'

Hoffmann waved a hand, 'Not your fault, Sergeant. That swine had it coming. This was never going to end well. Perhaps I was a little enthusiastic, but had he confessed I would have had to kill him anyway.'

Hoffmann pondered, to organise his thoughts. What to do next? Without the bank manager's confession that the Irish nuns were hiding the English and the gold, there was no way he could go to the generalmajor for permission to raid the abbey. He took off his fedora and ran his fingers through his dark hair. After a short pause he said to the sergeant, 'Get the mayor and the chief of police in here. I want them to see the body.'

'You wish to interrogate them here, Herr Captain?'

Hoffmann paused to draw breath, then his face slanted into a smile and said, 'No, just to scare them a little.'

The field policemen dragged in Rene Colaert and Marcel du Mont, their hands tied behind their backs. Both men were in bare feet, looking shabby and unshaven. They had been deprived of sleep, water, and food, and had been subject to their own rounds of questioning by Hoffmann. So far though, they had not been beaten. They stood in the dank cell room for several seconds, their eyes wide with horror, and their mouths open with shock, staring down at the gruesome sight of the tied up and badly beaten body of their friend, Henri Renard.

Hoffmann just stood there, his face impassive, allowing their fear to do the work for him. Colaert had tears in his eyes at his friend's unspeakable suffering before his death.

'It's like this, gentlemen,' Hoffmann eventually said in a casual tone, 'I need to find the gold, and I know it's still in this miserable town. So, not to waste anymore of my time looking for it, this is what we'll do.' Hoffmann stepped into their line of vision. 'You,' he pointed to Marcel, 'will be released. And you,' he pointed to Colaert, 'will remain here as my hostage.' Hoffmann walked up to Marcel, leaned into his face and stared into his eyes. 'You have three hours to find out where the gold is being hidden, along with the English soldiers, and to report back to me.' He then went behind Marcel and leaned over his shoulder and said softly in his ear, 'Otherwise, the mayor of this town will end up looking as gruesome as the bank manager. You understand that?'

Marcel slowly nodded his head.

'Good, and if you warn the English when you find them, you too will end up like this. You understand that also?'

Again, Marcel slowly nodded his head.

'Excellent! We have co-operation at last! You are the chief of police for this town so use your contacts. Otherwise ...' He turned quickly and gestured to the bloodied body on the floor, then with a cruel smile he said, 'I'm sure you understand.'

He saw Marcel look at Colaert, and there was fear in their eyes. Both their faces were pale with that look of dread. The look of men about to face their execution.

'You'll be released when the curfew ends in two hours' time,' Hoffmann told Marcel. He jerked his head at the guards and they dragged them both back to their cells.

CHAPTER 30

He heard footsteps, then a bolt sliding across his cell door. The door opened and the sergeant with the waxed moustache stepped in, with another big man behind him.

'Six o'clock,' he snarled, 'time to go.'

Marcel pushed himself up from the damp floor, wiping his hands on his trousers as he stepped out. The sergeant pushed him along the gloomy basement corridor, his bare feet padding along the flagstone floor, and up a set of stone steps to the floor above. A field policeman with a dark bushy moustache sat at a table and handed him his things: the belt to his trousers, his socks and boots, some small change, matches, a box of cigarettes, and his wallet. Marcel took them and sat down on a nearby chair to pull on his socks and boots. The sergeant and the other big man stood either side of him. When he was ready to go, they dragged him up, frog-marched him into another room, then shoved him out of a single door at the back of the Cloth Hall.

Marcel cursed them under his breath. He was the chief of police after all, and had an important position in this town, yet it counted for nothing to them, and they treated him like dirt. He yawned and looked up at the grey sky. It was drizzling. He felt cold, he turned up the collar of his coat and took deep breaths to gulp the fresh, sweet morning air deep into his lungs. He lived outside town, too far to walk if he was to wash and change his clothes and get back again in the time allowed. So, the first thing he thought of doing was to go to the house of Henri Renard and tell his niece that her uncle was dead; it would be a decent thing to do. Perhaps there he could have some coffee for his parched throat, clean himself up, and figure out what he was going to do next. As he headed to the house, he searched his pockets for his matches and cigarettes, found them, lit one, and took one long drag that sent him into a spasm of coughing. He took two more drags, coughed some more and threw the cigarette onto the road. The smoking had made his throat feel worse. He needed coffee.

*

Vanessa was startled awake by a fist urgently banging on the street door. Packard sat up in bed and quickly reached for the Webley on the small table beside him. 'Who the hell's that?' he said.

Vanessa quickly climbed out of bed and threw on a dressing gown. 'It's probably Uncle Henri. The Germans must have released him.'

'Doesn't he have a key?'

Vanessa went to the bedroom door. 'Never mind that, get up quickly,' she hissed. 'I don't want him to find you in my bed!'

Packard swung his legs out of bed, pulling on trousers and a shirt.

Vanessa made her way down the stairs to more urgent banging on the door. She unlocked it with a key and opened it. She gasped. Standing there was Marcel, in a dishevelled state, and not her uncle as she was expecting.

'I need to speak to you,' he said. 'Can I come in?'

She hesitated for a moment before she allowed him through and closed the door behind him. His clothes were damp and dirty, his face needed a good wash and he smelt like old food. He looked as if he'd slept in the gutter all night.

Once inside, he turned to face her. 'Thank you for letting me in, Vanessa. I'm sorry for my appearance but I've been imprisoned by the Germans since lunchtime yesterday, and they've just released me. They're not good hosts, as you can see.'

She stared at him for several seconds, wondering what condition her uncle might be in. 'If you've come to see Uncle Henri, I'm afraid he was also arrested, along with the mayor.'

Marcel nodded. 'I know,' he said, 'that's why I've come to see you.'

Floorboards began creaking above from footsteps. They both glanced to the ceiling. 'You have company, Vanessa?'

Vanessa lowered her eyes. 'He's a friend.'

'I see. Do I know him?'

She shook her head.

'Is he a local man?'

She shook her head again.

'Just a lover?'

She looked up angrily. 'Enough questions.' She scowled. 'What is your business here?'

Marcel held up his grubby hands. 'I'm sorry,' he said, 'I didn't mean to pry. Your private life is your business, and I've no right to ask, I know, but I need to speak to you alone.' He jerked his thumb upwards. 'So lover boy will have to go, whoever he is.'

She wrinkled her nose and dropped her voice. 'He can't. Well, not at the moment.'

Marcel looked at her closely. 'The curfew has ended,' he said, 'why can't he go home?' The question was intense.

'Look,' she said, her voice guarded, 'I'll make some coffee and explain. You look as if you could do with some. May I suggest you go to the washroom at the back to clean and tidy up? There are some of Uncle's clean shirts there, use one if you like. I'm sure under the circumstances he won't mind, just as long as you return it. You know how he likes his shirts, pristine.'

Marcel nodded. 'I will do that,' he said, 'and thanks,' but deep down he felt guilty.

After he had washed as best he could, he returned to the parlour. Vanessa had laid a tray of coffee and some cold ham. 'The bread is a little stale,' she remarked, and they both sat down at the table.

Full of apprehension, she asked, 'Why are you here?'

Marcel bit his bottom lip. 'Look, Vanessa, there's no easy way to say this, but your uncle has died, at German hands.'

Vanessa gasped, placing a hand to cover her mouth. Tears immediately formed in her eyes, then ran down her cheeks. 'Dead? What happened?' And then a picture formed in her mind of that beaten Belgian soldier in the bank, and she instinctively knew what had happened to her dear uncle. She threw both hands up to hide her face and began sobbing and wailing uncontrollably.

Marcel let her cry for about half a minute before he reached out to lay his hand on her shoulder, to give her comfort, and as he did so he felt the cold end of a pistol barrel pushed hard behind his right ear.

'Don't turn around,' said a voice behind him. 'One false move and I'll blow your brains all over breakfast. Just do as I say when I tell you.'

Marcel froze, said nothing, just nodded. From the tone of the voice behind him, he knew it was meant.

The pistol barrel pushed harder. 'Now slowly and carefully place both your hands on the table in front of you, where I can see them.'

Slowly and very deliberately, Marcel placed his other hand on the table in front of him.

The man slowly stepped around to face him, tightening his finger on the trigger as he did so, the pistol pointing directly at Marcel's head. He stood at the side of Vanessa, who was wiping her eyes with a napkin.

'Who is he?' he asked, very tense.

She looked up at the man, her cheeks streaked with tears. 'It's all right,' she said, 'he's a friend of my uncle.'

'Yes, but who is he?'

Marcel answered quickly, 'I'm Marcel du Mont, Chief of Police.'

The man raised his eyebrows in surprise, then said to Vanessa, 'You trust him?'

'Oh, of course, Harry,' she replied, 'he's with us. He helped my uncle hide the gold in the abbey.'

Harry gave a deep sigh of relief and lowered the pistol slowly to his side. 'My apologies,' he offered. 'When I heard Vanessa crying, I thought you were hurting her in some way.'

Marcel nodded his head, then shrugged. 'I was bringing her bad news about her uncle.'

Packard glanced at Vanessa, then back to Marcel. 'What have the Germans done to him?'

'He died during interrogation,' Marcel said, wiping his hand across his mouth. 'The Germans showed me his body. He was a very brave man; he gave nothing away.'

Packard tilted his head back and sighed. 'Oh, no,' he said. 'The bastards.' Then, turning to Vanessa, he leaned down and hugged her tightly. 'I'm so sorry for you, Vanessa, so, so very sorry.' They hugged for a long minute, Vanessa sobbing most of the time.

When she calmed herself, Packard stood up, still clutching her hand. 'I'm feeling better now,' she said kindly to him, forcing a small smile. 'The moment I set eyes on Hoffmann at the bank,' she said, 'deep down I knew it would somehow end like this.' She kissed Packard's hand softly, then let go. 'Come, sit down, have some coffee,' she said to him, drying her tears with the napkin.

Packard placed the Webley in his trouser pocket, pulled a chair from under the table and sat down.

There was an awkward silence as they began to eat and drink coffee before Marcel said, 'And what is your stake in all this, monsieur?'

Packard finished chewing the stale bread and replied, 'Purely a military one. What's yours?'

Marcel began looking questioningly at the dark suit Packard was wearing, and then he said, 'You're military?'

Packard nodded and then drank some coffee to soften the stale bread in his mouth.

For about ten seconds, Marcel sat there open-mouthed and then said, 'You are English army?'

Packard nodded. 'Indeed, I am,' he replied. 'I've come to rescue the gold.'

'Let me introduce you,' said Vanessa. 'This is Major Harry Packard of the Richmond Regiment.'

Marcel leaned back in his chair and sat there for about twenty seconds, gazing at them both with disbelief. 'You do know the Germans are aware of your presence in town?' he asked.

Packard stopped chewing and glanced at Vanessa, who also stopped eating. 'How do you figure that out?' he said. 'Henri Renard told Hoffmann that we had collected the gold and gone.' He looked at Vanessa for reassurance.

'That's right,' Vanessa confirmed. 'I was there in the bank when Uncle told him.'

'Then things have changed,' Marcel said. 'When I was seen by Hoffmann, the questions always centred on English soldiers in two lorries collecting the gold from the bank and hiding somewhere in town when the Germans arrived.'

Packard narrowed his eyes. 'So what did you tell him?'

Marcel shrugged. 'The truth of course. I had no idea that you were here until now. I thought Hoffmann had got that bit wrong. I told Hoffmann I was aware the gold was in the bank, waiting to be collected by the English, but had no idea what happened to it after that. The last bit I lied, of course.' He looked at Vanessa. 'Remember, I helped carry the gold into the abbey with your uncle and Rene Colaert, just in case the Germans came before the English got here.'

'Who's Rene Colaert?' Harry asked.

'The mayor, and right now he is being held hostage by Hoffmann until I deliver you and the gold to him.'

'So that's why you've been released this morning?'

Marcel nodded. 'And if I don't deliver you and the gold to Hoffmann, the mayor will end up like Henri – beaten to death.' He looked at Vanessa. 'I'm sorry,' he said, 'but that's how it was.'

Vanessa lowered her head, closed her eyes and nodded, swallowing hard.

'If Hoffmann thinks we're still hiding in town,' Packard said, 'why isn't he out looking for us? Why is he sending you?'

'Obviously, he can't find you,' replied Marcel. 'He told me to use my police contacts in town and report to him in three hours.' He looked at the clock on the mantel shelf above the fireplace. 'That was at six this morning, fifty minutes ago.'

Packard glanced at the clock and pushed his fingers through his hair while he weighed up his options. 'We've got until nine then?' he said.

'To do what?' Marcel asked.

'To get out of town with the gold.'

'And how do you think you're going to achieve that?'

'Load up and drive out – come what may, we'll just go for it and take our chances, whatever they may be.'

Marcel gave Packard a cold stare. 'Just like that, eh? And what about the Germans? What about Rene Colaert?'

Packard lifted his hands. 'I know, I know, but what else can I do? I can't sit here and wait it out. Hoffmann is bound to find us in the next few hours, and as for Colaert, well, there's nothing I can do for him. He'll have to take his chances – just like all of us.'

'Just like Henri Renard had to take his, you mean?'

Packard bit his lip and nodded slowly, then looked at Vanessa; there was no anger in her eyes, just sadness. 'Just like Henri Renard,' he repeated.

'It's a fool's plan,' said Marcel, 'but we don't have many choices. I'll have to go back to Hoffmann at nine and tell him where you are. You just make sure you've gone by then.'

'Why? Come with us. I'm taking Vanessa with me.' He looked into her eyes. 'You can't stay here,' he said to her. 'Not now.'

She gave a slight uncertain nod.

Marcel shook his head. 'Thanks, but no thanks. I'll take my chances here. Besides, I would feel I was deserting Rene. I couldn't do that.'

'I understand that,' Packard said. 'It's very noble of you, not to mention very brave.'

Marcel shrugged. 'And foolish,' he said. 'Don't forget, very, very foolish.'

'That's settled then,' Packard said. 'Vanessa and I will go straight away and get things organised.'

Marcel slowly stood up and offered his hand. 'Then good luck, Major, I think you'll need it.'

Packard stood up. 'Are you sure you won't come with us?'

Marcel shook his head. 'I can't. Whatever happens I must stay.'

Packard shook his hand firmly. 'Then my thanks, and good luck to you.'

'Thank you,' replied Marcel.

Vanessa stood up and gave Marcel a hug. 'Take care,' she said, and tears began rolling down her eyes.

CHAPTER 31

Sergeant Campbell was worried. It was 7:15 a.m., an hour and fifteen minutes since the curfew had ended, and still there was no sign of his officer. That was a constant thorn in his mind, and one he could not shake off. Understandably, the nuns wanted them to go now that Hoffmann had shown an interest in searching the abbey, but he couldn't see himself leaving without looking for his officer, especially at the bank manager's house where the Reverend Mother believed he was hiding, along with Vanessa. Over his shoulder he could hear the voices of Corporal Hedges and Ratcliffe, and he turned to see the two NCOs getting the men lined up in the corridor outside their room, ready to be taken for breakfast in the hall upstairs.

'All their kit packed, and the room cleaned and ready?' he asked.

'All done, Sarge,' replied Ratcliffe, 'and the room is ready for your inspection.'

Campbell knew that everyone was eager to get their breakfast, load up the gold, and get out of this claustrophobic crypt, even if it meant running the gauntlet of German fire in their escape from town. After his pep-talk to them this morning about the situation so far and what they were going to do, everyone felt the same, on edge but ready to go.

Campbell turned to Hedges. 'Sentries posted and briefed?'

'Yes, Sarge, by me. The two sentries are Steed and Joyce, as you suggested. They know the drill. They'll get breakfast while on guard.'

Campbell nodded. He wanted the two drivers on guard so that his own men could relax a little before they had to start humping heavy gold aboard the two lorries, not to mention maybe having to fight their way out of town. He didn't think the drivers would be used to much labour, and that way they could get rested before their long drive to Dunkirk.

If they got out of town in one piece.

Once the men filed their way along the corridor to the dining hall upstairs, he went to inspect the room they'd occupied, making sure it was as clean and tidy as they found it; with the bed ends neatly stacked against the far wall, the used linen folded and piled in one corner as requested by the nuns, and the floor swept clean. Their small-packs and webbing were laid out in a neat line along the floor, their rifles leaning against them. He was pleased that the two NCOs had made sure the men had made a good job of it.

All the men carried their revolvers to breakfast, despite the Reverend Mother's disapproval of guns at mealtime, but she didn't make a fuss when she saw them queuing for breakfast.

When he entered the hall, the Reverend Mother was standing by the food counter looking at the soldiers collecting their breakfast. He went across to her, hoping she might have some news about Major Packard and Vanessa. She acknowledged him with a polite smile as he approached, and he saw her take a deep breath as if to ready herself for his expected questions, but he realised she had second guessed what he was going to ask her. She said softly, 'Good morning, Sergeant, no news yet about Major Packard, but I'm sure we'll hear soon.'

Campbell saw her blue eyes shining with disappointment as she spoke and wondered what disappointment his own eyes were revealing. For a moment, he felt desperately alone. 'Thank you, Reverend Mother. Either way, I intend to be out of here this morning as soon as we have loaded the gold.'

'When you've had breakfast, I'll show you where it's hidden, and how to retrieve it.'

'Thank you, Reverend Mother,' he replied. 'Once we've gone, at least you won't be burdened with that responsibility anymore. That problem will be ours.'

'Before you leave, my sisters would like to offer you a prayer, for your safe journey back to England.'

Campbell rubbed his chin. 'A prayer you say? About how long will that take?'

'Don't worry, Sergeant, it won't be long, about ten minutes, that's all. I'm sure you can give the sisters that time before you go.'

Campbell thought about it for a few seconds then said, 'Sure, why not? The lads will appreciate it. Besides, we'll need all the help we can get once we leave here. Thank you, Reverend Mother.'

She made no comment, just nodded her head with a small smile and made her way over to the breakfast table, joining the other nuns who sat there. Campbell returned to the queue, grabbed his breakfast, and sat down with his men.

Twenty minutes later, when breakfast was finishing and everyone was about to leave, the bell rang from the main gate. The hall was stunned into silence. They all felt it. Driver Steed entered the hall and went straight to Campbell, telling him that Sister Mary had gone to answer it. He sounded breathless, as if he had just been running instead of walking back from the abbey entrance. 'Right,' Campbell ordered, 'let's get this all away in case it's Fritz. I want no give-away signs we've been here – not yet, anyway.'

With the help of the nuns in the hall, Campbell gave orders to scoop up all the dirty plates and cups from their table, bag them into the table linen, and carry them quickly into the kitchen. Above the clamour, he gave orders to split the men into three groups: one group with Hedges, one with Ratcliffe, and the third to hide behind the two doors that led into different parts of the abbey. He would hide with the two sentries. 'If Fritz has come for us,' he told them, 'shoot your way out and make for the lorries.'

The men scrambled away.

Campbell was joined by the two drivers, Steed and Joyce. He turned to the prioress and said, 'Reverend Mother, as we planned yesterday – right?'

'Of course.' She turned to Sister Teresa and said, 'Take Sergeant Campbell to our toilet just off the hall, so I'll know where he is.'

Campbell, heart racing, face set, unaware of his troubled expression, pulled his revolver, as did Steed and Joyce, and followed the young Sister Theresa to the nuns' toilet.

Once inside, they stood either side of the door, gun in hand. Steed and Joyce on one side, Campbell with Sister Theresa on the other. Campbell saw the nun cross herself. There was no disguising it, she looked scared to death.

'Didn't you do this yesterday, with young Norris?' he asked.

She looked up to him, her big brown eyes fearful, and just nodded.

Campbell forced his face to relax and smile a bit. 'All you girls have put yourselves in danger for us,' he said. 'That takes a lot of courage, and we're beholden to you for it.'

At first she didn't answer. Then she looked down, took hold of the rosary around her waist and held it up to him. 'This is where we get our courage, Sergeant,' she said softly, and kissed the cross.

Campbell grinned. 'I know,' he said, 'and this is where we get ours,' and he kissed the Webley. 'Right now we need both of 'em to work together if we're to get out of here in one piece.'

Her eyes widened as she looked at the gun in his hand, then she carefully dropped to her knees, placed her hands together, closed her eyes, and silently began praying.

Campbell looked down at her sympathetically, then looked across to Steed and Joyce. He placed a finger to his lips, then pointed to his eyes and then to the door, and all three steeled themselves to be ready for any German that came crashing through the door looking for them.

Three minutes had passed when they heard footsteps that stopped outside. Campbell tensed from a knocking on the door. As it gently opened, Steed and Joyce stiffened, and Sister Theresa's eyes went wide with horror until the prioress slowly leaned in. 'Sergeant, it's Major Packard with Vanessa,' she said, her voice a mere whisper. 'They're back.'

Campbell breathed a sigh of relief and glanced at Sister Theresa beside him as she crossed herself again. He relaxed and followed the prioress out into the hall. He saw his officer give a big grin as he approached. Vanessa was beside him, a suitcase between them. She stepped to one side to greet the prioress.

'Welcome back, sir,' Campbell said. 'You're a sight for sore eyes if ever I saw one.'

'Well I'm glad to be back, Sergeant, but things have been moving fast.'

'I'm fully aware of that,' Campbell replied, and recounted the events of Hoffmann's visit with General Vogel the previous evening. 'He suspects we're here alright,' he explained, 'so we've got to go, sharpish like. We're all ready to load. We're just waiting to collect the gold. If we stay here any longer, we'll be in serious trouble, that's for sure.'

Packard gritted his teeth and was a little taken aback by the news that Hoffmann had been within a whisker of searching the abbey, and that only Vogel had stopped him. Now he understood why

Hoffmann had tortured Henri Renard. He needed a confession from him so that he could go to Vogel to justify raiding the abbey before the Germans left the town this lunchtime. Packard told Campbell and the prioress what had happened to Henri Renard, and that the chief of police would be going to Hoffmann at 9 a.m. to tell him the gold was at the abbey, to save his friend's life.

'Our situation is like this,' Packard explained. 'We can't stay in this abbey any longer, we'll end up in a fight with Hoffmann and his bunch of thugs, and if that happens, we may never get out.' He looked around him, then back to Campbell, his face serious. 'If we go now, we may well have to fight our way out of town, but the element of surprise will be in our favour – for a short while, anyway.'

Campbell rubbed his chin thoughtfully and said, '9 a.m., you say? We've just over an hour to load the gold. Assuming we'll have to fight eventually, I agree with you. It's best we take our chances outside and run for it.'

The prioress approached, looking solemn, with a tearful Vanessa. They both turned to face her. She eyed Harry gravely and reached out, taking hold of his hand with extraordinary gentleness. 'I am appalled and saddened to hear the distressing news about my dear friend, Henri Renard,' she said with utter despair, fighting back her tears. 'He was a dear, kind man, a courageous man, and he sacrificed himself to keep us safe.' She closed her eyes tightly, released his hand and crossed herself. She opened her eyes. 'Now we must make sure that his sacrifice was not in vain. My sisters will show you where we hid the gold.'

'Thank you, Reverend Mother,' said Packard. 'We need to load it now. We're running out of time if we're to be gone by nine.'

'Of course, Major, my sisters are ready. Now if you would like to bring your men along and follow me to our cemetery corner, you can be loaded up in no time.'

Campbell called out to the NCOs to bring the men up behind them in single file. They all filed out of the abbey building into the cool morning air, Vanessa walking at Harry's side, still dabbing her wet eyes while he carried her suitcase. As they approached the cemetery corner, they could see that a group of nuns had erected a tall wooden triangular frame above one of the large square tombstones. The prioress waited until everyone had gathered around it. Four nuns stood by with ropes and pulleys. The large heavy stone lid of the tombstone was secured by a rope on each corner that led up to the pulley at the apex of the frame.

The prioress took a step forward and nodded to the three nuns holding the rope. They started pulling on the rope while the fourth one steadied the lid as it began to rise slowly with a slight swing.

Campbell turned to his two NCOs. 'Don't just stand there, give 'em a hand.'

They both went forward and took hold of a section of the rope, and helped the sisters raise the heavy stone lid about six feet into the air.

'That's enough,' said the prioress. 'Secure the rope.' They tied the rope to a heavy rusting metal rung screwed deep into the ground. The prioress stepped forward to the side of the open tomb. She looked in, then turned to face them, beaming with pride, and beckoned for Harry, Vanessa, and Campbell to join her.

They stood beside her in silence and craned their heads to look. This was the moment they'd been waiting for. Their faces were burning with curiosity and trepidation as they gaped open-mouthed while nosily peering over. A wave of pure satisfaction flowed through their veins when they saw dozens of small wooden slatted boxes neatly stacked, each containing two gold bars. The mesmerised silence continued as they stared in. The fear of having to fight their way out of town had suddenly disappeared.

Vanessa felt a thickness in her throat as a lump formed, and a pain in her heart that was bigger than anything she had experienced. 'So, this is it? What my uncle died for,' she said testily.

Packard turned to her and nodded. Feeling her pain, he said, 'It wasn't just the gold, it was more than that. Your uncle knew he had to stop the Germans from getting their hands on it, for the sake of Belgium's army and their fight to survive this war.'

Vanessa shook her head. 'What do I care for gold when Uncle Henri lies dead?' she said, a stab of resentment poisoning her words. Tiny tears formed in the corner of her eyes, which she wiped away with the back of her hand. 'I hate the gold; I hate this war.' She turned away and pushed through the gathered soldiers, she started to make her way back to the abbey.

Packard was about to go after her but the prioress put her hand on his shoulder to stop him. 'Give her some space,' she said. 'I will see to her. Leave it to me.'

He nodded, watching Vanessa walking back along the path in solitary gloom and disappearing into the abbey.

Hedges and Ratcliffe looked at each other, and with curiosity at a premium, they too stepped slowly forward, and peered over. Hedges took a sharp intake of breath as his eyes caught the light from the glinting gold. 'Blimey,' he said, 'wouldn't you just look at that. Isn't that just a wonderful sight?'

'Yeah, that's power, that is,' agreed Ratcliffe, and then with an admiring grin, he turned to Hedges and said, 'Wipers gold!'

The prioress turned to Packard. 'Two hundred years ago, this tomb, and the one next to it, were built to hide our precious items should the town come under siege, which it has several times, and to stop any marauding soldiers who were ransacking our abbey from stealing what we hold dear. It's been used many times. So, as you can see, the gold was perfectly safe.'

'It's perfect,' Packard said with a grin, 'and sensible too,' he added. 'No one would have thought of looking for it here.'

The prioress said, 'Over there we have four wheelbarrows and two small garden carts to load up and take them to your lorries.'

Packard and Campbell spun their heads around and saw the wheelbarrows and carts on the footpath. 'Excellent,' he replied, 'you've thought of everything, Reverend Mother. How will we ever be able to thank you?'

'That's simple,' she said, 'just get the gold safely to England, for my friend Henri Renard.'

He nodded and gave a half-smile. 'Of course, Reverend Mother, we will do our best.'

'That's all I ask.' Then, turning to the other nuns, she commanded, 'So, we ladies will leave you to it. Don't forget the barrels of coins in the other tomb. Let us know if you need any help.'

'We will, and thank you, Reverend Mother,' Packard said, as the prioress led her nuns back to the abbey.

Campbell noticed that the men behind them were getting impatient to look at the gold and making noise as they waited in line. He turned to his officer and said, 'The time, sir. We'd best get cracking and get this loaded if we're to be out of here before nine.'

'Of course, Sergeant, I'll leave this part to you. I'll get changed into uniform and be at the barns making sure they load an even distribution of the gold into both lorries. I'll take Steed and Joyce with me.'

'Very good, sir.' Campbell turned to the men gathered around him. 'Right, listen up!' He began to detail the men as to who was loading and who was carrying. 'And be sharp about it,' he said, 'we haven't got all day. I want this done in half an hour, so get sweating.'

Hedges climbed inside the tomb with Thompson and started to lift out the wooden boxes. 'Blimey,' said Thompson, 'they weigh a ton! I never knew just how heavy gold was.'

Campbell replied, with some authority in his voice, 'That's because each gold bar weighs about 25 pounds. So that's just over 50 pounds, or three and a half stone per box.'

Gower piped up, 'About the weight of your 'ead, Thomo.' Laughter broke out among the men.

'Very funny, Gower,' Thompson replied, 'very funny.'

'That's enough,' snapped Campbell. 'Save your breath – all of you! We've got work to do.'

CHAPTER 32

Hoffmann had been fast asleep in the chair when the sergeant with the waxed moustache placed a hot cup of coffee and a candle on the table beside him and gave him a nudge.

'It's eight o clock, Herr Captain,' the sergeant said.

Hoffmann startled out of his sleep, and it took a moment for his eyes to adjust from the darkness of the room to the light from the candle beside him. He rubbed his eyes, then the back of his neck with both hands. He yawned and stretched out his arms. He'd been asleep for four hours. He shivered before picking up the cup and sipping the hot coffee with relish. The hot liquid tasted bitter but it was wet, his dry mouth and parched throat and made him cough. When he stopped coughing, he said gruffly, 'Have we heard from the chief of police yet?'

The sergeant shook his head. 'No, nothing,' he replied.

'Pity, but we've still got time.'

'About an hour. Do you want me to look for him?' the sergeant asked.

Hoffmann laughed. 'No, Sergeant. I want him to speak to his contacts. He's a good friend of the mayor and he knows I'll kill Colaert, or he thinks I will, if he doesn't return at nine and tell me where the gold is hidden.'

'But we *know* where the gold is hidden. The bank manager refused to talk about the abbey every time you mentioned it. That's proof enough that he's trying to protect those Irish nuns. You should tell the general your findings. How could he refuse to search the abbey now that the answer is obvious?'

Hoffmann thought about it for a moment then suddenly beamed at the sergeant. 'You're right, Sergeant. I should've thought of that before.' He stood up, stepped into his boots, buttoned up his coat, put his hat on his head, and said, 'I'm off to see the general. You're in charge of the prisoners. I'll be back soon.'

He made his way across the square to the hotel. There were battalions and horse-drawn wagons forming and getting ready to leave town.

Hoffmann climbed the stairs to the first-floor office, where Haas was working. He told Haas he needed to see the general urgently. Haas went to the general's room, knocked on the door, and entered the room first.

Barely moments later, he opened the door again, standing to the side to let Hoffman in. Vogel was at his table, drinking coffee and smoking a cigarette.

Hoffmann removed his fedora, stiffened, and clicked his heels. 'Good morning, Generalmajor. Thank you for seeing me.'

Vogel puffed out some smoke, blowing it high into the air. Hoffman watched the generalmajor's eyes pan up and down, taking in his unshaved, bedraggled, and under-rested state.

'Ah, Hoffmann. Glad you're here. I was about to send for you. I've just received orders this morning to return to headquarters straight away. I'm leaving in an hour's time. My administration will follow later this afternoon. Before I go, I would like an update regarding the gold.' He gave a brief, sharp-edged smile. 'Not found, I take it?'

'No, Generalmajor, we have searched the town and found nothing, but things have changed. My questioning of the bank manager makes me even more certain that the gold, along with English soldiers, is being hidden in the Benedictine abbey by those

Irish nuns.'

Vogel gave him a long hard stare, leaning forward and slowly extinguishing his cigarette in the glass ashtray on his table. Then he sat back, folding his arms. 'We had this conversation yesterday, *Herr Captain*,' he said, his voice tone emphasizing his rank, 'and I think I made myself quite clear then. So, *Captain*, this had better be good.'

Hoffmann nervously cleared his throat. He had to get his point across and sound certain. If that didn't work, he'd use threats. 'Well, sir, when I questioned the bank manager on any subject he always gave a reply. But the moment I mentioned the gold being hidden in the abbey, he sat there like a stunned rabbit, and did not offer a single word, just silence. My experience in these matters tells me that when they do that, people are hiding something. The more I pushed him on the abbey, the more he stayed silent. The gold is there, Generalmajor, I know it. It's the last place in town where it could be; in the abbey hidden by those Irish nuns, and the only place I have not searched.'

'I see,' said Vogel, frowning. 'Your assumption that silence means guilt can be laudable in certain matters, I agree, but tell me, did you beat him?'

Hoffmann swallowed. 'I admit we roughed him up a little, but no more than usual.' He didn't want to admit to Vogel that Henri Renard was dead. Not yet anyway. 'He co-operated fully until I mentioned the gold in the abbey, then he said nothing, just a wall of silence.'

'Where is the bank manager now?'

'Under guard in the old prison cells of the Cloth Hall.'

'Is he still conscious?' Vogel asked in a mocking tone.

'He's resting,' Hoffmann replied, 'and I have no further use of him, but I won't release him until I have your permission to search the abbey.' He saw the fury form in Vogel's eyes, and kept on talking. 'I need to search the abbey, if only to eliminate it from suspicion. Of course, I would mention your co-operation in my report to Berlin if no gold is found and the English fled with it before our arrival – which I don't believe for one moment.' There was a silent pause as each man stared at the other in subdued, simmering anger. Hoffmann pushed on. 'But with your permission, in a few short minutes we could find out if the abbey is being used to hide the gold or not, as the case may be. If you say no, I would hate for you to be proved wrong after the fact. Just think of the outrage among the general staff in Berlin. They would blame you personally for the loss of the gold, and with good reason. My report to Berlin would have to reflect the decision you made here, particularly if it was discovered afterwards that the gold *was* stored in the abbey. It's just a small matter of your support. Say yes, and this matter would be resolved,' he snapped his fingers, 'just like that, and I will make sure that a favourable report about your support goes to Berlin.'

Hoffmann saw Vogel look at him with acid in his eyes. The look that came the captain's way said that, in particular, the threat about the report to the general staff in Berlin would not be forgotten.

Hoffmann read his man. He could almost see the thoughts going through Vogel's head. He was, after all, acting under the orders of the Kaiser himself to retrieve the gold or find out what had happened to it. It came down to who Vogel was more scared of, his God or his Kaiser. Hoffman saw the glare intensify as Vogel realised he had no choice, and that the abbey would have to be searched before they left town.

'Very well, Hoffmann,' Vogel muttered, his voice now more humble, 'you have my permission, but I insist that Lieutenant Haas goes with you as my personal representative to make sure that no impropriety takes place, and that you and your men conduct yourselves in a manner befitting the dignity of the German army.'

Hoffmann's faced burned with victory. 'Thank you, Generalmajor. It will be a pleasure to have your adjutant join us for the search this morning.' He stiffened, clicked his heels, and left.

CHAPTER 33

Churchill sat perched on the edge of a high-backed wing chair, leaning on his walking stick with both hands, drumming the fingers of one on the other. He glanced around the private secretary's office outside the cabinet room, while waiting for the prime minister to call him in for his 9 a.m. appointment.

This was not the first time he had waited in this office during his twenty years as a politician, and normally it was just a formality to wait until one was called through. But in the wing chair next to him were laid the military cap, gloves, and cane of Lord Kitchener, who was now in the cabinet room with the prime minister discussing the present situation of Antwerp as he saw it. Churchill's brows furrowed and his dyspeptic frown rippled.

Kitchener's priority was not good news for Churchill. Since his recall from Antwerp yesterday, he knew the prime minister was angry with him. He was accused by his political enemies in London of deserting his admiralty post for self-promotion and adventure, which was not the case. Although he had to admit, to himself if no-one else, that sending the prime minister a telegram offering to resign his post as First Lord of the Admiralty, in exchange for a general's rank along with staff officers so that he could take charge of the defence of Antwerp, would be seen that way. Questions were being asked in the Commons about Churchill's role in Antwerp. But the telegram had sealed his fate. Asquith had no choice and recalled him back to London.

Now news was coming in this morning that the situation in Antwerp had got worse since he'd left yesterday morning. The two mighty German guns were reducing the outer defensive forts to rubble very quickly, as he and Admiral Hood had predicted they would, but now artillery shells were constantly crashing down into the city centre itself, destroying hundreds of homes and businesses. With casualties mounting in the streets, nearly half a million panicked civilians had started rushing to the river that cut the city in half, west to east, in the hope of crossing the bridges into the northern half, which were now jammed to an almost standstill, or catch a boat to cross. Once across, they began the long journey along the roads to Ghent in the west or Holland to the east.

The Belgian government and all the other politicians had already gone, but King Albert and his wife intended to stay until the last moment.

And when would that last moment be? Today? Tomorrow? The next day after that? The Germans were holding a sharp knife at Antwerp's throat and were poised to slice it open at any moment. His one marine and two naval brigades would be at the forefront of any German attack at their seemingly fragile defensive lines. They would be squandered to buy time – and that time was fast running out.

He turned to look as a marble and gilt clock on a bookcase shelf whirred and struck 9 a.m. He removed the watch from his waistcoat pocket and checked the time. The private secretary, a middle-aged man with grey receding hair who'd been sitting behind his desk shuffling papers for the last thirty minutes, also glanced up as the clock chimed. He caught Churchill's eye, returned a force smile, and quickly returned to the papers on his desk.

Two minutes later, a low buzzer went off in the room. Churchill looked to the private secretary as he silently rose stiffly behind his desk, tugged at the jacket tails of his black frock coat, went to the door that led to the cabinet office, and opened it. Churchill felt his pulse race as he waited to be received, and squinted from the morning October sunlight flooding in through the door from the cabinet windows on the opposite side of the room that looked over the garden and Horse Guards Parade beyond.

'First Lord of the Admiralty,' the private secretary announced in a nasal tone, then stepped to one side.

Churchill got up, placed his silver-topped walking stick and his black hat on the chair he had just vacated, and stepped through into the cabinet room; the private secretary closed the door behind him. His pulse calmed as he stood at the end of the large cabinet table. The room smelt of cigarette smoke and stale whiskey. The prime minister was sitting at the cabinet table reading through some papers. Sitting next to him was Lloyd George in his usual pose, thumbs in his waistcoat pockets, looking him straight in the eye with a sly smirk on his face, and enjoying the moment. Lord Kitchener took his stance opposite with his back to the windows, hands clasped behind his back, keeping an eye on everyone. As Churchill stood there in that moment of silence, he felt as if he had just walked into the lion's den as a live meat offering. Kitchener moved first. His left eye twitched as he nudged his walrus moustache with a knuckle.

Asquith squared the papers and placed them down on the table. He looked up and turned to him. 'Come in, Winston, glad you're back in one piece.'

Churchill approached them and stood opposite, having not, he noticed, been asked to sit down. 'It is indeed an unexpected pleasure to be back in London so soon, Prime Minister.'

'Quite so, Winston. Still, I heard you visited almost every defence site around Antwerp during your short stay, even coming under fire a few times. Is that correct?'

He saw Lloyd George grin at the thought of him being under fire. 'When visiting troops on the front line, one has to put up with some inconvenience.'

Asquith quickly glanced at Lloyd George, and both men gave a small chuckle. 'Of course, Winston, bravo.'

'Thank you, Prime Minister.'

Asquith cleared his throat. 'Well, Winston, now that you're here we have war business to discuss.'

'Yes, Prime Minister. I understand that my time in Antwerp is a prime topic for malicious gossip in the tea rooms of the Commons at the moment.'

Asquith nodded, face serious. 'Indeed it does, Winston, and your telegram to me about offering to resign your post at the Admiralty and take command of Antwerp is the prime cause. Your enemies in the House are accusing you of abdicating your duties with the navy, and this,' he said, waving the telegram in the air, 'gives them that ammunition. What were you thinking?'

'Forgive me, Prime Minister, if I express this poorly, but during my inspection of Antwerp's defensive lines, matters military and politically deteriorated quickly. Within hours of arriving and speaking to the Belgium government to get agreement, they began leaving the city. Their military commanders felt let down by their political leaders and indeed, by their allies, with good cause. They could see no other solution than to abandon Antwerp by withdrawing westward to Ghent. To stay and fight … they would face the prospect of their army surrendering. Until I got there that was just a matter of time. I got together their senior high command, along with my own General Paris, and made a plan for a tactical withdrawal west towards Ghent when the time came to abandon Antwerp.' He noticed that they were staring at him suspiciously but he continued. 'Prime Minister, from the beginning I have always stressed to this office that holding Antwerp posed a barrier to the German advance along the coast. Delaying the enemy here is a far greater service to us now than its defeat in the coming months, so I took stock of the situation and sensed the need to take command before it broke down. To do that, I needed to be free of my post in the Admiralty, and be fully endorsed by this office with a field rank of general to assert my authority to do so ... thus saving the Belgian army from disaster, and our own forces from being cut off from their supply lines.'

Kitchener snapped, 'What about General Paris? He was your man in command of the naval brigades, was he not? If there were a need for an executive commander, why could he not take control? After all, you're just a politician.'

Churchill narrowed his eyes. He thought the question impertinent because he had served in the Boer War and was now an officer in a territorial regiment. He enunciated his answer, slowly. 'I needed General Paris to stay in command of my naval brigades to keep the continuity of their command when they retired from battle, otherwise their retirement could well develop into a rout, and control would be lost. *They*, as you know, are ill-equipped and trained, and he knows their limitations very well, so it was vital he stayed with them. Besides, General Paris has a military mind, not a political one. I have both!' That comment earned him a vicious look from Kitchener.

'There was also General Rawlinson,' said Asquith, intervening. 'Where does he fit in to this?'

'Lately, Prime Minister,' Churchill tutted. 'General Rawlinson arrived in Antwerp as I was about to depart. We met briefly of course. But he left Antwerp for Ghent. He felt that his two divisions would arrive too late to help defend Antwerp. It would be a lost cause, he said. I've just heard that his two divisions have landed in Belgium this morning and are currently en route to Ghent to cover the expected withdrawal along the coast … and the hope for French support with troops never materialised, despite their promises!'

Lloyd George said, 'Are you saying that Antwerp has been mismanaged?'

Churchill sensed the trap and considered his reply carefully. Lloyd George was a known intriguer, who saw himself as the next in line to accession as PM, and he would be looking to distance himself from Asquith if things went badly wrong in this war. Looking straight into the chancellor's eyes he replied, 'That may be the opinion of other people, but I do think we've missed some opportunities.'

'Such as?' Kitchener demanded.

'For one thing, I promised this office that I'd give our army seven days to reach the coast. I have delivered on that promise, and yet we've still been too slow to send sufficient reinforcements to support the Belgian army in Antwerp who, I may add, have been grappling to stay in this war.'

'Nonsense,' replied Kitchener. 'We've done as much as we can. If they fail, it's their doing – not our fault. We can't possibly prop up every little army in this war fighting the Germans. We have our own responsibilities to consider first.'

Churchill frowned. 'Say that and we surrender our future. We need those little armies to stay in this war and we must do our utmost to support them. Wars are won or lost by little armies, one wound at a time. If we do not support them … there could well be a sombre reckoning.'

Lloyd George gave him one of his mocking frowns. 'Are you saying, Winston, if we don't do anything, that this could end in tragedy?'

Churchill narrowed his eyes and said, 'When Antwerp falls, Ghent will be the next city to be attacked by the Germans. That I promise you.'

Asquith looked straight across to Kitchener. 'Is that right, Lord K? Ghent will be next?'

All eyes turned on Kitchener, whose left eye began to twitch again. Standing ram-rod straight and grim-faced, he sniffed sharply, stroked his moustache with a finger and after five seconds replied cautiously, 'We're hoping to send fresh troops from England to boost Rawlinson's two divisions that are currently on their way to Ghent, Prime Minister,' as if that explained it all.

Churchill saw Asquith nod his head, seeming impressed by his up-to-date knowledge of events, but Kitchener ... he was almost stunned into silence, so Churchill pressured him. 'And if the Germans take Ghent, it will be Dunkirk next, then on to Calais, and from Calais I fear they could make plans to cross the Channel.' They all looked straight at him with open mouths. He had stunned them all. 'We can't wait for new troops to arrive from England,' he argued. 'How long will it take to get them there and into position, a week, ten days even?! No. It will be too late. We have to act now! Once Antwerp falls, and King Albert's force, or what is left of it, retires to Ghent, we must rush reinforcements north to link with our Belgian allies and counterattack, to take the pressure off the Belgian army, if only temporarily. The Belgian army must live to fight another day.'

'A forlorn hope,' said Lloyd George, grinning.

'It's not as bad as that,' snapped Kitchener.

'Then how bad is it?' demanded Asquith.

Kitchener breathed, as though punched in the gut. 'If time is given, Prime Minister, we shall prevail.'

'If we fail to deliver the necessary reinforcements—' said Churchill, pushing on.'

'We won't,' Kitchener interjected. 'You have my word on that.'

'I trust that we have, Lord K,' said Asquith. 'King Albert has been loyal to us despite our lack of support for Antwerp. We can't let him down again at Ghent. We must do something to help. We must do something now.'

Churchill nodded approval at Asquith's words, feeling vindicated in sending his telegram. He said, 'I do not find favour with this situation, for our honour is at stake here. My naval brigades have been trusted with this mission, despite their lack of training and equipment, and are about to face a last-ditch defence of Antwerp against the full force of the German attack. They will do their duty. We must do ours.'

'Here, here,' said Lloyd George. 'Well said.'

Asquith was nodding. 'That's settled then,' he said, 'we push harder to the coast to support the Belgian army.' He turned to Kitchener. 'Anything to add, Lord K?'

'I've been pushing General French to stretch his forces to the coast for the last few days, Prime Minister,' Kitchener replied, 'especially now that a German brigade has pushed forward and occupied the town of Ypres ahead of us.'

'Ypres?' Asquith said. Then turning to Churchill with a frown he said, 'Isn't that where your gold is hidden, Winston?'

Churchill licked his dry upper lip. 'Indeed it is, Prime Minister. On my return to London yesterday, I was greeted with a telegram from Major Packard, the officer in charge of this mission. Just as he got to the bank, the Germans occupied the town, and he is now in hiding.'

Asquith flopped back into his chair. 'Dear God, is nothing going right? Do we know if the Germans have the gold?'

'Had the Germans got the gold, Prime Minister, I'm sure they would have shouted it from the rooftops by now. Their propaganda machine would have been in full swing.'

Asquith removed a handkerchief from his jacket pocket and wiped his face. 'So, what happens now?'

'I immediately sent a telegram back. Told him to get the gold out as soon as possible – at all costs.'

Lloyd George gave another of his complicated Devil's Advocate frowns. 'Now that Antwerp is about to fall, does it matter who has the gold?'

Churchill's face reddened and he bit back. 'Of course it matters! If that gold fell into German hands now it could cause the collapse of Belgian morale. It may just be the tipping point. It must be saved – *must!*'

The words hung in silence in the cabinet room a while until Kitchener spoke. He shook his head and said, 'Their chances of getting out of an occupied town with that gold are slim, and you know it!'

Churchill responded to Kitchener with a look that was cocked and loaded, and scowled. 'We're not finished with the gold yet. Not by a long chalk.' He banged the flat of his hand on the cabinet table as he said, 'Any chance, any chance whatsoever, is better than no chance at all. In pushing your army to the coast, you have to pass through Ypres.' Then, with a pleading edge to his tone, he said, 'That means putting pressure on the Germans around that town. That means the Germans taking their eye off the gold. That means we're in with a chance. That means the Belgian army stays intact, and that means we won't lose this dreadful war!'

There was an awkward silence for about ten seconds. Asquith was about to say something but Kitchener intervened. 'By driving on Ypres we may draw the Germans' attention of course, and doubtless you could be right. I hope you are right, Winston,' he replied indignantly, 'for all our sakes. Let's hope your man in Ypres can pull it off and make it happen.'

CHAPTER 34

It was 8.45 a.m.

From the moment the two lorries were loaded with the gold and the men's small packs with their rifles were neatly stowed under the bench seating in the back, Packard was anxious to leave. He felt a prickling of concern running up and down his spine of suddenly being faced with a firefight inside the abbey as Hoffmann and his thugs came crashing through the gate just as they are about to escape. His sixth sense told him not to hang around and to go now. Although Sergeant Campbell had promised the prioress that they would attend a short service of prayer before departing when he was absent yesterday, he objected to the idea. In his heart he knew that to be the right decision and went and found Sister Margaret. Both went to the prioress's office to tell her.

'We must get away now,' Packard stressed to the prioress. 'I don't think it wise for us to stay here any longer than is necessary.'

'I'm fully aware of the risk, Major, but my sisters would like to invite you all into our chapel to offer a prayer, wishing you all a safe journey. They're in the chapel now, giving their mid-morning prayers, just waiting for you and your men to join them.' Her chin tilted upwards, head to one side, her blue eyes pleading for him to relent. 'Just ten minutes is all it would take. Surely you can spare that time before you go?'

Harry spread his hands, and tried to sound composed, but it was hard to say no. 'With respect, Reverend Mother, I don't think you do understand the danger if we remain here. We can't spare five minutes. It's putting us at risk, not to mention your good selves. I'm sorry, but we should go right away.'

'Then at least allow us all to say goodbye,' she asked. 'Let me gather my sisters into the hall to bid you all a fond farewell and a safe journey home. One minute. You can't refuse that, Major, surely?'

Now he felt guilty for saying no to the prayers, especially after all the nuns had done for them, not to mention the risk. One minute to say goodbye? At least he could do that. Packard bit his lip, took a deep breath and, against his better judgement, reluctantly agreed. 'Very well, one minute, that's all. I'll get the men into the hall and say a few words of thanks to you and the sisters.'

She smiled. 'Of course.' She turned to Sister Margaret. 'Collect the sisters from the chapel and take them to the hall, quickly now!'

He stood aside to let Sister Margaret pass. He followed her out, going quickly through the hall to the entrance, he smelt the beeswax and fresh flowers as he passed through, his eye squinting at the bright daylight flooding in from outside. He looked up. Broken clouds slowly drifting along with the odd ray of sunshine breaking through. A pity it wasn't raining, he thought, it would help keep German heads down as they drove through town.

He saw Campbell standing in a bright ray of sunlight on the gravel driveway outside the hall entrance, talking with Vanessa, while the men were standing behind them looking like survivors from a recent disaster, smoking and talking in hushed whispers. They were all keyed up waiting for the order to depart and preparing themselves for the drive through a town full of Germans.

'Sergeant Campbell!' Packard heard the irritation in his own voice and saw his sergeant stiffen.

'Sir!'

'Get the men formed up into an orderly line inside the hall, quickly now,' Packard said testily. 'The nuns want to say goodbye. We've got one minute, that's all!'

'Very good, sir,' said Campbell, then added, 'I've just sent young Norris to your lorry with Miss Vanessa's suitcase. Told him to stay put as we're about to leave. Shall I–'

'Leave him there,' Packard interjected irritably, 'this won't take long.' He pushed out his left elbow for Vanessa to take his arm. She stepped forward and gave him a small smile, blushed, and linked her arm through. He caught a whiff of her perfume, soft, clean, feminine. They entered the hall together as the nuns began emerging. Campbell led the men inside and formed them into a line facing the nuns, just like mealtime. Packard and Vanessa stood in front of them. On the opposite side the gathering nuns parted, allowing the prioress, with Sister Margaret following behind, to squeeze through as they made their way to the front, the sisters all gathered behind them smiling.

Above the abbey, the sun shone through the broken cloud as it slowly drifted along. Morning sunlight suddenly came flooding in from the upper stained-glass windows, casting light and shadows in strips along the spacious hall. Dust particles were glinting, dancing, floating aimlessly in the warm filtered sunlight air, then quickly disappearing like magic as a cloud covered the sun and the light faded away.

Once Packard was satisfied that everyone was in place, the hall fell into a hushed silence. All looking at him, all listening intently, waiting for him to say a few words. He cleared his throat, took a short breath, and said, 'Reverend Mother, and sisters of the Holy Benedictine Abbey of Ypres, on behalf of my men, and of Vanessa –' He gave her a quick sideways glance. '–I would like to express our deepest gratitude for all you have done for us during our short stay at the abbey. You have made us feel very welcome, and in doing so, you have put yourselves in danger and shared some of our anxieties and fears. May we give you all our sincere thanks and best wishes, and pray that you remain safe after our departure, and that one day in the near future we can all meet again in much more convivial circumstances.'

All the nuns, their faces serene and smiling, clapped gently, while the men behind Packard clapped, cheered, and whistled.

When the noise died down, he saw the cheerful smiling prioress take the dangling crucifix from around her waist, clutching it with both hands, lifting it close to her heart. She began her reply, saying, 'Major Packard, and men of the Richmond Regiment–'

She never finished. The bell from the front gate rang for four continuous seconds. It sounded urgent. Demanding. The hall was stunned to silence. All heads turned sharply; their eyes fixed on the entrance to the hall. Nobody moved. They stood like silent, nervous statues.

The bell rang again, jangling nerves and making some of them jump. It seemed to grow louder, sounding more urgent this time, refusing to be ignored.

Packard heard fearful gasps from nuns just a few feet away. It took a moment for him to adjust his mind. That prickling feeling was running up and down his spine again from fear of knowing what would happen if it was Hoffmann at the gate. He shot a worried glance over his shoulder at Campbell as he unconsciously removed his arm from Vanessa and undid the catch to his holster, placing a hand on the grip of the Webley and withdrawing it into the ready position, barrel facing upwards. Campbell did the same.

Packard opened his mouth to say something to the prioress, but she pressed a finger to her lips to silence him. He saw the fear flare in her eyes.

'Wait here,' she said in a hushed whisper, as if the bell ringer at the gate could hear her. 'Sister Margaret and I will go to see who it is and deal with the matter.'

Packard nodded and watched them leave. He could see the worried look on their faces. Like them, there were no doubts in his mind who it was, and there were no doubts in all the anxious faces of the nuns that turned to stare at him, watching and waiting for him to act. He saw Sister Mary at the front, her hands pressed together in front of her grim face in prayer. He went across to her and she looked up to him, her eyes wide and nervous, almost paralysed by his presence. He lowered his head and said softly, 'No panic, Sister Mary, but I do suggest you get the sisters to leave the hall and go back into the chapel, just in case it's trouble.'

Sister Mary stood there, silent, just blinking at him as if she were unable to comprehend what he just said to her.

Then, on cue, the bell began ringing again, this time longer. It sounded louder and more threatening in the silent hall.

She nodded quickly, turned around, her hands gesticulating to usher the sisters away in a silent flurry of activity as they broke up and melted out of the hall.

Packard gripped the Webley tighter then turned to the two NCOs, who'd already split the men into two groups, pistols drawn and waiting for orders, their faces a mask of alarm. There was no time for any complicated tactics, no time for anything apart from what they had discussed the other day should a situation like this arise. *Ambush*. Ambush was the key to success, he had told them. His tactic was brutally straightforward – they would wait until Fritz was in the hall, then slaughter him where he stood in a hail of lead, surrounded, confined, with nowhere to go. Dead meat. Simple.

'You know the plan. Take the men behind those two doors either side of the hall and wait for my command. And remember your training! At close range, fire from the hip. As soon as you hear rapid gunshots, storm out screaming your heads off. In that instant they'll be confused, and we'll hit them with thunderclap surprise.' Then he narrowed his eyes. His strong features were set and determined. 'None of the bastards get away. They die here or surrender. Got that?'

'Yes sir,' they answered as one.

'Good, let's move into position.' He watched as they disappeared behind the doors, their hobnailed boots scrunching on the flagstone floor. Once they had gone, the hall fell into silence.

This was his nightmare scenario – a shootout inside the abbey. If they didn't get this right and end the firefight in seconds, Hoffmann could call for reinforcements from the town, they would be trapped inside the abbey, and that would spell curtains for them.

If only we had driven out earlier.

He hovered for a moment thinking about the consequences should the firefight end up in a stand-off, before turning on his heel to Vanessa, who was standing behind him, hand covering her mouth, silent, pale-faced and scared from what she'd just heard. He held his hand out to hers and squeezed it gently, reassuringly. Then the morning sunshine suddenly flooded through the upper stained-glass windows again, but only briefly this time, and he thought how the glow of sunlight in her hair made her the most beautiful thing he had ever seen.

'Harry …' she said, then took a deep breath and blinked back tears. 'I'm–' She didn't finish.

Before she could say any more, he tenderly put his finger to her lips, 'I know,' he said, 'we've been here before, haven't we?' It already seemed like lifetimes ago, that attack by the bridge when he'd wanted her to leave before the German battlegroup arrived.

She nodded, her watery brown eyes shining brightly as they fixed firmly on his.

He felt as if her eyes were trying to probe his innermost thoughts. 'Only this time, I can't send you away to safety,' he admitted, a quaver on inevitability in his voice.

She shook her head slowly, and her eyes were wet.

'When the time comes, Sergeant Campbell and I will hide in the toilet over there.' He pointed with the barrel of the Webley. 'It gives us a clear view of the hall. You'll be with us. When we rush out, there will be lots of yelling and gunfire, with bullets flying everywhere, so you stay inside and keep safe until I come for you.'

She nodded, the tears in the corners of her eyes starting to run down her cheeks.

He peered down at her, then flung his arms around her, hugging her tightly, kissing her wet cheeks, stroking her hair. He suddenly felt ashamed, because he knew the dangers only too well. Knew what may lie ahead in the next few minutes. It turned his stomach just thinking about it, but he had to be strong for her. He swallowed, and his throat felt bone dry.

'You'll be safe,' he whispered in her ear. 'I'll look after you.' He pulled back slowly, wiping a tear from her cheek with the tip of his finger, then taking her hand, he led her to the door and opened it. To his surprise, Sister Mary and Sister Theresa were hiding inside. 'Look after her,' he told them, then lifted her chin, kissed her on the lips, and closed the door.

Harry sighed as he stood outside. He knew how Vanessa felt but he couldn't allow himself to weaken now, he had to concentrate on putting those worries aside. He turned to find his sergeant at the hall entrance, almost on tip-toe, cap in hand, peering intently to see what was happening at the gate. Packard went to him and stood at his elbow, feeling distinctively edgy. 'Everyone is now squared away,' he told him. 'Our boys are ready. Anything happening here?'

Campbell shook his head. 'Not yet. The prioress and Sister Margaret are approaching the gate now.'

*

Her heart was pounding, her legs felt weak, her hands felt sweaty and shaky as the prioress approached the gate silently with Sister Margaret. Staring straight ahead and taking short bird-like steps, the prioress made sure they did not hurry themselves. Their approach to the gate was to be made in a dignified manner, she told Sister Margaret. When they got to the two black wooden gothic doors, the prioress paused. She felt a little lightheaded and ready to faint. She placed a hand on the gate to steady herself, and closed her eyes briefly, took three deep breaths to help calm her nerves and began to whisper a short prayer. Sister Margaret glanced at her and they both crossed themselves when the prioress had finished.

The prioress tried hard to compose herself, then pulled the viewing slider across to peer out. Standing a few feet away from the gate entrance was Lieutenant Haas. Tall, smart, looking immaculate in his field-grey uniform, his spiked helmet caught a ray of sunlight that sparkled in an orange glow. He leaned towards the slit in the door as it scraped open, and he peered in quizzically.

'Reverend Mother, is that you?'

Her mouth was dry, she swallowed hard, and almost stumbled out her words. 'Yes… yes, it is. How can I help you?'

Haas threw up a salute as a polite gesture of goodwill. Smiling, he said, 'Reverend Mother, good morning to you. Generalmajor Vogel sends his sincere apologies for this interruption, but I'm afraid it's necessary for these premises to be searched.'

The prioress noticed Hoffmann behind him, in his black trench coat and fedora hat, arms behind his back, impatiently pacing back and forth. She watched him for a few seconds with a fascinated horror … and behind him were two open-backed trucks full of mean-looking soldiers in spiked helmets with silver gorgets hanging on chains around their necks. Field police – all looking her way.

'What's this all about?' she asked, her voice shaky. 'We're about to start our mid-morning prayers, and we do not wish to be disturbed.'

Hoffmann almost shoved Haas to one side to peer in beside him. His dark piercing eyes narrowed. 'Prayers can wait, Reverend Mother. Open up, this is a military matter!' Then he stepped back and resumed his pacing.

Haas looked embarrassed and briefly glanced at Hoffmann over his shoulder. 'I do apologise, Reverend Mother. If you would allow us inside, I will explain.'

There was a moment's hesitation. She was glad that Haas could not see the anxiety in her face. 'As you wish, Lieutenant Haas,' she replied, her voice tone hiding a knot twisting in the pit of her stomach as she closed the slider. She turned to Sister Margaret, and in a low voice said, 'Quickly now, run back and let Major Packard know it's Hoffmann with his field police. They're going to search the abbey. Tell Sister Mary and Sister Theresa to wait in the toilet by the hall to assist Major Packard in case he requires them. Make sure the other sisters gather in the chapel. We will be safe there, and all pray together.'

Sister Margaret nodded, turned, grabbed handfuls of her black robe, lifting it above her ankles, and ran as fast as she was able to the abbey entrance.

The prioress saw Sergeant Campbell step out from behind the doorway to greet Sister Margaret as she approached him before disappearing inside. She was now alone at the gate. Her heart began pounding again, her breathing like a gallop. Her lips began to tremble. She felt rigid, immobile, and she swallowed hard. She knew that once she let in Hoffmann with his field police there would be a fight in the abbey hall. There would bloodshed, pain, and death – and after that, her sisters could be violated by the angry Germans seeking swift vengeance for their dead comrades, and for hiding and supporting the English soldiers. That thought horrified her the most.

From the other side of the two heavy doors came the sound of Hoffmann's harsh and irritated voice. 'Open up! What's taking so long?' His fist banged on the strong gothic door as if the devil himself was demanding access into this house of God. Thump! Thump! Thump! 'Open up, damn you! Let us in!'

She looked skyward, mouthing *'Dear God, give me strength this day'* before gripping the heavy cold iron bolt to slide it open.

CHAPTER 35

No sooner had Sister Margaret gone to join the other nuns in the chapel than Packard and Campbell heard dull hammering from the gate as they peered from the shadows of the abbey entrance.

'The bastard is impatient to get us,' Campbell said dryly.

'Then we'll have to give him a warm welcome when he comes, one he won't forget.'

Campbell glanced at his officer with a grin. 'Or regret, for that matter.'

Packard didn't answer but looked on worriedly. He had no idea how many Germans were out there. It could be a dozen or a hundred with Hoffmann outside, he had no way of knowing until they came through the gate.

The sun burst through a cloud, basking the gravel drive in sunlight. Packard and Campbell shaded their eyes with a hand as they watched the prioress slide the iron bolts across the heavy black wooden doors, first swinging the right side open, and then the left. The sunshine faded away.

Packard saw Hoffmann for the first time; tall, dark, and menacing, just as Vanessa had described him. A hatred for the man crashed over him like a cold wave. Beside Hoffmann stood a tall smart army officer with an adjutant's lanyard around his shoulder. He wasn't field police and seemed out of place. Packard studied both men. The adjutant was talking to the prioress and appeared to be relaxed, having a general conversation with her. The nodding of heads, a spread of his hands, a smile even. Then there was Hoffmann, who stood with his hands behind his back, still, impatient with narrowed eyes and a determined look on his face. His body language told him more than words. Hoffmann was bent on murder.

He watched Hoffmann gravely, giving instructions to the driver of the first truck and stepping aside while it moved onto the driveway and was followed by the second truck. Packard made a quick calculation; six in the back of each truck and two in the cab, including Hoffmann and the adjutant. Fourteen altogether. The field police carried rifles tipped with bayonets. He gave a small sigh of relief. The odds were even. They had a chance to win at least.

The two trucks came to a halt about twenty-five feet from the abbey entrance. Packard and Campbell shuffled closer together in the shadowed entrance, pistols at the ready, barely able to see with one eye without giving themselves away. The field police jumped from the back of the two trucks but didn't seem to have any urgency about them or think they might be in any kind of danger. They gave Packard the impression that this was just a routine search. They just gathered in groups beside the trucks, looking around. Packard felt as if their serene surroundings had lured them into a false sense of safety.

He heard a door slam on the second truck and a big sergeant with a waxed moustache, dark piercing eyes with a barrel chest appeared and stood with both hands on his hips, looking up at the abbey, scrutinizing the architecture as if he were an expert. He had no rifle, just a holster on his belt. He was joined by another big man, a corporal, who was about three inches taller. He too carried a holster on his belt. Hoffmann, the adjutant, and the prioress were walking slowly towards the trucks.

Hoffman called to the sergeant and took him to one side, out of earshot of the prioress to speak to him. He pointed towards the two barns over by the perimeter wall and then gestured to the abbey building. The sergeant nodded, saluted, turned, and called across two of his men to join him. Both men stood before him, their rifles slung over their shoulders. They both nodded and started heading towards the barns. The sergeant then gathered the rest of his men and headed for the abbey entrance.

'Two are headed for the barns,' said Campbell quietly. 'Norris is alone in there.'

'Shit!' Packard cursed between clinched teeth. 'I'd forgotten about him. Too late now. He'll have to take his chances like everyone else. Come on, let's get ready.'

They both stepped back carefully into the deeper shadows of the entrance, and Campbell quickly followed his officer across the hall into the toilet.

When Packard pushed open the toilet door to enter, Sister Mary, Sister Theresa, and Vanessa were huddled together in the corner, fearful and trying not to cry.

'Quiet now,' he said, his voice scarcely audible, 'Fritz is here.'

Packard prised the door open enough to peer with one eye through the slender opening. He felt his pulse drumming away in his neck, his face sweating and his breathing coming in short gasps as adrenalin pumped around his body.

The sergeant with the waxed moustache was the first to walk into the hall, looking up to the vaulted ceiling with the stained-glass windows, like a curious tourist. He stopped and directed his men past him into the middle of the hall. They moved along obediently and gathered in the middle. The big corporal stood beside him and he too was looking up and around. They just stood there, gathered in a bunch, waiting and looking around – but no Hoffmann. He must still be outside.

Packard cursed his luck. He needed them all in the hall together and it wasn't happening. He continued to stare, making his eye water. He turned to Campbell, wiping his eye with the back of his hand. 'We can't wait any longer for Hoffmann to appear, we have to go in now. I'll take out the sergeant on the left as we go in, you take out that big corporal behind him.'

Campbell nodded.

Packard waited until he was sure the Germans were not looking his way, then, taking a sharp intake of breath, he opened the door and stepped out at a sharp pace with Campbell right behind him.

The sergeant with the waxed moustached was at least twenty feet away with his back to him. As Packard lifted his arm and took aim, in that split second, he saw the sergeant turn his head, enough to see Packard's gun pointing directly at him. In that fraction of a second he saw the sergeant stiffen and hold his breath as the two men stood looking at each other. The sergeant began to turn, eyes wide with horror, his mouth opening to scream, but before he could shout a warning, Packard fired his two shots in quick succession. The first bullet smacked hard into the sergeant's right shoulder with a sickening thud, the bullet smashing into his collarbone and deflecting out of his back. The second bullet ripped into the side of the sergeant's neck in a crimson spray of blood. He staggered backwards from the impact, arms flailing and colliding with the big corporal behind him as he went down, arterial blood pulsing in long gushes from the neck wound. He was dead in seconds.

The burly corporal turned, froze, looking straight at Packard. Uncertain and shocked in that moment's hesitation, before stirring into life, his face twisting in anger, he reached for his holster. It was the last conscious thing he did.

Campbell saw the danger and was too quick. He fired. The bullet hit the corporal's forehead just above the left eye, jerking the head upwards, sending a spray of bone splinters, brain matter, and blood high into the air like water under pressure. Death was instant. He dropped to the flagstone floor next to the sergeant with a heavy crump.

Complete uproar broke out. With a wild chorus of screams and curses, Packard's hidden men poured out from the two doors either side of the hall, firing from the hip and shooting down three Germans before they even knew what was happening. A melee of shouts, gunfire, and screams echoed around the hall from the madness of a close-quarter gunfight. The struggling German figures in the middle of the hall were hit with a terrifying noise as a fusillade of bullets tore into their bodies, arms, and legs. It was pure hell as bullets banged and whizzed around them. Facing certain annihilation, some, seeing safety a few feet away, turned to escape via the entrance, but they tripped over the fallen rifles and bodies of their comrades around them, or slipped on the blood splashed across the stone floor. It was carnage.

The last standing German managed to get his rifle to his shoulder but he was cut down by a volley of bullets that peppered his body like hail, turning his insides to mincemeat. He went down heavily, with a horrifying scream among the rest of the other wretched wounded, writhing and groaning with the limp corpses on the blood-soaked flagstone floor.

Suddenly a dark figure in a spiked helmet and carrying a pistol appeared in the entrance, his back to the sunlight, making it impossible to see his features clearly. It was Haas. A gunshot rang out. Haas groaned, clutching his chest, slumping to his knees, his head tilting to one side before he pitched forward, stone dead.

Packard lowered his smoking Webley, his heart thumping, and his breathing hard.

It was over. Packard's men just stood and stared listlessly, contemplating the horror they'd just been through in a few short seconds that seemed like a lifetime. The floor around the dead and dying was covered in blood, like spilled red paint.

Campbell reloaded his Webley, snapping it closed before he moved about the writhing heap. At least three Germans were still alive, spread out on the floor, their whimpering and groans clear for everyone to hear.

He turned to Hedges. 'Get two men to remove the weapons from this heap and then drag the three wounded over there,' he pointed. 'The nuns can deal with them later.'

Packard stood by, watching his sergeant while he snapped his Webley in half to reload. Seconds were ticking by and there was no time to lose. Hoffmann and two other Germans were still outside. There was still unfinished business, and it had to be resolved quickly if they had any chance to get out of this town alive.

CHAPTER 36

Sitting alone at the back of the lorry in the dim, smelly interior of the barn, Norris began wondering why it was taking so long for the others to join him. After a while he heard voices, then a truck, possibly two, crunch on the gravel driveway outside. The faintest breeze brought him subdued voices – speaking in German.

He stood up, afraid and not sure what he should do. It was obvious, the Germans were here and about to search the abbey. Nervously, he wiped his mouth with the back of his hand. He decided to take a look at what was going on outside. He stepped over the tailgate and carefully lowered himself to the floor. As he made his way to the closed doorway at the front, hazy rays of morning sun probed through several gaps in the barn's dry old panelling. He stopped to peak out through a large crack beside the door and stepped back abruptly when he saw two German soldiers heading towards him. He looked around wildly. *Where to go? What to do?*

He turned around and, almost on tiptoe, silently went to the back of the barn to hide in a dimmed corner behind a stack of straw, automatically lifting his Webley from its holster and steeling himself to fight. He felt sick with fear and began licking his dry lips nervously. His right hand trembled as he gripped the Webley.

Suddenly the barn door opened halfway, flooding the interior with light. The first German soldier to enter the barn stumbled over something on the floor and began cursing in German, then paused just inside to allow his eyes to adjust to the dimmed interior.

Norris froze, hardly breathing, his gun hand still trembling, his nervous finger twitching on the trigger. He thought of surrender but rejected the idea. The next few seconds were vital. He felt as if he should shout something out, but what? For a few seconds he tortured himself with indecision, then he heard muffled gunshots, sounding like they were coming from the abbey. Both Germans spun around, unslung their rifles, and took up a kneeling position by the door, looking outwards. He heard them talking urgently in low voices but couldn't translate what they were saying. Then one got up, almost blotting out the light, and headed into the interior of the barn. Norris pointed the Webley at the dark shape with a trembling hand as it slowly approached him. For a second he panicked, then he squeezed the trigger and the revolver kicked and fired.

The gunshot sounded like a mini explosion in the confines of the barn, and his ears screamed from the deafening roar of the bang. The German soldier let out a startled cry and fell wounded to the floor in a heap. The other German was shocked into action, instantly throwing himself to the floor while Norris fired off another panicky shot in his direction. He missed but struck the metal hinge on the doorway above the German's head. It ricocheted off with a loud *zing*.

The fear Norris had felt was now gone. The fight for his survival had begun.

There was a scramble of sudden movements and curses from the wounded German on the floor in front of him. In one second, maybe two, the German soldier had lifted his rifle to fire a shot. He missed. But Norris felt the shock of the bullet whizzing past his face, and, in an automatic reaction, he took aim and fired two shots at the wounded German on the floor, killing him instantly.

From the German sprawled across the doorway he could hear muffled curses and a metallic sound like that of a rifle bolt being worked back and forth. His rifle had jammed, then suddenly, leaping to his feet, he gave a chilling cry and lunged forward. Norris saw a ray of sunlight gleaming along the edge of the bayonet, the pointed end rushing towards him with the dark shape of a mad demented man pushing behind it.

The animal instinct for survival rose quickly within him. He pointed the Webley at arm's length and fired at the dark shape rushing towards him. The German soldier cried out and fell dead at his feet. Despite his ears still roaring from the gunshots, and a layer of sweat now covering his face, he began reloading his gun. The tremble in his hands had stopped, and for the first time since he joined the army, he really felt soldier-like, something he hadn't thought he was capable of until now. With his newfound confidence, he got up and started looking around the barn for another way out.

He found none and made his way to the open door at the front to peek out. His eyes quickly grew accustomed to the bright daylight outside and he began looking around the driveway for danger and a way to escape. All he could see were two German trucks outside the abbey entrance, the prioress, and a man wearing a dark hat and coat waving a gun around. Suddenly the man grabbed the prioress and she let out a cry. She lurched to get away, but he was too strong for her. He gripped her tightly around the neck, after which she didn't put up too much of a resistance, but he could see she was in distress. The man then aimed at the abbey entrance and fired a shot.

CHAPTER 37

As Packard stepped over the body of Haas and crept up to the entrance, he heard a woman cry out and instantly recognised the voice of the prioress. He peered around the door frame gingerly. Bang! A shot rang out, slamming into the brickwork just above his head, sending a shower of dust and tiny fragments over him as he flinched back.

It was Hoffmann, and in that moment, Packard had seen he'd taken the prioress hostage and was using her as a human shield. He couldn't rush him, he would kill the prioress for sure, but he had to do *something*.

Campbell joined him at the entrance, kneeling by Packard's elbow. He was breathing heavily but not through exertion. One by one the men fell into line behind him, reloaded, keyed up and ready to fight it out. Campbell said, 'If that's Hoffmann, we'll rush 'im.'

Packard shook his head. 'Can't, he's using the prioress as a shield.'

'Bastard,' Campbell replied.

'Got any suggestions, Sergeant?'

Campbell ran a hand over his chin. 'Could try calling him and see what he has to say. He'll want something.'

Packard nodded. 'I'll give it a try, but I know he wants the gold.' He cupped a hand to his mouth and called out, 'Hoffmann! It's Major Packard, British Army. I want to talk to you. I'm coming out, don't shoot!'

Campbell grabbed his officer's arm. 'I said talk to him, not make yourself a shooting target! What are you expecting to do?'

Packard looked round and saw Campbell and all the others, grim-faced and staring at him. 'If the opportunity presents itself, I intend to kill the bastard.'

Campbell grinned. 'Oh, well that's more like it. Long as you've got a plan.'

'Stay here,' said Packard. 'I'll give it a try.' He stood up, stiffened for a moment, taking in a few short breaths to calm himself, then gingerly eased his head around the doorframe. Hoffmann was still there, tightly gripping the prioress, the barrel of his Luger pointing hard against her head.

Packard stepped out slowly, both hands raised, his right hand still holding the Webley. He stepped out onto the driveway and stood there for a moment to let Hoffmann scrutinize him, feeling vulnerable and scared and thinking of Vanessa.

Hoffmann took a panicked look at him, straining his eyes in an effort to see any tricks.

'What do you want, Major?' he called out.

Packard could see the anguished look on the prioress's oval face, with one hand gripping Hoffmann's arm around her neck, the other holding the crucifix around her waist. He could see her lips moving. She was praying.

'There's just one of you now, the rest are dead,' Packard said. 'Let the prioress go and I'll let you live.'

Hoffmann grunted, seeming rattled that all his men had been killed. His head moved fractionally sideways, his eyes darting to the barn then back to Packard. 'Let me live, you say?' he shouted back. 'Oh, I'll live, Major, as long as I have the prioress.'

'I give you my word as a British officer. In the circumstances, that's a fair exchange.'

Hoffmann laughed out loud, then narrowed his eyes, his features set and determined. 'Your word, Major, means nothing to me. You want the prioress; I want the gold. Now *that's* a fair exchange!'

Packard shook his head. 'No deal, Hoffmann. I'd rather eat my own liver than hand the gold to you. Besides, it's not my gold to give. It belongs to Belgium, and I'm entrusted to deliver it safely to England.' Inwardly, he cursed himself for telling Hoffmann that bit of information.

Hoffmann nodded. 'Very well, Major. Then I'll take my leave.' He slowly edged himself backwards towards the open gate, keeping a firm grip on the prioress as a shield, she having no option but to go with him. Once outside the gated entrance he turned right, heading for the town square.

Packard turned and called out to Campbell, 'Get someone to take a look for Norris in the barn,' then went to the gate and peered round carefully. He saw Hoffmann slowly edging backwards, still using the prioress as a shield, gun to her head. But he noticed something else – there were no Germans around and the town seemed quiet. Had they gone?

He ran back to the abbey entrance. 'Right, what's happening with Norris?'

'Corporal Ratcliffe took his section to the barn,' Campbell replied. 'Norris killed both Germans, but he's shaken up a little.'

Packard pushed up the peak of his cap and said, 'Norris! Well I'd be damned. Good for him.'

'Amen to that.'

Packard nodded, then tugged his cap firmly over his eyes. 'Right, Sergeant, get the men on the lorries, we're moving out now!'

'What about the prioress?'

'There's nothing we can do,' said Packard, then added bitterly, 'and I've made a big mistake. I've just told Hoffmann that I'm taking the gold to England. He now knows that I'll be heading for the nearest port.'

Campbell grimaced, recognising what his officer had done. 'Then we'd best get our skates on, sir.'

'Of course, we've no time to lose. I'll get Vanessa, you can get the lorries fired up and ready to leave.' He dashed into the abbey. The smell of fresh flowers and beeswax had been replaced by gun-smoke and blood.

Packard got to the door, knocked gently and opened it. The three women were still huddled in the corner, and he could see they'd been crying.

Vanessa's face lit up when he entered, and went forward quickly, throwing her arms around his neck, kissing him hard on the lips. 'My darling, my darling, you're safe, thank God.' Tears rolled down her cheeks.

He pulled back slowly. 'We're all safe,' he said, 'and about to leave.'

'And the prioress?' she asked.

He shook his head. 'Hoffmann got away, and he took the prioress with him.'

The three women gasped in horror, pressing their hands to their mouths.

'Is she ... hurt?' It was a catch-all term, a way not to say the things it meant, not to blame him.

'She's fine at the moment,' Packard replied, then his tone hardened. 'If we don't get away right now, we'll all join her, now come on!'

He grabbed her hand and quickly led her through the hall, and from the corner of his eye he could see Vanessa's eyes widen, her mouth gaping as she caught sight of the German dead, twisted or spread-eagled on the floor, bloodied and grotesque. They got to the entrance, where he guided her around a small puddle of blood that had seeped from under the body of Haas, sprawled across the floor. He hurried on as she put a hand to her mouth to retch. He was too troubled to care at that moment, but he knew that later, when things had calmed down, he would feel ashamed and angry with himself.

Campbell was on the drive as both lorries pulled out of the barns. Packard, face taut, said, 'If Fritz gets ahead of us, we're done for.'

Campbell jerked his head towards the two German trucks. 'They won't chase us in those,' he said. 'We've just emptied the engine oil. A couple of miles down the road and the engines will seize.'

Packard turned on his heel to look at the first truck. He could see a dark stain on the gravel beneath it. 'Good thinking,' he said.

'Thank our two drivers,' Campbell replied, 'it was their idea.'

The first lorry pulled up beside them. Packard helped to lift Vanessa into the back. 'It'll be much safer in there than the front cab,' he told her, then ordered the men in the back to keep a low profile unless they hit trouble. He went to the cab, stepped up into it, pulled the Webley from its holster, and checked it was loaded

Driver Joyce was ready, just waiting for the order.

'Let's get out of here, as fast as you like and stop for nothing.'

The lorry set off with a jerk, with Campbell's lorry right behind. They turned left at the gate entrance and headed for the Lille gate to the south. They passed a platoon of marching German soldiers, loaded down with heavy backpacks, who took no notice of them. The Germans were pulling out; most it seemed had already gone. As they approached the Lille gate, two German sentries wearing pork-pie hats, with their rifles slung over their shoulders, stood guard. One stepped into the road, raising his hand for them to stop.

Joyce shot Packard a sideways glance, looking for instructions.

'Easy Joyce, just keep going. Run the bastard down if necessary.'

Joyce nodded without answering.

Then Packard turned in his seat to the small hatch window behind him, saying, 'Corporal Hedges, prepare yourselves to engage two sentries on the bridge as we pass!'

'Will do, sir!'

They got closer but didn't slow down. It seemed to take an eternity before the sentry acted. Packard saw him narrow his eyes in disbelief as he quickly stepped aside and began to unsling his rifle. There were shouts of 'Halt! Halt!' but they sped past the sentries and kept on going.

Behind him, he heard the sudden clatter of pistols firing. Packard craned his head round to see. The two sentries were diving for cover. A cheer went up from the men. Packard chuckled.

Across the bridge, they turned right onto the road that skirted the southern perimeter of the town and took the sign post for Poperinghe, the next town – and an hour's drive from there lay Dunkirk.

CHAPTER 38

Jacques sat at his desk in the post office, taking a final draw of his cigarette before twisting it out in an overcrowded ashtray next to him. He scratched his snow-white moustache with a nicotine-stained finger and started to work. He opened a folder in front of him that was filled with dozens of telegram messages from local businesses that had been pushed through his letter box earlier, to be sent out that morning to their suppliers for urgent orders. The occupation by the German Army in Ypres had drained all the town's resources of bread, milk, meat, potatoes, vegetables, flour, rice, grain, petrol, straw, fodder, and almost everything else that they could buy, requisition or steal, including some private cars, horses, carts, and some delivery vans. Not to mention the cash taken from the bank, the jewellers, and his post office safe. Now that the Germans were leaving, and most had already gone, the business community of Ypres had to stock up quickly.

He was contemplating where to start when he heard the shop door open and then close, indicating that someone had entered. He frowned, took a deep breath, got to his feet, and suspecting that it was more urgent telegrams, he went out of the office door that led him to the front of his post office shop.

To his surprise, Hoffmann was standing in front of the counter, red-faced, sweating and almost breathless. Standing next to him was the prioress, also red-faced, hot, sweating, and almost in a state of collapse. He noticed that Hoffmann was gripping her arm like she was under arrest.

Jacques leaned on the counter, his hands clenched into fists. He trained his eyes on Hoffmann and felt a rush of anger that he could barely control. 'What is it you want this time?' he said.

Hoffmann released the prioress' arm, and his face looked rigid when he answered, 'Your services on the telegraph. I have urgent messages for Berlin.'

'I thought you pigs were leaving?' Jacques bit back.

Hoffmann narrowed his eyes, taking a menacing step toward him, and pointing a finger directly at him, he replied, 'You'll do well to watch your tongue, Herr Jacques. Some of us may stay a little longer, and it wouldn't do to antagonise us with your boldness just yet. I suggest you consider your words very carefully ... you might be *misunderstood*.'

Jacques tried his hardest to remain calm. It was a clear threat to his safety, and, not knowing how true it was that not all the Germans were leaving today, he swallowed his pride hard. He glanced at the prioress, taking in her demeanour as she leaned forward against the counter, her forehead resting on her outstretched arms. She was breathing deeply. It was clear that she just had an unpleasant experience.

Jacques leaned down to her and spoke softly. 'Are you all right, Reverend Mother?' he asked her. 'Would you like to sit down? Can I get you a drink of water?'

She raised her head enough to show her grim face. She looked at him, her eyebrows arched solemnly, her blue eyes bloodshot and tearful. 'Thank you, Jacques,' she murmured gratefully. 'Some water please.'

Hoffmann banged the flat of his hand on the counter, startling the prioress and Jacques into standing bolt upright. 'Enough of this nonsense!' he growled. 'We have not come here to socialise. Water and other pleasantries can wait. I have an urgent message for my superiors in Berlin that must be sent now!'

Jacques sniffed indignantly. 'Is that so? I too have many urgent messages to send this morning after your little army's occupation. What makes yours so important above all others?'

Hoffmann gave a cruel grin as he pulled the Luger from his coat pocket, pointed it directly at Jacques, then slowly swivelled it towards the prioress. He lowered his voice. 'She makes my messages important above all else, Jacques. I trust you understand that?'

Jacques glanced at the prioress as she clutched at her neck anxiously. He tightened his fists and swallowed hard. He understood and nodded his head.

'Good,' said Hoffmann. 'That was easy, now let's move into your office at the back. But be careful now, Jacques, no sudden moves. I'd hate for the prioress to come to any harm because of a moment's foolishness on your part.'

Jacques stood rigid, red-faced and angry.

Hoffmann gestured with his head towards the office door. 'Would you mind?' he said, then he grabbed the prioress's arm and pulled her in front of him, shoving her forward. 'The office door, Jacques, open it and step inside so that I can clearly see you.'

Jacques took a sharp intake of breath to control his anger, then did as he was told. He pushed opened the semi-closed door and went inside slowly. Hoffmann shoved the prioress towards a chair to his right. She let out a little cry, more in protest than pain.

'Sit there,' he ordered. Then Hoffmann went to a desk in the corner on his left that had two trays full of documents and message pads. He pulled out a chair and sat on it, gestured with the gun for Jacques to move further away from him until he was at his own desk with the telegraph, then to sit down. 'Good,' said Hoffmann. 'I can write my message and keep an eye on you both at the same time.' He reached inside his jacket pocket, took out a small black book like a diary and opened it. It was full of codes. Then he pulled a message pad in front of him from the tray, picked up a pencil from the desk and began to write, checking the code book while writing, and, every other moment, glancing up at Jacques. The office resumed its silence while he scribbled away.

Jacques sat there livid, his face burning red as he thought of ways to distract Hoffmann so that he could rush him. But his frustration was that he could not bring himself to act if it would put the prioress in any danger.

After about twenty minutes, Hoffmann stopped writing and began reading. When Hoffmann stopped reading, he looked up. He pushed back his chair, got up, and handed the message sheet to the prioress. 'Give him that,' he said.

The prioress took it, slowly stood up, and crossed the room to where Jacques sat at the telegraph desk. He could see she was nervous, her hands trembled as she handed the note to him. He gave her a reassuring smile, trying to put her at ease. She opened her mouth to speak but said nothing, just bit her lower lip. She turned to face Hoffmann.

Hoffmann gestured with the pistol for her to return to her chair, which she did immediately. She crossed the room and eased herself down on the chair.

'Well, go on, do your work and send it, word for word – and I'll wait for a reply,' snapped Hoffman, gesturing with his gun.

Jacques held the message sheet in his hand, seething. The prioress was scared. There was nothing he could do but obey. He looked at the address on the message sheet and hesitated for a moment:

To *Commander Walter Isendahl, Director of Naval Intelligence Department*

(N). Headquarters of The Imperial German Naval Service, Berlin.

Jacques' bushy white eyebrows arched quizzically as he looked across at Hoffmann. 'A reply to this could take a little time,' he said.

'Don't question it, Herr Jacques,' Hoffmann said with a wry smile, again emphasising his name, 'just send it.'

Jacques shot a glance at the prioress, who was still in the chair, wringing her hands nervously. He looked back at Hoffmann, shrugged his shoulders, turned his back on him, adjusted his chair under the desk, leaned forward, and began tapping.

*

At five minutes to nine, Marcel Du Mont left his police barracks and made his way to the Cloth Hall. He shivered and turned up the collar of his coat, not from cold but from his nerves. The town was unusually quiet, no one was around, not even the German patrols. Where were they? Then a trumpet call sounded far away, the other side of town at least. It was German; who else? He spat on the ground, cursing their occupation.

He passed through the empty square, empty because no Germans were there – had they really gone? A platoon of German soldiers with heavy backpacks were marching towards the Lille gate some distance away, their boots crunching on the cobblestones in a measured step as they headed out of town. Six German riders were standing near the corner of the square, waiting. Then a senior officer appeared on horseback and they saluted him as he trotted past. He saluted back, then they turned and spurred their horses after him, forming a double line behind like an escort, heading towards the Menin gate. It was hard to believe, but the Germans did look as if they were going.

When he got to the Cloth Hall to report to Hoffmann, the door was closed but unlocked. Unusual, because since the German arrival yesterday, a guard had stood outside. Come to think of it, he recalled, there was no guard outside the hotel in the square either. He opened the door and went in, expecting to see at least one field police NCO sitting at the desk. It was empty. No one about, the place was deserted but the candles were still lit. He called out but there was no answer. The place looked deserted.

Marcel saw the stairs that led to the cells in the basement where he had been held captive earlier and went down into the semi-darkness. A few lighted wall candles showed the way, flickering as he went past them. He found the cell that held Rene Colaert, the mayor. The door was ajar. His worst fears were that he would find him dead, tortured and mutilated. Carefully he pushed open the door a little, throwing some candlelight from the corridor into the shadowy cell. He peaked in. It smelt strongly of stale piss, damp, and neglect.

'Rene? Rene, are you in here?' he called. Then he saw him and took a sharp intake of breath. Colaert was tied up and sitting in a puddle against the far wall. 'Rene!' Marcel pushed the door open wide, entered the cell and knelt beside him. 'Rene, are you ok?'

Colaert was asleep, but he opened his eyes with a stare, then began blinking. 'Marcel, it's you, thank God. For a moment I thought Hoffmann had come back.'

Marcel set about untying him. 'There's no one here,' Marcel said. 'They all seem to have gone.'

'I know,' Colaert said, 'they all went to the abbey in a hurry and left me. I told them I needed the toilet before they went. Hoffmann just laughed and said, "We don't have time, just piss yourself." He said he would send someone back for me.' Colaert shook his head, 'I couldn't hold it any longer, Marcel, I'm pissed through,' he said, his face sour with shame.

'Don't worry about that,' Marcel said, 'it couldn't be helped.'

Colaert shook his head. 'I dread to think what has happened at the abbey with the nuns and the English soldiers there.'

'Your guess is as good as mine,' Marcel said, and he threw the rope to one side as he helped Rene to his feet. 'But it does look as if the Germans are pulling out of town. Most have gone already.'

'Then Hoffmann has the gold,' Colaert said dejectedly. 'That's what he came for, the gold, and now he has it.'

'It doesn't matter,' Marcel said. 'We're safe at least.'

'Safe?' Colaert said. 'And what about Henri Renard?'

Marcel nodded. 'I know, Rene, I know. Let's get you home and cleaned up. I'll return with a few of my officers to collect Henri's body.'

'The least we can do,' Colaert said. 'He's the town's hero now, that's for sure.'

They left the cell and went up the stone steps to the main door, and just as they stepped out into the empty street, they heard the muffled sound of a woman being chastised by a man's harsh voice. They turned to look, and in the distance they saw Hoffmann, his arm around the prioress's neck, dragging her across the square with a gun in his other hand. Marcel grabbed Rene's elbow and pulled him back into the shadow of the door to watch.

'My God,' said Colaert, 'Hoffmann has arrested the prioress!'

Marcel looked curiously at the spectacle. 'Maybe,' he said, 'but it doesn't make sense. Where are his field police? He looks as if he's running away and taking the prioress with him? Something's not right. Something's gone wrong at the abbey.'

They watched as Hoffmann disappeared from view.

'Look, go and get yourself cleaned up,' said Marcel. 'I'll follow Hoffmann discreetly to see where he goes and try and find out what's been happening.'

Colaert nodded. 'Good idea, but take care, my friend,' and they shook hands firmly before departing.

Hoffmann wasn't hard to follow; he was too occupied with dragging the reluctant prioress down the street to the post office to notice that Marcel was following some distance behind. Once they went inside, Marcel realised that Hoffmann would be sending messages. Why else would he go there? He decided to act and quickly made his way back to the police barracks to retrieve a pistol from his desk drawer. He sprung the magazine, took seven .32 bullets from a box and loaded it, then put the pistol in his coat pocket before making his way back to the post office. This time, he had no intension of meeting Hoffmann unarmed.

While he was making his way to Jacques' shop, he realised the town's people were staying at home until they were certain all the Germans had gone. In the circumstances it was a wise precaution. Nobody wanted to attract unwanted German attention now. As he returned to the post office, he'd hardly seen a soul, except from the odd twitch of a curtain as he walked the streets.

When he reached Jacques' shop, he carefully peered in through the glass panel of the door, shielding his eyes from the glare so that he could see inside. The front of the post office was empty. Beyond the counter, the door leading to Jacques' office at the back was open slightly. Hoffmann had to be in there with Jacques and the prioress, he thought. That's where the telegraph was housed. Marcel took the pistol from his pocket. Feeling the weight, he gripped it tightly before going in.

The moment Marcel was about to place his hand on the door handle he suddenly felt his heart race as a rush of adrenalin pumped around his body. Small beads of sweat broke out on his brow. To steady his nerve, he took two deep breaths, then he gripped the door handle with his free hand and carefully opened the door to step inside, closing the door gently and quietly behind him. Then he glided silently across the shop floor to a position behind the counter and next to the open doorway. He stopped and quietly listened. He was now sweating across his top lip. His hands were a little shaky. There was silence in the office apart from the distant *tap tap tap* of Jacques on the telegraph. He knew the layout of the office, so Jacques had to be at his desk at the far end. But where was Hoffmann?

Then the tapping stopped, and he heard Jacques say, 'That's the acknowledgement from Berlin, and I've replied that I've received it.'

'Good,' said Hoffmann. His voice confirmed that he was in the room, and guessed he was near the door and probably at the desk to the left. Then he heard a chair scrape across the floor. He guessed right; Hoffmann was near the door and was about to stand up. 'My work here is done,' the German said in a mocking tone. 'And your work has also come to an end.'

Marcel heard the prioress cry out, 'No!'

That was his cue to enter. Her cry spurred him into action. He stepped into the doorway, pushing the door fully open, and for that moment, Hoffmann had his back to him, pointing his Luger at Jacque. He saw Hoffmann shoot a glance over his shoulder as he stepped in, and as Hoffmann began to twist around, Marcel squeezed the trigger and fired. There was a loud bang. He shot him in the back, square between the shoulder blades. Hoffmann jerked from the impact, his eyes glazed over, but the Luger fired before he crashed to the floor dead. The gun went spinning across the floor.

Jacques, he saw, threw his hands to his face in horror, but not at Hoffmann sprawled dead on the floor – but at the prioress in the chair to his right. Jacques immediately rushed over to her. She was clutching her chest. The white wimple around her neck and shoulders was quickly turning red from blood. He knelt down to her. She was gurgling blood from her mouth. She gave one last gasp, and in that second her head slumped to the right. She was dead.

Marcel was frozen to the spot, his ears ringing from the two gunshots, his pistol still smoking, gripped in his hand.

CHAPTER 39

'My first piece of advice is don't ignore that letter,' said Packard.

Commander John Buckmaster, Royal Navy, looked perplexed as he surveyed the letter he was holding. The letter that was signed by The First Lord of the Admiralty, Winston Churchill. It gave the major standing in front of him the authority to secure a safe passage on *any* British warship to Dover.

About an hour ago, at ten thirty in the morning, Packard had arrived at the port of Dunkirk, demanding to be let inside. He and his troops were refused entry at the gate by a group of armed gendarmes, led by a tall sergeant with a long thin dark moustache, who kept snapping his fingers, demanding papers of authority to enter. Eventually, Packard got him to contact the harbour master's office. The harbour master had arrived ten minutes later. He was a short, dowdy, fat man in his sixties with an oversized bristling grey moustache, and like the gendarme sergeant, he wouldn't listen to what Packard was trying to explain to him. He rocked up and down on the balls of his feet, shrugging his shoulders and demanding official paperwork.

Packard, exasperated, showed him the gold in the back of the lorries and explained where it had come from. The harbour master raised his eyebrows, ordered the gendarmes to guard the lorries, and then rushed off back inside the port. Twenty minutes later, to Packard's surprise, he'd returned with a British naval officer. Aged about twenty-nine, with dark hair and grey eyes, he was dressed in a dark blue uniform with a single line of medal ribbons across the chest, and the cap that gave him his authority had gold leaf on the peak. His rank of three gold stripes with the distinctive loop on top was on his lower sleeve. It glinted in the light against the dark blue background of his uniform. In comparison, Packard felt dirty and unkempt.

'Hello, I'm Commander John Buckmaster,' he said, and shook Packard's hand firmly. 'What can I do for you?'

Packard thought Buckmaster had a look of being razor-sharp and very professional, and introduced himself. Then he took him to one side to briefly explain what was going on without going into too much detail. And then he handed him Churchill's letter to read.

Buckmaster read it, then rubbed his chin as he read it a second time.

'I'll have to contact London first, to verify your story and this letter,' he said cautiously.

'Of course,' said Packard, 'but make it quick, we can't wait long. This cargo has priority, and I want to be out of here and crossing the Channel in the next hour or two.'

Buckmaster shook his head ruefully, and said almost apologetically, 'An hour or two? Can't be done. My ship is not due to sail until tomorrow at zero eight hundred hours. We're refuelling and taking supplies on board. Besides, half of the ship's company are on leave until twenty-three hundred tonight. The first they've had for weeks.'

Packard sighed, then pointed into the port and said, 'Isn't there another ship in there leaving earlier that I could take?'

Buckmaster shook his head, 'Afraid not. Most of the merchant shipping are foreign. Our last merchantman sailed for Dover this morning. I'm next, once my ship's company are aboard, and supplies are loaded.'

'Dammit!'

'Look, I'll make that call,' Buckmaster said, 'and see what we can do.'

'Good,' said Packard. 'I'll come with you, if you don't mind, I have a password to give if it's necessary.'

'Very well,' said Buckmaster, handing the letter back to Packard. 'I'll give permission for you to enter the port and be parked alongside my ship, HMS *Gibraltar*. The "Gib", as we fondly call her. From there, we'll go to the harbour master's office to make the call. He has a direct line to Dover Harbour we can use. From Dover they can redirect the call to the Admiralty in London. In the last few weeks, we've had to use it often.' He turned to the harbour master and spoke to him in schoolboy French about the cargo and what they were doing. The harbour master nodded his head, then went to Packard, gave him a big smile and pumped his hand, saying, 'Viva la Belgique! Viva la France! Viva l'Angleterre!'

The two lorries stopped on the jetty where HMS *Gibraltar* was berthed. Packard stepped from the cab along with Buckmaster, looking the ship over.

'A beauty, isn't she?' Buckmaster said with pride.

Packard nodded. He knew nothing about ships but he did admire her lines. The ship looked lean, fast, and powerful, he thought. Right now, that made her the most beautiful ship in the world.

'Tell your men to wait here,' said Buckmaster, 'and join me over there in the harbour master's office.'

Packard went and spoke to Campbell in the second lorry about what was happening, then he went to the back of his own lorry to make sure Vanessa was ok.

'Not long now,' he told her. 'We'll be aboard in a jiffy. All safe and sound.'

He went to the harbour master's office and found Buckmaster on the telephone in a small room just inside the building. The harbour master was standing behind his desk. The office had a large dirty window that overlooked the jetty where the *Gibraltar* was berthed. The air smelt of cheap cigarettes and coffee. It was too small for Packard to stand inside comfortably and he decided not to squeeze in, so he stood just outside by the doorway. Outside the office was a larger room with three crude desks, chairs, and a line of tall filing cabinets against the far wall. Each desk had a telephone but only the harbour master's telephone had a line direct to Dover. A large wall clock hung above the harbour master's door, ticking loudly. A thin-faced, bearded, bespectacled man in a dark grey suit bent over his desk, working on papers. A small wooden sign on the top of his desk said, 'Chief Clerk.' He looked up as Packard entered, removed his spectacles, and scrutinized him intently.

'You have business here, monsieur?' he said to Packard.

Packard nodded. 'I'm seeing the harbour master,' he replied.

'Ah, I see,' said the chief clerk. Then stared at him for a few seconds more. 'Unusual?'

'Unusual? What is?' Packard said.

'To see a British army officer here. They are all naval men who come here to see the harbour master – not army. Your business must be important to be seen by the harbour master?'

Packard shrugged his shoulders. 'I'm just passing through, won't be here long.'

'The *Gibraltar*?' said the chief clerk, waving his spectacles nonchalantly towards the ship's berth.

'Hopefully,' Packard replied, and looked away, not wishing to engage with the man anymore. Something about the way he stared made Packard suspicious of him.

Buckmaster, phone at his ear, turned to Packard in the doorway and said, 'Dover is transferring me to London now.'

Packard nodded. 'Good.'

Ten seconds passed, then Buckmaster glanced at Packard and whispered, 'I'm through to the Admiralty. Ah, good morning, sir …' He introduced himself, recounted the events at the gate and began to explain about the letter. It was a difficult line and he had to keep asking whoever was on the other end to repeat themselves. 'What's that you're saying?' Buckmaster contorted his face as he listened intently. 'Yes, yes, I see, ok, got that. Leave it to me. I'll arrive in Dover tomorrow morning as planned. Yes, sir. Thank you, sir. Goodbye.'

'Well, what did they say?' Packard said, a sharp note of urgency in his breathing.

Buckmaster was beaming when he replied, 'You'll never believe it … but I've just spoken with the Admiral of the Fleet, Prince Louis of Battenberg. I explained everything to some pompous commodore at the Admiralty, and he goes and puts me through to the Admiral himself. Apparently, the Admiral was absolutely delighted by my call. He said, Mr Churchill will be "cock-a-hoop" when he hears about you making it to Dunkirk with the gold, and I'm to pass on the Admiral's hearty congratulations to you and your men, and, in his words, to "Splice the Mainbrace."'

Packard smiled back, pleased that this mission was almost at an end. Just a short trip across the Channel to England and home.

'Pink gins all round, I'd say,' said Buckmaster smiling.

'Ah, yes, pink gins,' said Packard. 'After what I've been through in the last few days, I'll certainly drink to that.'

As they made their way across the jetty to the ship, Buckmaster said, 'I'll speak to the first lieutenant about finding accommodation for your men, and a place to store the gold. How many are you?'

'Twelve men and a girl.'

'A girl?' Buckmaster said, suddenly serious.

Packard nodded. 'Too long to explain now, but she helped me secure the gold from Fritz,' he said. 'Her position in town was compromised, she couldn't stay. I offered her sanctuary with us. She took it.'

'A sort of ... *agent*, you mean?'

'Not quite,' said Packard, 'but there was a good chance she would have been executed by Fritz for what she did.'

When they reached the dockside, Campbell was standing by the first lorry.

'Wait here,' said Buckmaster. 'Once I've got things sorted on board, I'll give you a shout.'

'Fair enough,' said Packard. 'I'll let my men stretch their legs and have a smoke.'

Buckmaster went straight up the gangway. The Quartermaster saluted and piped the Commander aboard.

Fifteen minutes passed when a young sub-lieutenant with an older, grizzled-looking chief petty officer and six ratings stepped from the ship and approached the lorries. The sub-lieutenant saluted Packard. 'Good morning, sir. I'm Sub-Lieutenant Rogers, this is Chief Petty Officer Mulraney. The Commander's compliments, sir. Would you and the lady join him on board? The Chief will arrange to help unload the lorries and accommodate your men.'

'Thank you, Sub-Lieutenant.' Packard turned to take Vanessa's suitcase.

'Leave that to me, sir,' said the sub as he grabbed the suitcase handle and touched the peak of his cap, giving a big smile to Vanessa when he saw just how pretty she was. 'Follow me, if you please,' he added and made his way up the gangway.

Packard turned to Campbell, 'I'll leave you with the Chief to sort things out. Whatever happens, I want a guard on the gold even if it's under lock and key.'

'Leave it to me, sir,' said Campbell. 'I'll make sure it's done.'

On board, below deck, was a small wardroom where they were greeted by Buckmaster. A ward steward stood by with a tray of drinks as they stepped over the coving and entered. The room smelt of cooked food, stale pipe smoke, and polish.

'Welcome aboard the Gib,' said Buckmaster, smiling.

'Thank you,' said Packard, returning the smile. 'May I introduce Vanessa Renard. Vanessa, this is John Buckmaster, commander of this ship.'

Vanessa held out her hand. 'I'm pleased to meet you, Commander.'

Buckmaster took her hand. 'I'm delighted to meet you, Vanessa. Major Packard gave no indication to me that you were such a beautiful woman.'

Vanessa blushed slightly. 'You're very kind, Commander, but I trust I'm not the only pretty girl to have walked these decks.'

Buckmaster smiled. 'But indeed you are,' he said. 'The Gib was commissioned in late 1912. By the time she had her sea trials and returned to port, she was just in time for the outbreak of war. Since then I've been escorting troop ships and supplies vessels across the Channel for the army. Pink gin anyone?'

The steward stepped forward and Vanessa took a glass from the tray, then Packard, and then Buckmaster. 'Cheers,' said Buckmaster, raising his glass, 'and congratulations to you both for recovering the Belgian gold.'

'Cheers,' Packard and Vanessa said as one.

After they took a drink, Packard said, 'We're not quite home and dry yet. I've got to get that gold safely to London, and across the

Channel first to do that. Fritz knows I'm here. I would hate for him to have a go while we're crossing.'

Buckmaster waved his hand. 'You've nothing to worry about,' he said, 'the Germans don't have any capital ships or destroyers near here. At best, they have a few small torpedo boats that patrol the coastline up ahead but they wouldn't dare come this far south, too risky for them. We have too many ships patrolling these waters to secure the army's supply line. Since this war's started, we haven't seen sight of their navy apart from a few patrols in the North Sea, but they don't hang around for long once we show up, let me tell you.'

Packard nodded. 'That's good to know, but I still won't be satisfied until I'm putting that gold into the Bank of England tomorrow.'

Buckmaster laughed. 'Relax. We'll be fine. Another gin?'

They all drained their glasses and the steward offered them another from the tray.

Packard heard the clatter of feet somewhere on the ship and voices raised. Both he and Vanessa glanced round at the sound.

'That'll be the gold being loaded,' remarked Buckmaster. 'On a ship you hear everything. After a while you get to distinguish all the sounds and what they are. A ship is like a living, breathing thing. You get to know her intimately.'

'I'm sure you do,' Packard said, but despite Buckmaster's assurances, deep down he still felt a twinge of apprehension about the crossing tomorrow.

CHAPTER 40

Commander Walter Isendahl sat back in his chair and regarded the decoded telegram from Hoffmann. His desktop was covered with intelligence files and reports.

Aged forty-two, he had a round face, dark eyes, and was bald with a waxed moustache that turned upwards at the end, just like the Kaiser's. He had taken his position as Head of Naval Intelligence, Department N (news department) in Berlin just months ago. His department was interested in naval operations, particularly the British, their main rival, the French and American navies, their port installations, and port defensive positions. Most recently, he'd begun receiving reports of radio monitoring of British ships carried out by radio station Heligoland on the ship SMS *Zieten*. Until recently, British warships had often used plain language in the radio text and call address.

He frowned. What did Hoffmann expect him to do? They had no ships or submarines close enough that could stop the gold shipment, and besides, he had no way of knowing on what ship the gold would be carried or when. He had telephoned the fleet admiral to explain this. The admiral told him not to worry, that he would contact the Kaiser and explain the situation himself. As far as Isendahl was concerned, that was that and the matter was closed – finished.

There was a tap at the door and he called out, 'Enter!'

Oberleutnant Karl Beck, his signals officer, entered the office. He was tall and slim with fair hair, and he stood before Isendahl waiting to be acknowledged. Isendahl looked up. 'What is it, Karl?'

'Sir, I have an interesting signal we received over an hour ago from one of our agents in France. Dunkirk, to be precise. It has just been decoded. He said an English army major had arrived at the port with gold, and it has been loaded onto the destroyer HMS *Gibraltar*. She sails for Dover tomorrow morning at eight.'

'Let me see it!' Isendahl snatched the details from Beck and read them. Then he suddenly stood up, moved around his desk and began pacing his office, staring at the report he held in front of him. He paused at the window, then turned to face Beck and said, 'Get me the Fleet Admiral on the phone, right away … No, wait! First, find out the present locations of our torpedo boats near the coast of France and bring them to me. I'll decide then whether to call the Fleet Admiral or not. Hurry Karl, this can't wait!'

Thirty minutes later, Beck returned with a chart showing all the present locations of their torpedo boats. He handed it over.

'You see, sir, we have one patrolling as far as the Danish coast,' said Beck. 'If given the signal now it could be off Dunkirk by dawn, sea state permitting.'

Isendahl read the report, stood up, and the two of them went to a coastal map on the wall. He pointed with his short stubby finger to its position. 'Here it is,' said Isendahl. 'Perfect, just perfect.'

'A torpedo boat on its own is no match against a destroyer, sir,' Beck reminded him. 'Especially in daylight.'

Isendahl gave a sigh. 'I know Beck, I know, but there's a chance of surprise. The British will not suspect it. All our ships are too far north. Our torpedo boat could travel along the coast at night and be in the right position in the morning to ambush the British destroyer when she leaves harbour. At that time it will be at its slowest and least manoeuvrable, with little sea-room. The captain and crew might be paying more attention to harbour regulations than to looking out for a torpedo boat, no?'

Beck had to agree there was a chance, albeit a slim one. 'A sort of hit and run attack, you mean?'

Isendahl said, 'Yes, yes, a hit and run, a surprise.' He went to the window and looked out. 'Send a signal to the captain of the torpedo boat … go to Dunkirk and sink HMS *Gibraltar* as she leaves harbour – at all costs!'

CHAPTER 41

Packard was invited to the open bridge of *Gibraltar* by Buckmaster. When he arrived, he glanced about at the Special Sea Dutymen there. It all seemed a bit crowded with sailors and officers, most with large powerful binoculars hanging from their necks. Orders were constantly being shouted out. He had no idea what the naval language meant, but he found it fascinating. He went to the rail to see a derrick beside the ship gently lifting the gangway from *Gibraltar*'s portside. Dockside men crowded around, tugging on ropes to steady the platform as it was lifted away and landed safely onto the jetty.

'Gangway clear, sir!' someone called.

A tugboat lay hove-to to pull the bow away from the jetty and point *Gibraltar* in the direction of the open harbour and the sea beyond.

Buckmaster stood in the middle of the bridge, binoculars hanging from his neck, legs apart, hands on hips, twisting his head left, then right, watching everything happening. Packard didn't join him; he could see he was concentrating.

'Very good.' Then Buckmaster went to a voice pipe, flipped the lid, leaned over, and shouted, 'Bridge, engine room … Standby!' Looking up and around, he moved forward to stare over the rail at the front, then moved to the back of the bridge. He returned to the voice pipe and shouted, 'Bridge, engine room, slow ahead!' He went to the rail at the front again and waved his hand to the dockhands and his own ratings on the berthing parties. 'Let go forrard!'

Packard could feel the engines coming to life by the vibrations from the deck and the stern of the ship slowly easing away from the dockside.

'All clear forrard, sir!'

Buckmaster was back at the rear of the bridge, waving a hand. 'Let go aft!'

Buckmaster did another lap to the front of the bridge and leaned over the rail as the tug started pulling *Gibraltar* away from the jetty.

'All clear aft, sir!'

Gibraltar had finally slipped her berth. The ship shuddered and then began to move.

'Clear of the jetty, sir!'

Packard leaned over the rail to see a triangle of water appear between the ship and the jetty, getting larger by the second.

The officer of the watch shouted down the voice pipe, 'Slow ahead both engines. Revolutions, one three zero!'

Gibraltar started to nudge forward.

The coxswain replied, 'Wheel amidships, one three zero revolutions on slow ahead both engines!'

Buckmaster turned his head to shout, 'Cast off from the tug, Number One, and tell her thank you!'

'Aye, aye, sir!'

Packard watched as the harbour started to slip away. Dock workers were watching, some were even waving.

A watchman gave Packard a pair of naval binoculars. 'Commander's compliments, sir, thought you might like the view.'

'Oh, yes, thank you.'

Packard put the heavy binoculars to his eyes and focussed the lenses on the shore. He was staggered; they were far more powerful than his field glasses. He could see dozens of workers on the quay going about their business and completely ignoring *Gibraltar*'s departure. Then, in the circle of lenses, he spotted the chief clerk standing outside the harbour master's office, shielding his eyes with a hand, watching *Gibraltar* leave harbour. He felt a chill run up and down his spine. It made him shiver.

Buckmaster said, 'Less speed, Number One, we're moving too fast inside the harbour!'

'Aye, aye, sir.' Number One leaned over a voice pipe. 'Bridge, wheelhouse, revolutions one zero zero!'

The coxswain repeated, 'One zero zero revolutions, sir!'

Packard breathed the fresh chill of morning sea air deep into his lungs as *Gibraltar* got underway, slowly heading away from the jetty and out into the harbour. A flock of seagulls, some of them screeching, flew overhead. He stifled a yawn, having had a restless night listening to the shipboard sounds of the crew returning last night, the footsteps along the passageways of sailors going about their nightly duties, the creaks and groans of the ship as it slowly rolled back and forth in its berth when a small craft passed by, and the slight vibration of the ship's engine pulsating through the floor. Buckmaster was right about one thing, the ship's sounds; a heartbeat of a living being. He closed his eyes and pinched the fatigue at the bridge of his nose.

Buckmaster glanced at Harry over his shoulder, a big grin on his face. 'Morning, Major! We're back on duty. Thought you'd like to see us leave harbour before you have breakfast.'

'Yes, thank you,' Packard replied. 'Us landlubbers don't see this sort of thing often. Quite an experience from the bridge.'

Buckmaster nodded, smiling. He seemed very pleased and returned his attention to the ship just as it was leaving the harbour wall and easing itself into the open sea.

A broadcast came over the ship's tannoy. *'Special dutymen to stand down. Forenoon watchmen to close up. Both watches of the hands to muster on the quarterdeck. Hands to cleaning stations.'*

Packard started to feel the swell, the ship going up and down, the slender bow of *Gibraltar* cutting into the waves as she pushed past the harbour wall into the tossing whitecaps of open sea, and gradually began to pick up speed.

A wardroom steward appeared and stood stiffly at Packard's elbow. 'Breakfast is ready in the wardroom, sir. Miss Vanessa is waiting.'

'Ah, yes, breakfast. Forgot all about that. Thank you,' Packard said, handing him the binoculars.

Packard made his way down the ladder to the deck, then cut into a doorway at the side, and down the stairs to a narrow corridor that took him to the wardroom. As he stepped over the cowling to enter, he could smell bacon and eggs. Vanessa was sitting at the table waiting for him. She wore a dark skirt with a cream blouse that had a little lace collar edged in pink, and her hair was tied up into a bun, exposing the elegant curve of her neck. She looked pretty as a picture, he thought. He removed his cap and smiled at her.

'Good morning,' she said, returning the smile.

He pulled a chair from under the table, sitting down opposite her. 'And a very good morning to you. I've just watched our departure from the bridge. Fascinating stuff.'

'Tempted to transfer to the navy, then?' she asked in a jovial way.

Packard shook his head. 'Not me. I prefer to have my feet placed firmly on the ground,' he said. 'At least I know what I'm doing.'

A steward immediately went to Vanessa's side, holding two pots. 'Coffee, miss?'

Vanessa smiled and replied, 'Yes please.'

'White or black?'

'White please.'

The steward used the other pot to pour in some milk, then went round to Packard's side. 'Coffee, sir?'

Packard nodded. 'Yes please. White.'

When the coffee steward had finished, another steward entered the wardroom carrying two white china plates of bacon and eggs. He placed one in front of Vanessa, and the other in front of Packard. Then he stood by the door.

Packard smiled. 'Marvellous,' he said, rubbing his hands together gleefully. 'This is the life.' Then he picked up his knife and fork and began cutting the bacon. 'I trust you slept well?'

She didn't answer. It was at that moment the alarm sounded.

'Action stations! Action stations! Hands to action – assume damage control, state Zulu. Close all watertight doors. Batten down the hatches!'

Packard glanced round at the steward standing at the door, who was looking suddenly nervous. 'What's happening?' he said. 'What's going on?'

The steward hesitated, his eyes darting to the speaker on the bulkhead sounding the alarm and then back to him. 'It's an action stations, sir,' he said, then darted off.

Packard looked across at Vanessa. Her face was a mask of fear. He dropped the knife and fork quickly and stood up, his chair crashing to the deck behind him. 'Wait here, I'll find out what's going on.' He grabbed his cap, jammed it on his head, and tugged it down. He went to the door and, not realizing, he pulled his Webley from its holster, a natural reaction from a seasoned soldier. He got to the doorway in three strides, careful to step over the cowling.

Rushing into the corridor at the end, and up to the wardroom door, came Campbell, gun in hand. 'Sir! It's action stations! What's happening?'

The two men stood there looking at each other, realising just how ridiculous they both looked holding a revolver at the ready. Packard grimaced, and without a word they put them away. He stopped a sailor rushing by. 'Hey, you, what's going on?'

At first the sailor looked stunned, then quickly glanced at Packard's profile and said, 'Sir, enemy boat spotted, heading this way,' and dashed off.

Packard gritted his teeth. 'I knew it … this is Hoffmann's doing, got to be!'

Campbell nodded and said, 'What do you want us to do?'

Packard had to think fast. He glanced back into the wardroom. 'Take Vanessa back with you. Keep her safe. Tell the men to standby. I'll go to Buckmaster and see what's what.'

'Will do, sir.'

Packard moved along the corridor at a pace along with the sailors sprinting to their action stations. He went up the steps two at a time and out onto the deck into the harsh glare of daylight that took him to the ladder, and the bridge above it. It was still crowded – most of the Sea Duty Watchmen were looking with powerful binoculars to their right and searching for the small torpedo boat. Buckmaster was in the middle of them. Packard went to him. 'What's happening?'

Buckmaster lowered his glasses and looked round, his face serious. 'Just got a report from Nieuwpoort, just a few miles up the Belgian coast from here, that a German torpedo boat has just passed the lighthouse going at full speed, heading this way.'

'Ship spotted, sir, off the starboard bow!' a watchman shouted. 'Coming in fast!'

Everyone trained their binoculars on the horizon.

'I see it!' shouted Buckmaster. 'He's in a hurry alright and heading right for us!'

Packard watched as Buckmaster swiftly moved across the bridge to a voice pipe. 'Wheelhouse, bridge, full speed ahead. Revolutions two zero zero. Hard a-starboard, course to steer one four five!'

The coxswain replied, 'Revolutions two zero zero on. Course to steer one four five, sir!'

Buckmaster turned to his first lieutenant. 'We'll go straight at him. It'll make us a smaller target and difficult to hit. Tell guns to load and make ready.' Then he grinned and added, 'And hoist battle ensign, Number One, we're going to war at last!'

'Aye, aye sir!'

Buckmaster turned to the signals officer on the bridge. 'Sigs, send a signal to Dover – about to engage German torpedo boat outside Dunkirk harbour!'

'Aye, aye sir!'

'Enemy ship still bearing down, sir!' called a watchman. 'Still coming in fast!'

Packard rushed to the rail, his eyes glued to the torpedo boat in the distance throwing up a white spray either side of her sharp bow, that was cutting deep into the chopping waves at speed. He saw Buckmaster quickly move to another voice pipe, shouting, 'Guns, open fire!'

A brief pause, then Packard felt the deck jump as the forward four and three-inch guns fired with an almighty bang, and black acrid smoke belched out from the end of the two barrels, racing over the bridge and blotting out the light for a few seconds. He saw two great gushes of water lifting high into the air on either side of the torpedo boat. Then heard the two explosions thunder in the distance, but the torpedo boat cut through the gap in the spray like an open curtain.

'A straddle, sir!'

'She's launched a torpedo, sir!'

'And another! She's turning hard to starboard to get away!'

It looked like a hit and run, Packard thought, then he heard the distinct clatter of a machine gun in the distance from the torpedo boat as a defiant parting shot – the speeding white tracer arching its way toward *Gibraltar*'s superstructure. Packard's instinct as a soldier kicked in and he threw himself flat on the gratings as the bullets raked the ship – several banging into the bridge superstructure and sounding like a demented blacksmith was outside hammering on the steel plate.

'Aaaaargh!' screamed one of the watchmen as he was struck by a bullet. The impact spun him round, his right arm severed below the elbow, the stump now a bloodied mess. He fell to the deck, still screaming, blood pumping from dangling arteries. A medic on standby at the back of the bridge went straight to his aid.

Packard jumped to his feet, heart pounding. He had never felt as useless in a fight as he did now.

'Torpedo, sir! Dead ahead! Starboard bow!'

Packard swung round and rushed to the rail to look, as did Buckmaster. The first torpedo was rushing toward the ship, skimming through the water like a bullet under the surface and just passing the bow on the starboard beam, missing the ship by just feet before disappearing into the wake behind the stern.

'Second torpedo, sir!'

This one looked as if it were on target to hit the bow. Everyone held their breath but it too skimmed by, just missing the bow by a few feet.

A lookout cheered and shouted, 'It missed, sir, it missed!'

Packard breathed a deep sigh of relief as Buckmaster went to a voice pipe beside him. 'Bridge, wheelhouse, port twenty!' Into another voice pipe, he yelled, 'Bring the guns to bear and keep firing!

We're turning hard a-port! I want all guns to bear on that bastard with a broadside before it gets out of range! I want him nailed!'

Packard grabbed the rail as he felt the ship tilt almost on its side as *Gibraltar* swung round to the left. He could hear Buckmaster murmuring, 'Come on, come on,' urging the ship on as *Gibraltar* turned in a tight arc, her sharp bow biting hard into the sea's troughs. Thick black smoke was bellowing from the two short funnels behind the bridge, casting a shadow behind them across the sea.

The deck heaved again as all four guns, now in line, fired together as a full salvo. Packard saw it was another straddle – but very close this time. The gunners had the torpedo boat in their sights. One small adjustment, he thought, and they'll have her. Then another salvo fired, again a close straddle. At the moment, it looked to Packard as if Fritz still had luck on its side.

The *Gibraltar* fired again.

This time a great thundering explosion erupted in the distance, spewing bright yellow flames and black smoke high into the air. The torpedo boat was struck amidships and began grinding to a halt.

'A hit, sir, a hit!'

Packard turned to see Buckmaster beside him, now wiping sweat and grime from his face with his sleeve. He leaned across to a voice pipe to say, 'Well done, guns, you got her! She's dead in the water! Cease firing!' Then he turned to his first lieutenant. 'Prepare to pick up survivors, Number One.'

'Aye, aye, sir.'

Packard looked over the rail as *Gibraltar* almost came abeam with the stricken torpedo boat that was rolling from side to side and ablaze from bow to stern. Black smoke boiled up and blossomed into the air from the raging fire that engulfed the boat. Only four enemy crewmen were plucked from the sea. The rest had perished.

He heard Buckmaster say, 'Stand down action stations, set a course for Dover, Number One, and let's go home.'

He watched as Buckmaster went to the front of the bridge into the sunlight and raised his powerful glasses toward England. 'Home indeed,' he heard him murmur. 'Home indeed.' He said it with a special pride.

CHAPTER 42

Buckmaster stood on the bridge, allowing his Number One to handle the mooring preparations as *Gibraltar* slipped into Dover harbour. A tugboat was guiding the ship to the dockside. Packard stood next to Buckmaster and watched a swift exchange of signal lamps. Under Number One's command, *Gibraltar* was swinging nicely to the dockside.

The first lieutenant lowered his face to the voice pipe to the wheelhouse, 'Stop both engines and ring off the revolutions!'

Gibraltar gave a shudder and settled in her berth at the jetty.

'Secure forrard, secure aft!'

A gaggle of dock workers began tugging on ropes as the derrick swung the gangway across, placing it gently and safely between the ship and the jetty.

'At last,' Packard said. 'Home and dry. I hope we get some leave after this. We deserve it, by God, after what we've been through in the last few days, we truly do.'

Buckmaster turned to him, cleared his throat and said, 'Before we entered harbour, I received a signal from the Admiralty.' He grinned. 'It seems you have a VIP waiting to whisk you away.'

'For me?' Packard said. 'Who's that?'

Buckmaster pointed at a large black car that was waiting on the jetty, with four lorries parked behind it. Standing at ease in two lines were twenty marines, their rifles tipped with bayonets.

Packard said, 'Ah, must be the escort for the gold, I should think.

With a bit of luck I won't have the responsibility to escort the gold to London.'

Twenty minutes later, Packard was walking down the gangway with Vanessa. He was saluted by a waiting marine sergeant. They exchanged a few words, then the sergeant detailed half the marines to board the ship. At the top of the gangway they were met by Campbell, who took them to the ship's magazine, where the gold was stowed.

A marine lieutenant approached Packard, snapped up a salute, and said, 'Major Packard, would you follow me please? There is someone in the car waiting to see you.'

He led Packard and Vanessa to the large black car and, as they approached, the back door swung open.

Winston Churchill stepped out, puffing on a large cigar, his face beaming broadly through the smoke. He took Packard's hand and began to pump it like a man possessed. 'Major Packard, I can't begin to tell you how proud I am to be the first to congratulate you!' His voice was loud, excited. 'You have no idea how important your deeds in Belgium have been. Downing Street awaits you,' he told him, 'and I have the honour to escort you there.'

Packard began to blush; everything seemed to be happening like a whirlwind. He met Churchill's gaze and gave him a small smile back. He was not sure what to say at first. Then he gave a quick glance to Vanessa beside him, and said, 'We only got away with it because of this girl and others like her. Brave Belgian people to be proud of. Their help was invaluable. Regretfully, some made their final sacrifice so we could succeed. We have a lot of people to remember back there, and to be thankful for.'

Vanessa nodded her head slowly and smiled sadly.

Churchill nodded his head too and dropped his voice. 'Of course,' he replied, 'we'll have a full report from you in due course, and those in Belgium that merit recognition will be rewarded, be sure of that. Now, we must go. There are lots of people who wish to meet you, including the Prime Minister, the Belgian Ambassador, and King Albert's representative in England. Let's not keep them waiting.'

'Who's taking the gold to London, sir?'

'As from now, I'm taking full responsibility for the gold,' Churchill said. 'It will be loaded on a special train to London, and then on to the Bank of England, guarded by my marines. It's all taken care of.'

'And what of my men?'

'They will go to London in the same train, to join you later.'

Packard nodded, and, before he got into the car, he glanced at *Gibraltar's* bridge. Buckmaster was there; he gave a wave. Packard smiled and waved back, then he turned away, not sure of his feelings, whether they were elation or sadness, nerves or adrenalin. But it was over, and they had survived. He got into the car with Vanessa, the door slammed shut behind them, the engine started up, and as the car drove along the jetty, he gave *Gibraltar* a brief glance before the ship was gone from view.

THE END

HISTORICAL NOTE

The tide of war during October 1914 was very fluid. After the German advance was stopped by the Allies from reaching Paris at the battles of Marne and the Aisne, and a stalemate ensued, each side tried to outflank the other by heading north toward the Channel coast in a series of smaller battles. This became known as 'The Race to the Sea', and at the northern end was the British supply lines, the coastal ports of Dunkirk and Calais, and the town of Ypres.

When Belgium was invaded, its army put up a strong resistance against the massive German onslaught, but the odds were against the Belgians and about 80,000 soldiers fell back to the fortified city of Antwerp. King Albert and his government installed themselves there and the city and port of Antwerp came under siege, but it threatened the German advance into France as well as protecting the British supply lines from the Channel ports. The situation was precarious, and a meeting was held at Downing Street that included the Prime Minister Herbert Asquith, the Chancellor Lloyd George, Secretary for War Lord Kitchener, the Foreign Secretary Sir Edward Grey, and the First Lord of the Admiralty Winston Churchill to discuss the crisis. Antwerp needed help desperately to hold as long as possible to prevent the German thrust having a clear run along the coast and cutting off the British supply lines before that gap could be closed.

Churchill, fearing the fragile state of Belgian morale, offered up his two newly formed Naval Brigades and prepared them for embarkation. Likewise, Kitchener, having predicted that the Belgian army would have to retreat and would be no match against the German army's thrust into Belgium, promised an infantry Division and later the 3rd Calvary Division to Antwerp, but it would take them a good week to get over there. British high command worried about their supply lines from the Channel ports, asked the Belgians in Antwerp to attack the Germans holding the siege, and, in a series of sorties they made, the German thrust along the coast was diverted, temporarily, to deal with these renewed attacks on their flank. The Germans attacked Antwerp with vigour on 3rd October and it was clear that without urgent help the city would fall. King Albert sent a message to London that they could not hold out without help.

Churchill was on a train to Dover when it was stopped at a Kent station and ordered to return back to London, where a meeting was being convened at Kitchener's London home. It was here that Prime Minister Asquith asked Churchill to go to Antwerp with his newly formed Naval Brigades, who, through Churchill's foresight, were already on their way to help relieve the city, and he went that night, with Admiral Hood arriving the next day.

The state of the two Naval Brigades was as I described them, mainly reservists who were poorly trained and poorly equipped, but Antwerp's morale, and that of the Belgian army, was boosted greatly by their arrival and that of Churchill with Admiral Hood. Churchill was dressed in a Trinity House uniform, much to the amusement of some of the Belgian delegation in Antwerp who greeted him. The Festival Hall in Antwerp where Churchill met the King of Belgium still exists. During recent renovations a fire started that destroyed the internal architecture, just leaving the façade. It is now a popular shopping mall. After Churchill's inspection of Antwerp's defences, he telegraphed Asquith for permission to take full command of all British forces there. He was refused and ordered back to London.

The city held on for another five days. When the Naval Brigades were attacked by the Germans, they put up some stout resistance, despite their inadequate training and equipment, before they were given the order to withdraw. Just over fifty Naval Brigade men were killed in the clash. Two battalions, however, never received the order to withdraw, and had to flee to nearby Holland, where they were interred for the rest of the war. Those that got away and back to Dover were sent to Gallipoli the following year. Antwerp fell to the Germans on 9th October. But this had given the British that precious time to drive north to reach the town of Ypres by 13th October and secure their supply lines.

The town of Ypres (or Wipers as it was pronounced by the British Tommy) was once a very prosperous town and had got its wealth from the cloth industry, but this had declined in the last forty or so years before October 1914 and the town's population had halved to a mere 18,000 inhabitants. The Benedictine Abbey of our Lady of Grace was situated in Rue St Jacques (now renamed Sint Jacobstraat), and was run by a community of Irish nuns (Les Dames Irlandaises) for two hundred and fifty years. This town had been laid siege by the British (Cromwell's forces), and the French, the Dutch and Austrians prior to the Great War, and each added to its defensive walls with gates on all the entrances. This was reduced to just two gates (Menin and Lille) in later years.

At the beginning of October 1914, there were rumours of a German advance towards the town. Several villages outside had visits from the dreaded German Uhlans. German spotter planes flew over to survey the town for its defences. The mayor, Rene Colaert, ordered that no strong light should be seen in the town at night, and no bells to be rung from six in the evening until the following day.

The Germans arrived at lunch time on Wednesday 7th October.

All principal men of the town were ordered to present themselves to the Germans. They took hostage the mayor Rene Colaert, the bank manager, and the chief of police to ensure the town's good behaviour. The Germans took BF75,000 from the bank, BF200 from the post office safe, they broke in and took the contents of the safe from the main jewellers and literally emptied the town of food and valuables that included bread, rice, coffee, butter, potatoes, some horses, some carts, and the odd motor vehicle they found. They offered worthless tokens for some of these items.

The Germans also demanded shelter for their soldiers in peoples' homes overnight and housed their horses in the railway station waiting rooms. However, it is interesting to note they did not interfere with the Irish nuns in the abbey. By mid-morning on the following day the Germans had mostly gone, and the hostages were released.

Rene Colaert was a popular man and was made mayor of Ypres in 1900. He was born on 10th March 1848 in the next town of Poperinghe, and became a lawyer in Ypres. After the war in 1919, two English newspapers, the *Pall Mail Gazette* and the *Manchester Guardian*, published an article claiming that Mayor Rene Colaert had been a traitor when the Germans occupied the town. He took both newspapers to court in England and won £1,300 damages with costs and a full apology. There were calls at this time to leave the ruins of Ypres as a memorial to the British and Commonwealth war dead, but Colaert was against this and wished the town to be rebuilt. He got his way but he never saw this done, for he died aged 79 on 3rd October 1927. He is buried in Old Ypres Cemetery where his gravestone can be seen today.

Field Marshal Sir William "Wully" Robertson was born on 29th January 1860. In 1914 he was the British Expeditionary Force quartermaster-general. In 1915 he became the chief of staff. "Wully" was the first and only soldier in the British army to advance from private to field marshal. He died on 12th February 1933 and buried in Brookwood Military Cemetery, near Pirbright.

The British destroyer HMS *Gibraltar* was based on the Acheron class of ships built just prior to the war starting. It had a compliment of 70 men and during sea trials reached a speed of over 30 knots.

The German torpedo boat at this time was nothing like those in World War II. They were almost as big as a destroyer and lightly armed but had four torpedo tubes. They too could reach speeds of over 30 knots. Some were still in service during World War II but were upgraded with more weapons. They were often used in the Baltic Sea.

Commander Walter Isendahl, Director of Naval Intelligence department (N), of the Imperial German Navy during the Great War, served again in naval intelligence as an admiral during World War II. He died in Berlin in April 1945. The exact date is unknown.

The British arrived in Ypres on 13th October and shortly afterwards took part in a major battle for the town, which is now known as First Ypres (19th October to 22nd November 1914). During the second battle of Ypres (22nd April to 25th May 1915), the Germans used poison gas for the first time, that had a mild effect on the town – by this time, continuous heavy shelling had reduced it to a mere ruin; it was evacuated of all civilians by mid-May, including the Irish nuns of Ypres. What was left were stray dogs and the badly decomposing bodies of horses and soldiers among the devastation. The mayor and town council, including most of its inhabitants, settled in exile on the northern French coast, in the town of Le Touquet.

Ypres was rebuilt thanks to the efforts of Rene Colaert and was completed in 1967 when work finished on the Cloth Hall. The Irish nuns never returned to Ypres and made their way to England with the help of the British army, staying in Oulton Abbey in Staffordshire. In 1915 they returned to Ireland and in 1920 they purchased a large Victorian house called Kylemore Abbey in Galway, Ireland, where they remain today. The abbey in Ypres was never rebuilt and is now a row of houses and shops, but the Lille gate still exists. At the newly rebuilt Menin Gate, where the names of over forty thousand soldiers of Britain and its Commonwealth are carved into the stone panels, the last post is played each evening at 8 p.m. by the town's firemen. Each night it is well attended by tourists and local dignitaries.

Rear Admiral Horace Hood, who accompanied Churchill to Antwerp, went back to sea in late October 1914. He lived in a house in Mortlake, south-west London, that was demolished during the 1920s, where the area was redeveloped. The streets around this area are named after him. Hood died aged 45 during the Battle of Jutland on 31st May 1916 when his flagship HMS *Invincible* was struck by a shell that hit the magazine. The explosion broke the ship in two and sank it within ninety seconds. There were few survivors. In 1918, his widow lunched HMS *Hood*, named after one of his ancestors, the 18th century Admiral Samuel Hood, which went on to be sunk by the German battleship *Bismarck* on 24th May 1941. This too was hit by a shell that struck the magazine, then broke in two from the explosion and sank. There were only three survivors.

Secretary of State for War Lord Kitchener was a member of the East India Club in St. James's Square, London, and a portrait of him hangs in the club. He was sent on a diplomatic and military mission to Russia, to meet the Tsar. He boarded the cruiser HMS *Hampshire* at Scapa Flow on 5th June 1916. When the ship was about two miles off the Orkney coast it struck a mine laid by German Submarine *U-75* and sank in fifteen minutes. Lord Kitchener and his mission team were among the 737 others who went down with the ship. There were only twelve survivors.

Winston Churchill was also a member of the East India Club (and the National Liberal Club in Whitehall) and a portrait of him hangs in the club with the inscription, 'Never in the field of human conflict was so much owed, by so many to just one man' – a take on his speech as prime minister to the fighter pilots of the RAF during the Battle of Britain in the summer of 1940. In 1916, after the disastrous Gallipoli campaign, he resigned from politics and saw service in the trenches at Ypres for six months as an army battalion commander of the 6th Royal Scots Fusiliers, before returning to politics in 1917. He died in January 1965 aged 90 and was given a state funeral, the largest in English history up to that time. Along with many other members of the Churchill family, he is buried with his wife in St Martin's Churchyard, Bladon, near Woodstock, Oxfordshire.

ABOUT THE AUTHOR

Gary Parkins was born in North London and served in the Parachute Regiment in the early and mid 1970s with two tours in Northern Ireland. A member of The Western Front Association, he visits the battlefields of western Europe to both World Wars every year. Now retired after 42 years at Harrods, 32 of those years as the Security Operations Manager, he is married with one son and lives in South-West London.

Printed in Great Britain
by Amazon